TILLY BAGSHAWE

Scandalous

HARPER

Also by Tilly Bagshawe

Adored
Showdown
Do Not Disturb
Flawless
Sidney Sheldon's Mistress of the Game
Sidney Sheldon's After the Darkness

To find out more about Tilly Bagshawe and her
books, log on to www.tillybagshawe.co.uk

For James Bagshawe, the best brother in the world

HarperCollins*Publishers*
77–85 Fulham Palace Road,
Hammersmith, London W6 8JB

www.harpercollins.co.uk

Published by HarperCollins*Publishers* 2010
1

First published in Great Britain by
HarperCollins*Publishers* 2010

A catalogue record for this book
is available from the British Library

ISBN: 978 0 00 736255 4

Set in Meridien by Palimpsest Book Production Limited,
Falkirk, Stirlingshire

Printed and bound in Australia by
Griffin Press

ACKNOWLEDGEMENTS

Many thanks to everyone at HarperCollins for all your hard work on the book; in particular to my editor Sarah Ritherdon, to Michelle Brackenborough for the gorgeous cover, and to the terrific sales team, especially Wendy Neale. Also to my agent and friend, Tif Loehnis, and the whole team at Janklow and Nesbit in London, especially Kirsty Gordon and Tim Glister. *Scandalous* is partly set in Cambridge and inspired by my own years there. So this is probably an appropriate moment for me to thank St John's College for letting me in, giving me the time of my life, and changing my life forever. Finally, thanks as always to all my family for their love and support, especially my husband Robin and my brother James, to whom *Scandalous* is dedicated. Team Bagshawe for the win.

PROLOGUE

In a private screening room in Beverly Hills, a beautiful woman stared intently at the man on the screen. Flicking a switch, she allowed her luxurious red velvet chair to recline. Languidly extending a hand dripping in Neil Lane diamonds, she reached for the remote, freeze-framing the shot on the man's face. She smiled.

He was handsome, undoubtedly. Blond, blue-eyed, chisel-jawed, like every other television presenter in Los Angeles. But this woman had her pick of handsome men. Handsome, rich, powerful, she had had them all and grown bored of them all. Last month, for the third year in a row, *People* magazine had voted her 'Sexiest Woman Alive'. It was the sort of label that meant little to her, but everything to the producers and directors who lined up to be the next piece of man candy on her perfectly sculpted arm. Her looks had made her famous, and they had made her rich. Men were stupid.

But not this man. This man was different. He was an intellectual. Some even called him a genius. She wondered what he would be like in bed? How it would feel to sleep with a man who, on one level at least, was her superior? She found the concept thrilling, albeit rather difficult to imagine.

Hitting play, she watched the man walk towards the camera, talking about deep space and the cosmos and things she did not understand in his divine English accent. Slipping a hand beneath her cream silk La Perla negligée, she began to touch herself, imagining him making love to her.

Theo! Oh Theo. Don't stop.

As always when she pleasured herself, she came to orgasm almost instantly. Yet another thing she did better than the men in her life. Opening her eyes, she sighed. How inconvenient that she'd only just got married again.

She would have to do something about that . . .

Three thousand miles away and some years later, in New York, another wealthy, beautiful woman watched the same man on the cinema-sized plasma television in the master bedroom of her palatial Upper East Side apartment. Just as she had watched him every night for the last five years.

Unlike his admirer in LA, this woman *did* understand what Professor Theodore Dexter was saying. Listening to him pontificate in the fake, fireside-chat voice she knew so well, she thought, *I hate you. Why are you still alive? Why aren't you suffering, the way you made me suffer, you treacherous son of a bitch?*

One day, she vowed, Theo Dexter would get what was coming to him.

When that day came, she would show him no mercy.

PART ONE

Eight years earlier . . .

CHAPTER ONE

'Are you sure you want to do this Sasha? It's not too late to change your mind.'

Sasha Miller looked at Will Temple's naked body – the six-pack stomach, broad rugby-player's shoulders, sturdy legs, and of course *it* – and marvelled again that such an Adonis had chosen her to be his girlfriend.

'I'm completely sure. I just . . . I hope you won't be disappointed, that's all.'

Will Temple was nineteen and *very* experienced. At least, that's what he'd told Sasha. *Oh God, yeah. I lost my virginity when I was twelve. It was with the au pair. Bodil. Gorgeous Swedish bird, couldn't keep her hands off me. She's a top model now.* Sasha was wildly impressed. Not that that was why she had fallen for Will. All the girls loved him because he was captain of the rugby team at school, handsome, rich and insanely popular. But Sasha Miller was drawn to another side of Will Temple. He was funny, and spontaneous. When he wasn't with 'the lads', his posse of sycophantic hangers-on from Tonbridge, the local public school, he could be loving and sweet.

Sasha and Will had been an item for three months now. If Sasha didn't do the deed soon, she knew there'd be a queue of girls from St Agnes's waiting to take her place. She'd only been putting it off because of the rumours.

Rumours about *it*.

For weeks Sasha had been hearing that *it* was so huge, an appendage of such superhuman girth and elephantine length that sex was bound to be agony. So it was with immense relief that Sasha had watched Will drop his Simpsons boxer shorts to reveal a modest five and a half inches of manhood. Eager, certainly. Ready for action, unquestionably. But hardly the Eiffel Tower.

'You could never disappoint me, darling,' Will assured her. 'Just follow my lead. I'll take care of you.'

Kicking aside a pile of dirty sports kit, Will led Sasha to the bed and started taking off her clothes. Sasha closed her eyes. Downstairs she could hear the *thump, thump, thump* of music from the party and wondered if all Will's friends knew what he was up to. *Did boys talk to each other about things like that?* She tried not to think about it, or about the faint but pervasive smell of mildew rising from Will's sheets.

'What's wrong with this thing?' Will fumbled with the clasp of her bra. 'Why won't it . . . open?'

'Sorry. It's quite old.' Hearing the exasperation in his voice Sasha wriggled out of the offending garment herself. Two perfectly round, full, eighteen-year-old breasts tumbled into Will's hands like ripe fruit from the tree of heaven.

'Bloody hell, you're gorgeous,' he gasped.

He was right. With her flawless, milky skin, gleaming mane of black hair and sparkling, intelligent eyes, the same pale green as mint ice cream, Sasha Miller was a knockout. But she was also . . . different. All Will Temple's previous girlfriends had been the cool, popular girls at school.

Standard-issue blondes with tight jeans and the latest Topshop heels. With her Marks & Spencer's cardigans and sensible lace-up shoes, and her nose permanently stuck in a science book, Sasha Miller was a card-carrying nerd. But that was what Will loved about her. He'd had his fill of dating prom queens. Sasha knew even less about fashion than Will did, and either didn't know that she was beautiful or set no store by her looks. She also had no interest in the local Sussex party scene, a scene of which Will Temple was the undisputed king.

But even kings could get bored.

Sasha gazed up at him, naked and adoring.

'Thank you. You're gorgeous too Will. I . . .'

The pain was sharp but it was over in a second. Sasha didn't even remember Will taking her knickers off, but he must have because before her head hit the pillow he was inside her, pounding away like a jackhammer. Tentatively Sasha ran a hand over his bare back. She was debating whether or not it would be bad form to reach lower and stroke his bum – perhaps she ought to have spent more time reading the *Just Seventeen* problem pages when she was younger like the rest of her friends? – when Will let out a strange, yelping noise and pulled out of her.

'Would you like a condom?' Sasha offered helpfully. 'I've got one.'

'A bit late for that, I'm afraid.' Will grinned. 'Sorry, darling. You're so sexy I couldn't help myself. I didn't hurt you, did I?'

'Erm, no. Not really.'

Wow. So that was sex. It was quite a lot shorter than I expected. But that's probably only because Will's so good at it, it doesn't take him as long as other people.

'Shall we go back down and join the party?' Will was

already pulling on his jeans. 'Of course I'd much rather be here, making love to you.' He kissed Sasha on the forehead. 'But I feel a bit rude. You know, being the host and everything. Jago's probably nicking the silverware as I speak.'

Will's parents were on holiday in Spain. With a faith in their eldest son that owed more to love than judgement, they had left Will in charge of Chittenden, their beautiful sixteenth-century farmhouse in the Sussex Weald. Tonight's party was his third in as many days.

'Oh, gosh, totally. Of course. You should go down.' Sasha scoured the floor for her underwear. 'I have to get home anyway.'

'You're not staying over?' Will looked genuinely crestfallen. Sasha sighed. *He's so lovely.*

'I can't. It's my dad's birthday, remember? I promised him I'd be home for supper. Mum and I always watch him unwrap his presents.'

'Hmmm. Well, I suppose that's fair enough. After all, I've already unwrapped *my* present.' Will pulled Sasha to her feet and kissed her on the lips. She felt ready to burst with happiness.

Will Temple loves me.

Will Temple has made love to me.

I am a woman at last!

Chittenden was in the village of Tidebrook, about a ten-minute drive from Sasha's parents' cottage in Frant. It was just past seven o'clock, and the last rays of summer sun were still sinking into the woody, Sussex horizon. *I love it here,* thought Sasha, driving through the familiar countryside. *I'll miss it when I go away to Exeter.*

In a few weeks Sasha would have her A-level results. Not

that there was ever much doubt what her grades would be. Sasha Miller had been a straight-A student since she started school at four years old. By that age she could already read fluently, and knew considerably more about the solar system than her primary school teacher, Miss Rush.

'I hesitate to use the word "obsession",' Miss Rush told Sasha's father at her first parent–teacher meeting. 'But Sasha is inordinately interested in space. I'm wondering if you could try to introduce some other interests? Just to create a balance.'

'Such as what?' Don Miller, Sasha's father, was a keen amateur astronomer himself. He shared his daughter's delight in the unknown world of stars and planets, and wasn't sure he liked the cut of Miss Rush's jib.

'A lot of the little girls are keen on princesses.'

'Princesses?'

'Yes. Princesses. Mermaids. Even the dreaded Barbie!' Miss Rush let out a tinkling little laugh. Don Miller shot her a withering stare.

'It might help her make friends, Mr Miller. Sasha . . . how shall I put this? She doesn't quite fit in.'

Sasha never did learn how to fit in. Princesses, mermaids and Barbies passed her by in much the same way that in later years drugs, nightclubs and celebrity culture remained a deliberately closed book. Thankfully, as she grew older, her teachers became more encouraging of Sasha's 'obsession' with astronomy, and her emerging genius at physics.

'Your daughter is a uniquely gifted scientist, Mr and Mrs Miller.' Mrs Banks, the headmistress of St Agnes's, stated the obvious. 'We have high hopes for her at university.' Don and Susan Miller had strained every financial sinew to afford their daughter's private school fees. They had high hopes too.

'What about Oxbridge?'

'Well.' Mrs Banks shifted uncomfortably in her high-backed wooden chair. 'That's certainly a possibility. Of course, Oxford and Cambridge both require interviews.'

Nobody doubted Sasha's intellectual ability. It was her social skills that had always been the problem. Speaking in public was her worst nightmare. But even speaking in private could be a challenge, if the subject didn't interest her. These days, Cambridge colleges were looking for more than straight-A grades. They wanted 'rounded' students. Pretty, confident girls who could hold their own at interview. Sasha was fine once you got her onto particle physics or the latest debates raging in game theory. But she had no facility for small talk. As for the dreaded UCAS form, with its two pages devoted to 'Hobbies and Other Interests', Sasha could only stare at it in bafflement. *Why would somebody need to have* another *interest, when their specialist subject was the entire universe?*

Sasha applied to the five universities with the best reputations in her subject. None of them required interviews. All five offered her a place. She decided that, if Cambridge rejected her, she would go to Exeter, and she did her best to look forward to the prospect. But deep down she knew that the Cambridge physics faculty was the best in the world. She desperately longed to get in.

The staff at St Agnes's suggested she go to an interview coach to address her weaknesses as a candidate. 'Even something as simple as wearing the right clothes can be crucially important.' But Don Miller was having none of it.

'Ridiculous. It's a travesty. Sash wants to be a scientist, not a television presenter. It's blatant sexism.'

He was right. It *was* blatant sexism.

Unfortunately, the school was right too. Sasha's interview

at St Michael's College, Cambridge, was an unmitigated disaster.

On the drive back to Sussex, Sasha glumly ran through a postmortem for her dad.

'They asked me about politics. What I thought about the latest G7 summit and whether I had strong views on globalization.'

'Why?'

'I've no idea, Dad.'

'Well, what did you say, love?'

'I said "no".'

Fair enough. Bloody silly question anyway.

'What else did they ask?'

'The Tutor for Admissions asked me what I thought I would bring to St Michael's.'

Don Miller brightened. 'And what did you say to that?'

'Books.'

'Ah.'

Oh well. Exeter's a fine university. I'm sure she'll be happy there.

The Millers' cottage was a tiny, higgledy-piggledy tile-hung gem overlooking Frant village green. All Sasha's classmates from St Agnes's lived in far grander houses – houses like Will's – but Sasha would not have traded her childhood home for Buckingham Palace. She loved everything about it: the hanging flower baskets dripping jasmine on either side of the front door; the minuscule leaded windows that let in almost no light, but that gave the house the look of Hansel and Gretel's cottage; the long, sloping back garden, a tangled mish-mash of weeds and wild flowers, with the shed at the bottom housing Sasha's precious telescope, her most treasured possession.

By the time Sasha parked her dilapidated red Golf beside the green, it was twilight. The church's ancient Saxon steeple jutted proudly over the village roof tops, a benevolent giant bathed in the blue light of evening. As Sasha got out of the car, a single note of the church bell marked the half hour. Summer smells of warm earth, freshly mown grass and honeysuckle hung heavy in the air. Sasha breathed them in, dizzy with happiness. *Will loves me.*

Before tonight, she'd been nervous about leaving him in October. Will had gone straight from school into his father's estate agency business – *I never fancied uni, Sash. I'm not the type.* The idea of leaving him in Sussex, prey to all the St Agnes's girls in the year below, filled Sasha with horror. Especially as Exeter was so terribly far away. But now that they were sleeping together – *Goodbye, virginity! I won't miss you* – she felt blissfully secure in the relationship. She would read books on the subject and become a fabulous, inventive lover. Will, consumed with desire, would hurtle down the A303 every weekend, desperate to be with her. Afterwards they would lie awake at night, staring at the stars, talking about . . . Hmmm, the fantasy got a little vague at that point. But anyway, it would all be wonderful and perfect and . . .

'Sasha! Where have you been? We've been trying your mobile all day. Dad was about to call the hospitals.'

Sue Miller, Sasha's mother, was a plumper, shorter version of her daughter. Her once black hair was now heavily laced with grey, but her pale skin was still smooth. More worldly and sensible than Sasha (not that that was hard; the family poodle, Bijoux, had more common sense than Sasha), Sue had no idea how she and Don had produced such an intellectual powerhouse of a child. Don reckoned it was his genes. But then Don was out of his mind.

'Sorry. I must have switched it off. Or something . . .'

Sasha rummaged absentmindedly in her handbag. Where *was* that phone? 'Is it birthday-supper time? I'm starving.'

'Not yet.' Don Miller appeared in the hallway. He was holding a large envelope. 'This arrived for you in the after-noon post, Sasha. I think you should open it now. Get it out of the way.'

Despite herself, Sasha's heart lurched when she saw the Cambridge postmark.

'St Michael's.'

She already knew she hadn't got in. But the weight of the envelope confirmed it. Everyone knew that if you were accepted, they sent you a fat package full of bumf about grants and accommodation and reading lists. This, quite clearly, was a single sheet of paper.

Sasha wandered through into the kitchen. Don started to follow her, but Sue held him back.

'Leave it, love. Give her a minute. She doesn't need an audience.'

In the kitchen, Sasha stood with her back to the Aga, turning the envelope over in her hands. Sensing her anxiety, Bijoux heaved his fat form out of the dog basket and sat loyally at her feet.

'Thanks, boy.' *Why did the stupid rejection have to arrive today?* She wanted to remember this as the day Will Temple made her a woman. Not the day that St Michael's Stupid College rejected her because she didn't know about globalization and her cardigan was buttoned up wrong.

Wrapping her anger around her like a cloak, Sasha tore open the letter.

On the other side of Frant village green, the Carmichael family was enjoying a summer barbecue with friends when they heard the scream.

'What was that?' Katie Carmichael put down her beer and moved towards the garden gate.

'Nothing.' Her dad, Bob, turned over the last batch of Wall's pork sausages. 'Just some kids playing silly buggers. Any chance of another jug of Pimm's out here, Kelly? It's thirsty work, you know, slaving over hot coals.'

But Bob Carmichael's wife wasn't listening. She was standing at an upstairs window, staring open mouthed at the spectacle unfolding before her.

'Oh my God!' Katie Carmichael had reached the gate. 'It's Mr Miller. He's got no clothes on.'

'You what? Don Miller?'

Bob Carmichael dropped his tongs. Half the village was outside now, pouring onto the green. Some of them were taking photographs. Most of them were laughing, or screaming, or both. Everyone knew Don Miller. He'd run the local post office for the last fifteen years, not to mention heading the Frant Neighbourhood Watch Committee.

Now it was Don that the neighbourhood had come to watch. Stark naked, whooping for joy, he tore round the cricket pitch screaming. 'She did it! She bloody did it!'

'He's flipped his lid.'

'I don't believe it. Don Miller!'

'That's put me right off me sausages, that has.'

'Where's Sue?'

A few moments later Sue Miller's solid, dumpy figure could be seen waddling towards the growing crowd of spectators, most of whom were now cheering loudly. The last time Don had felt compelled to take all his clothes off had been the night of his twenty-second birthday when England had beaten the All Blacks at Twickenham. It was a sight Sue would never forget, and one she'd hoped she'd never have to see again. Don, however, was clearly having the time of his life, playing

to the crowd with a series of pirouettes and other impro-
vised ballet moves. His plié left nothing to the imagination.

'I'm sorry about this, everyone.' Sue Miller smiled sheep-
ishly. 'I'm afraid Don's gone rather off the deep end.'

'No kidding!' Bob Carmichael wiped away tears of
laughter. 'It's his birthday, isn't it? Is he drunk?'

'Not yet, but he will be. We just heard.' Sue's smile turned
into a grin. 'Sasha got into Cambridge.'

Three hours later, Don Miller was in bed, snoring loudly. The
combination of the excitement, Sue's homemade chocolate
fudge birthday cake and at least a bottle and a half of the
best red wine the Abergavenny Arms had to offer had finished
him off, poor man.

'I knew you'd do it. I jush knew it!' he told Sasha repeatedly as he staggered upstairs, leaning on her for support like
an exhausted boxer. 'You're going to be the greatesht scientist this country's ever prd'ced. My daughter. You're gonna
change the world. I *knew* it.'

'D'you think he'll be all right, Mum?' Sasha closed the
bedroom door.

'Don't worry about your father,' said Sue. 'It's the rest of
the village that's going to need counselling. Post-traumatic
shock, I think they call it. I'm used to seeing your father's
wedding tackle swinging in the wind, but poor Mrs Anderson.
She looked like she was about to have an aneurism. I mean,
she is ninety-two, the dear old stick.'

Sasha got ready for bed in a daze. She'd had a few drinks
herself, but that wasn't the reason. In the last few hours,
her life had changed forever. She'd called Will to tell him
the good news as soon as she got back from the pub.

'Great, babe,' he yelled over pounding music. Evidently
the party at Chittenden was still in full swing. 'Cambridge

is miles nearer than Exeter. That means I can still play rugby on Saturday afternoons once the season starts, then drive up and take you out for dinner. Wicked.'

If it wasn't quite the reaction she'd hoped for, Sasha tried not to be disappointed. *I can't expect him to understand. He's not academic. He has other qualities. And at least he's making plans to come up and see me. That has to be a good sign, doesn't it?*

Pulling on a pair of scratchy cotton pyjamas she'd had since she was fourteen, Sasha turned out the light and crawled under the covers of her single bed. Above her, a solar system of glow-in-the-dark stickers shone a comforting green. It was a child's bedroom and Sasha loved it. *But I'm not a child. Not any more. I'm a Cambridge undergraduate! I'm Will Temple's lover!* She hugged her excitement to her like a priceless treasure. *I don't want to fall asleep. I don't want today to be over.*

Outside, the church bells struck midnight.

The day was over.

Sasha Miller slept.

CHAPTER TWO

Professor Theodore Dexter was having a wonderful day. The sun was in the sky. Cambridge, ever beautiful, had looked particularly lovely this morning as he cycled along the Backs into college, its spires and turrets bathed in early autumn sunlight. His rooms, the most beautiful in St Michael's, had been newly cleaned and filled with vases of fresh flowers. (Professor Dexter's bedder was more than a little in love with him. But then, who wasn't?) And waiting in his bed was Clara, a German postgraduate student with the sort of oversized jugs rarely seen outside of specialist porn mags and a mouth that God had clearly created for the purpose to which she was now so gloriously putting it.

'That's right, sweetheart. Nice and slow.'

The blow job was so good it was almost painful. Clara was an average physicist, but thanks to her extraordinary oral abilities her PhD thesis on galactic anisotropy was rapidly edging its way to the top of the class. Trying to prolong his pleasure, Professor Dexter moved higher up the bed so that he could see out of the window. His rooms in First Court looked out over St John's Street and the splendid redbrick portcullis of Trinity College. Trinity was larger and more prestigious than St Michael's, but St Michael's was consistently voted the most beautiful college in Cambridge, with its wisteria-clad medieval courts, romantic formal gardens and exquisite, walnut-panelled Tudor Hall. It also had far and away the best reputation in astro and particle physics. Which was why so many of the faculty were astonished when Theo Dexter was offered the fellowship there.

To the world at large, Theo Dexter was a brilliant scientist. He'd published two books with titles that no ordinary mortal could understand (His debut, the catchy *Prospective Signatures of High Redshift Quasar HII Regions*, sold a very creditable five hundred copies), he had a first from Oxford and a PhD from MIT and he was still only thirty-five. To the physics faculty at Cambridge, however, he was an amateur. A mere popinjay. Not only were his ideas rehashed versions of other people's research, but the man *dyed his hair*, for God's sake. He wore Oswald Boateng bespoke suits – in Cambridge! – and was even rumoured to undergo regular facials, whatever those were. Female students flocked to his lectures to catch a glimpse of that rarest of all known mammals – a sexy scientist – when just down the hall, infinitely more brilliant and innovative minds were being ignored. A combination of envy and intellectual snobbery had made the golden boy of Cambridge physics deeply unpopular amongst his peers. Being offered the St Michael's fellowship was the final nail in Theo's coffin.

Not that he cared. At least, that's what he told himself. *I've got the cushiest job in Cambridge, rooms that any other junior fellow would kill for, and a revolving door of willing, educated pussy at my beck and call. Not to mention a lovely wife and a pretty house*

18

off the Madingley Road. What more could a man ask for? And yet despite his smugness, lack of scruples and almost limitless physical vanity, deep down Theo Dexter *did* want to be taken seriously by his fellow scientists. *One day,* he vowed. *One day I'll show them all.*

Feeling himself building to a climax, he reached down and grabbed Clara's hair, forcing himself deeper into that heavenly mouth. Instinctively she pulled back, but as he started to come Theo held her head firmly in place. *If you want top marks for your crappy dissertation, angel, you're going to have to swallow.* Afterwards he watched her get dressed, physically lifting each of her enormous breasts into her bra. *Beautiful.* He'd been worried he might not be 'up to it' for today's pre-term tryst with his student. Theresa, his wife, had pounced on him earlier that morning, waving a positive ovulation stick as if she was trying to bring a plane in to land. It was sad, really. The doctor had told them that their chances of conception were low to nil, but Theresa couldn't let it go. For his part, Theo had never understood the big deal about kids. Sleepless nights, dirty nappies, the mind-numbing boredom of the playground. Who in their right mind would sign up for that? Then again, he was by no means sure Theresa *was* in her right mind. She always seemed to be away with the fairies these days, so lost in her Shakespeare that she barely registered his presence – or lack of it. But Theo Dexter was not a man to look a gift horse in the mouth. Tomorrow was the first day of Michaelmas term. That meant a new year, and a new crop of nubile, naïve young freshers, all of them in search of a mentor. If there was one thing Professor Theodore Dexter prided himself on, it was his ability to mentor. Just look how far dear Clara had come.

* * *

Fifteen minutes later, Theo was on his way to Formal Hall for lunch. Two shags in six hours had left him ravenously hungry, and the smells of garlic and onion wafting up the stairs from the college kitchens were like a siren call to his stomach. Only about half the St Michael's fellows ate in Hall on a regular basis, but Theo Dexter went every day. Partly out of meanness (meals in college were free), but partly because he had yet to find anywhere he preferred to dine than in the dark, Tudor splendour of St Michael's. Everything about it, from the rituals of the Latin grace and standing to welcome the Master to high table, to the strict rules about the passing of wine and water, gave Theo a deep and abiding thrill. To eat in college was to become part of history. It was to claim one's place amongst the chosen ones, the privileged few whose intellect set them above the rest of humanity. Theo Dexter grew up in a nondescript semi in Crawley, but he had made it to the table of the Gods, and he relished every second.

'Morning, Dexter. Off to enjoy the condemned man's final meal? Depressing, isn't it?'

Professor Jonathan Cavendish, Head of History at St Michael's, was in his late fifties. A handsome man in his youth, one of the university's most successful rowing blues, he had long since run to fat. Renowned as a bon vivant, Jonathan wore his paunch with pride, and didn't seem remotely concerned by his thinning hair, or his fattening arteries. Everybody at St Michael's loved him. Everybody except Theo Dexter. Jonathan Cavendish made Theo's skin crawl. *Why the hell doesn't he go to the gym? Can't he see he looks like Friar Tuck?*

'I don't know what you mean, Johnny.'

'The bloody undergraduates coming back, of course. Don't tell me you're not dreading it. Tomorrow morning they'll be crawling all over college like vermin.' Professor Cavendish shuddered. 'I suppose one shouldn't complain. They are our bread and butter, after all. But really, it's so difficult for college life to run smoothly with so many drunken children underfoot. And to do one's *work*.'

Theo was silent as the two men crossed the cobbled bridge that led into Second Court. He was aware that most of the fellows at St Michael's shared Johnny Cavendish's view of undergraduates as an inconvenience, a necessary cross to be borne. But Theo Dexter didn't see it that way. Just the thought of all those earnest eighteen-year-olds in cheap miniskirts, away from home for the first time, was enough to put a spring in his step and a song in his heart.

Dressed in their long, black academic robes, the professors filed into Hall like penguins on the march. Theo looked around at the familiar faces as grace was said and they sat down to eat. Most of them were elderly and wrinkled, a curmudgeonly group of old farts. Almost all of them were male. Watching them slurp their soup and scatter breadcrumbs through their thinning beards, Theo was conscious of being a class apart. Not only was he half their age, but he was clearly the only senior member of college who took care of himself. With his streaked blond hair, naturally athletic physique and bland, almost soap-star handsome features, Theo took great pride in his looks. His wife Theresa had annoyed him last week by giggling when he came home from a four-day academic symposium in Los Angeles with a mouthful of bright white porcelain veneers.

'What? What's so funny?'

'Sorry, darling. They're jolly nice teeth. It's just that they make you look so . . . American. Were they awfully expensive?'

'Of course not,' lied Theo. They'd actually cost him the better part of fifteen grand, but he wasn't about to tell

Theresa that. In America where Theo had spent most of his postgraduate years, no one criticized you for spending money on your appearance. If anything, good personal grooming was considered a sign of self-respect. This was one of the many things Theo preferred about the States. Here you were made to feel like a vain, shallow idiot. 'Besides, I'm a fellow now. It's part of my job to look professional.'

Unlike his wife, Theo's young mistress Clara had been wildly impressed with his Hollywood smile when she saw it this morning. *Young people appreciate me*, thought Theo. *The sooner the undergraduates breathe some life into this place, the better.*

'My goodness, Professor Dexter. You're ready for your close-up.'

Margaret Haines was smiling. One of only two female fellows in the entire college, Margaret made Theo uncomfortable. A Latin scholar, she was cleverer than he was and only a few years older. He could never quite tell if she was being sincere or taking the piss. In this instance he rather suspected the latter.

'I don't think I've ever seen such a perfectly pressed gown in my life. It looks good with your tan though. Have you and Theresa been away?'

'*I* was away,' Theo said cautiously. 'California, for work. T had to stay here, unfortunately. She's at a crucial stage with her book.'

'Oh. *How* unfortunate.' That smile again. 'You must have been lonely.'

Definitely taking the piss. Stupid old dyke.

'I soldiered on, Margaret.'

'I'm sure you did, Theo. I'm sure you did.'

Margaret Haines had vociferously opposed Theo Dexter's appointment last year, but she'd been shouted down. Anthony Greville, the Master, in particular had been a big supporter. 'Dexter's glamorous. The under-graduates worship him. And he's a natural teacher. We need a bit of vigour at St Michael's, Margaret my dear. A bit of *pizzazz*.'

'The man is ghastly. He's vain and arrogant. Not to mention an inveterate womanizer.'

Greville ran his rheumy old eyes lasciviously over Margaret Haines's body. In her early forties she was still trim and attractive, albeit in a motherly sort of way.

'I can think of worse crimes,' he oiled, smiling to reveal a set of crooked, yellowing teeth. 'Let he who is without sin and all that . . .'

The fellowship had supported him. Margaret Haines wondered how many of them were regretting it now, forced to share high table with Theo's insufferable vanity. The man's self-satisfaction needed a seat all to itself.

'I saw Clara Hausmann leaving your rooms earlier.' Margaret Haines felt a guilty rush of satisfaction watching the smile die on Dexter's lips. 'Back early, is she?'

Theo hesitated for a moment before answering. 'Yes. Clara's been struggling with her dissertation. I've been doing what I can to help.'

'I must say, it's very generous of your wife to share you so freely with your students. Not even term time and already you're giving private tutorials.'

Bitch. If she says anything to make things difficult for me with Theresa . . .

'You forget, my wife teaches herself,' Theo said smoothly. 'She understands the pressures of the job.'

'But not the perks of the job, I imagine.' The meal was over. Margaret Haines got to her feet. 'Something tells me she would be rather less understanding of those. Enjoy the term, Theo.'

Theo Dexter watched her go, feeling something close to hatred. It was no good. St Michael's wasn't big enough for the both of them. He would have to figure out a way to get rid of her.

CHAPTER THREE

Sasha Miller sat in the back seat of her parents' old Volvo, gazing out of the window in wonder.

'There's Downing!'

'Oh my God. That's King's!'

'Look, Dad, that's Trinity. J.J. Thomson was Master there.'

'J.J. who?'

'*Thomson*, Dad.' Sasha shook her head in wonder. 'J.J. Thomson? He discovered the electron in 1897?'

'Oh.' Her parents exchanged smiles. '*That* J.J. Thomson.'

Sasha had been so quiet on the M25, her parents started to worry that something was wrong. She'd mumbled a few words in the Dartford tunnel – something about Will, the lad she was seeing from Tidebrook – then reverted to mutedom all the way up the M11. It was only when they pulled off at exit 11 and made their way through the flat East Anglian landscape towards the ancient city itself that Sasha miraculously sprang back to life.

'It's all so beautiful.'

And it was. Sue Miller wasn't a fan of the featureless countryside they'd driven through on the way here. No hedges, no nice old dry-stone walls, just acres of industrially cultivated rape-seed fields cutting a garish yellow swathe through the landscape. But Cambridge itself was adorable, a medieval, redbrick wonderland with charming cobbled streets and alleyways all tumbling down towards the river and the vast, green expanse of the Backs beyond. Everyone seemed to be on bicycles, not surprisingly given that the roads were so tiny. Twice Don almost scraped the paint off his wing mirror trying to squeeze the Volvo down some wafer-thin alley or other, in search of St Michael's. As for the ludicrously complicated one-way system, at one point they wondered whether they would have to give up on the whole enterprise and go back to Sussex, so impossible was it to get within a mile of Sasha's college. But at last they did get there. Sasha sprang out of the car like a shot.

'Wow.' It was like stepping into a scene from *Brideshead Revisited*. Young men in rugby shirts and college scarves chatted to pretty girls with piles of library books under their arms. Bikes with wicker baskets leaned against every available wall. The spire of St Michael's College Chapel cast a long shadow over the Porters' Lodge. Across the court, Sasha could just glimpse the tops of the punts as they made their sedate way upriver.

I've died and gone to heaven. Just think, on Monday I'm going to see the Cavendish Laboratory, the greatest physics lab on the planet. Twenty-nine Cavendish researchers have won Nobel prizes. Twenty-nine! Imagine if I were the thirtieth?

While Don unloaded the suitcases from the car, Sasha closed her eyes and indulged in her version of the Oscar-night fantasy. Instead of the Pavilion Theatre, Hollywood and an Hervé Léger bandage dress, Sasha was in Oslo City Hall, dressed in . . . well, who cared what she was dressed in, the point was she was receiving her physics prize for her pioneering work in . . . something. There were her parents, teary-eyed with pride. And Mr Cummings, her lovely physics teacher from St Agnes's. And of course Will, looking gorgeous in black tie, escorting her up to the dais . . .

Sasha had said a tearful goodbye to Will last night. For all their plans and promises to each other over the summer, they both knew that her going away would be a giant test for their relationship.

'I've never felt like this about anyone,' Will said truthfully, squeezing Sasha's hand. They were walking through the woods that adjoined Chittenden. Now that his parents were back there was little privacy to be had at Will's house, and none at all at Sasha's shoebox of a cottage. A few weeks ago it was warm enough to make love in the woods at night, gazing up at the stars. (Sex, if she was honest, was still not all Sasha had hoped it might be. Although Will asked her each time if he was 'taking her to heaven and back' and Sasha always loyally replied in the affirmative, the truth was that the celestial round trip was still distinctly short haul.) But now the nights were closing in, it was much too cold for outdoor shagging. Even Will seemed to have lost his enthusiasm.

'I'll miss you so much, Will. But at least we'll be busy.' She tried to look on the bright side. 'You'll be working with your dad. And I'll be in the lab all day and studying all night.'

'Not *all* night, I hope.' Will laughed. 'You have to have some fun, Sasha.'

She looked at him curiously. 'Studying *is* fun. I mean, nobody goes to Cambridge to get drunk and party. It's all about the work.'

'Oi, you lot!' A loud, angry voice from the Porters' Lodge brought Sasha back to reality. 'Bugger off before I send you to the Dean. And stop harassing my freshers!' A group of drunk, semi-naked young men dressed (or half-dressed) as Roman soldiers staggered giggling out of the Lodge, pursued by the irate Head Porter, a beadle-like figure in black suit and bowler hat. As they left, two of them dropped their togas, flashing a pair of unappealingly white and hairy bottoms in Sasha's general direction.

'So sorry, miss.' The panting porter returned. 'Not what you need on your first day at St Michael's.'

'Local yobs from the town, I suppose?' asked Sue Miller disapprovingly.

'Them lot? No, ma'am. They're classics scholars. Ours, unfortunately. What are you reading, miss?'

'Physics,' said Sasha.

'Lovely. We like the scientists. Nice and quiet, your lot. Apart from the medics, of course. You don't want to go out with any of them.'

'Oh, I won't be going out with anybody,' said Sasha earnestly. 'I have a boyfriend. I'm here to study, not socialize.'

The Head Porter looked at her pityingly.

Poor little thing. Like a lamb to the slaughter.

Theresa Dexter watched in exasperation as, one by one, the papers fluttered to the ground.

'Bugger!' Her soft Irish accent rang through the crisp Cambridge air. 'Bollocks. Come here, you stupid . . . oh, no, please don't . . . shit.' She was standing outside her front door, car keys in her mouth, mobile phone wedged between her ear and her shoulder, clutching the most enormous stack of essays escaping from an elastic band. Not only had the first stray papers made a break for freedom, but as the wind picked up, they began to dance around the front garden, taunting Theresa. Two sheets were heading dangerously close to the road. 'I'm sorry, Ma. I'll have to call you back.

Somebody's dissertation is about to get run over by the Madingley bus.'

Dressed inappropriately for the chilly weather in a floaty summer skirt and one of Theo's old shirts, with her tangled mane of pre-Raphaelite curls held precariously in place by a pencil, Theresa dropped everything on the doorstep and began running after the errant essay papers, like an over-excited puppy chasing a butterfly.

'You all right, T? Can I help?'

Jenny Aubrieau, Theresa's next-door neighbour and closest friend in Cambridge, stuck her head over the gate. Jenny was an English scholar, like Theresa, and was married to Jean Paul, a research fellow at Jesus. Jean Paul was always urging Jenny to tell Theresa the truth about her philandering husband – Theo Dexter's extra-curricular love life was the worst-kept secret in the university – but Jenny couldn't bring herself to do it. For one thing they hung out as couples, which made the whole situation doubly awkward. But more importantly, Theresa was so madly, blindly in love with Theo, the truth would destroy her. Besides, maybe Theo would come to his senses and get over his mid-life crisis soon. Jenny Aubrieau hoped so.

'No, I'm all right,' said a flustered Theresa. 'Actually, yes. Grab that one. That one, that one, that one! Oh God.' A single, handwritten sheet flew over the garden gate and dived directly beneath the wheels of an oncoming car. Seconds later more muddy tyres pounded it into oblivion.

'Not the next Shakespeare, I hope?' Jenny helped Theresa retie the remaining papers and carry them out to her car.

'I very much doubt it,' sighed Theresa. 'Still, it's not very professional, is it? *Sorry, what's-your-name, I threw your essay under a car. We'll call it a 2:1, shall we, and better luck next time?* God, I hate teaching.'

'No you don't.' Jenny chucked the files on the back seat of Theresa's Beetle and stood back to wave her off.

'I bloody do. All I want is to be left alone to write.'

'Drink after work? I have to put Amélie and Ben down at seven, but I'm free after that if you are.' Jenny still felt awkward talking about her children in front of Theresa. She knew how desperately her friend wanted kids. Each pregnancy felt like a betrayal. But there came a point when *not* talking about them felt even more awkward. Particularly as these days Jenny's every waking hour seemed to revolve around the little sods.

'I can't. Not tonight. Theo's taking me out for dinner at the University Arms hotel. It's a start-of-term celebration.'

Jenny Aubrieau watched her friend drive happily away and thought, *I wonder what the bastard's feeling guilty about this time?*

Nobody was more surprised when Theo Dexter asked Theresa O'Connor to marry him than Theresa O'Connor herself. Born into a dirt-poor Irish farming family in County Antrim, Theresa had always been a dreamer. A hopeless romantic who couldn't help but see the good in everyone, she appeared to have nothing in common with the worldly, ambitious, self-confident young Englishman whom she first met at a friend's wedding in Dublin five years ago. Nor could she believe that anyone as handsome and brilliant as Theodore Dexter, by then already in his last year at MIT and sporting a mid-Atlantic accent as fake as his gold Rolex, would be interested in her. Theresa had always considered her life to be an endless series of lucky accidents – the acceptance into grammar school and later to Cambridge; her starred first in English literature; and now her soon-to-be marriage to the most eligible man in academia. She never believed herself worthy of the wonderful things that kept happening to her. Still less could she accept that she herself was responsible for them.

But Theo Dexter *did* love Theresa. He loved her wild, Celtic beauty, her white skin and fiery red hair. She was artistic and sensitive, two qualities that he utterly lacked, but was capable of admiring in others, particularly women. She was passionate, terrific in bed and, most important of all, she worshipped the ground he walked on. Other physicists might be reluctant to take Theo Dexter seriously, but Theresa O'Connor was never in any doubt as to his genius. Sleeping with her, just being around her, was like plugging himself in to an inexhaustible ego-recharger. Those who thought that Theo Dexter's ego couldn't possibly *need* recharging did not really know the man. His arrogance and his insecurity had always gone hand in hand.

They were married in Cambridge, in the ancient Holy Trinity Church on Bridge Street. Theo would have liked a more lavish affair, but they couldn't afford it. Theresa would have been happy in a register office in Slough, so great was her joy at becoming Mrs Dexter. She wore a plain white dress from Next for the service, teamed with flat ballet slippers (Theo hated her in heels; they made him look short). Despite her simple attire, or perhaps because of it, the bride couldn't have looked more radiant. At the reception, a simple affair at the Regent hotel, Theo's best man, Robert, made a joke about how much the happy couple had in common.

'Theresa loves Theo. And Theo loves Theo. They're a perfect match!' Theo laughed thinly, but the rest of the guests roared. 'The only two people in Cambridge who think Theo's cleverer than Theresa are Theo and Theresa.' More laughter. 'Here's hoping the kids have Mum's looks *and* Mum's brains.'

Theo thought: *Note to self: Drop Robert Hammond as a friend.*

Theresa thought: *I wonder how long it'll be before I get pregnant?*

'Polycystic ovaries.'

'I'm sorry?'

'Poly – cystic – ovaries.' Dr Thomas, Theresa's Harley Street consultant, sounded irritated. A gruff, bullying man in his sixties with overgrown caterpillar eyebrows and a pink bow tie, Dr Thomas was a brilliant gynaecologist. But he had the bedside manner of a Stalinist general. 'Your ovaries produce fewer eggs. In addition, in your particular case, the quality of those eggs you *do* produce is extremely poor.'

'I see.' Theresa bit her lower lip hard, trying not to cry. *My life is perfect. What right do I have to blub over one tiny setback?*

'So what do we do from here? IVF? Donor eggs? What's the next step?' Theo spoke brusquely, trying to sound in control. Deep down he was overwhelmed with relief that the problem wasn't on his side. Not that he wanted kids, far from it. But no man liked the idea that they were shooting blanks.

'I would give IVF a very low chance of success in your wife's case.'

Theresa swallowed. 'But there is *some* chance?'

'Less than five per cent. You'd be wasting your time,' said Dr Thomas brutally. Despite herself, Theresa felt her eyes well up with tears.

Theo asked, 'We can still try naturally, though, can't we?'

'You can try.' Dr Thomas shrugged. 'Otherwise I would steer you towards considering adoption.'

Theresa's eyes lit up, but Theo shook his head firmly.

'No. Not for us, thank you, Doctor. I've no interest in raising another man's mistake.'

On the long drive back to Cambridge, Theresa stared out

of the car window in silent misery. As always in times of trouble, her mind turned to Shakespeare:

'The miserable have no other medicine but only hope.'

I will not give up hope. I will keep trying.

She'd been disappointed by Theo's hostility to the idea of adoption. But then why *shouldn't* he want a child of his own? After all, she did. It was her fault they couldn't conceive, not poor Theo's. Suddenly she was seized with panic. What if he left her? What if he left her because she couldn't have children?

'Of all base passions, fear is the most accursed.'

I can't let the fear defeat me. I have to believe. We will have children. Somehow. We will.

By the time Theresa got to the new English faculty building on West Road she was fifteen minutes late. Running across the car park, she felt sweat trickling down the back of her neck and an unpleasant wetness spreading under her arms and breasts. Panting from the exertion, she pushed open the door of the lecture room.

'Sorry, everyone. Terrible traffic. I'm afraid I've had a bit of a disaster with . . .' She looked up. Three faces looked back at her.

'Where are the others? Is this it?'

Mai Lin, a sweet Asian-American girl from Girton, said kindly, 'Maybe they got stuck in traffic too?' But all four people in the room knew this was a lie.

Theresa knew the dropout rate for her seminars was high. Students complained that they were too chaotic, that they strayed too far from the parameters of Part II Shakespeare and the topics that they needed to cover for finals.

'But there's more to life than exams!' Theresa pleaded with the head of the faculty. 'Where's their soul? Where's their passion? How can they possibly expect to cover something as breathtaking as *Macbeth* in two one-hour sessions?'

'Because if they don't, my dear, they won't cover the rest of the tragedies and they'll fail their degrees. You *must* stick to the syllabus, Theresa.'

'But I thought teaching was about inspiring people?'

'Oh, my dear.' The Head of English doubled over with laughter. 'Whatever gave you that idea?'

Still, Theresa thought glumly, looking around the empty room, *I can't inspire them if they're not here. If only I had a vocation for teaching, like Theo. His lectures are always packed to bursting.*

Depressed, she opened her notes.

'Right, well, for those of you who *have* made the effort. Let's get started, shall we?'

Sasha's first week at St Michael's went by so fast, and there was so much to take in, it was like being in a particle accelerator. She was tiny. Cambridge was huge. And everything was moving at light speed.

Her room was a bit disappointing. A small, featureless box in the only ugly part of the college, a concrete seventies accommodation block that had apparently won loads of architectural awards despite looking like the multi-storey car park in Tunbridge Wells, it was hardly the ivory tower of Sasha's fantasies.

'I wouldn't worry about it if I were you.' Georgia, a drop-dead-gorgeous blonde architecture student from across the hall, told Sasha cheerfully, helping herself to the last of the homemade biscuits Sasha's mum had left. 'You're not going to be spending much time in your room.'

'I suppose that's true,' said Sasha, thinking of the physics library and the Cavendish labs.

'Course it's true. The JCR bar doesn't close till midnight, and there's always a party somewhere afterwards.' Georgia bounced up and down on Sasha's bed with excitement. 'Have you joined any societies yet?'

'Societies?'

'Yes, you know. Like the Union or Footlights.'

'God, no.' Sasha shuddered. The Cambridge Union was a debating society and the Footlights a comedic dramatic club. The very thought of speaking in public under any circumstances brought Sasha out in a rash. How anyone could sign up for such a thing *by choice* was incomprehensible.

'Well, what sort of things are you interested in?' asked Georgia. 'These biscuits are delicious, by the way.'

'Thanks.' Sasha smiled. 'I'm interested in physics. Radiophysics, cryophysics, physics of phase transitions and magnetism.'

Georgia's eyes widened. Sasha went on.

'You know, all of it really, quantum optics, semiconductors and dielectrics . . .'

'So not a big cookery fan, then?'

'Cookery?'

'That was a joke.' Georgia looked at her new friend with a combination of admiration and pity. Clearly she was going to have to introduce Sasha to the concept of fun. 'Look, I get it. You're Einstein.'

'Oh, no.' Sasha was mortified. 'I didn't mean to imply . . . I'm nothing special. Certainly not by Cambridge standards.'

'Bollocks to Cambridge standards,' said Georgia robustly. 'You're obviously an evil genius or you wouldn't be here. You've probably got a *laser* in your room. *Do you have a laser, Scott?*' She put on her best Dr Evil voice but it went right over Sasha's head. 'Never mind. The point is, we're at St Michael's now.' Grabbing Sasha's hand she dragged her over to the window. Outside, the college's picture-postcard courts and bridges lay spread out below them like a wonderland. 'Our mission is to have the time of our fucking lives,' said Georgia. 'Are you with me?'

Somehow Sasha knew instinctively that this was a rhetorical question. Georgia Adams was a force of nature. Sasha was with her whether she liked it or not.

From that day on the two girls were inseparable. The outgoing, flirtatious blonde and the quiet, mysterious brunette were the talk of freshers week. Party invitations flooded into Georgia and Sasha's pigeonholes – all the third year Casanovas had bets on who would be the first to get one of them into bed – but even Georgia found that she had less time for partying than she'd hoped, what with all the paperwork and reading lists, supervisions, seminars, and, of course, exploring Cambridge itself.

'It's an architect's paradise,' sighed Georgia, wandering from college to college, where exquisite Gothic buildings huddled cheek by jowl with some truly stunning modern architecture. Treasure troves that they were, there was more to Cambridge than the colleges. There was Kettle's Yard Gallery, centuries-old pubs like the Pickerel with its low beams and roaring log fire. There were the grand museums on Downing Street, and Parker's Piece, and the teashop at Grantchester that let you moor punts in the garden. There were quaint cobbled alleys, magnificent churches, twee pink-painted cottages and outrageous neo-classical mansions. And it was *theirs*. It was all *theirs*.

For Sasha, the highlight of her first week was the tour of the Cavendish laboratory. Possibly the ugliest building in England, and certainly the ugliest in Cambridge, to Sasha Miller it was the most mesmerizing thing she had ever seen. This was where the magic happened! This was the Emerald City of Oz. The third-year physicist from Magdalene who showed her around didn't appear to share Sasha's enthusiasm. A skinny, greasy-haired boy with a Birmingham accent and acne so severe that he was more spot than face, he led Sasha from room to room with a look of pained ennui. *Doesn't he realize that we're standing on the frontier of experimental physics? That we're walking in the shadows of the great Cavendish professors, of Maxwell and Thompson, Bragg and Mott?* Sasha couldn't wait to call Will tonight and tell him all about it.

They emerged into the daylight – to Sasha's regret and her guide's relief, the tour was over – and Sasha noticed an extraordinarily good-looking blond man surrounded by an admiring throng of female undergraduates.

'Who's that?'

'Professor Dexter.' The boy's Brummie accent made him sound even more bored. 'Fancy him, do yow?'

Sasha blushed. 'Don't be so ridiculous. I wondered what the fuss was about, that's all. The man's being mobbed.'

'Well. You'll find out for yerself soon enough, won't yow?'

'What do you mean?'

'You're at St Michael's?'

Sasha nodded.

'So's he. Physics fellow. He'll be your Director of Studies.'

Sasha looked at the man again – what she could make out of him through the herd of miniskirts and low-rise jeans. *He looks very young to be a fellow. I hope he knows what he's talking about.* How awful it would be to have made it to Cambridge only to be taught physics by someone second-rate. Still, one shouldn't judge by appearances. Lots of people thought Will was a standard-issue, shallow, rugby-obsessed, public school boy when they first met him.

Which only went to show how wrong first impressions could be.

*   *   *

Professor Theo Dexter sat in his rooms at St Michael's hunched over his computer in a foul mood. Last week's optimism about the new term already felt like a distant memory. So far, this year's intake of undergraduates had been dismal. Barely a single good-looking girl amongst them. As for the physicists, it made you wonder what the hell the government's two hundred million pounds of extra education spending was being spent on. Certainly not hiring decent science teachers. To think that these kids were the best that the English school system had to offer. Morons the lot of them. God, it was depressing.

He turned back to his book. *Cursed bloody thing.* As an academic, you were expected to publish your own work at least every few years. Most scholars, including Theresa, considered this 'the fun part' and saw teaching as a distraction to their studies. For Theo it was the other way around. He found the obligation to continually reinvent the wheel and come up with new theories an immense drain on his time and energy. The truth was, he wasn't much of an original thinker. He was bright, naturally. Unlike most of his colleagues he was also a good communicator, with a gift for expressing the most complex ideas in theoretical physics in simple, human terms. But Theo Dexter had yet to stumble across that one, seminal thought that would forever be identified with his name. Deep down he was wildly envious of his wife's ability to come up with new angles on Shakespearean criticism over her Special K every morning. Not that he'd ever have told *her* that. Inspiration seemed to explode out of Theresa involuntarily, like a sneeze. Theo Dexter knew that his fellow physicists considered him a 'plodder'. If only he had half his wife's instinctive, unstructured brilliance, they might start taking him seriously. As it was . . .

A knock on the door disturbed him. *Who the hell could that be? I don't have any supervisions this morning.*

'Yes?' He sounded less than welcoming. Tentatively the door creaked open.

'Professor Dexter?'

'Yes? For God's sake, come in whoever you are. Don't skulk in the corridor like a thief.'

A young girl shuffled nervously into the room. Theo's first thought was, *She's escaped from the circus.* Dressed in baggy, striped trousers teamed with a multi-coloured, polka-dotted shirt, dark hair flying all over the place, mascara smudged, she looked like a lunatic. His second thought was, *She's pretty.* It was hard to make out much of her figure beneath the billowing clothes, but the face was angelic. Porcelain-white skin, wide-set green eyes, hair as black and gleaming as liquid tar.

'Can I help you?'

'I'm Sasha Miller. I've got a supervision with you this morning. Eleven o'clock?'

So she's a physicist! One of mine. Thank you, God. At last.

'Ah. Miss Miller. Well, your supervision was actually scheduled for yesterday morning. But do come in.'

'Oh God. Was it?' Sasha blushed scarlet. 'I'm terribly sorry. I'm afraid I can be a bit disorganized sometimes. I'm working on it.'

Theo offered her a chair. In a fluster, Sasha somehow managed to miss the seat, lowering her bottom into mid air and only just righting herself before she hit the floor.

'Sorry.' She clung to the chair's arms like life rafts.

Theo smiled. *She's adorable. So gauche. I wonder if she's even eighteen yet?*

'Don't worry,' he said kindly. 'A lot of people get muddled in their first week. How are you finding Cambridge?'

'Oh my goodness, it's perfect,' Sasha gushed. 'Just magical, thank you. St Michael's is like a dream come true.' She thought, *He seems very kind. I shouldn't have judged him so harshly the other day.*

'It's certainly a very special place,' said Theo. *I wonder if her nipples go darker when she blushes?* 'Especially for we physicists. These are exciting times, Sasha. World-changing times. And Cambridge is right at the heart of it.'

Sasha felt a rush of excitement and pride so strong she had to grip the chair even tighter. She loved the way he said 'we'. Professor Theodore Dexter, a Cambridge physics professor, her tutor, was addressing *her*, Sasha Miller from Frant, as an equal. She felt like a co-conspirator in some wonderful, top-secret plot. Looking at him close up for the first time, she had to admit that Professor Dexter really was terribly good looking. Better looking than he'd seemed across the car park at the Cavendish labs. He reminded her of an American actor . . . she was so bad with names, she'd never remember which one . . . one of the doctors from *ER* perhaps? He was certainly very young. She'd been right about that the other day. *But that doesn't necessarily mean anything. Isaac Newton discovered the generalized binomial theorem at twenty-two. Mozart wrote his first concerto at six. You can't put an age limit on genius.*

'Listen, Sasha, I'm afraid I'm a bit busy just at the moment. I wasn't expecting you, you see.'

'Oh. Of course.' Embarrassed, Sasha got up to go. 'I'll get the notes from one of the others and I'll, er . . . I'll come back next week. Sorry.'

'Please, stop apologizing,' said Theo smoothly. 'If you like I could meet you somewhere for a drink this evening? We can talk through the course, what's expected of you, the lecture schedules . . . that sort of thing.'

It was such an unexpected suggestion that for a moment Sasha didn't say anything. She was supposed to be calling Will this evening for a proper chat. She'd even blown off Georgia, who'd been on at her to come to some quiz night at Caius, because she wanted to focus on Will. It had only been a week, but already Sasha felt as if the distance between them was growing. All the magazines said that long-distance relationships took work.

But she couldn't exactly turn down her professor. Not after he'd been so understanding about her coming at the wrong time and all that.

'All right. Thanks. Where should I . . .?'

'I'll leave a note in your pigeonhole.'

Sasha left and Theo turned back to his book. All of a sudden his spirits had lifted exponentially.

Perhaps inspiration was about to strike after all?

CHAPTER FOUR

Michaelmas term seemed to race by. Sasha hadn't ever known time to pass so quickly. Once the excitement of freshers week was over, St Michael's got back to work. The bar was still packed every night, but by eight thirty in the morning a steady stream of green-faced undergraduates could be seen on their bicycles heading for labs or libraries. Even Georgia, whose dedication to partying was the stuff of legend, dutifully trekked off to the architecture faculty building every morning with a back-breaking stack of files under her arm.

When she didn't have a supervision – one-on-one teaching with Professor Dexter – Sasha spent her days shuttling between the Cavendish lab and the university library. After a brief panic in the first two weeks, when she'd worried she might be out of her depth intellectually (Professor Clancy's 'introductory' lecture on nanophotonics was so impenetrable, he might as well have been speaking Urdu), she soon relaxed and began to delight in her studies. Not only was the teaching phenomenal – physics lessons at St Agnes's felt like another lifetime already – but the facilities and technology at her disposal were the stuff of Sasha's dreams. Of course, it was the Astrophysics course that really excited her: the formation of stars and planets, observational cosmology, evolution of galaxies, active galactic nuclei. Sasha had been obsessed with space before she knew how to say the word. She felt incredibly lucky that her own Director of Studies at St Michael's, Professor Dexter, was an astrophysicist himself. Not to mention a wonderful teacher and mentor.

Sasha's respect and admiration for Professor Dexter had grown exponentially since their first drink together in freshers week. Not only was he clearly an *amazing* physicist, but he really went the extra mile to nurture and encourage his students. He was constantly offering Sasha extra help with her assignments. When she began her first solo research project, into astrophysical plasmas, he even took time out of his weekend to come round to her rooms and check her work. How many professors did that? Of course, he was probably only too glad to get out of the house for a while, poor man. Over the past few weeks Professor Dexter – Theo – had opened his heart to Sasha about his unhappy marriage. His wife's drinking problem and affairs had clearly wreaked a terrible emotional toll. But he was loyal to a fault, putting up with her blind rages. Bipolar disorder could do terrible things to a person. Sasha felt that, on some unspoken level, she and Professor Dexter had become friends. Their twice-weekly supervisions were the highlight of her week.

By contrast, one of the hardest parts of Sasha's week was her regular Sunday-night phone call to Will. Every week she looked forward to hearing his voice. And every week they seemed to run out of things to say to each other almost immediately. It had got to the point where Sasha had taken to writing bullet-point lists before each call, pieces of news she could tell him, questions she could ask to keep things going. Twice he'd promised to come up and visit her, and twice he'd cancelled because of rugby.

'I do miss you, babe. But I can't let the lads down. Maybe you could come back to Sussex for a weekend? We're playing Saracens' Second Fifteen on Sunday, there's gonna be a huge party at High Rocks afterwards.'

'I can't, darling. Not this weekend. I've got so much work to do,' said Sasha. Then she felt guilty all week because she'd lied to him, and she didn't know why. *What's happening to us?*

At last, one Saturday in late November, Will made it up to Cambridge. Sasha met him at the station, wrapped up in so many layers of sweaters and scarves he almost didn't recognize her.

'Christ on a bike, it's cold up here,' he shivered, hugging her tightly on the platform. 'This *wind*. It's like bloody Siberia.' Dressed in his favourite Diesel jeans and Tonbridge rugby shirt under a cool leather bomber jacket, he looked even more handsome than Sasha remembered him. He smelled of Givenchy aftershave and mouthwash, and his arms felt so strong and wonderful around her. *What an idiot I've been,* thought Sasha. *He's perfect. Everything's going to be fine.*

In the taxi, he reached under Sasha's duffel coat and put a cold hand on her thigh.

'I can't wait to unwrap you, my darling. Have you missed me?'

'Of course I have,' said Sasha, adding guiltily, 'there's been so much to do here, that's all, work and finding my way around and stuff. I can't wait to show you St Michael's. Isn't Cambridge beautiful?'

They were driving down Trumpington Street, in the heart of the old university district, but Will wasn't interested in sightseeing.

'Mmmm,' he yawned. 'You're not on your period are you?'

Sasha blushed. 'No!'

'Good.' Will's hand crept higher. 'I'm sorry to be blunt, but this is the longest time I've gone without sex since I was like, twelve. The only part of St Michael's I'm interested in is your bedroom.'

Don't be annoyed, Sasha told herself. *He's trying to pay you a compliment. You should be grateful he's stayed faithful. There'll be plenty of time to show him around tomorrow.*

At Will's request, they spent the afternoon squeezed into Sasha's minute single bed. Sex felt awkward at first. Sasha had forgotten how perfect Will's body was, taut and athletic and muscular, like a Michelangelo sculpture. She'd also forgotten how fit he was. As much as she fancied him, after the third round of shagging she was starting to feel not just bored but exhausted. And sore. Will's idea of foreplay was to kiss each boob once before launching himself into her like an Exocet.

'Are you hungry, darling?' she asked tentatively as he came loudly for a third time before rolling off her, spent. If rugby was Will's favourite thing in the world and sex his second favourite, Sasha had learned early that food ran a close third. 'I thought we might wander down to the Pickerel. It's a really lovely old pub. They do a good lasagne, and you could meet some of my friends.'

'Sure.' Will bounded out of bed like a Labrador. Lasagne sounded wicked. Sasha's nerdy science-geek mates would be less wicked, but he could put up with them for an hour or two if he had to. 'We'll regain our strength before tonight!'

He grinned.

Good heavens, thought Sasha. *At this rate I'll be in a wheel-chair by the end of the weekend.*

Half an hour later Sasha walked into the pub with Will and was immediately dragged to the loo by Georgia.

'Oh. My. *God. That's* Will? That boy-band hottie with the Justin Timberlake arse?'

Sasha laughed. 'I told you he was attractive.'

'*Attractive?* He's Brad bloody Pitt, Sash. If I had a bloke like that at home I'd have told St Michael's to stick their offer. How could you bear to leave him?'

Half an hour later, Georgia was beginning to understand how Sasha could have borne it. Will Temple was one of the most handsome boys she'd ever seen. He was also vain, self-centred and a complete cretin.

'I've never seen the point of university myself, to be honest. Obviously I'm pleased for Sasha. But I'm more interested in the real world. The UOL.'

'I'm sorry?' Georgia smiled politely.

'University of Life. I'm all about experiences, you know. Travel, other cultures.'

'I see. And have you travelled much?'

'Oh God yeah. I've been to France, loads of times. And I've been on rugby tours all over. Australia, Samoa, New Zealand . . .'

'Three hotbeds of culture . . .' Georgia muttered under her breath, but Will wasn't listening. Will never listened.

'Sport's the one true international language,' he went on. 'It can totally bring people together. But you know what I'm talking about. You must be a sportswoman, right? You don't get *that* kind of body stuck in a library all day sitting on your arse, that's for sure.'

Georgia winced. *How can Sasha stand this guy? He's been shamelessly flirting with me all evening right in front of her. And he's totally ignored the rest of our group, Lisa and Josie and all the boys. All he cares about is impressing women. Well he certainly doesn't impress me.*

'Josie's been to New Zealand,' Georgia changed the subject.

'Have you?' asked Sasha.

'Last year. For a biology field trip. It was incredible.' The chubby, chipmunk-faced redhead began to talk about the rainforests. Will feigned interest for about twenty seconds, then yawned pointedly and turned to Sasha.

'I'm really knackered, babe. Let's go back to yours.'

Sasha looked at her watch. 'But it's only nine o'clock, Will. It's a bit early to go to bed isn't it?'

'Don't worry. We won't be going to sleep.' He winked at Georgia.

Prick.

'I'll have a quick slash and we can make a move. Nice meeting you all.' Getting to his feet, Will made his way to the men's loos.

'Sorry,' said Sasha. She was clearly embarrassed. 'He doesn't mean to be rude. It's just we haven't seen each other for ages.'

No one said anything. In the end Danny, a wry engineer from Glasgow, said gently, 'You know, Sasha, it's none o' my business. But I wouldnae say the two of you have an awful lot in common.'

'We do,' Sasha shot back automatically. 'Honestly. At home we do. I think he feels a bit out of place here, that's all. He'll get used to it.'

I hope not, thought Georgia. The thought of Will Temple

becoming a regular feature of their weekends was enough to make her bring up her lasagne.

On the walk back to college, it started to snow. Thick, soft flakes drifted down onto the cobbles, their progress illuminated by the warm orange glow of the street lamps. In front of them, King's College Chapel rose out of the darkness like a fairytale castle. Sasha snuggled tighter into Will's body.

'You can see why I love it here, can't you?'

'Sure.'

Not a flicker of interest. Sasha tried again.

'I mean, there's a magic to it. Something in the air. Do you know what I mean?'

'The air?' said Will absently. 'The air's arctic. How far are we from your college? My nuts are about to drop off. '

For the first time all day, Will noticed that Sasha was upset. She'd pulled away and started walking faster up ahead of him.

'What's the matter?'

'It's you. *You're* the matter.' She turned around. Snowflakes began to settle on her shoulders. 'You were really rude to my friends back there.'

'Oh, come on, Sash. They weren't exactly the most exciting bunch. Apart from the blonde.' He smiled knowingly.

'They're my *friends*, Will. Do you know how bored I am with *your* friends? But at least I make an effort.'

Now it was Will's turn to get angry. 'An effort? Don't talk to me about making an effort. At least I came up here to see you, which is more than you've been bothered to do all autumn.'

'Well, why *did* you come? You don't want to see me. All you want to do is have sex!'

'So? What's wrong with sex? Jesus, Sasha. If you want

to go out with a fucking intellectual why don't you go and marry Stephen bloody Hawking? It's not me that's changed. It's you.'

That night they lay together in stony silence. Will fell asleep after about an hour, but Sasha lay awake, staring at the ceiling, trying to sort through her conflicting feelings. *Is he right? Have I changed?* She couldn't bear the thought that she'd abandoned him. They'd been so happy last summer, in the woods at Tidebrook. Was this how Professor Dexter felt, lying in bed next to his mean, bipolar wife? A stranger in his own life?

The next morning they patched things up, on the surface anyway. Will's train was at two, so they spent the morning walking along the snowy Backs and had a goodbye lunch at Wagamama.

'How are your noodles?'

'Fine, thanks. Would you like another Coke?'

'Oh, I'm OK. Thanks.'

The politeness was awful.

By three o'clock, Sasha was back at St Michael's. It was properly winter now, and the sky was already beginning to fade to a bluish twilight that made the snow-covered college look like a Christmas card. But Sasha couldn't enjoy it. She'd blown things with Will. It was over. In a few weeks she'd be home in Sussex for the holidays, and he'd be out with some other girl. *Carolina Fuller probably. She'd been after him for months. Slut.* Would Sasha regret it once she got home? Here, at Cambridge, her life in Sussex felt like a dream. But what if it was the other way around? What if home and Will were her reality, and her undergraduate life was just a passing phase? What if she never found love again?

'Penny for your thoughts?'

Theo, looking ruggedly gorgeous in a blue cable-knit sweater and jeans, emerged from his rooms on First Court.

'It can't be that bad, surely?'

Sasha shrugged. 'I don't know if it's bad or not. I think I just broke up with my boyfriend.'

With immense difficulty, Theo suppressed a grin.

'Poor Sasha. That's hard. Break-ups are always hard.'

Sasha smiled. *He's so nice. Maybe it's because he's younger than other professors? He can still remember what it's like to be our age.* 'How come you're in college on a Sunday, Professor Dexter? Isn't it your day off?'

'Sasha, if I have to tell you again I'm going to throttle you. It's Theo, OK? You're not in sixth form now.'

'OK,' Sasha giggled. 'Sorry.'

'And yes, it is my day off, but to be perfectly honest with you I couldn't face the silence at home.' His handsome brow furrowed. 'I don't really want to talk about it,' he said stoically. 'What about you? Where are you off to?'

'The library,' said Sasha. 'Thank God for research, eh? You can really lose yourself. There's nothing like astrophysical plasmas to take one's mind off things, don't you find?'

Theo laughed aloud. She was so earnest.

'I tell you what. I've got a better idea. How about we cheer each other up? Have you ever seen the St Michael's wine cellars?'

'Of course not.' St Michael's College was renowned for having one of the best-stocked, most valuable wine cellars not just in Cambridge but in all of Europe. For obvious reasons, undergraduates were not allowed access to them. Only a very small number of fellows had keys, and even they had to sign in to a log book and follow certain, time-honoured security procedures.

'Would you like to?'

Sasha nodded eagerly. She wasn't much of a drinker, but her dad was a keen amateur wine buff. If she passed up this chance he'd never forgive her.

'Good. Follow me.'

Theo led her over the bridge into Second Court. Pulling out a cluster of keys, he unlocked the heavy oak door to St Michael's Formal Hall and pushed it open. Sasha had eaten in Hall a few times. Like Theo she loved the formality and tradition of it, getting dressed up in her gown and all that. But she'd never seen the place empty. Being here now, alone, she felt like Beauty exploring the Beast's enchanted castle. It was illicit and exciting.

'This way.'

She followed Theo up the steps to the high table, where the Master and all the senior fellows sat. Sasha couldn't resist running her fingers along the polished mahogany table as they walked its length, eventually coming to some steps that led down to a red velvet curtain. Behind the curtain was another door.

'It's like Oz!' Sasha laughed.

'Isn't it?' Theo unlocked the second door. A smell of damp stone, musty and ancient, hit Sasha in the face like a punch. Behind the door everything was dark. Theo fumbled for the light switch and a dim, thirty-watt bulb flickered to life, revealing a winding stone staircase. 'Either that or Scooby Doo. When I first came down here I confidently expected a mummy to leap out of one of the alcoves and start chasing me.'

Sasha thought, *He's so much fun.* Guiltily she realized that she'd forgotten about Will already. His train wouldn't even have reached London yet.

Edging their way down the staircase, leaning on the stone wall for support, they finally emerged into a vaulted, redbrick crypt. Fumbling in his pocket for a lighter, Theo pulled it out and to Sasha's delight reached up and lit an old-fashioned oil lamp bracketed to the wall. The effect was marvellously Dickensian. Hundreds, no, thousands of dusty bottles danced in the light of the flickering flame. Theo lit another lamp, then a third. In the middle of the room was a simple refectory table with two benches and a single, high-backed chair with a cushion at the head. It was laid with about twenty wine glasses, long stemmed and each topped with bowls almost as big as Sasha's head, and an exquisite ivory corkscrew. At the back of the room was a rather tatty sofa and a rattan ottoman with a lid. Idly, Sasha wandered over and opened it. Inside were piles of neatly stacked blankets.

'It can get pretty cold down here,' Theo explained. 'You should put one on. And get one out for me.'

He was writing something in a thick, leather-bound log book by the door. Signing his name with a flourish, he smiled and turned to Sasha.

'Can I offer you a drink, Miss Miller?'

'Oh, no, we can't.' She handed him his blanket. 'Won't you get in trouble?'

'Don't worry about me,' said Theo. 'The Master's an old friend. Red or white?'

Sasha hesitated. This felt like the sort of thing you could get sent down for. On the other hand, if Professor Dexter said it was all right ... what the hell. After the weekend she'd had she deserved a drink.

'Red.' *Georgia's always telling me to be more impulsive and let my hair down. If only she could see me now!*

'Red it is.'

Theo selected a bottle thick with dust and pulled it out. 'This should do to get us started.'

Sasha looked at the label and gasped. It was a Château Pétrus Bordeaux, 1984. 'Pétrus? No, no, no, we can't possibly. Do you realize how much this is worth?'

'I do,' said Theo, expertly drawing the cork with a gentle pop and pouring two glasses. He handed one to Sasha. 'The question is, Sasha: do you realize how much *you're* worth?'

He was staring at her, holding eye contact. Sasha felt her insides liquefy and her knees start to wobble. *Is he coming on to me?* But no, he couldn't be. He was her professor. Her married professor. Besides, even if he wanted to be unfaithful (understandable in his situation) a man like Theo Dexter could have any woman he wanted. He wouldn't be interested in a teenage nobody like her.

Holding out his hand, Theo stroked her cheek. *Oh my God.* Sasha felt as if she was about to pass out. 'Sasha. Beautiful Sasha . . .'

'Professor Dexter, I . . .'

'Shhhh.' Leaning forward, he put down his wine glass and stopped her with a kiss. It started as a tender brushing of the lips. But before Sasha knew it their whole bodies were entwined, pressing against one another. Theo's tongue felt hot inside her mouth, caressing her, teasing her. The only other person Sasha had kissed was Will, and that had felt . . . well, nothing like this, that was for sure. It was all very disconcerting. Her limbs seemed to be acting with a mind of their own. Were those her fingers in Professor Dexter's hair? Theo pressed his hard thigh between Sasha's legs and she jumped like a flea on a hotplate.

'Stop! We can't.' Panicked, she pulled away from him. 'I'm . . . you're . . . this is definitely against the rules.'

'Whose rules?' Theo kissed her again. *God, it was heavenly.*

'Everybody's rules!' She squirmed free again. 'I'm your

student, Professor . . . Theo. You're my teacher. And you're married.'

Theo's quick mind was working overtime. He had to tread very carefully here. He'd put in a lot of groundwork with Sasha all term and he didn't want to blow it at the last hurdle. *I mustn't be the bad guy. I have to make her feel sorry for me.*

'I know.' He sat down on one of the benches and put his head in his hands. Sasha tried to feel relieved, but part of her – a big part – wished he would waive aside her objections and start kissing her again. *What am I getting myself into?* She took a big slug of her wine, choked, then took another, draining her glass. She sat down next to Theo, who wordlessly reached for the bottle and poured her another.

'I'm being selfish,' he said. 'I know that. You've got your whole life ahead of you. I shouldn't be burdening you with my marital problems. Sometimes I just feel like . . .' He paused, as if struggling to find the right words. 'Like I'd like some happiness for myself for a change. It sounds awful, doesn't it?'

'No. Not at all.' Instinctively, Sasha put her arms around him. 'And you're not burdening me. I'm happy to listen.'

The mothering instinct, thought Theo. *Women can't resist a bird with a broken wing.*

'You've been so kind to me since I got here, Pro . . . Theo,' she blushed. 'The least I can do is return the favour.'

Theo swirled the Pétrus around in his glass, gazing into the deep purple liquid as if the secret to his life's problems might lie hidden in its depths. Then he took a slow sip and said quietly, 'You're not attracted to me. Well, why would you be?' He flashed Sasha a sweet, self-deprecating smile. 'In your eyes I'm probably only a few years away from my pension.'

'That is absolutely not true!' Sasha touched his cheek, turning him to face her. The Pétrus must have gone straight to her head or she would never have been so forward. But her inhibitions seemed to be deserting her. 'I think you're extremely attractive. Everybody does,' she added, immediately regretting blurting out the last part. She didn't want to sound like some sort of groupie.

'I can't help it Sasha.' Tears welled up in Theo's eyes. 'When I'm with you, I feel like I can glimpse my future. And for the first time in years, I see happiness.'

'Oh, Theo.' Sasha leaned forwards and kissed him. There was no hesitation this time. Slipping his hands under her shirt, cupping her magnificent teenage breasts, it was all Theo could do not to punch the air in triumph. Swiftly, joyously, his practised hands unclasped her bra and helped her out of her jeans, stripping off layer after layer of clothing like an erotic game of pass the parcel. Bending his head to kiss her belly, then tracing his tongue slowly down to her smooth, creamy thighs, Theo felt Sasha's back arch and heard her gasp involuntarily, lost in pleasure and too inexperienced to hide it.

'You're shaking,' he whispered. 'Are you cold?'

'A little,' murmured Sasha.

Theo grinned, 'Let's warm you up then, shall we?'

Hastily throwing one of the blankets down on the table, he lifted her up as easily as he might a rag doll and lay her down on her back. Still dressed himself – there was no need for both of them to catch hypothermia – he unceremoniously unzipped his flies to release an erection that put poor Will's in the shade. Grabbing Sasha's hand he curled her fingers around it.

'Good God.' Her eyes widened. 'It's huge!'

Could this get any better?

'It is all yours,' he whispered, thrusting himself inside her with so much force that she slid two feet up the table. Her body was exquisite, perfectly proportioned, slim yet succulent. He couldn't keep his lips off those perfect breasts, and his hands groped greedily for her buttocks as he fucked her harder and faster, racing towards climax. But best of all were Sasha's responses. So desirous, so uninhibited! She made him feel like Mick Jagger.

Theo had been bored of Clara for months now. The porno body that had once so excited him now seemed grotesque. It was like fucking a pregnant sow. When sex with your wife was more exciting than sex with your mistress, something was very wrong. But now dear, sweet little Sasha Miller was here. And everything was very, very right.

With one final jerk of the hips, Theo Dexter closed his eyes and came. He felt the glorious tightening of Sasha's muscles around him, heard her moaning with her own orgasm as she bucked and writhed helplessly beneath him.

This was going to be a great year after all.

Back at home, Theresa was putting the finishing touches to her signature chocolate fudge cake. It was Theo's favourite, and she'd spent the entire afternoon baking it, neglecting her book, in the hope of cheering him up. He'd disappeared after breakfast this morning in a foul mood, mumbling something about going into college, and hadn't so much as texted her since.

Staring out of the kitchen window at the snowy front garden, Theresa watched a little robin hop tentatively across the lawn, eyeing the bird feeder in her apple tree.

Poor thing. I forgot to fill it. Theo was always getting cross with her for her forgetfulness. But how was one supposed to remember not to forget things, that was the question? *I'll do it as soon as I've iced the cake.*

Biting her lip, eyes narrowed in concentration, she began tracing a perfect, italic *T* in icing sugar across the gooey chocolate. *Like snow on a ploughed field.* Jenny and Jean Paul had gone out to Grantchester to make snowmen with the kids. Sensing Theresa's loneliness, Jenny had asked her to join them, but Theresa didn't feel like playing gooseberry. Besides, Theo might be back any minute. Whatever was troubling him, he wouldn't want to come home and find a dark, empty house.

She finished the cake, and then disappeared to hunt for kindling so she could light a nice, welcoming fire.

She'd completely forgotten about the robin.

In St Michael's wine cellar, curled up naked on the sofa under a big pile of blankets, Sasha Miller lay in Professor Theo Dexter's arms in blissful shock.

Will Temple's Casanova reputation would never recover.

'What are you thinking?' Theo softly stroked her hair.

I'm thinking about what my wedding dress will look like. I'm thinking about waking up with you every morning for the rest of my life. I'm thinking about spending long, heavenly days in a laboratory with you by my side, unravelling the mysteries of the universe together. I'm thinking that maybe I do *like sex after all . . .*

'Nothing. Only that I'm happy.'

He smiled and kissed the top of her head. 'So am I, Sasha. You do realize we're going to have to be discreet about this? *We* know we're not doing anything wrong. But the university authorities might not be so understanding. And Theresa . . .'

Sasha put a finger to his lips. 'I completely understand.'

I'm a mature woman now. I'm in love with an important, brilliant, troubled man. I must handle this like an adult and show Theo that he can trust me.

The truth was, she didn't want to tell anybody anyway. Some nameless, inner voice told her that Georgia and the rest of her undergraduate friends might not have understood. Keeping it a secret somehow made it all the more precious. As for Theo's wife, well, life was complicated. They'd have to cross that bridge when they came to it.

CHAPTER FIVE

Before her first year at Cambridge was over, Sasha Miller was already being spoken of amongst the physics faculty as a rising star. Not only did she gain the top first in the university in her first-year exams – her independent research project on astrophysical plasmas was easily PhD standard – but she consistently showed an instinctive flair for experimental physics that was rare in one so young. Especially a woman. Girls at Cambridge tended to play it safe, dutifully learning and regurgitating the prevailing academic wisdom of their elders and betters. But Sasha Miller took risks. She was an original thinker, a scientist not just of the mind but of the soul. If she fulfilled just half of her early promise, she might well have great things ahead of her. As long, that is, as she didn't blow it by doing something reckless.

There was no such thing as a secret at Cambridge. Like all universities it was a hotbed of gossip and intrigue. Within a month of their first tryst in the St Michael's wine cellar, news of Professor Dexter's love affair with his star pupil began to spread. Rumours in the Senior Common Room became whispers at high table. Soon every science fellow in the university knew – or thought they knew – about Dexter's latest extramarital escapade. Among Sasha's friends, however, the affair was still a deadly secret. As instructed by Theo, Sasha had told nobody, not even Georgia. The Chinese wall between fellows and undergraduates meant that the gossip was effectively contained. Theo got to bask in the envy of his peers, safe in the knowledge that nothing could be proved against him, while Sasha found herself becoming more and more isolated from her friends, unable to confide in them or share what was rapidly becoming the most important part of her life.

As for Theresa Dexter, cocooned by her own blind love and distracted by the twin imperatives of her Shakespeare research and her efforts to conceive, such whispers as did reach her ears were dismissed as malicious nonsense. Theresa was used to other women fancying her husband. But as for Theo having an affair, well, that was just nonsense. Theo loved her. They loved each other. Besides, why would he want an affair when their sex life was undergoing such a renaissance? Recently it was as if they were newlyweds again. He could barely keep his hands off her.

'I can't bear it. How can it be summer already?'

Sasha lay her head back against the picnic blanket and gazed up at the cloudless blue sky. Theo had driven her out to Houghton Mill, an idyllic village about a forty-minute drive north-west of Cambridge, for a romantic afternoon. Keen to discuss her latest research findings, Sasha had brought her laptop with her. Theo, needless to say, had other ideas. Unfolding the blanket in a secluded field, hidden from the lane by a high hedge on one side and a beech copse on the other, he'd asked her to take her top off and started taking pictures; from the front, from the side and (his favourite) from behind, a glorious shot of her naked back with Sasha looking shyly at the camera over one shoulder. That had got him so hard he'd had to take her on the spot, bringing her to climax after climax with his mouth and hands before finally allowing himself to come. A light lunch of champagne and smoked salmon sandwiches had restored both their strength, after which they made love again with noisily blissful abandon. It made a nice change from sneaking around in Theo's rooms at college, always half listening for a knock at the door.

'I know.' Rolling onto his stomach, Theo picked seeds out of Sasha's hair. 'Every year seems to go quicker than the last. This term was over in a blink.'

'It's all right for you,' moaned Sasha. 'At least you get to stay here and carry on with your work. I'm banished from the lab for *fourteen weeks.*'

She made it sound like a prison sentence.

'Oh, so it's the Cavendish you'll be missing? Not me?' It was childish, but Theo felt piqued.

'I'll miss both of you,' said Sasha truthfully. 'More than you know.'

The thought of going home to Frant for the long summer filled Sasha with despair. Of course the village was still lovely. And she knew how much her father was looking forward to taking her round to the Abergavenny Arms and pumping her for information on St Michael's and her friends and the progress she'd made on her research. Sasha still loved her dad as much as ever, but the prospect of their long-awaited chat made her sad. Intellectually she was now so far ahead of Don, it was impossible to talk to him about her studies in any meaningful way. As for her personal life, the one thing she longed to share with her parents – her relation-ship with Theo – was completely off limits. Sasha and her father had always been so close, this growing apart was painful. Most painful of all though was being separated from her beloved research laboratory. And, of course, from Theo.

Sasha knew he'd agreed to start IVF with his wife, against her doctor's advice and quite clearly against his own wishes. It was incredible to her how Theo could be so strong in all the other aspects of his life, but so weak when it came to Theresa's bullying.

But maybe I shouldn't call it weakness. Compassion, that's what it is. He knows how desperately she wants a child and he's too soft-hearted to refuse her. Especially when she keeps blackmailing him with her depression, threatening to kill herself all the time. I don't know how women like that live with themselves.

Theo had assured her that the chances of them actually conceiving a child were nil. That it was all a question of managing Theresa's mental illness. That when she was well enough and able to take the blow, he would begin the process of leaving her. By then, they hoped, Sasha would have graduated. Theo would no longer officially be her professor. Everything would be easier.

Even so, the thought of leaving him in Cambridge for the summer, knowing that he was sharing a bed with his wife, was a bitter pill to swallow.

'It hurts me as much as it does you,' Theo was fond of telling her. 'You can't think I *enjoy* sleeping with Theresa?' Sasha tried to take comfort in his words, but it wasn't easy. Part of the problem was that she'd never actually *seen* Theo's wife. There were no photos of Theresa in his rooms at St Michael's and Mrs Dexter never stopped by the college to see her husband. In one way, of course, Sasha was thankful for that. But in another, it made it easier to fill the wife-shaped void with some supermodel-beautiful goddess of Heidi Klum-like proportions. Theo always described Theresa as 'ordinary' or even 'plain'. But Sasha found this hard to believe. As he clearly couldn't have married her for her personality, she simply must be beautiful. Images of the two of them together haunted Sasha nightly, to the point where they were threatening to disrupt her research. She had to get a grip.

'Here. I wanted to show you something.'

Still naked, the sun dancing on her pale, now lightly freckled skin, Sasha leaned forward and pulled her laptop out of its case. Turning it on, her fingers raced nimbly across the keyboard, pulling up a string of impenetrable graphs and equations.

'You're not serious. Now?' Theo groaned. Sometimes Sasha's passion for physics was too much, even for him. The summer holiday would provide a welcome break from her relentless enthusiasm. Not to mention a chance to make some progress on his own work. It was a little unnerving how much more productive his nineteen-year-old girlfriend was than he.

'Please, darling. It'll only take a minute,' she cajoled. 'I don't want to overreact. I mean, I mustn't get ahead of myself. But I feel as if I've stumbled on something really important. Remember, I told you on Tuesday?'

Theo scratched his head, then his balls. *Tuesday. Tuesday . . . We had a supervision at noon. Can't remember what it was about. Then I fucked her on the couch. Was that Tuesday?* Reluctantly he focused his attention on the screen of Sasha's computer.

Five minutes later, he was still staring at it.

And five minutes after that.

Was it possible? He read the equations again and again. Each time the adrenaline in his veins coursed faster and faster. *Jesus Christ.*

'What do you think?' Sasha's voice was so tentative that at first he didn't hear her. 'Theo?' She tapped him on the shoulder. 'You've gone awfully quiet. I said, "What do you think?"'

Theo's mind was racing. Shock, excitement, disbelief at what he was reading made it hard to find the right words. Unless he'd made some very fundamental misunderstanding – which he might have done; he was tired after all – Sasha had stumbled across a theory so simple, and yet so radically *new* . . . it could change the face of modern astrophysics. No, not could. *Would*. More than that, it would alter the way that human beings thought of space. Of their own planet's place in, and relation to, the universe. Theo Dexter could have worked twenty-four hours a day, seven days a week for the rest of his life and he would never, ever, not in his wildest fantasies hope to come up with something so brilliant. Blindingly, *obviously* brilliant. Like all profound ideas, once he'd grasped it Theo couldn't imagine why it had taken someone this long to come up with it. But there it was, in front of him on Sasha's computer, in black and white: the theory of his dreams.

And all at once, sitting naked in that field, it came to him.

I could claim it. I could say that it was my idea. Who would know?

A theory like this would make him as a physicist. It would silence all the envious mutterings about him being a phoney academic, a pretty face with a head for numbers but not a *real* scientist. It would change his life. But would he get away with it?

Why not? It'd be my word against hers, a professor against an infatuated undergraduate.

'Theo!' Sasha's voice brought him reluctantly back to reality. She'd pulled on a t-shirt and knickers, but still had that flushed, tousled, post-coital look that never failed to give him a hard on. 'Are you all right?'

'I'm fine.' He closed the file, making an effort to keep his tone casual. 'There's some interesting stuff here. Definitely.'

Sasha's face lit up.

'But it does need work. Particularly in the first section, some of your equations look shaky to me. Given how much you're extrapolating from those foundations . . . Hey, don't look so crestfallen.' He kissed her. 'This is good stuff, Sasha. You can't expect to get it pitch perfect on a first draft.'

'I suppose not.'

'Look, I tell you what. Make me a copy of it. If you like I'll look at the problems in more detail over the summer.'

'Would you really have time?'

'Well, not really. But I'll make time,' he said magnanimously, pulling on his jeans and buttoning up his shirt. Sasha looked so utterly ravishable, he was half tempted to screw her again. But until he had that document safely in his possession, he knew he wouldn't be able to think about anything else.

'I'll email it to you when we get back to college,' said Sasha.

'No, no, don't do that,' said Theo hastily. 'I hate email. Just stick it on a disc and drop it in my pigeonhole before you go.

Sasha watched him stand up and brush the grass and dust off his clothes.

He's so perfect. Handsome, brilliant, kind, the whole package. How on earth am I going to survive the summer without him?

Two weeks later Theresa Dexter sat at her desk at home, watching Theo scribbling feverishly at *his* desk, and said a silent prayer of thanks.

Thank you God for making him happy again. For bringing him back to me.

Eighteen months ago Theo had been as miserable as she'd ever known him. Theresa knew that the spiteful gibes of his fellow physicists were hurtful to him. She also suspected that her husband felt the absence of a child in their lives much more keenly than he admitted to her. But she felt sure that his depression was more than that. Something was wrong, and as hard as she tried to discover what it was and to reconnect with him, she couldn't.

Then miraculously, around Christmas of that year, Theo's spirits had lifted. He still came home tired. But he *left* home full of the joys of spring, bouncing out of the house like Tigger. It made Theresa's heart sing to watch him. By the spring, their sex life had begun to revive, and in the last six months it had positively exploded. It was like dating a teenager, the energy, the *enthusiasm* . . . Theresa's hands had been shaking when she screwed up her courage and asked Theo if they could try IVF. Ever since the meeting with Dr Thomas, he'd been implacable on that score: it was expensive, and it wouldn't work. But to Theresa's delighted amazement, he agreed right away, even taking her out to their favourite curry house to celebrate the decision with chicken jalfrezi and two large Cobras. Walking home hand in hand, happily bloated on naan bread and beer, Theresa realized what had been missing in her marriage for so long: fun. She didn't know what had wrought the change in Theo and she didn't care. *We're going to be happy again.*

Theresa finished her own book in the spring. *Shakespeare in Hollywood: The textual implications of filmed adaptation.* Only a handful of specialist academics bought it, but that didn't matter. It was critically well received, and cemented Theresa's position as a leading expert in her field. Theo, meanwhile, was still struggling with his follow-up edition to *Prospective Signatures*. It was the one part of his life that clearly still troubled him. And the one area where Theresa, whose knowledge of physics would have fit comfortably on the back of a stamp, was completely unable to help him.

But God, apparently, had another miracle in store for the Dexters. Two weeks ago to the day, Theo came home in tearing spirits, bursting through the front door like Rhett Butler and scooping Theresa up into his arms.

'What on earth is it?' she giggled. 'Have we won the lottery?'

'Yes,' he laughed. 'In a way we have. Well, *I* have. But I'll be happy to share my winnings with you, darling.'

Theo had come up with a theory – he tried to explain it to her but it was all way over Theresa's head, something about planets and the birth of the universe and quantum something-or-other. Anyway, the point was it was clearly brilliant, Theo had thought of it, and he seemed to think it had potential not just to boost his career, but quite possibly to make them a lot of money into the bargain.

Theresa couldn't have cared less about the money. She loved their little house in Cambridge, their battered old car, their charmed, ivory-tower life. But to have Theo's genius recognized at last? Well, that would be amazing, wonderful and long overdue. Apart from being pregnant, she couldn't think of a single thing she would have wanted more.

'Are you hungry, darling?' she asked him. 'Shall I make us some lunch?'

'Lunch' meant a sandwich. Theresa loved to cook, but not when she was working. She spent ninety per cent of her time at home in this room, dubbed 'the office' because it had both their desks in it, but really the only proper recep-tion room in the house. Beneath her feet, a tattered Persian rug was almost invisible beneath the mess of books, papers, mugs of cold, half-drunk tea and empty packets of custard creams ('the thinking woman's biscuit' as Jenny so rightly called them). The Dexters' home was a modest, solidly built Victorian semi, with high ceilings, bay windows, and lots of what estate agents called 'original features'. Jenny and Jean Paul's house next door was a carbon copy, except that theirs had had the benefit of Jenny's design flair, so the grand old fireplaces and thick white cornicing looked impressive, whereas Theresa's just looked – what was the word? – ah yes. Filthy. In the past Theo had moaned constantly about the un-Cath-Kidston-ness of their kitchen and what he impolitely referred to as Theresa's 'dyslaundria' (he never seemed to notice his own). But these days Theresa could do no wrong.

'I'd love to eat with you, T,' he said, typing the last few words with a flourish and snapping shut his computer. 'But sadly, I can't. Big meeting today. Massive.' Scooping up his laptop and papers, he came over and kissed her on the lips. Seconds later he was out the front door.

He's like a cyclone, thought Theresa. *A happiness cyclone.*

She wondered what the big meeting was, and hoped it went well. But it would go well. Of course it would. Theo was on a roll.

'I've done it, Ed. I've bloody done it.' Theo Dexter triumphantly slammed a thick, bound manuscript down on the table. 'Read it and weep, my friend. Tears of joy for all the money we're going to make!'

Ed Gilliam was a literary agent, the biggest name in the huge 'popular science' market. A short, unprepossessing man in his mid fifties with thinning red hair and a high-pitched, nasal voice, it was Ed Gilliam who had helped make Stephen

Hawking's *A Brief History of Time* brief: hence accessible to laymen; hence one of the highest-grossing books of the twentieth century in *any* genre, never mind science. These days Gilliam wasn't just about books. He had a finger in every pie, from TV to film to new media. Ed Gilliam had been interested in Theo Dexter since they first met at an MIT symposium in America six years ago. The kid was bright, charismatic, and with those blond, preppy good looks of his he'd be wildly telegenic – rare qualities indeed in a scientist. All Theo needed was some substance. An idea, a book, anything that Ed could use to launch him onto the unsuspecting public. *A sort of Steve Irwin for nerds.*

For six years, Theo had been promising to deliver. Now, just when Gilliam had begun to despair of ever making any money from him – by forty, Dexter would be losing his hair and spreading round the middle and the game would be up – Theo had called in high excitement, summoning him to Cambridge.

'This had better be good, Theo.' Gilliam's high-pitched, child's voice quivered with irritation. 'I'm not in the habit of making day trips. Why can't you come to London?'

'Because I'm still working on it and I need to be here. It is good, Ed. I'm emailing you a rough draft now.'

He was right. It was good. Better than good. Ed Gilliam was not a physicist himself, but if Theo Dexter really had proved what he claimed to have proved in this document . . . this could be as big as Hawking. Bigger.

Ed flipped through the manuscript as he sipped his white wine.

'Who else has seen the material?'

'No one. You, me . . .' Theo hesitated.

'And?'

Theo picked the crust off a warm piece of bread. 'I showed

pieces of it to a student of mine. A girl. She . . . we've talked through some of the concepts together.'

'I see. Anyone else?'

'Well, my wife. But she can't understand a word of it, it's way over her head.' Theo laughed dismissively.

'Good,' said Ed. 'From now on, don't show this to anyone and don't discuss it with a soul. If I'm going to try to put together a multi-platform deal, I'm going to need complete control.'

'Multi-platform?' Theo was salivating. 'You mean TV?'

'Of course. Book deal. TV. The works. We'll start with a simple press release in the *New Scientist*. Let the idea build up some steam amongst your fellow eggheads. Then, when the scientific community's behind you, we take it mainstream: you're on the news channels. Once the commissioning editors at Sky and ITV get a good look at that pretty face of yours you'll be beating off offers with a stick, I promise you.'

'Here's hoping . . .' Theo ordered a petit filet and green salad – expensive, as befitting his soon-to-be new lifestyle, but mindful of his six-pack. Ed went for spaghetti vongole, which he drank noisily whilst outlining his action plan to his client.

'You need to come to London as soon as possible. Tomorrow, if you can swing it. I'll get you in front of our intellectual property lawyers.'

'Lawyers?' For the first time since they sat down Theo's shit-eating grin began to fade. 'Is that really necessary?'

'It's a formality,' slurped Ed, garlicky clam juice dribbling down his receding chin. 'But yeah, it is necessary, especially in this case. You know what it's like with ideas. Some people only have to read them once to think that they came up with them in the first place.' He laughed. 'This is your theory, Theo. We need to make that iron clad from the get go.'

'Right. Of course.'

Theo felt a momentary stab of guilt, but quickly banished it from his mind. In the two weeks since Sasha had first showed him her theory, he'd worked on it so tirelessly and with such all-consuming passion, correcting even the tiniest errors, improving and polishing the text until it flowed like molten gold, that he'd almost come to believe it really *was* his work. Yes, Sasha had produced the original spark that inspired him – a spark that *his* teaching had so patiently nurtured and encouraged in her. But it was he, Theo Dexter, who had transformed that spark into *this*: a volcanic eruption of genius that had Ed Gilliam sitting across the table, eating out of his hands.

This is your theory, Theo. We need to make that iron clad. And they would. Ed Gilliam's fleet of top lawyers would protect him. They'd know what to do if Sasha got nasty. But she wouldn't, would she?

Just at that moment, Theo's phone buzzed to life on the table. He grabbed it, read the text and quickly deleted it.

'Nothing important, I hope?' asked Ed.

'No. Go on.'

Ed did, but Theo was beginning to find it hard to concentrate. The text was from Sasha, her third today. Even without the added pressure of the theory (mentally Theo had stopped referring to it as *Sasha's* theory) strains in the affair were starting to show. In the beginning Sasha had been wonderful, adoring in the way that only very young women ever were. The sex had been incredible too. That combination of innocence, desire and total malleability were a huge aphrodisiac, especially for an ego as rampant but fragile as Theo's. But as time wore on the dynamic between them inevitably shifted. Sasha might be young but she was far from stupid. Recently she'd started to question him more and more about Theresa, the state of his marriage and the future – *their* future. It had reached the point where Theo had been actively looking forward to the summer break. Not that he wanted to end things with Sasha. At least, not until a more attractive prospect came along. But the last thing he needed in his life was a second 'marriage', the sort of complicated, emotional relationship he had with Theresa.

Oddly, things were better with Theresa sexually than they had been in years. Perhaps it was his affair with Sasha that had given him a new lease of life? Or perhaps agreeing to IVF had unleashed a passionate gratitude in Theresa that translated to a whole lot more fun between the sheets? Either way, Theo found himself irritated by Sasha's endless, needy phone calls from Sussex, and actively looking forward to going home tonight and sharing today's triumph with Ed Gilliam with his wife. Theresa's body might not have the youthful perfection of Sasha's, but she knew what turned him on. Sometimes it was a relief not to have to be the teacher.

'So you can make it? Tomorrow afternoon, Berkeley Square? To meet with the lawyers? The press release?'

With a jolt Theo realized that Ed Gilliam was still talking.

'Oh, yes, yes. Of course.' He smiled. 'I'll write something up tonight.'

I've waited so long for this. My entire career. It's time to get this show on the road.

A week later, Sasha was sitting on the sofa in her parents' living room flipping through yesterday's copy of the *Sunday Times* Style Magazine.

Mrs Mills answers your problems

Dear Mrs Mills,

I've been seeing a married, older man for nearly a year now. He claims he loves me, but during a recent separation he's barely returned my calls. What should I do?

Yours,

Desperate of Frant

Dear Desperate,

If he loved you he'd call you back. Or even visit. Why are you being such a moron? Why are you letting this man take over your life? If he cheats on his wife he'll cheat on you. Once a liar, always a liar . . .

As hard as she tried to shake them, the voices in Sasha's head would not go away. Something was wrong. She'd dreaded the long summer holiday for ages, but not even in her worst nightmares had she pictured such a rapid unravelling of whatever it was that she and Theo had together. They used to *talk* at Cambridge, about everything. Life. The universe. She could live without the lovemaking. But the lack of communication was killing her.

'Are you sure you won't try the blue one? It's a perfect colour on you, Sash.' Her mother had tried vainly to interest her in a shopping expedition in Tunbridge Wells that afternoon. They were in Hooper's department store, looking for a dress for Sasha's cousin's wedding. *A wedding. That's all I bloody need.*

'Sure, I'll try it. But you pick, OK, Mum? You know I've got no head for fashion.'

In the changing room, she jumped for joy when she got a new text from Theo. But as soon as she read it: 'Cnt tlk

73

now. 2mr, OK?' she was plunged back into depths of despair she hadn't known she was capable of. She'd tried everything to put him out of her mind, going riding, spending time with school friends who knew nothing about her Cambridge life, even sorting out her bedroom, alphabetizing her CD collection and colour coding her knicker drawer in an attempt to create some feeling of order and control over her own life. *But I'm not in control. I'm out of control. I'm turning into a stalker!*

Just before supper that night – her favourite Moroccan lamb and homemade strawberry ice cream; Mum was pulling all the stops out to try and cheer her up – Sasha called Georgia.

'The summer's so *long*. I'm missing St Michael's more than I thought I would,' she admitted. Not able to tell her friend about Theo, she hoped Georgia would read between the lines and offer some sympathy. 'Do you find that?'

'Not really.' Sasha could hear the sound of laughter in the background. A student party. How long was it since she'd been to one of those? Let her hair down with people her own age? 'A lot of the gang from college were in Turkey two weeks ago. You should have come.'

Maybe I should have.

'Josie and Danny are here now. D'you want to say hi?'

Sasha said hi, but she hung up the phone feeling even more lonely than she had before. *We've grown apart. Even me and Georgia. We used to be so close.*

Seeing his daughter on the couch, lost in thought, Don Miller turned on the TV. He could see she was upset, but long experience had taught him that distraction was a safer bet than the dreaded 'talking' when it came to women's problems.

'*Only Fools and Horses*, *Gardeners' World* or *Law & Order*?' he asked cheerfully.

'Hmmm? Oh, I don't mind, Dad. Whatever.'

Don plumped for *Law & Order*. Sasha tried to focus on the twisting plot and the laboured tension of the detectives' banter, but it was a losing battle. She didn't even notice when Don switched over to the ten o'clock BBC news until her mother walked in and asked her a question about the Middle East. A few seconds later, however, and the TV had Sasha's full attention.

'Isn't that your professor, love? The fellow from St Michael's?'

Sasha felt her heart drop into the pit of her stomach. Theo's face on screen looked even more handsome than it did in her dreams, if that were possible. He was doing that half-frown, half-smile thing that he did when he concentrated. It was the same face he pulled when he made love, right before he came.

'What's he doing on the news?'

It was a good ten seconds before the pounding of Sasha's heart quietened enough for her to hear what Theo was saying. He was talking about some sort of breakthrough. Something that would change the face of physics and astronomy. Odd words and phrases leapt out at her . . . *Einstein's field equation, but seen through a mirror . . . changing our perceptions of existence . . . space-time continuum re-imagined . . .*

Sasha felt a momentary swelling of pride. *Those are my words. I wrote that.*

The report then cut to a ludicrously simplified CGI of the Big Bang and the formation of earth. Above the graphic of the spinning planet was an equation. And that's when it hit Sasha: *It's my theory. He's gone public with my theory. It's on the news.*

Her hands and feet began to tingle with excitement, as if someone were passing an electric current through her body. Wordlessly she grabbed the remote from the coffee table and turned up the volume, waiting to hear Theo mention her name.

Is this why he's been so distant? He wanted to surprise me.

Theo was talking. 'Sometimes an idea is so profound, but so simple, you can't quite believe it yourself . . .'

He knows how to handle these things better than I do. He didn't want me to screw it up.

'. . . culmination of years of work . . .'

Only six months actually.

'. . . grateful to all those who have supported me. Especially my wonderful wife Theresa.'

Excuse me?

'Science can be a lonely profession, but Theresa has been there for me through thick and thin. It's easy to get caught up in competition with one's peers. But clearly this is not about me personally. This isn't Theo Dexter's triumph. It's a triumph for the whole physics community. For the human race, in a way.'

Cut to various eminent physicists from around the globe. Sasha watched their mouths move, but her ears were ringing. Slowly, hideously, the truth began to dawn.

Oh my God.

'I'm just the lucky man who happened to be sitting in the right place when inspiration struck.'

Yeah you were in the right place! Naked in a field with ME. You stole my idea!

'Bastard,' Sasha muttered, getting unsteadily to her feet.

The report was finished. Huw Edwards was saying something about the Special Olympics. Sasha grabbed the arm of the sofa for support. The room was starting to spin.

'Are you all right, darling? Sasha?' Don gave her a worried glance.

'I need some air.'

*   *   *

Outside in the garden, warm summer scents of jasmine and freshly mown grass assailed Sasha's senses. The world looked and smelled and sounded familiar, but everything had changed. Her hand shook as she dialled Theo's number.

He won't answer. He'll see it's from me and he won't answer. He . . .

'Sasha. How are you, angel? Look, I'm sorry I didn't call you back earlier. It's been a manic day.' He sounded so calm, so normal, for a moment Sasha wondered if she'd imagined the news report. There was no hint of guilt or apology in his voice.

'I saw you. On the news. Five minutes ago.'

'Oh.' There was a long pause. Irrationally, Sasha's spirits soared. *This is where he's going to explain everything. It's all some sort of ghastly mistake and he's going to put it right.* 'Listen, all that stuff about Theresa . . . I had to say it. She's been so low recently, and she was desperate to be a part of all the excitement. You understand, don't you?'

Sasha shook her head in disbelief. This was getting more surreal by the second.

'*Theresa?* What are you talking about, Theo? You stole my theory! I just saw you on the BBC bloody news, telling people my thesis was *your* idea.'

'I think you're a wee bit confused, sweetheart.' There was an edge to Theo's voice that hadn't been there before. 'I've been working on this theory for years. Long, long before I met you. Now, granted, you developed a couple of my ideas further than I had. Your paper really got me thinking . . .'

'Liar!' Sasha exploded. 'I didn't develop *your* ideas! They were my ideas and you know it.'

'Come on, Sash. This is nonsense. I don't know anything of the kind. Listen, I'm jumping into a cab now. Can we talk about this tomorrow, when you've calmed down?'

Sasha hung up on him.

When Don Miller walked into the garden ten minutes later, he found his daughter pacing the stone path, mumbling to herself like a lunatic.

'Sash, love? What is it? Your mum and I are worried about you. Won't you tell us what's happened?'

Sasha stopped mumbling, stared at him and burst into tears.

When she finally stopped crying, she told him everything. Her affair with Theo, how it had started, his marital problems, the secrecy, and how it had alienated her from her friends and family. Finally she told him about her theory, a simplified version but Don got the gist. How she had trusted Theo to advise her on it and he had stolen it and was trying to pass it off as his own work.

Don Miller listened in silence. When Sasha finally finished talking, he said gently, 'I see. So what are you going to do?'

'Do?' Sasha looked at him blankly. 'What do you mean?'

'I mean what are you going to do? I hope you're not thinking of letting this wanker get away with it. Are you?'

'But Dad, it'll be his word against mine.'

'So?'

'He's a fellow, a respected, professional scientist. I'm just a student about to start her second year.'

'So?'

'So no one will believe me.'

Don Miller took his daughter's hand. 'I believe you, Sasha. You've got right on your side. The truth will come to light in the end, but not if you don't fight for it. Mum and I will be behind you all the way. We'll get you a lawyer. We'll sell the house if we have to.'

Sasha was so touched she started to cry again.

'I loved him, Dad.'

'No, love. You just thought you did.'

Her dad was right. She couldn't just sit back and let Dexter get away with this.

I'll take him to court. I'll win back my theory and expose him as a liar and a fraud.

Theo Dexter was going to curse the day he underestimated Sasha Miller.

CHAPTER SIX

Sasha squeezed both her parents' hands as the members of the Regent House filed back into the room. The Regent House was the official governing body of the University of Cambridge. Usually it only ever met in the grand, neo-classical Senate House on King's Parade to award degrees, or to elect a new chancellor. But today, sensationally, the Master of St Michael's had summoned a special congregation – Cambridge's equivalent of a court martial – to settle the increasingly embarrassing and bitter dispute between Professor Theo Dexter and his second-year pupil, Sasha Miller.

Of course, today was only the university's decision. Theoretically, Sasha could still pursue Theo in the British courts. But the six-hundred-pounds-an-hour lawyer Don Miller had engaged was blunt about her chances.

'If the university goes against you, it will be very difficult to win a civil case. I hesitate to say impossible. But if you pursue Dexter and you lose, the court will most likely award him damages *and* costs. Add that to your own legal fees and you could be looking at a bill running into millions of pounds.'

'We'll do whatever it takes,' Don said defiantly. But they all knew it wasn't an option. Everything rested on today's decision. Up until a couple of hours ago, Sasha had been sure she was going to lose. In the last two months, since the British press had got hold of the juicy story about the hunky Cambridge professor and his teenage undergraduate lover, Sasha had seen her good name raked through the mud. Like flies swarming round a turd, the university establishment had rallied around Theo Dexter. No one, other than Sasha's student friends, had agreed to speak up for her.

Until this afternoon.

Harold Grier, a senior American physicist on secondment from Harvard, had been one of Sasha's lab partners at the Cavendish. Grier had witnessed much of Sasha's early research work on what was already now being referred to as 'Dexter's Law'. If *he* spoke up for her, she had a shot. Unfortunately for Sasha, Harold Grier was also a pathologically private man and so shy he was borderline autistic. He had refused all her entreaties to testify at the Senate House. 'I can't be dragged into a s . . . scandal. I'm sorry. My work is too important.'

Sasha had given up trying to change Harold's mind weeks ago. But today, after the lunchtime recess, a miracle had occurred. Walking out of the ladies, she saw Harold Grier standing alone in the grand foyer of the Senate House with a sheaf of papers in his hand. Harold saw her too, and smiled.

'Who's that?' Sasha's dad asked her, watching Harold take his seat. Don noticed the way that the Dexter camp's eyes had all turned to follow him as he made his way to the front of the court.

'I very much hope that's my knight in shining armour,' whispered Sasha.

The Master of St Michael's took his seat. *'In curia nostra, hodie est dies juridicus. Sedete silentio si commodum est.'*
This is it.

Theresa Dexter held her husband's hand and kept her eyes fixed firmly on the robed figures in front of her. Sometimes the urge to turn around and look at Sasha Miller was so strong it made her neck hurt. But she knew that if she made eye contact she wouldn't be able to restrain herself from running over and strangling the girl with her bare hands. *Better to be here than down the road in the Crown Court, on trial for murder,* Theresa told herself. *In an hour this nightmare will be over.*

The last two months had been the worst of Theresa Dexter's life. It was August when Theo had come home, ashen-faced, and told her that he was afraid one of his undergraduates was going to try to lay claim to his theory.

'But why? I mean, that's ridiculous. How could she possibly lay claim to it?'

'We worked together.' Theo shrugged. 'I trusted her. You know, she's a bright girl, she showed a lot of promise. I thought it would be exciting for her to be involved with something like this. Something ground-breaking.' He shook his head sadly. 'I suppose I was naïve.'

Theresa had been outraged on Theo's behalf, sympathetic and practical. 'We'll talk to Ed Gilliam. He'll know what to do. Try not to worry, darling. At best this girl's delusional and at worst she's a liar. Either way, she can't hurt you. The truth will out.'

The next morning, Theo gave the same spiel to Ed Gilliam. When he'd finished, Ed said, 'You prick. You were sleeping with her, weren't you?'

'Sleeping with . . .? Of course I wasn't sleeping with her!' Theo blustered. 'How dare you imply . . .'

'I'm going to give you five seconds to stop talking shit and tell me the truth. And if you don't, I'm going to hang up, play a nice round of golf, and forget you ever existed. OK?'

Theo hesitated. 'All right. Yes, OK, I did sleep with her. A couple of times. But it was nothing, a silly fling. She seduced me. Sasha can be very persuasive, you know.'

'That's what I'm afraid of,' said Ed. 'Pretty young girl plays the victim on Richard and Judy's couch and next thing you know you're a paedophile. No one will give a fuck whose theory this is after that. By the way, just out of interest, *did* you nick it?'

'No! Of course I didn't. The whole thing's preposterous.'

'Good. Now listen, you leave the PR side of this to me. It's a nightmare, but I've handled worse. The trick is to hit back first, not wait for Lolita to leak the story. I'm going to tell you what to do, and you're going to do it, no questions asked. We can salvage this thing but we have to act fast. And, Theo?'

'Yes, Ed?'

'Stop lying to me. Save your energy for all the other people you're going to have to lie to.'

Following Ed Gilliam's instructions, Theo admitted his affair with Sasha to Theresa that evening, albeit a heavily edited version.

'But . . . but . . . we've been so happy.' Theresa blinked back tears.

'I know.' Theo hugged her. 'I've been a fool, T. I *am* happy with you. Sasha was just so vulnerable and so needy. She kept on and on, pursuing me, begging me to be with her.

83

It was relentless. I didn't realize how psychologically disturbed she was until it was too late. Can you ever forgive me?'

His remorse was so heartfelt Theresa couldn't help but forgive him, but she was desperately hurt. There was no time to process her feelings, however. The very next morning, a double-page spread ran in the *Daily Mail*, salivating over British science's newest star's liaison with his beautiful protégée.

At the breakfast table, Theo shook the newspaper angrily. 'Bitch. I can't believe she's gone public already. Has she no shame? I mean it's not just me she's hurting. It's you, and St Michael's. The whole physics community gets tainted with this *shit*. How could she?'

'It's all right, darling.' Theresa touched his arm consolingly. 'We'll get through it together.'

Half an hour later, Theo called Ed Gilliam from the car.

'Nice piece.'

'Yeah. It should do the job. Remember, say nothing to the press, not till I get you that statement. If they doorstep you, keep your cool and look remorseful.'

'Remorseful. Got it.'

'This is only the opening salvo, you know. The war hasn't begun. Now we have to get the university on side.'

'Leave that to me,' said Theo.

When Sasha read the *Daily Mail* article she was nearly sick.

'Where do they get this stuff? And who the hell are these "insiders" I'm supposed to have confided in? They make it sound like *I* leaked the story.'

It was only two days since she'd watched Theo on the evening news. She hadn't even worded her formal complaint to the physics faculty yet, never mind talked to the press.

'He's playing hardball, isn't he, the creep,' said Don Miller contemptuously. 'We need to get you a lawyer, pronto.'

Theresa sat at Jenny and Jean Paul's kitchen table, sobbing. Jenny put her arms around her. 'It's all right, lovie. You can cry. Theo's put you through hell.'

Theresa looked up, wiping her nose on her sleeve like a child. 'Oh no. You mustn't blame Theo. It's this vicious girl. I mean, yes, Theo made a mistake . . .'

Jenny raised an eyebrow. 'A bit more than a mistake, T.'

'If you could see how sorry he was, Jen. He hates himself for it. And now he stands to lose everything, everything he's ever worked for. It's much harder for him than it is for me.'

Jenny's eyebrows disappeared into her hairline.

'I know I've got to be strong, to hold it all together for him. But I . . . I . . .' Theresa broke down again. 'I started bleeding this morning. I haven't been to the doctor yet, but I just know. I really thought this time we might be lucky.'

Jenny put her arms around her friend. She knew how hopeful Theresa had been about this new round of IVF. 'Oh, darling, I'm so sorry.'

'It's the stress. Reading all this stuff in the newspapers. This little cow Sasha just doesn't care. She doesn't give a damn.'

Jenny was silent. There was so much to say, but she knew Theresa didn't want to hear any of it.

Theo Dexter had a lot to answer for.

'So you've made a formal complaint to the college authorities and to the physics faculty?'

'Yes.' Sasha's eyes wandered over the lawyer's office. It

looked more like a five-star hotel suite than a place of work, all antique armoires and cashmere-covered cushions. No wonder with the fees he charged. All around the room, silver-framed photographs of his ridiculously photogenic family beamed perfect smiles at her. They looked like a tooth-paste advertisement.

'And their response was . . .?'

'They've taken it under advisement.'

Don Miller lost his temper. 'Look, Mr Farley. We've been through all this. You know what happened. You've seen Sasha's evidence, her research files. The university's doing nothing. What we want to know is, can *you* help us?'

The lawyer sighed. 'I'd like to, Mr Miller. It does appear that Sasha has been very poorly treated by this chap. But the problem is, from what I've seen so far, it's going to come down to a case of Sasha's word against his.'

I told you so.

'What you really need are witnesses.' He turned to Sasha. 'Was there anyone other than Dexter who observed you developing this theory? Anyone who could prove that you came up with it first? We'd need dates.'

Sasha immediately thought of Harold Grier. 'There was one person. But I don't know if he'd want to get involved.'

'Convince him,' said the lawyer. 'That's the best advice I can give you.'

Fat chance, thought Sasha.

'This is very bad for the college, Dexter. *Very* bad.' Anthony Greville, St Michael's Master, stated the obvious. 'In a few weeks the girl's going to *be* here, beginning her second year. We'll be overrun with reporters and cameramen. The Porters' Lodge is already overwhelmed with calls from the gutter press.'

'I know, Master. And I'm truly sorry, believe me. But Sasha's the one stirring this up in the media, not me. I think we need to keep sight of the bigger picture here. My theory could change the very nature of our understanding of the universe. It's huge. *Huge.* If we don't let this scandal over-shadow it, it could bring immense cachet to the college. Just think what an incredible fundraising tool that could be.'

Anthony Greville thought about it. St Michael's, as ever, was in dire need of new funds. The chapel was not going to reroof itself. Trinity and St John's were both swimming in money, but the smaller St Michael's had always had to make-do and mend. *Perhaps Dexter's theory could change all that? If one tiresome, sex-mad undergraduate didn't ruin it for all of them.*

'What would you have me do, Theo? I can't send her down and keep you here. How would that look? Especially since she's still claiming you stole her work.'

'Call an emergency session of the Regent House. You can chair it. Let the university decide whose theory this is.'

'What good will that do?'

'It will put an end to all this once and for all. But on *your* terms. If, God forbid, the congregation rule against me, I'll resign and go back to America. If they don't, then you're free to send Sasha down. She'll be out of St Michael's, out of Cambridge, out of all our lives.'

'I'd just like her out of The *News of the* bloody *World*,' grumbled the Master.

'Once the case is closed the press will lose interest,' Theo assured him. 'Especially when they start to realize just how seismic this theory is. If the college and the faculty back me, we can kill this thing. We want the same things, Master.'

'Absolutely not.' Margaret Haines was livid. 'Why the hell should I lie for that arsehole?'

'My dear Margaret. Is such fragrant language really necessary?' The Master sat at his desk, radiating pomposity. 'No one is asking you to lie. Merely, to focus on the matter in hand and not encourage the Regent House to be distracted by, shall we say, the more *salacious* elements of this whole sorry affair.'

'You mean the fact that Dexter's been boning his students, in clear violation of the university's code of ethics? Sasha Miller wasn't the first, you know.'

'Be that as it may, this theory of Professor Dexter's could prove extremely important. And not just to the scientific world. To the *college*.'

Anthony Greville said this last as if it silenced all further conversation on the matter. Margaret Haines disagreed.

'And what if it really was this young girl's work? Have you considered that? What if she's telling the truth and Dexter ripped *her* off?'

'You can't honestly believe that.'

'Can't I? Why not? We already know Dexter's a liar with the morals of an alley cat and the discretion of a town crier.'

'She's an undergraduate.'

'Yes, and by all accounts a brilliant one. Unlike your friend Professor Dexter. No, Master. I won't be silenced on this. We should be backing the girl.'

Anthony Greville's eyes narrowed. He'd always lusted after Margaret Haines. He liked her feistiness and her sharp wit and the way her bosom jiggled underneath her sweater when she got agitated, as she was now. But if she threatened the reputation of St Michael's, he would have no compunction in getting rid of her.

'The Senior Common Room are all in agreement. If you go against us on this, Margaret, your position here may become very difficult.'

Margaret Haines looked at the squat, elderly toad sitting opposite her. Her contempt oozed from every pore. 'Is that a threat, Anthony?'

'Not at all, my dear. But as Master I must think of the good of the entire college. Testifying on young Miss Miller's behalf would not be in any of our best interests. Including yours. Think about that, Margaret.'

Margaret Haines did speak up for Sasha. But it didn't help. For one thing, the overwhelmingly male Regent House already knew that Theo Dexter was an inveterate woman-izer who preyed on his prettier students, and they couldn't have cared less. For another, by the time the Cambridge authorities finally sat down to hear evidence, Ed Gilliam had done such a thorough character assassination of Sasha in the press it was a wonder her own mother was still speaking to her.

'TEENAGE LOLITA WRECKS GENIUS PROFESSOR'S MARRIAGE'

'HOME-WRECKING FANTASIST STALKED DEXTER "FOR MONTHS"'

Margaret's only regret was having to add to poor Theresa Dexter's anguish by publicly running through the litany of Theo's student conquests. She needn't have worried. Theresa didn't believe a word of it.

'I swear on my life, T, it isn't true,' said Theo. 'Margaret's always had it in for me, the old battleaxe. She's jealous of my success. She knows Sasha's weakened me so she's moving in for the kill.'

After Margaret's testimony, the court broke for an hour's lunch. Not wanting to brave the hordes of press outside, Sasha and her family ate their sandwiches on a bench in the Senate House lobby. None of them spoke. It was pretty clear which way the congregation was leaning. *It's like the condemned man's last meal,* thought Sasha.

And then Harold Grier showed up.

Harold took his place on the dais. Anthony Greville, St Michael's Master, was chairing proceedings. He read out some lines of Latin, and Harold replied.

I'll be gracious in victory, thought Sasha. *I'm not interested in fame and glory. All I want is to be allowed to finish my research in peace.*

'Professor Grier, you worked as Miss Miller's laboratory partner at the Cavendish during the Easter term, is that correct?'

'Yes.'

Throughout the proceedings, Sasha had resisted the urge to look at Theo. A few short months ago, just the sight of him across a room would have made her heart race. Now his proximity made her physically ill. *He's so fake. So vain and bland and . . . empty. What did I ever see in him?* But as Harold Grier began his testimony, she couldn't resist stealing a triumphant glance. *I've got you now, you lying bastard.*

Feeling her gaze, Theo turned around. Sasha wasn't sure what she'd expected. Fear, perhaps, at the prospect of his imminent exposure and disgrace? Guilt? Regret? Instead the look on her one-time lover's face could only be described as . . . *pity. That's odd. Why would he feel sorry for me? He must know what's coming. He must know Grier's testimony is going to blow his case out of the water.*

Harold Grier was talking. 'She was very excited about working with Professor Dexter. She told me she felt inspired by him, and fortunate to have him as a supervisor.'

'And how familiar were you with Miss Miller's research work?'

'Very familiar. We worked together over a period of weeks. It was an exciting time.'

'You recognized the importance of the work she was doing?'

'Oh yes. Absolutely. And so did she. As I say, she was thrilled Professor Dexter had given her the opportunity to work with him on it. Not many undergraduates would have been given such a chance.'

Sasha cocked her head to one side. Had she misheard him?

Anthony Greville leaned forward eagerly in his seat. 'Miss Miller implied to you that the theory was, in fact, Professor Dexter's? That he had invited her to assist him?'

No!

'Yes. Well, she didn't imply it. She was quite explicit about it.'

'That's not true!' Sasha was on her feet, yelling from the gallery. The black-robed figures of the Regent House glared at her as one.

'Sit down please, Miss Miller, or I will have to ask you to leave.'

'But he's lying! Tell them the truth, Harold, for God's sake!'

Sue Miller took her daughter's hand and pulled her physically down into her seat. 'It won't help, love,' she whispered. Sasha sat down.

Harold Grier kept talking, calmly, rationally, convincingly. Every word was a bullet in Sasha's heart. She was too stunned to take in much of the Master's summing up, but the few words that sunk in left no room for doubt . . . *tragic, unnecessary case . . . slanderous claims . . . overwhelming evidence to suggest . . . confused, troubled young woman . . .*

The black-robed men began filing out. All around Sasha,

people were on their feet. She tried to stand up but her legs had turned to water. Her dad put an arm around her waist. 'It's all right Sash. Let's go home.'

It wasn't all right.

Outside the Senate House, King's Parade was choked with reporters. Theo Dexter stood on the steps, hand in hand with his wife, holding court. 'No, I don't feel victorious,' he told the *Times* correspondent. 'I'm relieved this is over. I'm relieved I can get back to work. I'm heartbroken at the pain I've caused my wife.' He looked at Theresa, his eyes welling with tears.

'How do you feel about Sasha Miller?' another journalist shouted. 'Will you be pursuing any legal action against her?'

Theo shook his head magnanimously. 'I think it's clear that Miss Miller is a gravely troubled young person. I have no desire for vengeance. I wish her the best and I hope her family are able to get her the help she needs.'

As he finished speaking, Sasha emerged from the building, propped up like a drunk between her bewildered parents.

'Are you going to make any statement, Sasha?'

'Will you be going back to St Michael's?'

'The university has asked for a formal retraction. Any comment on that?'

'No comment!' Don Miller roared. It was like walking through a pack of wolves. 'Get the hell away from my daughter.'

'Are you sorry, Sasha?'

Sasha looked up. *Am I sorry? Yes, I'm sorry. I'm sorry I ever laid eyes on Theo Dexter. I'm sorry I put my family through this. I'm sorry that none of you can open your eyes and see the truth.*

The mob followed her to the car. Cameras clattered against the sides of Don's tatty Volvo as the family drove away. Sasha stared out of the window at the colleges, their towers and steeples and portcullises bathed in late afternoon light. She remembered the day she had first arrived at St Michael's, full of hope and promise and excitement, her head full of thoughts of Will Temple, the boy she'd left back home. It was only a year ago. But it felt like a lifetime.

That girl is gone forever, thought Sasha.

She knew she would never return to Cambridge again.

It was almost midnight before Theo had a chance to call Ed Gilliam. What with all the press to deal with, and the celebratory drinks party at the Master's lodge, followed by a romantic, thank-you-for-standing-by-me supper with Theresa, he hadn't had a second alone since the verdict.

'I didn't wake you, did I?'

Gilliam laughed. 'Not likely. I'm so wired I don't know if I'll ever sleep again.'

'So come on, put me out of my misery. How did you do it?'

'Harold Grier, you mean?'

'When I saw him after recess I thought we were sunk. How did you get him to change his mind?'

'The same way you get anyone to change their mind. I made him an offer he couldn't refuse.'

'Money?'

'Better than that. I told him I'd get him a book deal for his new thesis. That and a sponsor for his next five years of research.'

'But Grier's research is impenetrable. Not even physicists can understand it.'

'Hey, I didn't say the book would sell. I told him we'd publish it.'

'Who's going to sponsor him?'

'You are, Theo. Or rather, your TV production company. Once your show gets syndicated globally, believe me, the payments to dear old Harold will be a drop in the ocean.'

'My show? What show?'

Ed Gilliam laughed out loud. 'Get some sleep, Theo. You're about to become a very, *very* busy man.'

PART TWO

CHAPTER SEVEN

New York, five years later

Jackson Dupree emerged from the elevator like a rock star walking on stage. With good reason. On Wall Street, Jackson Dupree was a rock star. And Wrexall Dupree, the commercial real estate giant founded by his great-grandfather, was his stage. Striding confidently towards the boardroom, past the desks of swooning secretaries, Jackson smiled. He was about to give the performance of his life.

A regular in the gossip columns and New York society press, Jackson Amory Dupree was one of America's most eligible bachelors. The only son of real estate mogul Walker Dupree and his socialite wife, Mitzi, Jackson was born a prince. As befitted royalty, he was not only rich beyond most ordinary people's imagination. He was also supremely gifted in every other aspect of his life: academically, physically, socially and, as he grew into adulthood, sexually. Despite being a brilliant sportsman – polo and tennis were his games of choice, but Jackson made the first team at everything – he was the antithesis of a jock. With his wild, jet-black hair, his lean, almost skinny figure, high cheekbones and sensual, predatory, almond eyes, Jackson looked more like the product of two passionate gypsy dancers than what he actually was: heir apparent to one of the oldest families on the east coast.

Now twenty-eight, Jackson's reputation as the most lusted-after playboy of his generation was well established. Famously estranged from his father (Walker Dupree found his son's womanizing and partying a grave embarrassment), Jackson's exploits in the bedrooms (and bathrooms and kitchens and offices and cars) of some of the world's most desirable women, many of them married, had become part of Manhattan folklore. Less well documented was his prowess as a scholar. Jackson graduated top of his section at Harvard Business School (despite spending two-thirds of his final semester satisfying the bottomless sexual demands of the dean's wife, Karen). He was fluent in French, Italian, Spanish and German. A natural communicator, with an easy, unpretentious manner, Jackson won over friends, teachers and later clients as effortlessly as he alienated husbands across the land. Husbands and, it had recently emerged, the twelve-man board of Wrexall Dupree.

It's my own fault, Jackson thought bitterly, the night he heard about the coup. *I took my eye off the ball.*

If it hadn't been for Liana, the improbably proportioned personal assistant to Bob Massey, Wrexall's irascible head of sales, he would never have known what the board was up to. As it was, Jackson was on the floor of Bob's office last month, happily exploring the smooth, waxed heaven between Liana's quivering thighs, when the girl burst into tears.

'It's all right, angel,' Jackson said comfortingly. He was used to women sobbing after he brought them to orgasm. Who wanted to come down from that sort of high? 'We can do it again in a minute.'

'It's not that,' snivelled Liana. 'It's Mr Massey. I overheard him talking with Mr Peters and some of the other board members. He made me swear to keep it to myself. He said if I told anyone, I'd lose my job.'

'Told anyone what?' asked Jackson, bored, running the tip of his tongue over Liana's left nipple. He wasn't in the mood for careers counselling.

'That they're going to veto your promotion.'

Now she had Jackson's attention. Dropping her breast like a dog that's lost interest in its chew-toy, he sat bolt upright. 'What do you mean "veto" it? They can't. I have an automatic right of entry to Wrexall Dupree's board after five years of service. It's in the statutes.'

'According to Mr Massey, there's a sub-clause in there that says if you fail to meet some target or other, I can't remember . . . and if the veto were to be unanimous . . . I shouldn't have told you. But now that we're a couple, you know . . .' She reached for his cock.

All Jackson knew was that he had to reread the company statutes. Almost knocking her out in his rush to get out of there he stood up, pulled on his clothes and ran out the door. Liana gazed longingly after him. *I hope I haven't made a mistake.*

An hour later, back home at his loft apartment on Broadway and Bleecker, Jackson found the passage Liana had been referring to. He'd been praying she'd somehow got her wires crossed. After all, she wasn't the sharpest knife in the drawer. But no. Here it was in black and white.

If the nominated family representative should fail to generate revenue equivalent to a minimum of five times his annual compensation; and if such a decision is unanimously supported by all members of the governing board; the said representative's appointment to board level may be denied. This would in no way affect the representative's rights as a shareholder.

Bastards, thought Jackson. *They set me up.* Another part of him thought, *Maybe I deserved it.*

The truth was that Jackson was one of the biggest revenue producers at Wrexall. In his first year alone he'd brought in $25 million. Unfortunately, he was also one of the highest earners. Bob Massey, in particular, had encouraged him to take the maximum allowable bonus in the last three years.

'Why not?' he told Jackson genially. 'You're only young once. Besides, you've earned it. Go buy a yacht or twenty.'

Jackson grinned. 'I'm tempted. But won't it look bad? Aren't we all supposed to be showing corporate restraint this year?'

'Says who? Look, sure, the media's up in arms about big payouts. But aren't they always?'

The rest of the board had concurred. *All this time I thought they were being generous. But all this time they were just waiting to stiff me.*

Wrexall Dupree had long been famous on Wall Street as a snake pit, one of the most aggressive, unpleasant, macho firms on the street. To that extent, it was not surprising to see Wrexall board members turn on one another. What was surprising was to have all twelve of them unite against a member of the family.

The truth was that while Jackson Dupree had the charm of the devil when he wanted to, and was undeniably good at his job, he could also be insufferably arrogant. At twenty-eight,

Jackson was a decade younger than the youngest Wrexall MD, but he'd never made so much as a token effort at humility. Swaggering into the office at ten or eleven in the morning, having clearly just rolled out of some model's bed, he would typically put in a few hours of phone calls (at least half of them to women), before pissing off to some spurious lunch meeting from which he frequently never returned. The fact that he made as much money as his superiors, whilst blatantly putting in a fraction of the effort, did not endear him to anyone.

Tonight, reading the company statutes, Jackson had a rare moment of self-awareness. *I fucked this up. All twelve of them hate me.* But he didn't dwell on it. Getting out a pen and paper he made a quick calculation. There were two weeks to go until his board appointment was supposed to become official. *How much more revenue do I need to bring in to stop the veto?*

He wrote down the number. It was huge. Short of selling a hotel chain for twice what it was worth, he had no chance of . . . A slow smile spread over Jackson Dupree's face. He picked up the phone.

Bob Massey stretched out his short legs, leaning back smugly in his leather-backed chair. Today was the day he was going to nail that arrogant little turd Dupree's balls to the floor. Jackson was late for the meeting as usual, but this time Bob Massey didn't care. Nothing could dim the pleasure he was going to have in bursting the boy's bubble once and for all.

At first Bob Massey had worried he might not have been able to persuade the whole board to back him. Especially Lucius Monroe, the chairman. Lucius was an old friend of Jackson's father, Walker. Doing the dirty on Walker Dupree's only son might make things a little awkward at the golf club. Then again, it might not. Old man Dupree was said to be wildly disapproving of his son's dilettantism, however much he might love him. But Lucius, like the others, had needed no persuading.

'The boy's a liability. He's crass, he's flashy. Did you see that piece on page six last week? About Jackson driving away naked from Senator Davis's mansion?'

'Oh God, yes.' Dan Peters frowned disapprovingly. 'The senator came home to find Dupree in bed with his wife *and* the Puerto Rican housekeeper. At it like rabbits, the three of them. Davis came at him with a shotgun, apparently.'

'I don't blame him. Wasn't Jackson dating the daughter at one point? Lorna? Lorretta?'

'Lola. Lola Davis. Yeah. That was the week before.'

Jackson's embarrassing public sexploits gave the board the moral high ground. The company statutes gave them the legal high ground. But everyone knew the real reason behind Bob Massey's coup: Jackson Dupree was an insufferable, arrogant prick. This would be the last day they'd have to put up with his entitled, self-satisfied swagger. The last day they would have to hear their secretaries salivating over how much they wanted to go to bed with him. The last day . . .

'Sorry I'm late.' Jackson loped into the boardroom with his usual sheepish grin. He was wearing torn drainpipe jeans, a vintage t-shirt and a black Spurr jacket. His dark hair was even more wildly dishevelled than usual and a dark shadow of stubble matched the circles under his eyes. He couldn't have looked more post-coital if he'd come in wrapped in a sheet and holding a used condom. 'Rita Halston got into town last night. She needed a lot of entertaining.'

Twelve pairs of envious eyes bored into Jackson as he took his seat. Rita Halston was a well-known 'adult entertainment' actress. There wasn't a man in America who hadn't fanta-sized about banging Rita, and the Wrexall board members were no exception. Her body was a Manga cartoon made flesh, and her face, with those ludicrously full lips and inno-cent Bambi-brown eyes made Angelina Jolie look sexless. Since she bought a string of West Village townhomes last year, Rita Halston was also officially a Wrexall client. Specifically, she was Jackson's client, which meant spending the morning in bed with her could be classified as 'work'.

Gloat while you can, jerk-off, thought Bob Massey. *By the end of this meeting we'll have wiped that smile off your face.*

Lucius Monroe launched into the order of business. Most of Wrexall's profits came from US commercial real estate: time-share condominiums in Florida; strip malls and business centres across the country in Denver, Dallas, Atlanta, Seattle; prime retail in Manhattan and Beverly Hills. Occasionally they did residential work, like Jackson's acquisitions for Rita Halston, or took pieces of real estate deals abroad, in Europe or Asia. Around the table, each board member updated the group on their division's progress. At the end of the meeting, Jackson's accession to the board would be formally ratified. *Or so he thinks.* It was all Bob Massey could do to not rub his hands together with glee.

At last Darryl Jeffries finished his deathly dull update on the latest retail deal. It was time. Bob Massey glanced triumphantly at Jackson. He was furious to see that the boy had fallen asleep at the table and was snoring quietly with his head in his hands.

'Are we boring you, Mr Dupree?' Lucius Monroe's voice shook with anger.

'Huh? Oh, sorry.' Jackson grinned disarmingly. 'I must have nodded off. Is it time yet, for the big announcement?

I guess we should get this over with. So, I'm very grateful to all of you, yada yada yada, it's a huge honour and all that. But I'd *really* like to get back to bed.'

Prick.

Bob Massey stood up. 'Actually, Jackson, there's been a change of plans.' The smile he'd been suppressing for the last hour and a half spread across his face now like a fungus. 'You may not be aware of this, but in the company's founding statutes there are a couple of stipulations concerning your appointment to the board.'

'There are?' Jackson feigned ignorance.

'I'm afraid so. One of them concerns the ratio of your revenues to earnings.'

'You don't say. Well, what does it say?'

Bob Massey lifted a piece of paper from the pile in front of him. He began to read, slowly, savouring every word. Around the table, his colleagues smiled and nodded. By the time Bob had finished, they were positively glowing with triumph. 'I have your numbers here, Jackson. And I'm sorry to say, they don't look good.'

Lucius Monroe got to his feet. 'Well, in the light of this, I suppose it's my duty to put Jackson's promotion to a vote. Would all those in favour of appointing Jackson Dupree to full membership of this board, with immediate effect, please raise their hands now.'

Nobody moved.

Bob Massey looked as if he might spontaneously combust with joy.

'I see. And all those against?'

Twelve hands shot into the air.

'Well,' Lucius Monroe sat down again, 'I realize this must be quite a shock for you, Jackson. You'll need some time to consider your options. Whether you wish to continue at Wrexall, in a more junior position of course, or . . .'

'If I could just interrupt you there, Lucius.' Jackson got calmly to his feet. 'No discredit to the detailed research that you've obviously done, Bob.' He smiled sweetly at Massey. 'But I think you'll find you've made a small error in your figures.' The door opened and Liana sashayed into the room, carrying twelve newly bound documents. 'Thank you, angel.' Jackson kissed her on the cheek, eliciting a blush of pleasure. He passed the documents around the table.

'What's this?' Bob Massey snarled. He'd been over those figures hundreds, thousands of times. There was no mistake.

'A new transaction I've been working on, turning around a chain of failing beach hotels in Hawaii. Great land, crappy businesses. I didn't tell you because I wasn't sure I'd be able to pull it off. But as you can see, it's a whopper. Two hundred and eighty-five million dollars, to be precise.'

Jackson watched as the twelve men turned the pages. With each line they read, more colour drained from their faces. Fucking Rita Halston last night had been fun. But it was nothing compared to this.

'But how . . .' spluttered Dan Peters.

'This price . . . it makes no sense,' said Darryl Jeffries. 'Why would anyone pay that for these hotels? They've been making a loss for five years.'

'Yes. It *was* rather a good price, wasn't it?' Jackson beamed. 'I had to put in a lot of . . . what should I call it? *Ground work.* Yes. A lot of ground work with the buyer. But she was happy to do the deal in the end.'

She. Of course it was a she.

Bob Massey's face had turned a colour that Jackson had never seen before. He was pretty sure it didn't occur in nature.

'It doesn't matter,' he said through tight lips. 'It's too late. The deadline for your revenues to improve was this morning. There's no way the fund could have cleared in that time.'

'You'd think so, wouldn't you?' said Jackson. 'But Alana's been terribly organized about it all. We closed the deal on Wednesday. The money hit Wrexall's account at eleven o'clock last night.'

'Alana?' Lucius Monroe looked up. 'You don't mean Alana Davis? Senator Davis's wife?'

'That's right.' Jackson smiled. 'It turns out she's hugely wealthy in her own right. Why? Do you know her? I'm meeting her tonight as it happens for a celebration dinner. I'll give her your best, shall I?'

Later that night, in bed at Jackson's apartment, Alana Davis closed her eyes and tried to remember the last time she had felt so alive. Feeling Jackson's huge dick inside her and his powerful thighs clamped around her own, rippling with strength and power and virility and *youth*, she gasped with pleasure, surrendering to her third orgasm of the night.

'That was incredible, baby,' she purred.

'You're incredible,' said Jackson, nuzzling into her neck.

At forty-five Alana Davis had believed that the days of mind-blowing sex were behind her. But in the space of a few short weeks Jackson Dupree had changed all that. On the night stand, her cellphone started to buzz. Alana turned it off.

'The senator?'

'No. My lawyer. He's been getting dreadfully antsy about this hotel deal. You are going to do that buy-back on Monday, aren't you, darling?'

'Of course,' Jackson assured her. 'As soon as my board approval's official, I'll take them off your hands. I'm sure I can turn them around for a small profit eventually.

Somewhere in the twenty-million range with any luck.'

'If you turn *me* around,' Alana looked at him naughtily, 'you can make a big profit right away.'

Jackson Dupree grinned. It was the perfect ending to a perfect day.

CHAPTER EIGHT

Theresa Dexter strolled across the UCLA campus towards the parking lot, where her hundred-thousand-dollar Mercedes convertible gleamed in the sunshine. Above her, a perfectly blue California sky stretched cloudlessly to the horizon. Theresa thought, *I've just given a seminar on Shakespeare to a packed lecture hall. I'm rich. I'm healthy. I'm doing my dream job in a beautiful, sun-drenched city and I'm married to the most gorgeous man in the world.*

She had never felt more unhappy in her life.

It was four years since Theresa and Theo Dexter had moved out to LA. Four years in which Theo had gone from being a minor British celebrity (his first TV series for Channel Four, *Space*, started shooting days after his dispute with Sasha Miller ended and had quickly become a ratings winner) to a world-famous television star. At first Theo had been reluctant to leave England. Dividing his time between Cambridge, where he still taught a half-weekly schedule at St Michael's, and London, he revelled in the sensation of being the biggest fish in a relatively small pond. Unlike Theresa, who avoided it as much as possible, Theo found the London media scene wildly exciting. He joined the Groucho Club and Soho House, and got invited to private screenings at the BBC and book launch parties at the V&A. His book, *The New Universe*, had kept its position in the *Sunday Times* Top Ten Bestseller List for a record twenty-two consecutive weeks, and ITV were already bidding against Channel Four for a second series of *Space*. It was only after *TV Times* magazine described him, much to Theo's chagrin, as 'Science's answer to Alan Titchmarsh' that he began to take Ed Gilliam's entreaties seriously.

'You're wasting your time over here, Theo. We need to take you to America. Start flirting with the big boys, NBC, CBS. Unless of course you're happy to end your career as a guest DJ for Radio 2.'

The Dexters' 'Goodbye to Cambridge' party was filled with enough celebrities to warrant a full page in the *Daily Mail* and a six-page photo special in *Hello!* magazine. Theo looked blonder and more glamorous than ever, his newly streaked hair perfectly offsetting the blue linen of his Paul Smith suit. Theresa, swollen-eyed from crying, stood beside him in an orange Next maxi-dress that did nothing for her figure, a lone ugly duckling amidst the twenty-something TV presenters in their Luella mini-dresses and Vivienne Westwood boots.

'For God's sake, cheer up, T,' Theo snapped at her between photo calls. 'Anyone would think I was dragging you to Beirut, not Bel Air.'

He was right, of course. LA would be an amazing opportunity. Theresa already had a teaching job lined up at UCLA that paid three times what she was earning now, and a grant to continue her Shakespeare research. Just because Los Angeles didn't have thousand-year-old libraries, or original

Shakespeare folios, or churches with entombed medieval knights, or dry-stone walls, or Christmas carols in King's College Chapel . . . She started to cry again.

They flew out first class on Virgin. That part was fun. Theresa got tipsy on free champagne and blubbed loudly watching chick flicks on her personal in-flight movie screen, in between stuffing her face with warmed (*warmed!*) cashew nuts. Theo, doing his best to look like a world-weary, regular first-class traveller, put in his earplugs and pretended to go to sleep. He longed to make his bed go flat so he could rest properly, but didn't want the sexy Asian stewardess to think he didn't know how to operate the seat. As a result, by the time they landed at LAX, Theo was tired and irritable and Theresa badly hungover. It took them an hour to hire a rental car, and another two to reach their rented property in Bel Air, thanks to traffic on the 405 and Theresa's poor map-reading skills. On first impressions LA seemed to be little more that a giant network of freeways, vast, supersized eight-lane roads endlessly intersecting beneath a flawless blue sky. *It's hideous,* thought Theresa bleakly. It wasn't until they reached Sunset Boulevard that the city began to look more like the tourist brochures. Tall, skinny palm trees swayed regally above them, and on both sides of the road, immac-ulately manicured mansions vied to out-do each other in the conspicuous consumption stakes. The West Gate of Bel Air was, it turned out, conveniently situated directly oppo-site the UCLA campus. As Theo and Theresa's car weaved its way up the hillside into the confusing maze of streets – Chalon, Somera, Roscomare, back to Chalon – the prop-erties seemed to become more and more sumptuous. Theresa spotted two with what looked like gold-plated gates, and one that *appeared* to be an exact replica of the

Disneyland castle. When they finally arrived at the address they'd been given, they both thought it was the wrong house.

'This can't be it,' gasped Theresa. 'It's enormous. It looks like the Ritz Carlton.' But a telephone call to Ed Gilliam confirmed that the sprawling, French country mansion was indeed 'home'.

'Welcome to the big time, Theo. Now get some sleep, for God's sake. You've got a meeting at NBC at eleven o'clock tomorrow morning. Six months' rent is paid but if you want to stay there longer than that, you're going to have to start earning.'

And Theo did. Within three weeks, the contracts were inked on his new American science series, *Dexter's Universe*. The combination of his unquestioned genius as a physicist, his telegenic looks and, best of all, his panty-melting British accent had the commissioning editors at NBC salivating with excitement. *People* magazine gave *Dexter's Universe*'s pilot episode a five-star review, dubbing Theo 'Brad Pitt with Brains'. Theo was ecstatic. It sure beat 'Science's answer to Alan Titchmarsh'. He celebrated by going out to Hyde, Hollywood's hottest nightclub, and getting off very publicly with Molly Meyer, the nineteen-year-old star of Disney's latest hit show *What Molly Did Next*. The following week, the pictures were all over *US Weekly*. Theresa was horrified, but Theo was unapologetic.

'You were the one who didn't want to come out with me.'

'I was working! I had fifteen papers to mark that night! Besides, does that give you the right to go and snog whoever you like? Look at her. You're old enough to be her father.'

'I can't help it if young women are attracted to me,' said Theo, crossly. 'Anyway it was only a kiss. Stop overreacting.'

Theresa thought, *Am I overreacting?* Countless people had

warned her that Theo being on network television would mean him getting a lot of unwanted attention. Lisa Jay, the wife of Howard Jay, *Dexter's Universe*'s executive producer, told Theresa over dinner, 'You need the hide of a rhino to survive in this town. Women here are shameless. They'll throw themselves at your husband right in front of you. I get it with Howard all the time.' Theresa looked over at the five-foot, bald figure of Howard Jay as he slurped his soup and tried to picture him being hounded by Hollywood hotties. 'As long as you and Theo trust *each other.* That's the key,' Lisa smiled.

Since the affair with Sasha Miller, Theresa had worked hard to rebuild her trust in her husband. In the immediate aftermath, it was easy. Theo was remorseful and grateful and had made a real effort to get things back on track between them. But as the months went by and his fame and confidence grew, things began to change. Theo spent more and more time shooting on location, or at the studio, and less and less at home. Since they moved to LA, being at work meant being surrounded by model-perfect women 24/7. Researchers, PR girls, stylists, every single one of them seemed to Theresa to have walked off the pages of *Sports Illustrated.* Even at UCLA, where Theo taught one day a week to 'keep his hand in' and his academic credentials current, his students all looked like cheerleaders.

What happened to all the nerds? Theresa wondered. *Were they exterminated at birth? Or sent to some secret farm-of-shame beyond the borders of Southern California?* It was the same story with the staff as with the students. At Cambridge, most professors rode knackered old bicycles, had arthritis or piles or both, wore shoes with holes to match their socks and held their trousers up with string. At UCLA, the teachers all looked like newsreaders, rich, shiny and as polished as their expensive sports cars. Worse still was the faux, have-a-nice-day friendliness. Everyone on campus sucked up to Theresa, because she was Theo Dexter's wife. But even after a year working there, there was no one whom Theresa could confide in or share a laugh with the way she used to with Jenny and Jean Paul, or her colleagues in the English faculty at Cambridge. Nor was she buffered by the cocoon of protective silence that had kept her in the dark about Theo's affairs back home. Cambridge was like a giant family. People were kind and tactful and discreet. UCLA was the opposite, sleek and cut-throat and riven with politics, like a corporation. Here, no one shielded Theresa from the gossip about Theo's philandering. Eventually it reached a point where even Theresa could no longer ignore it. Theo was sleeping with every good-looking woman who crossed his path: students, colleagues at work, waitresses, models, air stewardesses (on his long trips to promote *Dexter's Universe* in Europe and Asia), fans, journalists. When she challenged him about a specific rumour he would either deny the liaison outright, or turn things around to try to blame his wandering eye on Theresa. She was unsupportive. She was miserable. She embarrassed him with her frumpy clothes. She never made an effort. Depressed, lonely and demoralized, Theresa had started comfort eating, and drinking, knocking back her first strong gin and tonic the second the clock struck six each night. By the end of their second year in LA, she had gained almost forty pounds.

'Dr Dexter!'

Theresa spun around. She'd finally been awarded her doctorate six months ago. It still felt strange, and gratifying, when people referred to her by her new title.

'Do you have a second?' Theresa recognized the girl from her seminar on *As You Like It*. Even by UCLA standards she was strikingly beautiful, with flawless, dark Persian skin and an oil slick of lustrous black hair, like Aladdin's Princess Jasmine.

'Of course,' Theresa said kindly. Shakespeare's comedies were more complex than many scholars gave them credit for. Theresa always enjoyed leading a new generation of students through their mysteries. 'How can I help?'

The girl blushed. 'Actually, I was kinda hoping you would give this to Theo . . . Professor Dexter for me. It's a copy of my résumé. He said he might be able to put in a word for me about an internship at the studio?'

Theresa thought, *Why do American girls insist on pronouncing every statement as if it were a question?* Then she thought, *I wonder if Theo's already slept with her?*

'Sure.' She took the résumé, not knowing what else to do. 'I'll pass it along.'

Driving home in the expensive car Theo had bought for her – how she missed her old Beetle! – Theresa fought back depression like King Cnut fighting back the waves. Tonight was the Make-A-Wish charity fundraiser at the Beverly Hills hotel, one of the most glamorous social events in the Hollywood calendar. For once, Theo had insisted Theresa go with him. 'It's a family event. People will expect to see you there. But do *please* try to make an effort. All sorts of bigwigs from our sponsors are going to be there. I need to look credible.'

'Credible' was Theo's latest buzzword. Theresa wondered, *Credible to whom, and for what?* She failed to see how squeezing her fat rolls into a Spanx bodysuit and plastering on the make-up was going to make the slightest difference to Theo's career. Especially as, no matter how hard she tried, she could never hope to compete with the size zero, Hervé Léger shrink-wrapped bimbos that thronged to events like these.

But I must try. I must. He's only running around with other women because I always look such a fright. Passing a hair salon in Brentwood that had 'Walk-Ins Welcome' embossed in cheery red paint across the front window, Theresa pulled over.

Theo leaned on his horn. 'Bloody traffic,' he moaned. 'This city is ridiculous. It's seven at night and you still can't move on bloody Sunset.' He beeped again, setting off an echo of irritated replies from the cars in front of them.

'Try to keep calm, darling,' said Theresa. 'We're only five minutes late.'

Theo looked over at the passenger seat. Theresa, for once, looked half decent tonight. She could still stand to lose a couple of stone, at least. But the floor-length, silver Elie Saab dress she was wearing flattered her figure, making her look womanly rather than fat and showcasing her undeniably marvellous (and natural) cleavage. Her red hair was swept into a sixties-inspired up-do, a look that was topped off with thick black Marilyn Monroe eyeliner. All in all the effect was a satisfactorily fifties sex-siren. *I might even screw her tonight,* Theo thought idly. *God knows it's been a while.*

He was in a bad mood thanks to an email he'd received that afternoon from the editor at the *New Scientist*, politely but firmly rejecting his offer to write a regular column on the changing face of physics. The little dweeb had had the temerity to imply that Theo's academic credentials weren't lofty enough for his shitty, second-rate magazine. 'It's an amazingly generous offer, Professor Dexter, especially from a figure as high profile and, I don't doubt, busy as yourself. But our readership is primarily research scientists, working in the field. I'm sure you'll understand that their needs and interests are very different from your audience's. As editor, I need to be mindful of that.'

'Mindful.' Pretentious little turd. So because I'm on television, all of a sudden I'm not a 'proper' scientist? Not 'cutting edge' enough for your readership of losers and nerds, because MY research has been published and fêted around the world, and theirs hasn't?

Theo adored LA. He adored everything about working in television, the fame, the money, the travel, the hot girls falling over themselves to bed him. But it still irked him that his fellow physicists refused to take him seriously. As he'd told the interviewer from *Men's Vogue* only this morning (right after stressing how important it was for men in the public eye to make brave fashion choices): the scientific community was deeply unforgiving of commercial success.

Theo was still moaning to Theresa as they pulled into valet parking. 'I wonder what that up-himself editor would give to be attending an event like this? He'd probably have to hock his apartment just to buy a ticket. Twat.'

'Hmmm.' Theresa wasn't really listening. She was watching all the size-zero twenty-two-year-olds unfurling themselves from the back of limousines. Twenty minutes ago she'd felt beautiful, sexy and on top of her game. Now she felt old and fat and . . .

'Theo! Darling! I didn't know you were gonna be here. That's so awesome.' A brunette in a gold Dolce & Gabanna micro-mini whom Theresa had never seen before jumped on Theo as he got out of the car, draping her arms around his neck and kissing him on the lips. Theresa looked at the girl's pin-thin legs and thought, *My right breast weighs more than you.*

'Oh. Hi. You must be Theo's . . . wife?' The girl looked at Theresa as one might look at a mangy dog, her face torn between pity and disgust.

'That's right.' *And you must be . . . one of the sluts who work for him?* 'And you are . . .?'

'Camille. Theo and I are colleagues. This is my boyfriend, David. He's a producer.'

Theresa only just managed not to laugh. From behind the gazelle-like Camille, a fat dwarf of a man waddled over to shake hands. A foot shorter than his date, and a minimum of three decades older, David still managed to stick his chest out and preen as if he were Steven Tyler. Walking up the stone steps into the famously pink, kitsch hotel, Theresa leaned into Theo and giggled. 'Poor man! Talk about Beauty and the Beast. I suppose there's no fool like an old fool.'

'David Weinberg is nobody's fool,' said Theo pompously. 'He's one of the highest-paid TV producers in the world. He's the brains behind *Teen Queen Wrestling* and *Celebrity Surgery Face-Off*. You shouldn't be so quick to judge people by their looks you know, T.'

'*Me?*' Theresa spluttered. But Theo was gone, air kissing another gaggle of preposterously pretty girls as he worked his way through the crowd. Knowing no one and feeling homesick and depressed – she'd made a titanic effort to look her best tonight, but what was the point? – Theresa did what any sensible Irish girl would do. She headed to the bar.

'What can I get you? Watermelon vodka? Sour apple martini? Sex on the Beach?'

'Whisky. No ice, no water.'

She downed the first drink, then a second and third. Instantly the room became a little hazy, as if she were watching the party through a lens and someone had smeared it with Vaseline. So this was it, the long-awaited Make-A-Wish Ball. *I'm making a wish: I wish I were at home, listening to Classic FM on my computer. I wish I were two stone lighter. I wish I could make Theo fall in love with me again.*

'Would everybody please take your seats for dinner.'

*   *   *

Dinner was served in the hotel's famous art deco Crystal Ballroom. Above Theresa's head a lavish chandelier twinkled naffly over the pink and white tables, where Hollywood's elite sat sipping soda water and nibbling half-heartedly on plates of tuna tartare. 'I feel like I'm at Jordan and Peter's wedding,' Theresa joked to Theo. 'There are enough sequins in this room to make Liberace wince.' Once upon a time Theo had shared her irreverent sense of humour. No longer. Since moving to LA, he seemed to have had his appreciation of the absurd surgically removed.

'Don't be facetious,' he hissed at her. 'Who's that on table nineteen? The woman everyone's crowding around?'

Theresa looked. She didn't recognize anybody.

'That's Dita Andreas,' said the girl on Theo's left. 'Her new movie, *Heaven's Gate,* just had the biggest September opening weekend on record. *Variety*'s calling her the new Angelina.'

It wasn't a soubriquet that Theo would have picked. If anything, Dita Andreas looked more like an older, more womanly version of Scarlett Johansson, though she did share Angelina's trademark full-lipped pout. Her simple, black L'Wren Scott sheath and Neil Lane diamond drop earrings contrasted dramatically with her pale colouring. Blonde and sultry, with unfashionably fair skin and blood-red lips, she was not the most beautiful woman in the room. But she exuded sexuality like a stoat in heat, and she had that *something,* charisma, star-quality, whatever you wanted to call it, that eclipsed all the younger, taller, more regular-featured girls surrounding her.

'Is she married?' Theo asked bluntly.

'*Theo!*' Theresa blushed.

'Uh huh. Newlywed,' said the girl on his left. 'To Brett Graham, the director on *Heaven's Gate.* He's her fourth husband. Dita collects husbands the way Angelina collects orphans. Doesn't keep 'em as long though.' The girl laughed.

Theo stared across the room at Dita. He wasn't alone. The entire party seemed to be fixated with her. But some sixth sense made Dita look up and notice him.

'Who is that man?' she asked her husband.

'Which man? The blond?' Brett Graham glared at Theo. 'He's nobody.'

'No, really. You don't know him?'

'No, I don't know him. Which means he isn't in the film business. I know everybody in the film business.' Brett Graham was used to having girlfriends hang off his every word. With Dita Andreas, it was different. He was constantly having to prove himself, to try to impress her and keep her interested. Every day he spent with her he felt his heart growing tighter and his dick growing harder. It was torture.

'He's a physicist.' The man opposite Dita interjected helpfully. 'Theo Dexter. He has a TV show on NBC.'

'You see?' said Brett, smugly. 'I told you. He's in TV. He's nobody.'

Dita smiled at Theo, and turned away.

Not long after dinner ended, Theresa was back at the bar, alone again. Dita Andreas and her entourage had already left. No doubt they had another, more important party to go to. Theresa had seen Theo talking to Dita earlier, introducing himself, but Dita's husband had dragged her quickly away. *If only I could control Theo like that*, Theresa thought sadly. He was on the dance floor now with yet another young NBC staffer. Theresa watched the pair of them glide across the polished marble, their perfect bodies pressed close, feeling like Sandra Dee watching Danny and Cha Cha win the dance-off in *Grease*. She downed another whisky.

'I'd go easy on that if I were you.' A distinguished-looking man in his early sixties appeared at Theresa's side. 'Take it from someone who knows. Drink isn't the answer.'

Theresa looked up at him. He seemed kind. He was handsome too, for an old bloke. Like a tall Inspector Morse. Except that Inspector Morse would never have told anybody that drink wasn't the answer. He would also never have come to a party full of posers at the Beverly Hills hotel. *What am I talking about? I must be drunker than I thought.*

The man followed her gaze to where Theo was dancing. 'He'll grow out of it. Believe me. Hollywood, fame, all this, it's dazzling at first. He just needs to realize what a great thing he's got going at home. You're gorgeous.'

It was such a kind thing to say, Theresa felt her eyes well up with tears.

'Oh, God, sorry. I don't know why I'm snivelling. I think I'm a little drunk. Then again, I think you must be too. Either that or blind. I'm the fattest woman here by a million miles.'

The man looked at Theresa's glorious figure poured into her slinky silver dress and laughed. 'Nonsense. You've lost your confidence, that's all. Trust me, most men aren't attracted to anorexic airheads with two bags of silicone glued to their ribcage. Not for more than a few seconds anyway. Harry Meister.'

'Theresa Dexter.' Theresa shook his hand. Harry was a TV presenter, also at NBC. It turned out he knew Theo slightly through mutual colleagues.

'So what is the answer, Mr Meister?' Theresa asked him. 'If it's not to be found at the bottom of a bottle of Famous Grouse?'

'My advice? Get pregnant. I've seen hundreds of guys like your husband, new in town and all starry-eyed. Give them a family and they soon settle down.'

He couldn't have known it was exactly the wrong thing to say. Theresa barely managed to mumble a 'nice to meet you' before she ran outside into the parking lot. Slumped against the service doors to the kitchens, she broke down in tears.

He's right! The one thing that could save my marriage is the one thing Theo knows I'll probably never be able to give him.

Alone beneath the stars, Theresa wondered how much longer she would be able to hold her marriage together. Years? Months? Weeks? She tried to think back to where it had all begun to go wrong. Immediately one, single, unforgettable image loomed in her mind.

It was Sasha Miller's face.

CHAPTER NINE

Sitting in the front row at McCollum Hall, Harvard Business School's newly renovated auditorium, Sasha Miller waited excitedly for her name to be read out. As the top graduate in her section, she would have a long wait. Her name, as was the tradition, would be called last, and would undoubtedly prompt a standing ovation from her classmates and professors. But that wasn't why Sasha was excited.

She was excited because now, at last, she could take the first step towards fulfilling her destiny. The destiny that had brought her to Harvard in the first place. The destiny that had made her quit physics and take an MBA. The destiny that had brought her to America.

Now I can start to destroy Theo Dexter.

After the university ruled against her, things unravelled quickly for Sasha at Cambridge. She didn't stick around to be formally sent down. She'd suffered enough humiliation for one lifetime. Instead she quietly dropped out, intending to write to the physics faculties at the five other universities who'd accepted her, and finish her degree in peace.

It wasn't to be. It took six months of pleading letters, phone calls and personal references from every teacher she'd ever met to convince *any* university to admit her. In the end, University College London took pity on Sasha, mainly because the Head of Admissions, James Trethwick, used to go out with St Agnes's Deputy Headmistress, Diana Drew, and still held a torch for her.

'I don't know what happened with this Dexter fellow, but Sasha's never done anything remotely like this before,' Diana told James over dinner. 'And the girl truly is the most gifted physicist I've ever taught.'

That much was true. But James Trethwick still came to regret his decision to admit her. With Theo Dexter's star inexorably rising, media interest in Sasha refused to die. 'She's like Monica Lewinsky to Dexter's Clinton,' James complained. 'Dexter gets interviewed on *Parkinson* and suddenly there are a hundred photographers loitering outside our labs, trying to get a shot of the Miller girl looking sad or defiant or whatever story they're peddling this week. It's distracting.'

Luckily, Sasha's fellow UCL students weren't distracted for long. She graduated with a top first not much more than a year after enrolling. Her parents took her out for a celebratory meal in Tunbridge Wells.

'What now, love?' Sue Miller asked. 'You'll be looking for a research fellowship, I suppose?'

'With your degree scores you can go wherever you like,' her dad said proudly. 'You'll be beating off offers with a stick.'

'Actually,' Sasha took a big slug of red wine to steady her nerves, 'I've decided to go to business school.'

'*Business school?*' Don Miller couldn't have looked more horrified if she'd said she was enrolling in pole dancing academy or jetting off to a jihadist camp in Afghanistan. 'That's ridiculous. You're a scientist, Sasha. You have been since you were knee high.'

Sasha shrugged. 'Maybe I grew up.'

'No.' Don stood up. He was shaking. 'I can't let you do this. You'll regret it for the rest of your life, Sasha. You can't just give up on physics.'

Sasha looked at her father sadly. He'd never got to live out his own dream of becoming an astronomer. Instead, he'd lived through her. All her life, she'd been a channel for his hopes. Now she was about to dash them. But she knew she had no choice.

'I didn't give up on physics, Dad. It gave up on me. It doesn't matter how brilliant I am, how hard I work, how many times I prove myself. I'll always be the girl who tried to steal her professor's theory. I need to start again.'

Don opened his mouth to speak, but Sue interrupted him. Unlike Don, she had never been obsessed with their daughter's academic career. All Sue Miller wanted was for Sasha to be happy. If that meant a change of direction, then so be it.

'Where were you thinking of going? For your MBA? Have you applied anywhere yet?'

Sasha took another slug of wine. This was going to be the hardest part of all.

'Actually, I've been accepted. At Harvard.'

'*America?*' This time her parents' horror was mutual. 'You're going to America?'

I am. Theo Dexter's in America. I'm going to move there and work my arse off and make a success of my life. I'm going to become rich and powerful. Then I'm going to figure out a way to ruin that bastard's life, the way he ruined mine.

*　　*　　*

Sasha's only concern about going to Harvard was that it might remind her too painfully of St Michael's. She needn't have worried. Cambridge's charm lay in its slightly dilapidated old-worldliness. Everything was falling down, crumbling and overgrown, from the lecture halls to the underpaid professors' rickety bicycles. Harvard, especially the business school, was like a well-oiled corporation. Everything was new and perfect and gleaming. At St Michael's, the libraries smelled of dust, ancient stone and woodworm. At HBS, they smelled of money.

No one, Sasha learned, studied business out of passion. It wasn't like physics or history or literature. People came to business school for one reason and one reason only: because they wanted to be rich. Unlike in England, where the naked pursuit of wealth was considered vulgar and unseemly, here it was openly celebrated. Of course, there were a few deluded souls who liked to pretend to themselves and others that business really *mattered*. The 'I want to make America great again' brigade, or the 'I'm doing this for feminism, breaking the glass ceiling for the good of womankind' bores. For some inexplicable reason, the business ethics seminars were always oversubscribed. *They're trying to justify their greed,* thought Sasha. She herself had no need of justification. She knew exactly why she wanted to be rich. She woke up every morning and looked at his picture, Blu-Tacked to her bathroom mirror.

While the rest of her classmates partied and slept around, availing themselves fully of the wild nightlife that Harvard had to offer, Sasha became more and more reclusive, studying by day and waitressing by night to help pay for her tuition. 'Help' being the operative word. HBS was prohibitively, insanely expensive – another difference with Cambridge. After three years, becoming rich was no longer an option for most students but a necessity, to pay off their six-figure student loans. At Sue's Steak House, the restaurant where Sasha worked, customers hit on her nightly. Some of them were good-looking guys, but Sasha wasn't interested. After Theo Dexter, her libido seemed to have evaporated completely. She'd had sex twice in four years, both one-night stands, both deeply unsatisfying. After that, she gave up.

I'm a born-again virgin. But who cares? I don't need a man to keep me warm at night. I have the flames of my hatred and the fire of my ambition. I'm complete.

Already a Baker Scholar after her second year, no one was surprised when Sasha Miller graduated top of her section. Least of all Sasha herself. By the time her results came through, she'd already accepted a job at Merrill Lynch in New York. Not because she had the remotest interest in investment banking, but because it offered the highest starting salary and fastest track to directorship of anything else she'd been offered.

'Miss Sasha Miller.' The Dean's voice rang out around the auditorium. Sasha turned and smiled at her parents, seated a few rows behind. This wasn't their dream, any more than it was hers. But they were here, and proud, their love for her unwavering. *One day,* Sasha thought, *I'll repay them for everything they've done for me.* The little cottage in Frant where she'd grown up, and once been so happy, felt farther away than ever. It was almost inconceivable to think that tomorrow Don and Sue would be on a plane back there. And Sasha would be on a plane to New York.

All eyes were on Sasha as she made her way to the podium. One pair of eyes in particular thought, *Now that's a great-looking girl. Why haven't we interviewed her? If she's the brightest HBS graduate, she should be with us.*

Jackson Dupree made a note in his BlackBerry. 'Sasha Miller.' He would make her an offer she couldn't refuse.

Jackson hadn't really enjoyed his own years at Harvard. He couldn't shake the feeling that he was killing time, spinning his wheels until the real work of his life began, at Wrexall. What he *had* enjoyed was the sex. All the girls from Harvard College and Wellesley wanted boyfriends from the biz school, rightly perceiving them to be the next generation of American super-rich. Of course, New York had no shortage of stunning women. But at Harvard, the girls had been stunning *and* bright. Occasionally, bed-hopping from one airheaded Elite model to the next, Jackson missed his college lovers.

That was why he was here. He'd met Rachel at a party in the Hamptons last summer. She was eighteen then and due to start Harvard in the fall. After two blissful weeks of screwing in her stepfather's guesthouse, they'd parted ways, but Jackson made a point of keeping in touch. When Rachel called him last week to invite him up for the end-of-term celebrations, he'd jumped at the chance. After successfully quashing Bob Massey's would-be coup and winning his place on Wrexall's board, he deserved a vacation. The end-of-year celebrations at Harvard were always fabulous, debauched parties on the boathouses along the Charles, drunk, celebratory students running half-naked around Harvard Square, enjoying their brief window of freedom between their finals and the imminent beginning of working life. If he stopped by the Business School to do a spot of recruiting, he could even write it off on expenses. How much would Massey and his cronies love *that*?

Landing on the lawn outside Spangler Hall in a royal blue Wrexall Dupree chopper, Jackson arrived minutes before the graduation ceremony was due to commence. For once he'd dressed formally, in a dark Armani suit and grey Hermès silk tie, his wild black curls slicked into place and a crisp white handkerchief peeking the regulation half-inch above his breast pocket. All the graduating students and their guests on the way to McCollum Hall turned and stared as Jackson jumped nimbly to the ground, the women lustfully and the men enviously.

'Who's that?' Don Miller asked Sasha. 'He loves himself a bit, doesn't he?'

Sasha shrugged, bored. Over the course of the past three years she'd grown used to watching handsome young Americans chest-beating their way through college. Admittedly landing a helicopter on the lawn was pushing it to new extremes. But these men were the golden children, the chosen ones, and they knew it. Showing off was a way of life for them.

'Some trust-fund brat, I expect,' she said dismissively. 'Come on. Let's get you seats before all the good ones are taken.'

After the ceremony, Sasha put her parents in a taxi back to the hotel. Her mum was still jet lagged and wanted a catnap before they met up again for dinner. She was just heading back to her own rooms in Baker Hall when she felt a tap on her shoulder. Spinning around, she found herself face to face with helicopter guy.

'Sasha, right? Sasha Miller?' Up close he was even more ridiculously handsome. *And even more self-satisfied.* 'I'm Jackson Dupree.'

He didn't elaborate. If the name was supposed to mean something to Sasha, it didn't.

'Can I help you?'

'Actually I have a feeling I might be able to help you.' Jackson fixed his mesmerizing almond eyes on Sasha's dispassionate, pale green ones and waited for this to have the usual effect.

Nothing.

'I'm on the board of a little company named Wrexall Dupree. You may have heard of us?'

Sasha gave him a look, as if to say, *And?*

'Here.' Jackson handed her a business card. 'Meet me for dinner tonight and I'll tell you a little more about us. For now, suffice it to say that we're the best in our field. And we make it our business to hire the best. I know you'll have had other offers, but I'm confident we can more than match them. I'm staying at the Ritz Carlton on Newbury Street. Shall we say eight o'clock?'

It was so breathtakingly arrogant that for once in her life Sasha was speechless. Not that it mattered anyway. By the time she'd come up with a suitably withering reply, Jackson had walked away, jabbering into his cellphone nineteen to the dozen.

Dickhead, thought Sasha. No amount of money on earth would persuade her to work for a man like Jackson Dupree. Besides, she was already committed to her job at Merrill. She walked back to her rooms without giving him a second thought.

'I don't understand, Jacks. What sort of business? This is your first night. I made plans.'

Rachel pursed her adorable, cupid's bow lips into a pout and tousled her honey-blonde hair in irritation. They were in Rachel's dorm room – her roommate, Helen, had thoughtfully agreed to evaporate for the four nights of Jackson's visit, and Rachel had made the place as love-nesty as possible, throwing all her clothes into the laundry hamper and lighting scented candles on every inch of surface not covered with vases of flowers. Jackson walked over and slipped his hand inside Rachel's American Apparel tanktop, cupping a small but perfectly formed breast and gently caressing her nipple with his thumb. Despite herself, Rachel closed her eyes and moaned with pleasure.

'I promise you,' Jackson whispered, nuzzling her neck and softly kissing her earlobe, 'this is the last piece of work I have to do here. I'll be an hour. Two hours, tops,' he promised, mentally calculating how long it would take him to woo Sasha, get her up to his suite at the Ritz Carlton, fuck her *and* persuade her to come and work at Wrexall. 'After that I'm all yours.'

'What about *before* that?' Rachel's lips parted, her pupils dilating with lust.

Jackson grinned, pushing her down on the neatly made twin bed. Maybe he did miss his college days after all?

'You should go.'

'Don't be ridiculous, Dad.' Sasha took her mother's shopping bags as they crossed the street. Sue Miller wanted to do a 'lightning' stop at Banana Republic and various other American stores before their farewell dinner at Marco's. 'I'm not interested in the job, and I'm certainly not interested in him.'

'How do you know you're not interested in the job? He hasn't told you what it is yet.'

'If it involves working within a ten-mile radius of Jackson Dupree's ego, I'm not interested,' said Sasha firmly.

'Your father's right,' said Sue. 'Go and have a drink with him. We'll meet you afterwards. It's silly to close doors before you . . .'

'Oh my God.' Sasha interrupted her, pulling her off the street into a Starbucks. There was Jackson, kissing a young, blonde co-ed on the other side of the street. And not just kissing. His hands were everywhere. 'Look at him! That's disgusting.'

Sue and Don Miller exchanged glances. How long was Sasha's anti-men phase going to last? She hadn't had a boyfriend in years.

'He's very good looking,' said Sue.

'He's a lech.'

'I thought you wanted to be a businesswoman?' said Don. 'That you were selling your services to the highest bidder?'

'I am.'

'Then stop being so daft and go and meet him. Let him bid.'

Sasha opened her mouth to protest, then closed it again. *Fine. I'll go. But it'll be a cold day in hell before I work for Jackson Dupree.*

At eight on the dot, Sasha walked into the bar at the Ritz Carlton. Jackson was nowhere to be seen. *I'll give him two minutes,* she thought crossly. *I'm not hanging around for that vain, self-important . . .*

'You came.' In the twenty minutes since she'd last seen him, Jackson had showered, shaved and changed into a pair of cream linen Armani pants and a coffee-coloured Interno 8 shirt that perfectly offset his butterscotch tan. For a split second his handsomeness, combined with his broad, apparently genuine smile, disarmed her.

'I can only stay for a drink. It's my parents' last night in town. But I figured I'd hear what you have to say.'

Jackson frowned. He'd been planning on getting her tipsy in the bar, excited about Wrexall over dinner, then sealing the deal in bed. Now he would have to move straight to phase three. Languidly stretching out his arm, he stroked Sasha's hair.

'Let's cut to the chase, darling, shall we? I can tell you about Wrexall when you have more time. There's a job for you with us if you want it. But right now I think we both know it's not the job you want.'

Before Sasha had a moment to protest, Jackson swooped in and kissed her passionately on the mouth. He smelled of lemons and soap and toothpaste. Feeling his body pressed against hers, for a moment Sasha felt a stab of longing. Old feelings flooded her body, familiar yet strange, like a frozen river cracking in the first spring thaw. Then, out of nowhere, an image of Theo Dexter naked and making love to her popped into Sasha's mind. She pushed Jackson violently away.

'Get off me! Are you out of your mind?'

'I don't think so.' Jackson was maddeningly unperturbed. 'I want you. You want me. We're both adults. You're not attached, are you?'

'That has nothing to do with it!' said Sasha furiously.

'Good. Neither am I.' He leaned in for another kiss.

'Stop it! What are you, some kind of sex pest? I saw you on the street half an hour ago. With the blonde? So for one thing, you *are* attached.'

Jackson grinned. 'Ah. You're jealous.'

'I am not *jealous*. I came here to talk about a job, you jerk. Clearly I made a huge error of judgement.'

'Look me in the eye and tell me you're not attracted to me. That when I kissed you just now you weren't imagining the two of us in bed together.'

'You're deranged.' Sasha turned on her heel and stormed out of the hotel. As she came out of the revolving doors onto Newbury Street, she saw Jackson's blonde. Clearly the girl couldn't keep away from him. 'Excuse me,' said Sasha on impulse. 'I'm sorry to intrude. But are you the girl dating Jackson Dupree?'

A look of pride spread over the blonde's face.

'That's right,' she smiled. 'I'm Rachel Cooper. Do you know Jackson?'

'Not at all,' said Sasha. 'But that didn't stop him trying to get me into bed right now. He asked me here to talk about a job with his company, then he stuck his tongue down my throat and begged me to sleep with him.' Colour drained from the blonde's face. 'Look, I'm sorry to be so blunt. But you seem like a nice girl. You can do a lot better than that arsehole.'

Don and Sue Miller couldn't believe it.

'You should report him. That's sexual harassment.'

'It's worse than that. He kissed her. That's sexual assault.'

Sasha thought back to Jackson's kiss and her own response. She hadn't exactly slapped him round the face. Not for the first few seconds anyway. Sexual assault was probably pushing it.

'Forget it. He's a moron, but I'll never have to see him again. Besides,' she smiled, 'I think I've already ruined his evening.'

'Come on, Rach. You're being ridiculous!'

'So you didn't try to sleep with her? She's lying, is that what you're saying?'

The entire bar, restaurant and lobby had turned to tune in to the screaming match between Jackson Dupree and the gorgeous blonde girl. So far it was blonde fifteen, Jackson love.

'I don't *try* to sleep with anyone,' said Jackson coldly. 'If I want to sleep with a woman, I do.'

Fifteen all.

'Do you want to sleep with me?'

A slow smile spread over Jackson's face. 'Of course I do, angel. That's why I'm here. Let's not let a silly misunderstanding spoil our vacation, OK?'

Rachel turned sweetly to a woman at the bar. 'Could I borrow that for a second?' Picking up the woman's ice-cold vodka tonic, she threw it in Jackson's face.

'Well you can't. Not now, not ever, you lying son of a bitch.'

Game, set and match blond.

It was too late to get a flight back to New York that night. Lying in bed alone, staring at the ceiling in his palatial hotel suite, Jackson was too angry to sleep.

How dare Sasha Miller rat him out to Rachel? He knew damn well she'd been attracted to him. He'd seen it in her eyes. If there was one thing Jackson Dupree knew how to do, it was to spot desire in a woman. All that feminist anger, it was just a way of acting out. *She was angry at herself. She knew she didn't come because of the job and it killed her.*

The irony was, he didn't even want her that badly. Sasha Miller was pretty, more than pretty, but she was pricklier than a porcupine's hide. Rachel, dear, sweet, uncomplicated, teenage Rachel, she was much more Jackson's type. He'd only gone for Sasha because she presented a mild challenge, and a little variety. Jackson did like variety. What he did not like was rejection.

Fuck it. Tomorrow he'd go back to the city and bang a few models to restore his equilibrium. *Harvard girls are more trouble than they're worth.*

The next morning, Sasha opened her college mail to find a handwritten letter in a Ritz Carlton envelope.

An apology. Better late than never, I suppose.

Inside was a two-line note. 'You start as an Associate Vice President. $750,000 p/a plus bonus. JD.' There was a phone number at the end.

Sasha leaned unsteadily against the wall. Seven hundred and fifty thousand dollars. *Base!* Merrill had offered her $250,000, which was a third more than all the other banks. She thought about Jackson Dupree and how much she loathed him. Then she thought about Theo Dexter, and everything that he'd taken from her. She called the number.

'I won't report to you directly.'

'Fine.'

'I need to be in a different division altogether.'

'That can be arranged.'

'I can't start for two weeks.'

'Don't push it, Sasha. You start on Monday.'

The line went dead.

Sasha looked at the note again and laughed out loud. Seven hundred and fifty *thousand* dollars! Jackson Dupree must want to sleep with her very badly indeed.

CHAPTER TEN

Jackson Dupree did not want to sleep with Sasha Miller. Right at this moment he did not want to talk to her, see her, hear her, or be forced to acknowledge her existence in any way. Sasha had just lost them a huge deal, and Jackson was furious.

'What the fuck is wrong with you?' he exploded. 'Do you know how valuable Morgan Graham's business is to us? You can't even be polite.'

'Oh, I can be polite.' Strutting down Wall Street in a severely cut black Donna Karan suit and power heels, Sasha was equally angry. 'What I can't be is coquettish and fawning and flutter my eyelashes like Bambi just because Graham needs his dick massaged.'

'Jesus Christ. It was an anecdote. A funny story.'

'That story wasn't funny. It was cruel. He screws his poor wife over and I'm supposed to laugh at that? I'm supposed to be impressed?'

'You called him a prick, Sasha. To his face. You called the head of Goldman Sachs's Private Equity Group a prick, and you blew up a joint venture that's worth hundreds of millions of dollars to this firm.'

Sasha shrugged. 'He is a prick.'

'Yeah? Well so are you,' snarled Jackson. They glared at each other.

It was six months since Sasha Miller had joined Wrexall Dupree. Six months since Jackson had been deafened by the howls of protest from the board about her exorbitant salary. Six months since Sasha's hostile, truculent little face had appeared in the doorway of Jackson's office, demanding to see her contract and to be seated as far away from him as was feasibly possible within the confines of the building. In that time Jackson had grown to respect and dislike Sasha in equal measure. Her intellect was astonishing. Jackson was no slouch himself in the brains department, but he had never seen another human being assimilate information so quickly. Her maths skills were outrageous.

'No way she's a business major.' Jimmy Noakes, who ran Wrexall's highly regarded modelling group, told Jackson in an awestruck voice. 'She's a quant. I've never seen anyone crunch numbers that fast and with that degree of accuracy. She should be working at NASA, not wasting her life here.'

The marketing department was equally impressed. 'Clients love her. Seriously. John Walsh practically ate the girl up with a spoon. And it's not just men. Angie Jameson called Bob Massey to tell him how impressed she was with Sasha. *Angie Jameson!*' A brilliant businesswoman and one-time knockout beauty, Angie Jameson famously loathed working with other women, especially pretty ones. Her entire company, Jameson Estates, was staffed by men, right down to the secretarial and catering staff. But somehow Sasha Miller had won Angie over, scoring her first big deal for Bob Massey's commercial real estate division by selling Jameson

Estates a chain of strip malls. Soon after that, the board stopped bitching about Sasha's salary. For once, they agreed, Jackson had done well.

When he offered to take Sasha out to celebrate, she turned him down flat.

'Come on, now,' he said smoothly. 'I know we got off to a bad start. But don't you think it's time to bury the hatchet? I was really proud of your work today. We all were.'

'Thank you,' said Sasha.

'So you'll come out for a drink?'

Sasha smiled sweetly. 'Absolutely not.'

She was never unprofessional, or overtly rude. She avoided Jackson where possible, and where not possible worked alongside him with a cool detachment that would have made Henry Kissinger proud. But her distaste for the company of Wrexall's heir apparent was not lost on anyone at the firm. Jackson couldn't shake the feeling that he was being laughed at behind his back, and that it was all Sasha's fault.

Lottie Grainger, a Yale graduate with short chestnut hair and an enchanting, freckled, pixie-like face, couldn't understand Sasha's continued hostility. One of the few other female executives at Wrexall and a rising star in the PR and communications group, Lottie considered Sasha a friend and confidante. But she also liked Jackson.

'Don't you think you should give him a chance? Compared to a lot of the old farts on the board he's a good guy, you know. And you have to admit he's great at his job.'

'I never said he wasn't.'

Over the last few years, Jackson had developed something of specialization in high-end residential work, focusing on uber-wealthy private clients and developers. Sasha officially worked in the commercial group, under Bob Massey, which meant their paths rarely crossed. Recently, however, she'd been roped in to help with a potential joint venture in the hotel sector. The deal with Goldman Sachs's Private Equity Group was Jackson's baby. To Sasha's surprise and irritation, he had specifically requested to have her work on it with him.

Lottie Grainger would have given her eye teeth to have been Jackson's right-hand woman and couldn't understand Sasha's bitching.

'I know Jackson's a player and all that,' said Lottie.

'Quite the legend. In his own mind,' Sasha replied scathingly.

'But I've been here four years and he's always respected the boundaries.' Lottie couldn't entirely hide her disappointment. For some reason Jackson had made a pass at every attractive woman to walk through the doors at Wrexall . . . except her. 'Besides, like it or not, Jackson Dupree's going to run this place one day. If you want to make it to the top at Wrexall, you're going to have to make peace with him at some point.'

This was true. It was one of the reasons that Sasha had no intention of making it to the top at Wrexall. Her plan was to learn all she could, take the firm for as much money as possible, then get out and start her own firm. There was a popular saying at HBS: 'No one ever got rich on a salary.' Of course, that all depended on how one defined 'rich'. But Sasha wasn't interested in making a few million, the sort of money to keep her in big houses and couture clothes. She needed serious money. The kind that could buy and sell companies and make or break futures. The kind that could destroy a man.

Looking at Jackson's furious face after today's meeting, Sasha thought, *Maybe I'll have to bring the whole "quitting*

Wrexall" plan forward a few years. Morgan Graham, the big cheese from Goldman, had pissed her off royally with his self-aggrandizing, sexist bullshit. But deep down, Sasha realized she'd gone too far. Jackson had been working on this JV for six months. If he went to the board and told them what happened, they'd have every right to fire her.

Jackson stormed back into his office, slamming the door so hard that the framed photograph of his grandfather, Randall Dupree, crashed down off the wall. Lise, his secretary, knocked with trepidation.

'Can I, er . . . can I get you anything?'

'You can get me Sasha Miller's head on a plate,' snarled Jackson. 'Tell Bob Massey I need to talk to him. She's gone too damn far this time. And get Lottie in here,' he added as an afterthought. 'We need to figure out a damage-control strategy for the media. Everyone expected us to announce a deal this week. If we don't put something convincing out there our share price is going to drop faster than Paris Hilton's panties.'

'Yes, sir. Right away.'

Lise scuttled off. A few minutes later, Lottie Grainger walked in. In a simple, grey turtleneck sweater from J. Crew and Stella McCartney wool pants, with her face almost completely free of make-up, Lottie still managed to look radiant. *She's so lovely,* thought Jackson, warmly. Seeing Lottie was often the highlight of Jackson's working day. There was something pure and innocent and innately decent about her that had kept him from trying it on with her. Not that he hadn't thought about it. The girl had no idea how fabulous her figure was, with those gazelle legs and perfect little apple breasts. But Jackson knew that if he slept with Lottie, the easy friendship between them would be gone forever. He'd wind up hurting her – Jackson could no more 'do' commit-ment than he could fly to Mars – and he didn't want to be that guy, not with Lottie. Sasha, on the other hand, he would *love* to get into bed and then drop from a height. Boy did that chick have tickets on herself.

'You wanted to see me?'

'Yes.' Jackson took a deep breath. Just being in Lottie's presence seemed to calm him. 'Sasha Miller just walked into Morgan Graham's office and told the guy he was a prick and that she didn't blame his wife for leaving him.'

Lottie gasped. 'She didn't!'

'So I think it's safe to say that our Goldman deal is well and truly dead.'

Lottie looked at Jackson's clenched jaw and hunched, tension-filled shoulders and longed to walk over and touch him. *I could make you better. I could make love to you so perfectly you wouldn't stop smiling for a week.*

Aloud, she said 'You want a damage-limitation strategy?'

Jackson nodded. 'We need to get a statement out by tomorrow morning. Something the street will swallow, before Goldman put their spin on it, or some trigger-happy equity analyst starts making shit up.'

Lottie grabbed a pen, her quick mind racing, 'OK. This is what I suggest.'

Half an hour later, the press release was ready to go. 'Should I send it out now?'

Jackson hesitated, looking at his watch. It was already six o'clock. He was due at the Met in half an hour, attending yet another fundraiser, this time with a stunning French girl called Pascale. She was the new face of Chanel Mademoiselle and she was new to New York, bless her.

'No. We'll do it in the morning. I ought to sleep on it, anyway. Do you have plans tonight?'

For a moment, Lottie's heart soared. 'No! Not at all, I'm free as a bird. Why?'

'Oh, no reason,' said Jackson. 'You did a great job today, Lottie. Unlike some people I could mention. Go home and get some sleep. You deserve it.'

Lottie watched him leave. It was as if someone had shut off the power to the building. Or at least to her heart. She knew she wouldn't get much sleep tonight, whether she deserved it or not. Although she suspected she'd get more than poor old Sasha. *What on earth was she thinking?*

Sasha sat on the couch in her poky Brooklyn apartment, eating Cherry Garcia Ben & Jerry's out of the tub and feeling sorry for herself. On her salary, she could have afforded a much nicer place than the drab one-bedroom walk-up with its magnolia walls and dated, old-ladyish, avocado bathroom. But she preferred to invest her money in stocks, following a model she'd designed herself at Harvard. Everything was about making money, as much money as possible as fast as possible. Which was why Sasha was so disappointed with herself about today.

OK, so the guy was an arsehole who totally deserved it. But why couldn't I have held my tongue?

As much as she longed for the day when she would set up on her own, Sasha knew that right now she was too young and too inexperienced to attract the sort of serious investors she would need to get her own business off the ground. It wasn't about talent. It was about a proven track record. This Goldman deal would have been a major feather in her cap, a big step towards the type of experience she needed. It wasn't just that she had angered Jackson and put her job at risk. She'd also thrown away money, and kudos. Jackson had offered her a big step up the ladder and she'd pulled out a hacksaw and cut off the crucial rung.

Depressed, she flipped on the TV. One of the many things Sasha missed about England was the television. Where was a good old BBC period drama when you needed one? Where were Judi Dench and Julia Sawalha? The only British face you saw on American screens was Simon Cowell's, which was enough to put anyone off their Cherry Garcia ice cream. That and, of course, Theo Dexter's.

Unable to stop herself, like a child scratching a chicken pox sore, Sasha turned on her TiVo and clicked on the latest episode of *Dexter's Universe*. The show, originally based on *her* theory, had since morphed into a general look at space and the planets and was a huge ratings puller. Visually it was a work of art, an intergalactic version of David Attenborough's acclaimed *Planet Earth*. Although of course, in place of Attenborough's comfortable, fireside manner, there was Theo, young, impossibly handsome, energetic, funny, full of enthusiasm and *joie de vivre*. No wonder American women were all in love with him.

'Astronomy is like a drug.' Theo was talking directly to camera. 'More than that. It's like a love affair. For physicists like me, the universe is not just infinite. It's infinitely beautiful. There are many times when I've thought I'd rather give up breathing than give up science. Because it *is* breathing. It *is* life.'

Yes, Sasha thought bitterly. *And you stole my life from me.*

She looked at the cheap IKEA clock on the wall. Seven o'clock. Switching off the TV she jumped off the couch. If she dressed quickly, she might just make it.

Morgan Graham was preparing to leave the office for the day. He was meeting Anna, his new Russian mistress, for dinner at Elaine's, a prospect that would normally have put a smile on his face, however bad his work day. But today's meeting with Jackson Dupree and the girl from Wrexall had soured his mood beyond repair.

Tall, distinguished and (he flattered himself) quite attractive in a powerful, older-man sort of way, Morgan Graham was used to having young women fall at his feet. Admittedly, he wasn't a young stud like Jackson Dupree. But with two hundred million in the bank, a division of a hundred and fifty people reporting to him and a reputation as one of the sharpest dealmakers on Wall Street, Morgan Graham expected adulation and demanded respect. But this girl, Sasha, this *child*, had torn a strip off him in front of his team, as if he were some idiot she'd met at a bar! In his own office, too!

What rankled most was that the girl was extremely sexy. Morgan had always loved that dark-haired, green-eyed, Catherine Zeta-Jones look. He'd also heard rumours that she was immune to Jackson Dupree's charms and that Jackson was secretly livid at this rejection. For months now, Morgan had nursed a fantasy of bedding Sasha Miller, purely so that he could boast he had succeeded where the legendary young Dupree had failed. He'd been going to invite Sasha out to dinner tonight, in front of Jackson, to seal the finalizing of their long-awaited joint venture. Instead, he'd been made to look a fool and a laughing stock. The jokes were already doing the rounds on the trading floor.

'I'm sorry to disturb you, Mr Graham.'

'Then why are you disturbing me?' Morgan Graham bit his assistant's head off. 'I'm going home, Kate. Whatever it is it'll have to wait until the morning.'

'There's a young lady here, sir. She says it's urgent.'

Morgan Graham frowned. If he'd told Anna once, he'd told her a thousand times. He did not *like* being surprised at the office. He did not *want* to walk home with her and talk about his day, as if they were man and wife. Morgan Graham had just got rid of a wife, his third. All he wanted from Anna was for her to keep her weight under a hundred and twenty pounds and to open her legs whenever, and wherever, he told her to.

'May I come in?'

The secretary stepped aside. Sasha Miller stood in the doorway. In a backless black Ralph Lauren dress and spiked Jonathan Kelsey heels, her dark hair pulled starkly back in a ponytail and her exquisite, mint-green eyes ringed with smudged black liner, she looked more like a supermodel than a real estate executive. For a second, Morgan Graham forgot to be angry, standing and staring like a schoolboy. But he quickly regained his composure.

'What do you want?' he barked. 'Don't you think you've caused enough trouble for one day?'

'I want to do the deal,' said Sasha coolly. 'I think you do, too.'

Morgan Graham laughed in her face. 'Forget it. I wouldn't work with Wrexall now if you were the last firm on earth. You think I need you? I don't *need* you. We're Goldman Sachs. We can get another partner like *that*.' He clicked his fingers imperiously.

'You could,' agreed Sasha, walking slowly towards him. 'I know you don't need us. But that's not the point, is it, Mr Graham?' She was only two feet away from him now, close enough for Morgan to see her flawless skin against the clinging black jersey of her dress and to smell her Rive Gauche perfume. He stopped packing away his papers and looked at her, his eyes sweeping hungrily over her glorious body.

'The point is,' Sasha paused for effect, 'do you *want* us? And *I* think you do.'

Morgan Graham thought about Anna. He thought about the way Sasha had humiliated him today. He thought about the joint venture with Wrexall, and how excited he'd been about it until this afternoon. Finally he thought about Sasha's body, and how much he wanted to see her out of that expensive dress.

'If I sign,' he ran his hand languorously down her bare back, 'will you sleep with me?'

Wow, thought Sasha. *This guy doesn't beat around the bush.* She flashed him her best, come-hither smile.

'Put it this way, Mr Graham. If you *don't* sign, I *won't* sleep with you.'

Morgan Graham grinned. He liked a woman he could spar with, a woman who liked the chase. Anna's attempt at playing hard to get was wearing panties under her dress. And he *did* want to do this deal with Wrexall . . .

'Do you have the paperwork with you?'

'Of course.'

'Good. Let's see if you can convince me over dinner, shall we?' Morgan Graham's mistress was in for a long, lonely evening at Elaine's.

'You're sure this is what you want, Jackson?'

'Quite sure.'

Bob Massey was depressed. He didn't want to lose Sasha Miller. Not only was she a superstar in the making, not to mention easy on the eye, but she'd halved Bob's personal workload since she'd joined his division. The girl appeared to have no life whatsoever outside the office and cheerfully put in sixteen-hour days whenever they had a deal on. But even Bob Massey had to admit that yesterday's fuck-up was a firing offence. It was Dupree's deal that the girl had nuked. Which meant it was ultimately his decision.

'Couldn't we stop her bonus and, I don't know, give her a written warning or something? If we fire her she'll go straight to one of our competitors. In a few years she'll be a huge revenue generator for someone.'

'I don't care,' Jackson said stubbornly. 'If I see her face around here any more, I won't be responsible for my actions.'

He'd had a fitful night's sleep. The sex with Pascale had been terrible, largely because Jackson couldn't get Sasha out of his mind. He was still livid about her outburst at Graham. What made him even angrier was the way she got under his skin sexually. He never knew it was possible to dislike someone so much and want them so much at the same time. In the end Pascale had got up and gone home in the small hours of the morning, and Jackson knew he wouldn't be seeing her again. Before long word would no doubt be spreading throughout Elite: Jackson Dupree had lost his touch. Yet another thing he blamed Sasha Miller for.

It was time to face facts. Yes, she was bright, but hiring Sasha had been a huge mistake. She was too wilful, too much of a wild card.

Jackson's phone started buzzing. *Morgan Graham Cell* flashed across the screen. *That's all I need,* thought Jackson, *another ear bashing from Graham.* He turned it off. 'Let's get her in here. I want to get this over with.'

A few minutes later, a sober-looking Sasha walked into the boardroom. Ignoring Jackson, she smiled at Bob Massey and a couple of her other board-level supporters. They all avoided eye contact. *Uh oh,* thought Sasha. *This is it, then.*

If only she'd been able to seal the deal with Morgan Graham last night! She came so close. She could feel him weakening. But in the end, she realized, it was the power game he was interested in. He'd toyed with her all through dinner, but he wasn't going to sign the paperwork unless Sasha went home with him. No deal was worth that.

'I imagine you know why you're here?' Lucius Monroe, the chairman, said grimly.

'Actually, no.' Sasha looked at Jackson. She wasn't going to let him off the hook that easily. *If you want to fire me, then go ahead and fire me. I'm not falling on my sword to save you the trouble.*

'This firm lost a very valuable piece of business yesterday, Sasha,' said Monroe. 'Now we've heard Mr Dupree's version of events. Before we take any definitive action, we'd like to hear yours.'

'Why?' asked Sasha. 'Do you think Mr Dupree might be lying?'

Jackson exploded. 'OK, that's it.' He got to his feet. 'I've given you every chance, Sasha. We all have. But this is the end of the line. You're fired.'

'Hold on a minute, Jackson . . .' said Bob Massey. But Sasha didn't need a defender.

'And what am I fired for exactly?' She glared defiantly at Jackson. 'Losing us the Goldman deal? Or refusing to go to bed with you?'

'*What?*' Jackson roared. 'In what alternate universe do you think I would want to sleep with a ball-breaker like you?'

'*Jackson!*' Old man Monroe had gone white. He was imagining the sexual discrimination lawsuit. Sasha Miller standing outside the Supreme Court with a fifty-million-dollar Wrexall cheque in her hands.

'It's all right,' said Sasha. 'I'm used to it. And to think, *I'm* the one being fired because I don't know when to keep my mouth shut.' She knew she was in the wrong. That this wasn't about Jackson's ego, it was about her screw-up. But guilt and anger at herself only fuelled her aggression. Besides, what did it matter now? They were firing her anyway.

'Excuse me.' Lottie Grainger burst in looking flushed. 'I'm sorry,' she mumbled. 'I don't mean to intrude. But have you seen this?' She waved a piece of paper at Jackson. Taking it from her he saw it was a printout from Bloomberg news. It was less than a minute old.

'I don't believe it.' He read it twice more before handing it wordlessly around the table. Sasha watched the board member's faces light up one by one, like a string of Christmas lights. Jackson turned to her accusingly. 'How the hell did you pull that off?'

Sasha looked at him blankly. 'What are you talking about?'

'Goldman Sachs's Private Equity Group just put out a press release,' explained Lottie. 'Morgan Graham said he signed a joint venture with Wrexall Dupree this morning. He says he's excited to be moving into the growing boutique hotel market and that he's looking forward to working closely with the Wrexall team. He even mentions you by name.' Lottie beamed at Sasha.

So it's a reprieve! No wonder Jackson looks so pissed off.

'Does this mean I'm un-fired?'

Bob Massey hugged her. 'It certainly does. Congratulations, Sasha. You can go back to your desk now. We still have some other business to discuss.'

Twenty minutes later, Jackson stormed out of the board-room with a face like thunder. He found Sasha by the water cooler and pulled her to one side.

'That must have been quite a blow job you gave Morgan Graham,' he hissed.

'How dare you!' said Sasha.

'Oh, cut the Pollyanna crap, would you,' Jackson shot back. 'The rest of them might not see through you, but I do. Hiring you was the worst decision I ever made.'

'Why? Because now you have to interact with one woman who doesn't think you're God's gift? Anyone else would be pleased I salvaged that deal.'

'It's because of you that it needed salvaging!' snapped Jackson. 'You get to keep your job. For now. But you will have no further part in this joint venture.'

'You can't do that!' Sasha flushed with indignation. 'I worked my arse off on that deal.'

'I can do whatever I like. This is *my* company,' said Jackson. 'And *I* don't want to work with you. The sooner you get that through that thick, feminist skull of yours the better.' He looked at her, and for a moment Sasha saw a flash of genuine pity in his eyes. 'You know, whoever the guy was who did a number on you? He really screwed you up.'

'I don't know what you mean.' Sasha blushed.

'Sure you do,' said Jackson. 'Some guy broke your heart and you've never gotten over it. Well guess what, sweetheart? *It wasn't me.* Maybe if you pulled your pretty head out of your ass some time, you'd realize that.'

After he walked away, Sasha stood by the water cooler, shaking.

She ought to feel happy. Morgan Graham had caved, *without* her having to sleep with him. She would keep her job. She would keep her bonus. But Jackson's words stuck in her heart like a flick knife. '*Some guy broke your heart and you've never gotten over it.*'

He thinks I'm a victim.

Jackson's anger she could take. In some twisted way, she even enjoyed it. But his pity? That was unbearable. Even more unbearable was the fact that he was right. Everything came back to Theo Dexter in the end. Until she made Theo suffer, as she had suffered, she would never be able to move on. But the truth was she still had no idea how to do it.

Sasha was lost.

And Jackson Dupree knew it.

CHAPTER ELEVEN

'And *ease* forward into the downward dog.'

The yoga teacher's voice wafted mellifluously through the light-filled room. Theresa Dexter stuck her bottom in the air and thought that 'ease' was probably not the word she would have chosen. Yoga was about as much fun as having root-canal work. She couldn't understand why everyone kept smiling.

'Breathe. Find your centre.'

My centre. Presumably that's somewhere under all the rolling layers of fat?

It was the Make-A-Wish ball that had prompted Theresa to sign up for the torturous Ashtanga class at Maha Yoga in Brentwood. She left the house that night feeling like a million dollars, then realized that, even at her best, she was still an appalling blubbery heifer compared to every other woman in Los Angeles. Her depression was compounded by a visit to Dr Yeardly's office the following morning. Stanford Yeardly was *the* top fertility specialist in Beverly Hills and he'd spoken to Theresa sharply about what he called her 'lifestyle choices'. She could hear his disapproving, headmasterly voice now as she contorted her limbs into the even more torturous plough pose.

'I'm struggling to understand why anyone who's serious about having a baby is still drinking,' he looked down at his notes, 'two to three units of alcohol *a day*, and taking zero exercise.'

Because they're homesick, lonely and depressed, their husband's too busy fucking around to come home at night and if it weren't for the double gin and tonic at six o'clock, they'd probably have jumped out of a window two years ago? thought Theresa. Out loud she mumbled something about work pressure and promised to join a gym. Not that it mattered. Since starting yoga again four weeks ago, Theo hadn't come near her sexually. Short of an immaculate conception, there would be no baby, however many early nights she had or wheatgrass shots she gagged on.

'Hold on to that strength now as we move into plank pose.'

Theresa's upper arms began to shake. She could feel a collective sneer from the limber, flat-bellied blondes all around her. *It's not just for a baby. It's for Theo. And for me. If I don't get a grip soon I'll lose him.*

Tomorrow morning Theo was leaving for a promotional tour in Asia. He'd be gone for almost three weeks, signing books, making public appearances, and trying to sell *Dexter's Universe*'s third season to all the major networks in China and Singapore. To Theresa's utter amazement and joy, he was also going to visit two orphanages in Singapore, having done a complete about-turn on the idea of adoption.

'Maybe we should consider it,' he said one morning at breakfast, out of the blue, pouring skimmed milk over a half bowl of Kashi GoLean cereal. Theresa almost choked on her bacon sandwich.

'Really?'

'Sure. Ed thinks I need to soften my image, particularly in the Far East. I mean, I wouldn't want to go crazy and adopt an entire Benetton advertisement. But one kid . . . you could cope with one kid, couldn't you?'

It wasn't exactly the romantic outpouring of paternal love Theresa had fantasized about. But she still danced onto campus that morning. *He wants a child! He wants a child with me!* Surely, Theo wouldn't have brought up adoption if he were contemplating divorce? It wasn't too late after all.

The Asia tour was three weeks long. If she went on a properly hard-core, crash diet, laid off the booze and went to yoga *every single day*, Theresa reckoned she could lose a stone in that time and tone herself up. By the time Theo came home she'd be a new woman. He would have met an orphan child and fallen in love. Harry Meister's words still rang in Theresa's ears: '*Get pregnant. Give them a family and they soon settle down.*' She couldn't get pregnant. But she could give Theo a family. *When he sees what a loving, devoted mother I'll be, he'll fall in love with me all over again.*

Dita Andreas looked at the clock on her dashboard: *12.55 p.m.* She should have been on set over an hour ago. Carl Sams, the director of *Lies*, Dita's latest blockbuster, (not to mention her sometime lover) would be spitting teeth. But that was no bad thing. Recently, Carl seemed to have got it into his head that he was Dita's boss. Dita checked her flawless make-up in the rear-view mirror of her vintage Aston Martin and thought, *I'm the star of this picture. It's about time somebody reminded Mr Sams of that fact.*

Not that today was about Carl. Carl Sams was an afterthought. Even more of an afterthought than Brett Graham, Dita's soon-to-be-ex-husband and the director of her last film, *Heaven's Gate*. *Note to self,* thought Dita, *stop sleeping with all your directors. Or at least stop marrying them.* Dita's passion for matrimony was proving to be one of her more expensive hobbies. Her divorce attorney, Lorna McIntyre, had become one of her closest friends. Lorna had told her in no uncertain terms that her divorce from Brett would be the most costly yet. 'He'll go for the house, Deets. You do realize that?'

'I don't care,' Dita shrugged. 'He can have it. All I want is my freedom.'

It was unlike her to be so devil-may-care, at least when it came to money. Born to working-class parents in Detroit, the youngest of four children and the only daughter, Dita Andreas knew what it meant to be poor. Sure, she had always had a roof over her head and food on the table. But there were never any luxuries in the Andreas household. No brand-name sneakers, no hired limos on prom night, no out-of-state vacations. No vacations at all. Dita's parents were good people who worked their fingers to the bone to provide for their kids. Dita loved them, but did not understand their choices, especially her mother's.

'But you're beautiful, Mom,' Dita used to tell her, watching her mother brushing her hair before bed. 'You could have married anyone. A millionaire or a rock star. You could have gotten out of here.'

It was true. With her Swedish blonde hair, endless legs and full, sensual mouth, Mimi Andreas had been the prettiest girl at every school she'd ever been to. She could easily have married or modelled her way out of Motor City. But Mimi was a romantic. One smile from Georgious Andreas, Dita's charming car mechanic father, and it was all over.

'Why would I want to marry a rock star, baby? Your dad's worth a hundred Mick Jaggers to me. Besides, where you live is just geography. And you can't measure happiness in dollars and cents. You'll learn that as you get older, Dita.'

Dita hadn't learned it. In fact she'd learned the opposite. Geography was important. Who wanted to waste their life in Detroit, a dying city full of factories and despair, whose very name sounded like a *grind*, when they could choose to live in Malibu or Bel Air or Beverly Hills? And why would anyone choose to love a poor man, when there were so many rich men out there to love? *Too* many, Dita sometimes thought. At fifteen Dita signed her first modelling contract, courtesy of a married, forty-two-year-old agency boss named Nick Capri. Nick Capri was obsessed with the young and (he thought) innocent Dita, moving her into an apartment downtown and eventually leaving his wife for her on Dita's eighteenth birthday. By then Dita was already earning a seven-figure salary as the face of Lancôme's teen make-up line. A few months later, Nick was showing her off to one of his Hollywood friends at a party, a producer named Mike Reynolds, and boasting about how incredible his teenage girlfriend was in bed. Dita celebrated her nineteenth birthday in Los Angeles, in Mike Reynolds' bed. She got her first leading role in a movie the next morning and never looked back.

But as far as Dita Andreas had run from her past, there were pieces of it that she still carried with her. She would never forget what it felt like to be poor and anonymous. Unlike most of the leading box office actresses of her generation, Dita had no interest in making the occasional art-house movie, still less in taking a prestigious but low-paid role on Broadway. Not only did she never lower her fees on a movie, no matter how awesome the director, but she always clawed herself a piece of the action on merchandising as well, milking the studios she worked for every last possible cent. If Dita Andreas showed up at a party, or a club opening, the chances were she'd been paid to be there. Her avarice and business acumen were matched only by her extortionate spending. The girl who'd gone to grade school parties in Target jeans and K-Mart sneakers now dropped more on designer clothes in a week than her parents spent on food and rent in a year. Dita's closet was full of Marc Jacobs originals and exquisite vintage Chanel pieces, still with their price tags attached. She spent not for the pleasure of owning things but for the thrill of buying them. With every purchase her craving intensified, like a junkie coming down after a hit.

As much as she spent on herself, Dita Andreas was notoriously mean when it came to spending on others: her staff, her friends, even her family. In the case of her latest divorce, however, she'd thrown caution to the wind. Brett could take whatever he wanted, just as long as he disappeared. All Dita cared about was being with Theo.

Theo Dexter was unlike any of Dita's previous lovers. For one thing, he was a genius. Dita had always been more of a six-pack-abs and eight-figure-bank-balance girl than an IQ-whore, but Theo had it all: fame, looks, money *and* brains. *I'm maturing*, Dita thought with a smile. *I've outgrown Brett and his shallow aspirations. Brett Graham wants to change Hollywood. Theodore Dexter wants to change the universe.*

But it wasn't only Theo's intelligence that attracted her. It was his arrogance. In Theo Dexter, Dita Andreas had found something she had come to believe did not exist in nature: a human being more ambitious, more self-obsessed than she was. Dita was used to holding all the cards in her relationships and having the men in her life do all the running. Being with Theo made her realize how *bored* she'd become of being the goddess. For the first time in her life, she'd found a man who wasn't prepared to jump when she said jump. Yes, Theo adored her, yes, he worshipped her. But when Dita asked him to come on vacation with her he'd point blank refused.

'I'm a married man, Dita. I can't just take off to Bermuda with you. What if we were photographed together?'

'What if we were?' Dita pouted. 'Do you care about your miserable fat wife's feelings more than mine? I need you.'

'Too bad,' Theo said brutally.

It was wonderful!

Dita quickly learned that it wasn't spousal devotion that kept him true to tiresome Theresa. It was a pathological concern for his image, and what a scandalous affair and divorce might do to *Dexter's Universe*'s ratings.

'For heaven's sake, darling,' Dita complained. 'Do you think you're the first TV star to dump his wife? No one cares.'

'Not in LA, they don't. Perhaps not in America. But *DU* airs all over the world. It's huge in Muslim countries. I'm not prepared to risk that, not when I don't have to.'

Oh yeah? Well, now you do have to. I'm divorcing Brett and I'm going to tell the world I'm in love with you. Screw your precious image.

As much as Dita delighted in Theo's take-it-or-leave-it attitude, and apparent nonchalance about their affair, she was not prepared to put up and shut up. She was tired of being his mistress. She wanted to be his wife. And what Dita Andreas wanted, Dita Andreas always got in the end.

Turning right off Sunset Boulevard through Bel Air's ornate West Gate, Dita sped up Bellagio towards the Dexters' mansion. Her plan was simple. She would walk into Theo's office, rip his clothes off, fuck him like the superstar that she was until he was screaming for more, then tell him that she was leaving Brett and going public about their affair, whether he liked it or not. Together they would be a power couple unrivalled on the world stage.

I wonder if he'll put up a fight? she thought, feeling a frisson of sexual excitement pulse between her legs. *I do hope so.*

Theresa looked at her face in the mirror and panicked.

'But . . . it's all blotchy! I look like a fourteen-year-old with hives!'

She'd booked herself in for a facial, the first of her life, in hopes of looking fresh-faced for Theo on the last night before his big trip. Instead she looked as if she'd been mugged.

The dermatologist at Allen Edwards looked as patronizing as she could through a face full of Fraxel. 'It's an oxygenating deep cleanse and peel, Mrs Dexter. You don't see the results right away. Especially with older, neglected skin, there *can* be redness.'

Can be? There's no 'can be' about it! My chin looks like a baboon's backside.

'It'll calm down.'

'When?'

'Within a day or two. That'll be two hundred and sixty dollars. Would you like to leave a gratuity?'

It was a ten-minute drive back to UCLA, where Theresa had a class to teach at two thirty. Home, and her minimal make-up supplies, were twenty minutes away. She looked at her watch: *1.15 p.m.* Theo was supposed to meet her after class today. He had a list of things he needed her to do while he was away ('*Please* try to remember, T. I really can't keep doing everything') and wanted to run through it with her, item by item. *I can't let him see me looking like this.* She made a left at Barrington and headed up the hill towards Bel Air.

*   *   *

Theo lay on the floor of his home office, a vast, wood-panelled room that Theresa called the Beauty and the Beast library, because it looked like something out of a Disney cartoon, with his pants around his ankles. Above him, Dita Andreas's magnificent breasts jiggled from side to side as she straddled him, arching her back and expertly moving herself up and down his cock. He was tempted to pinch himself. *I'm fucking Dita Andreas. Dita Andreas!* But he was too caught up in the moment to focus on anything but the wave of pleasure drowning him.

'Tell me you love me!' Dita commanded, clenching her muscles more tightly around his erection and reaching down to play with his asshole. Theo had had scores of lovers since he came to LA and learned a number of new and exciting party tricks. But no one came close to Dita. If she hadn't been a world-famous movie star she would have made an astonishingly successful hooker. He groaned.

'Christ, Dita. I'm coming!'

'No!' She stopped dead, releasing him. 'Not till you tell me you love me.'

Reaching up, Theo pulled her head down to meet his own and kissed her full on the lips. 'You know I love you,' he whispered. 'Don't stop.'

Theo was many things but he was not stupid. From the first time he laid eyes on her at the Make-A-Wish ball, surrounded by sycophants and hangers-on, he knew that he would have to differentiate himself from every other suitor if he wanted to have a shot at Dita Andreas. What he didn't know was how easy that would be; that the key to Dita's pussy, if not her heart, was as simple as putting himself first. If there was one thing Theo Dexter knew how to do, it was to put himself first.

Dita started to rock her hips again, and Theo closed his

eyes. *It doesn't get any better than this. I've got the world's sexiest woman balancing on my balls, a hit TV show that just keeps getting bigger, and tomorrow I'm off to Asia for three wonderful weeks.* Most western celebrities loathed promoting in Asia. They hated the jet lag, the humidity, the soulless hotels and weird-looking food. Theo loved it. As excited as he was by Dita, he thrived on variety. In Tokyo, even the hookers acted like virgins, demure and submissive and so *young.* It was like owning Le Caprice, but being invited to dinner at Nobu. What's not to like? After a few weeks of on-demand sex from Japanese teenagers, he would return to Dita hungrier than ever. And of course, she'd have missed him . . .

Neither Dita nor Theo heard the front door open. Theo was lost in his own, ecstatic world and Dita was letting out little rhythmic gasps of pleasure as he thrust deeper inside her. She would tell him about Brett and the divorce after-wards. This was too good a fuck to be interrupted.

By the time Theo opened his eyes, Theresa had already been standing in the office doorway for a full twenty seconds. Too shell-shocked to speak, she watched the pair of them writhing on the parquet floor feeling like a zoologist observing the mating habits of some rare species. The girl was stunning, at least from behind. Irrationally, Theresa found herself thinking, *That's what I'd like my body to look like. I wonder who her trainer is?*

'Theresa!' Theo stared at her. The look on his face was more irritated than ashamed, as if he resented the inter-ruption. 'What are you doing here?'

'Getting my make-up,' said Theresa. Her voice sounded like someone else's. *Is this really happening?* Wriggling out from underneath Dita, Theo pulled up his trousers. Only then did Dita turn around, and cast a languid eye over her lover's wife.

'She's exactly like you described,' she said bitchily to Theo.

'You're Dita Andreas,' Theresa gasped.

'Last time I checked.' Dita stood up, stark naked, and held out her hand. Theresa couldn't help but stare at her crotch, which had been waxed completely hairless. It looked horrible, like a baby bird hatched too soon. 'How do you do.'

Numb with shock, Theresa shook Dita's hand. 'I'm fine, thank you.'

No. I'm not fine. This is not fine. I'm shaking hands with a naked film star who's just shagged my husband on the floor of our home.

Shaking, Theresa turned to Theo. 'I don't understand. I thought things were better. You seemed so much happier. The adoption . . .'

'He was happier because he's been with me,' said Dita. She'd been planning on using her divorce from Brett to force the issue with Theo. But his wife catching the two of them in flagrante was even better. Theo would have no choice but to end his marriage now.

'Shut up!' wailed Theresa. 'And put some clothes on, for Christ's sake. This is between me and my husband.'

Dita looked to Theo for support. Instead he threw her her clothes and said, 'Perhaps it's best if you go, darling. I'll handle Theresa.'

'You will not *handle* me,' sobbed Theresa. 'I'm not some bloody puppy you need to house train! I'm your wife.' She was getting hysterical.

'Fine,' Dita pouted, stalking into the hallway. Still naked, she didn't seem in the least perturbed that the cleaning staff had all stopped to stare at her. 'I'll leave. For now. But this isn't over.' She glared at Theresa. 'Theo and I love each other. We're going to be together and there's nothing you can do about it.'

After Dita had gone, Theo locked the study door. Then he poured a glass of whisky and handed it to Theresa.

'No, thank you.'

'Drink it,' he insisted. 'It'll help.'

Theresa drank. The amber liquid scorched her throat and made her eyes water. She sat down on the couch, feeling more disorientated than ever.

'I can't believe this is a surprise to you,' said Theo.

'Can't you?'

'We've been unhappy for years now. The best thing will be to work out a clean, quiet divorce. There's no need to let things get ugly or confrontational.'

'"The best thing?" The best thing for whom? For you and that slut?'

'Don't be puerile. Insulting Dita isn't going to make this any easier,' said Theo piously.

'Actually it makes things a lot easier for me. Are you in love with her?'

Theo hesitated. Eventually he said, 'We're similar, Dita and I. I need someone like that in my life, T. Someone ambitious and vital and strong and . . .'

'. . . thin?' said Theresa bleakly.

'I was going to say confident. But I won't deny that image is important. Come on, Theresa. When we met, we both lived in a different world. We've come a long way from Madingley Road. *I've* come a long way,' he corrected himself. 'Can't we just say we had a good run of it and call it quits? End this as friends, with dignity?'

Dignity? thought Theresa. *Five minutes ago you were on the floor with your trousers around your ankles.* If it weren't happening to her she would have laughed.

'I don't want to be friends, Theo. I love you. If you were planning to leave me, why did you tell me you wanted to adopt? Why did you set up those appointments with the orphanage in Singapore?'

Theo ran his hands through his hair. 'I don't know why. I was trying to do the right thing, I suppose. Obviously it was a mistake.' He couldn't tell her the truth. That a week ago he'd had no intention of divorcing her. That what happened today had brought things to a head. That he was as trapped as she was, because there could be no way back with Dita now. 'Look, I'm going to stay in a hotel tonight. We'll talk more when I get back from Asia. Work out the practicalities. That'll give us both time to get our heads around things.'

Theresa sat like a statue, watching him walk out of the room.

I don't want to get my head around things. I want you, and a baby, and my life back. Theo's dalliances with researchers and students had hurt her. But she knew that none of those girls meant anything to him, not really. While his affairs remained casual, she'd been able to cling to the hope of reviving her marriage. This was different. This was Dita Andreas! How on God's earth was Theresa supposed to compete with that?

Ten minutes later she heard the trunk of Theo's Lamborghini slam shut and his car roar out of the gates. Standing up, she walked unsteadily over to the drinks cabinet and poured herself another whisky. It tasted smoother this time, and the burn was less intense. The third was even better. The fourth was bliss. By the time she staggered out of the house and got back into her own car, the sun was starting to set. She turned on the ignition. *I'll be late for my class. The students will be waiting. I can't let everyone down. I have to be organized. I have to show Theo I can cope. That I'm strong, like Dita Andreas.* The gates at the end of the driveway opened automatically as her car approached. Theresa was dimly aware of Manuel, the gardener, in her rear-view mirror, waving his arms frantically as she drove out onto Chalon Road, scraping the side of her Mercedes on the gate post. But then he was gone and she was rolling down the hill, early-evening light dappling the windscreen as she sped past palm trees and mansions and manicured lawns and sprinklers. She didn't even see the stop sign.

The driver of the big rig slammed on his brakes but it was too late. Swerving wildly all over the road he saw a second's flash of black as Theresa's car disappeared beneath his wheels. He felt the sickening crunch of metal. Then his head slammed into the dashboard and everything went black.

CHAPTER TWELVE

First there was blackness. Then there was light. It came in flashes, blinding and painful. There were voices too. Some that she recognized.

Theo: *'I can't believe this is a surprise to you.'*

Dita Andreas: *'Theo and I love each other.'*

Others that were unfamiliar.

'Mrs Dexter? Can you hear me?'

'Her heart rate's dropping.'

'We're losing her again. Mrs Dexter!'

Theresa longed for the light to fade and the peaceful comfort of the blackness to return. Instead, as her lucid periods grew longer and more frequent, so did her awareness of the pain. Her chest felt as if a herd of elephants had trampled across it. Every intake of breath was agony. Her face was badly bruised and she had no feeling at all below the waist. But none of these things compared to the pain in her heart. To the desperation of knowing that Theo was gone, that she'd pushed him into the arms of another woman by being so useless and ugly and miserable and . . .

'Mrs Dexter. Welcome back. You look a lot better, my

dear. A *lot* better. You know the nurses have nicknamed you Lazarus?'

Theresa recognized the doctor's face. He was young and preposterously handsome with the same regular features and straight, gleaming-white teeth that everybody seemed to have in LA. Everybody except her.

'You're lucky to be alive.'

'Am I?' Tears rolled down Theresa's bruised cheeks. 'The other driver . . .?'

'He's fine,' the doctor reassured her. 'Minor bruises. We discharged him three weeks ago.'

'Three *weeks*?' The accident felt like hours ago. She'd had no inkling of time passing. Was Theo back from Asia already? But of course, he wouldn't have gone to Asia. He'd have been told of her accident as next of kin. He was probably outside now, waiting to see her, to tell her that this whole ridiculous affair with Dita was over, that it was her, Theresa, he really loved. 'Do I . . . have I had any visitors?'

The doctor's handsome face fell. 'Not in person. But the nurse's station is starting to look like a florist. Your mom's called every day. And a lady named Jenny.'

'So my husband . . .' The words died on her lips.

The doctor perched on the edge of the bed and took her hand. He was a kind man. Like the rest of the staff at St John's Hospital, he'd been outraged by Theo Dexter's callousness. Not only had he flown off to Asia while his wife was still critical, but he'd since gone public about his love for Dita Andreas, painting Theresa as an out-of-control drunk whom he'd been forced to 'stop enabling' however much it broke his heart. 'Dita and I both pray that this accident will be the wake-up call to Theresa to start getting the help she needs.' *Yeah, right. Dickhead.*

'Your husband has paid the bills. He's also written to you.

There's a registered letter waiting outside. But listen to me, Mrs Dexter. If ever there were a time to focus on yourself, this is it. You broke both your legs, fractured four ribs and suffered a potentially fatal brain bleed. Don't worry,' he added, seeing the colour drain from Theresa's face, 'we ran every scan under the sun, you're fine. But as clichéd as it sounds, you *are* lucky to be alive. You won't be able to leave here for at least another two weeks. Even after that you're going to need intensive physio. You can't afford to let your husband, or anyone else, set back your recovery. Thinking positive is half the battle.'

It's the half of the battle I'm going to lose, thought Theresa. She knew the doctor was right. But she couldn't help herself. As soon as he left her, she pressed the call button for the staff nurse. 'I'd like to see my messages please.'

The vast stack of get-well cards and presents, most of them postmarked from England, brought a lump to Theresa's throat. But there was only one letter that really interested her. Pushing the rest aside, she tore open the stiff FedEx envelope with Theo's handwriting on the address sticker.

He'll have written to apologize. He probably went to Asia because he was scared. Maybe he thought I wouldn't want to see him? That I wouldn't forgive him?

She pulled out the letter, five typed sheets with a 'Korol & Velen, Attorneys at Law' letterhead. It took her a few moments to cut through the legalese and process what she was reading.

Divorce papers. I've been lying here, fighting for my life, and Theo's filed for divorce.

Too numb to cry any more, she closed her eyes and prayed for the darkness to return. *Why did I have to survive? Why couldn't God have put me out of my misery?*

*   *   *

In fact it was almost a month before Theresa was allowed out of hospital. She returned to find the Bel Air house empty – Theo and Dita were in Los Cabos, Mexico, enjoying a very public romantic vacation – and a note on the marble kitchen counter.

Two months' rent and all the staff wages are paid. After that you'll have to make other arrangements. You can reach me through my lawyer, he's very efficient.
Best, Theo

It was the 'Best' that hurt the most. As if she were some secretary or acquaintance. As if all the years of love and support and passion had been for nothing. Unable to stop herself, Theresa had devoured the TV and magazine coverage of Theo and Dita's affair from her hospital bed. The strangest part was seeing herself being painted as some sort of unhinged lush, a depressive lunatic whom poor, devoted Theo had cared for as long as he could.

'You should hire a PR firm,' Amihan, Theresa's feisty Filipina nurse insisted. '*He* obviously has, the bastard. You need to fight back, or people are going to believe this rubbish.'

Theresa hadn't the energy to argue. Amihan wouldn't have understood anyway, any more than Jenny or her friends back home. *I don't care what people believe. I don't care about anything. All I want is my life back.*

A week after she got out of hospital, Thomas Bree, the head of the English faculty at Cambridge and her former boss, threw Theresa a lifeline.

'Good news!' Thomas's dry, acerbic English voice crackled down the phone line, like a message from another planet. Theresa could instantly picture him in his rooms at Jesus, knocking back his third Glenfiddich of the afternoon as he marked a stack of Chaucer papers. 'You remember Harry Talbot-Smith, from Jesus?'

'Of course,' said Theresa. 'Dear old Harry. How's he doing?'

'He's dead,' said Thomas Bree brightly. 'Which means there's an English fellowship open. Of course legally we have to advertise. I'll have to interview a lot of morons from UCL, I dare say, might take a few months. But after that the job's yours if you want it.'

Theresa burst into tears. 'I . . . I don't know what to say, Thomas.'

'Well don't get all American and schmaltzy about it, Theresa. Just get yourself on an aeroplane and come home.'

Theresa did.

For the first month she stayed in London with friends. Theresa had known Aisling O'Brien since their teenage days in County Antrim. Now married to Richard, a successful investment banker, and living in a sprawling house in Fulham with their three sons, Aisling had changed little from the naughty, life-and-soul-of-the-party schoolgirl that Theresa remembered. She was still a ball of energy and determination, just a slightly more middle-aged ball.

'First thing we do is get you a decent bloody lawyer. Fiona Shackleton, that's who you need, love. Or someone senior at Mishcon de Reya.'

Theresa laughed. 'Do you know what their fees are, Ash? I can't possibly afford that.'

'Bollocks. Theo can pay. Or they can subtract their fees from the whopping settlement they're going to get you. No, stop arguing. You're going, even if I have to frogmarch you into their offices myself.'

Theresa went. Charles Newton-Haughbury, the partner who took her case, had so many plums in his mouth that at first Theresa struggled to understand him. But as certain words floated through to her: 'outrageous . . . laughable . . . vigorous counter-attack . . .' she began to get the gist. Charles wanted her to file her own petition with the UK courts, citing adultery, and to reject Theo's paltry financial offer out of hand. He also wanted her to hire a public relations firm to address the slanderous things her husband had been saying about her.

'Whoever's been looking after your interests up till now should be shot. It's a shower, Theresa, an absolute shower.' He pronounced it *shah*, which made Theresa want to giggle. 'You've had a long marriage to an extremely wealthy man. His money may be able to buy him public sympathy across the pond, but it won't wash in a British courtroom, I can assure you of that. It's time to get the old boxing gloves on and land a few punches.'

But for once Theresa was firm. 'I don't care about the money, Charles. I don't want to fight with Theo. All I want is for this nightmare to be over.'

'But, Theresa . . .'

'No. Please. Just accept Theo's offer and let's be done with it.'

It had taken all Charles Newton-Haughbury's powers of persuasion to convince her to make accepting Theo's terms contingent on a gagging order, preventing either Theo or Dita from speaking about Theresa in the media. 'You're walking away with a fraction of what he owes you. At the very least, protect your reputation. You may not care about money, but a part of you *must* care about being slandered in this manner. For your family's sake, if not your own.'

Reluctantly, Theresa agreed. Generally speaking, she'd been sanguine about Theo's rewriting of their marital history, not because it didn't hurt, but because it hurt less than everything else, less than him being gone. A week ago, however, she'd been dreadfully upset by an interview Theo gave to

Barbara Walters, that showed footage of him touring a Singaporean orphanage. The orphanage *they'd* been talking about adopting from, just days before her accident.

'Dita's really changed my mind about the whole idea of adoption and parenthood.' Theo smiled wistfully to camera. 'You know, Barbara, when you're in a relationship with an addict, an alcoholic or whatever, someone who isn't functioning, you can't allow yourself to think about children. But Dita's so maternal, so *caring*. She's truly opened my eyes.'

That interview opened Theresa's eyes. She still loved him and missed him terribly. She couldn't help it. But the time had come to protect herself, or at least let Charles do it for her.

The divorce came through a few weeks later. Theo paid her legal and medical bills, signed a gagging order, and gave her a one-off, lump-sum payment of seven hundred thousand pounds. Aisling took Theresa out to celebrate.

'We're not toasting the money,' she said sternly. 'That settlement was daylight robbery and we both know it. We're celebrating your freedom. Here's to the first day of the rest of your life!'

Theresa raised a glass sadly.

'When does the job start at Cambridge?'

'November,' said Theresa. 'But I'm going up there on Friday. I need to start house hunting. And working. I haven't written a line since the accident. I'm sure my brain must have turned to mashed potato.'

'Ah, bollocks,' said Aisling. 'You'll be back in the saddle in no time, dating some good-looking Shakespeare scholar or playwright or whoever it is you genius types like shagging. You'll see.'

Theresa laughed. She had no intention of dating anyone,

still less shagging. Besides, there was no such thing as a good-looking Shakespeare scholar. Everyone knew that.

Dita flipped over onto her back and did a few, languid strokes across the swimming pool. Theo watched her flawless naked body, her breasts bobbing on top of the water like two buoys, her legs slightly parted to reveal a tantalizing hint of coral-pink labia as she wiggled her toes, and felt his dick start to harden.

'Come here,' he called across the splashing.

'Why?' Dita smiled coquettishly, opening her thighs wider. 'Is there something I can help you with?'

Theo grinned. *How the hell did I get this lucky?*

He'd moved out of the Bel Air house last month and rented this place in Beverly Hills, nominally for the privacy (Theo and Dita were 'so tired' of the relentless press attention) but actually because George Clooney used to own it and Theo thought that was cool. Though smaller than the Bel Air mansion, the house managed to be even more impressive, largely thanks to the gadgetry in every room. This was a bona fide LA party house. Vast outdoor TV screens surrounded the pool, rising up out of the stone at the touch of a button. In the master bedroom, the heart-shaped bath filled from a hidden pump in the ceiling, and the Jacuzzi turned on when you said 'bubbles'. But the greatest luxury of all was Dita herself. It wasn't just her perfect, made-for-sex body or her relentless, unstoppable libido that excited Theo. It was her fame. Being with Dita Andreas was like being sprinkled with Hollywood fairy dust. Overnight, Theo had gone from being a celebrity to being a star. And to think, he'd almost passed on all of this because he was too scared of hurting his image with a divorce. What a fool he'd been!

'You have ten seconds to get out of that pool,' he growled

lustfully at Dita, 'or I swear to God, I'm coming in to get you.'

'Really?' Dita hauled herself up out of the water and walked towards him dripping, like Ursula Andress without the bikini. Perching on the edge of Theo's sun lounger, she wrung out her hair, deliberately dropping cold water onto his erection.

'Bitch.' He kissed her, reaching between her legs.

'Uh uh.' Dita stood up and grabbed a towel. 'Sorry, baby. We don't have time. We're meeting Ray, remember?'

Theo groaned. Ray Angelastro was a movie agent, one of the biggest names at CAA. Dita was convinced that Theo had a future on the big screen and had been pushing for this meeting for weeks. Theo wasn't so sure.

'I'm not an actor, Dita. I'm a scientist.'

'You *were* a scientist,' Dita corrected him. 'Now you're a brand. Especially since the new Asia deal, a very marketable brand.'

It was true, Theo's trip to Asia had been successful beyond even his wildest fantasies. Not only had *Dexter's Universe* been syndicated in every major market, but he'd been offered an endorsement deal by Canon cameras that would catapult his earnings into the stratosphere. And it didn't end there. Theo's combination of all-American good looks, British James Bond suaveness, and scientific credibility was the Holy Grail for Asian consumers. He returned to LA overwhelmed with offers to promote everything from aftershave to coffee to computer games.

'Studios love brands,' Dita assured him. 'Any idiot can act.'

Watching her dry herself with a towel and pull a bright yellow, micro-mini sundress over her head, Theo resented the meeting with Angelastro more than ever. All he wanted to do was take Dita upstairs and bang her till she begged him to stop. Not that that would ever happen. But at the same time, he loved her for pushing him. Theresa had never understood his ambition. She was always wanting to hold him back, hankering after the simpler life they'd left behind in England. Well, now she could have it. On the paltry divorce settlement he'd given her, she'd be able to live very simply indeed. Briefly, Theo wondered where Theresa was at that moment and whether she was happy. But only briefly.

Now then. What to wear to this morning's meeting? Ray Angelastro was a flaming homosexual. *I'll wear my new Gucci suit. The one with the tight-fitting trousers. It's formal for Hollywood, but it should get Ray's motor running.*

Theo stood up, stretched and followed Dita indoors.

'Oh my God. *Oh*, my *GOD!*' Jenny Aubrieau stood on the front step of Theresa's new cottage in Grantchester, gasping for breath. A medieval longhouse painted palest pink with a low thatched roof and stone mullioned windows, it was ridiculously, Disney-idyllic. 'It's exquisite. Like something out of a *Flower Fairies* illustration.' Turning to her children she roared, 'Ben, Amélie! Get *out* of that flowerbed, *now*. If you trample so much as one of those gorgeous hollyhocks I will personally run over your PlayStation with your father's lawn-mower.'

'Great place.' Jean Paul, Jenny's husband, kissed Theresa on the cheek and handed her an expensive bottle of Chablis as his son and daughter charged past them into the house. 'We would 'ave left the kids at home, but no babysitter will take them,' he grinned.

'I'd have shot you if you left them behind,' said Theresa. 'There's a tree house in the back garden with a rope swing that goes right out over the river. They'll love it.'

'Daaaaaad!' Ben's whoop of delight could be heard all the way to Trumpington Street. 'Come and see this!'

To a soundtrack of happily screaming children, mingled with late summer birdsong and Handel's *Messiah* on Radio 3, Theresa gave Jenny a tour of the cottage. Inside it was all low beams and inglenook fireplaces. Theresa had only moved in a few weeks ago, but already she'd made the place a home, filling it with books and framed botanical prints and jugs stuffed with wildflowers from the riverbank. She'd left LA with nothing, no furniture, no clothes. Moving to Willow Tree Cottage was a fresh start in every sense of the word. Thanks to her divorce settlement, she'd been able to buy it for cash, with money to spare to spend on furniture, rugs and the like. Putting the place together had been a godsend, the first thing she'd actually enjoyed doing since Theo left her. She was proud of it.

'Bed's a bit small,' said Jenny, bouncing on the faded rose-patterned quilt covering Theresa's barely queen-sized four-poster.

'It's a small room.'

'Why didn't you take the bigger one, at the front? There's easily room for a king in there.'

'I like the view. And the window seat,' said Theresa, unlatching the ancient tiny window to reveal a glorious vista of open fields with King's College spires in the distance.

'Wow,' sighed Jenny. 'If I divorce JP and dump the children, will you adopt me?'

Theresa smiled. She hadn't added that she had no need of a king-size bed. That she'd slept in one at Aisling and Richard's and woken up every morning reaching for an absent Theo.

Sensing a shift in her mood, Jenny put her arms around her friend. 'Are you eating? You feel like skin and bone.'

'I'm drinking. Does that count?' Theresa joked. It was ironic. All those failed diets and yoga regimens in LA, trying endlessly to get thin for Theo, and the moment he left her the weight fell off like flesh from a well-steamed sea bass. 'I made us paella for tonight and tomato salad from the garden. Will the children eat fish?'

'Amélie will. Ben will eat anything if you drown it in ketchup.'

Theresa's face fell. 'Oh dear. I'm not sure I have any ketchup.'

Jenny reached into her capacious, mother's handbag and pulled out a red plastic bottle. 'Never fear. We bring our own. Like insulin.'

Supper was a riot. It was wonderful to be with Jenny and JP again. Theresa hadn't seen Ben and Amélie since they were toddlers, and while the kids were unrecognizable, their parents were the same funny, charming, understanding people they'd always been. After Theresa's accident, Jenny called the LA hospital every day and was the first to offer support, both practical and emotional, when Theresa announced she'd be moving back to Cambridge. After a month in her new job at Jesus she still cried about Theo at least once a day and thought about him constantly. But it was a relief to dive back into the cool, restorative waters of her beloved Shakespeare. As for Cambridge itself, the city never failed to lift her spirits.

When the estate agent first drove her out to Grantchester, Theresa was resistant. A pretty hamlet a few miles from the town centre, best known for being home to the poet Rupert Brooke and latterly to Jeffrey Archer, it would mean driving into work every morning. Living in Los Angeles had left Theresa with an abiding hatred of commuting, however short the distance. 'I'm sure it's a charming property. But I really am set on finding something closer to college. I wouldn't want to waste the vendor's ti—' They turned a corner and there it was: Willow Tree Cottage with its overflowing cottage garden, its lichened gate, its thatch and its winding swathe of lawn rolling down to the river and the eponymous willow tree.

'It's perfect,' Theresa sighed. 'That's the one.' To the agent's delight, she wrote a cheque for the full asking price on the spot.

'The starter was delicious,' pronounced Jean Paul, finishing off his third enormous helping of paella while Theresa opened a third bottle of wine. 'What is the main course?'

His wife hit him over the head with a napkin. 'Ignore him, T. *Il est un cochon.*' They kissed and Theresa thought, *They're like teenagers, so in love. Were Theo and I ever like that?*

As if in answer to the question, Jenny asked brusquely, 'So is it all over now, the divorce paperwork and stuff? You're done?'

'Yes,' said Theresa, unable to keep the note of sadness out of her voice. 'We're done.'

'Good. You're well shot of him, T, isn't she, darling?'

JP nodded through his last mouthful of rice.

'Honestly, I could never say it at the time. But he was always an arsehole, even before he was famous. Now he's a plastic, airbrushed, American arsehole, which is even worse.'

Theresa tried to smile.

'Ooh, this will make you laugh,' said Jenny. 'Guess what I read the other day? The name "Theodore" is Latin for "God's Gift"! Do you think he christened himself?'

Amélie wandered in from the garden. At eight years old she already looked distinctly teenage, with her blue chipped nail polish and a Girls Aloud t-shirt that clung to the two tiny, nascent mounds that would eventually become her breasts. Bored of the rope swing, she was deep in some sort of gossip magazine. Quick as a flash, her father yanked it out of her hands.

'*Qu-est-ce que c'est*, Amélie, this rubbish? What do you read this for? Whatever 'appened to My Little Horses?'

'My Little Pony,' said Jenny. 'Give it back to her, JP, don't be annoying.'

But father and daughter were already caught up in a familiar game, with Jean Paul holding the magazine at arm's length, out of Amélie's reach, and reciting passages in his embarrassing-dad voice while she screeched at him to stop.

'Oh my God, you are so *sad*, Dad,' she howled. 'Mum, make him give it back.'

'Listen to this,' laughed Jean Paul. '"Six things your man wants you to do in bed but is too scared to ask". Zat one is followed by "Ange and Brad, why it's *really* over" and . . .' He turned the next page then stopped abruptly, blushing. Seizing her chance, Amélie snatched the magazine while his guard was down and dropped it onto the table. There, grinning up at Theresa, were Theo and Dita. They looked picture perfect, with their matching white smiles and blond haircuts, radiating happiness and love and success.

'Don't look at it,' said Jenny, reaching for the offending object. 'Don't give them the satisfaction.' But Theresa stopped her arm. It wasn't the picture she was looking at. It was the headline:

AND BABY MAKES THREE

CHAPTER THIRTEEN

'More wine?'

Sasha looked across the table at the man sitting opposite her. In the soft glow of the candlelight he looked even better than he had in the gym last week, when he'd asked her out after spinning class. Tall, athletic, faintly rugged in a hot-plumber-from-*Desperate-Housewives* sort of way.

Positives: He's seen me at my worst, hyperventilating and dripping with sweat, and he still fancies me.

He's handsome, charming and a good conversationalist.

He hasn't tried to grope me or stick his tongue down my throat . . . yet.

Negatives: His name is Grover.

Grover! What possessed people to do that to a perfectly innocent little baby? Sasha tried to imagine herself screaming it out in the throes of passion. *'Oh, Grover, that's so good! Don't stop, Grover!'*

'You're laughing. What, do I have spaghetti sauce on my chin?'

'Oh, no!' Sasha blushed. 'I'm sorry. I was, er . . . I was thinking about something else. Please, go on.'

'Go on with what?' Grover cocked his handsome head to one side, puzzled.

'With what you were saying.'

'I wasn't saying anything. I was offering to refill your glass, but maybe you've had enough? Is everything OK, Sasha?'

Oh God, thought Sasha. *I mustn't sabotage this. I mustn't.* OK, so his name *was* Grover. And he did over-use the word 'awesome'. And vote Republican. But really, he was a decent, solvent, straight and apparently kind man, and he'd asked her out on a date, and for once she'd actually gone because if she didn't have sex again soon she was pretty sure some weird biological process would start to kick in and she wouldn't be *able* to do it . . .

'Sasha?'

'I'm fine, thanks. Just a lot going on at work, you know. It's hard to switch off.'

It was ironic. In her professional life, Sasha was completely together and successful and brilliant. For the last year, she'd specialized exclusively in retail development, and had become one of Wrexall Dupree's biggest producers. In business meetings Sasha had no trouble conquering her inner-geek, the social awkwardness that had dogged her since childhood. She was charming, funny, professional, a natural saleswoman. But put her in a purely social situation – like a date with hot gym guy for example – and she flailed around helplessly like a fish out of water.

Theo Dexter still her haunted her dreams at night. She was still no nearer exacting her revenge. With every passing season Theo seemed to become *more* famous, *more* successful, *more* happy with his film-star girlfriend and *more* out of Sasha's reach. But by day it was Jackson Dupree who consumed all her mental energy. The rivalry between

Wrexall's future chairman and Sasha Miller, the firm's undisputed star, was an open secret on Wall Street. Within Wrexall itself, the sparring between Jackson and his one-time protégée acted as a sort of atomic generator at the heart of the company, spewing out energy and igniting a feverish fireball of deal-making that had catapulted them to the top of the market. Jackson's 'team' were the hotel and residential divisions. The relationship between his executives and Sasha's retail group was akin to gang warfare, with both sides vying daily and hourly to out-perform the other. At first, the rest of the board was wary of the open hostility that blazed between Jackson and Sasha. But as the results rolled in and the stock price continued to rise, they backed off. A controlled nuclear explosion was clearly exactly what Wrexall Dupree needed.

Between fighting with Jackson, building her business and obsessing about Theo Dexter, Sasha had had neither the time nor the energy for a personal life. But it was January, and her New Year's resolution was to stop turning down flat every male who approached her and to force herself to go on at least three dates a month.

The first one had been a disaster: a lawyer called Simon Tooley who had been on the other side of one of Sasha's M&A deals. At work he'd seemed completely normal, blond, clean cut, perhaps even a little preppy. But over a four-hundred-dollar dinner at Masa, a pretentious Japanese restaurant with no menu in the Time Warner Center, he waxed suicidal over the edamame about his broken marriage, drank his bodyweight in sake, then collapsed in tears, confessing to Sasha that he was a life-long cross dresser and how would she feel about maybe letting him wear her panties later? When Sasha politely declined, he took umbrage and stung her for half the bill.

Grover Hammond was a *lot* better, not that that was hard. He was thirty-five, worked in publishing, had never been married and (at least by the time dessert arrived) had not asked to borrow any of Sasha's clothing, not even her outerwear.

Grover had just started telling her a funny story about one of his authors' diva-fits when the door to the restaurant opened and a mind-blowingly attractive redhead sashayed in. Close to six feet tall and pin thin, she was obviously a model. Even dressed down in Hudson jeans and an Abercrombie polo neck sweater, with no visible make-up, she was the sort of beauty people couldn't help but stare at. Every man, woman and child turned to look at her, including Sasha.

'Wow,' she said admiringly. Sasha wasn't given to envy. 'I think that may be the best-looking human being in the universe.' But her smile faded when she saw the redhead's date walk in behind her, and wrap a possessive arm around her waist.

'We'd like your best table.' Jackson's arrogant voice jarred on Sasha's nerves like nails on a blackboard.

'I'm sorry, sir. There's nothing available at the moment. As you can see, we're fully booked. Did you have a reservation?'

'I don't make reservations. Tell Marcel I'm here, he'll make room. And you can bring us two glasses of Cristal while we wait.' Pulling the redhead closer, Jackson turned around to survey the room, smiling proudly, like a tribal king showing off his latest bride to his adoring subjects. His eyes soon fell on one less-than-adoring subject, however, and the smile vanished. He walked over to Sasha's table.

'Sasha.'

'Jackson.'

'I'm surprised to see you out and about so late. Surely you should be hanging upside down in a cave somewhere by now? Or home polishing your cauldron?'

In vintage Levi's and a thick, blue cashmere Ralph Lauren sweater, with snowflakes still clinging to his wild black hair, Jackson looked as effortlessly desirable as the stunner he'd walked in with. Unlike the girl though, who seemed sweet if a little bit vacant, Jackson knew it. He positively radiated vanity.

'Waiting on a table for three, are you, Jackson? Just you, your lady friend and your ego. How romantic.' Sasha turned back to Grover. To his surprise, she took his hand. 'Jackson, this is Grover Hammond, a friend of mine. Grover's a publisher.'

Jackson nodded a curt acknowledgement.

'Grover, this is Jackson Dupree, a work colleague. Jackson's a penis.'

It was so unexpected, and so totally rude, Grover burst out laughing. Jackson glanced over his shoulder to see if the redhead had heard, but she was engrossed in her BlackBerry. At that moment Marcel, the restaurant owner, rushed over and began fawning over Jackson, clapping his fat little hands excitedly as a new table and linens were carried out from the kitchens. Jackson contemplated firing a shot back at Sasha. If she wanted to embarrass him in front of his date, two could play that game. But the moment had passed. Besides, he'd look a lot cooler to Leilani, the redhead, if he laughed it off and didn't stoop to Sasha's level.

Once Jackson and Leilani were seated, at the opposite end of the room, Grover asked Sasha, 'What was that about? You just blew that guy out of the water. Is he an ex or something?'

'An ex?' Sasha looked disgusted. 'Eeeugh. I wouldn't date Jackson Dupree if the survival of the human race depended on it. No, I told you. He's a colleague. And he's a penis. That's the kindest word I can use to describe him.'

'He's famous, right?'

'In his own mind,' Sasha scoffed.

'No, really. I'm sure I've heard of him.'

'You might have. When you get home tomorrow, google "world's biggest penis" and see if his face pops up. I'm just going to run to the ladies. Should we get the bill first?'

Now it was Grover's turn to look disgusted. 'Please. *I'll* get the check. I may not be as rich as your buddy Jackson Dupree, but if I take a girl out for dinner, I pay.'

Sasha smiled. Maybe dating wasn't going to be such an ordeal after all?

A few minutes after Sasha and Grover left, laughing, into the night, Jackson was about to order appetizers when Leilani suddenly stood up.

'What's the matter?' he asked. 'You look pale. Is everything OK?'

'Yeah. Sure. Look, I'm sorry for what you've been through, OK? Really. But I can't help you. No one can.' She started putting on her scarf.

Jackson looked blank. 'What?'

Leilani squeezed his hand sympathetically. 'Being gay. It's not something you can be cured of. It's genetic. I have two gay brothers, I know what I'm talking about.'

'Well that makes one of us. What on earth makes you think I'm gay?'

'Look, it's OK, truly. Your friend told me everything, in the ladies' room. I know you're really super Christian, and you probably think you're trying to do the right thing by fucking it out of your system. But if it's Brian you love . . .'

'*Brian?* Who the fuck is *Brian*? If I were going to be gay, you think I'd date someone called Brian?'

'You need to start loving yourself for who you are,' Leilani said earnestly. 'And I need to do the same.'

Jackson sat and watched as she walked out into the street. Slowly, he felt his anger start to rise, like a building wave about to break.

OK, so it probably wouldn't have worked out with Leilani anyway. Yes, she was a knockout, but she had the IQ of a small piece of cheese, not to mention that gentle, save-the-whales vibe about her that, in Jackson's experience, invariably translated to being shit in bed. But even so. That little bitch Sasha Miller had successfully sabotaged his evening. He pictured Sasha in a cab right now, laughing at him in between getting down and dirty with Elmo or whatever the fuck the guy's name was.

Fine, sweetheart. You want this to get personal?

Just you watch how personal I can be.

Two weeks later, a package arrived on Sasha's desk. It was beautifully wrapped in expensive, silver paper with an over-sized red silk bow on the top.

'Where did this come from?'

Jeanne, her secretary, shrugged. A middle-aged matron from New Jersey with a sharp eye for detail and an even sharper tongue, Jeanne Grogan was Sasha's right-hand woman. Other than Lottie Grainger, who wouldn't have hurt a fly if it were injecting her with malaria, Jeanne was the only person at Wrexall whom Sasha totally trusted.

'I have no idea. I was picking up a fax from the machine and when I got back to my desk, there it was. It's not ticking, is it?'

Sasha held it up to her ear. 'I don't think so. Should I open it?'

'No. You should marinade it in chilli sauce and slow roast it for six hours. Of course you should open it! What else are you gonna do?'

The wrapping was so perfect, Sasha almost felt guilty tearing into it. For a moment she was transported back to childhood Christmases in Frant, and her mother carefully saving the nicest wrapping paper, smoothing it out under the encyclopaedia to be used again another year. These days Sasha was comfortably earning seven figures a year. *If I ever have children, they won't need to save wrapping paper,* she thought idly. For some reason the thought made her sad.

'What is it?' Jeanne's harsh, nasal tones brought her back to reality.

'It's DVDs.' Sasha sounded nonplussed. 'A box set.' Turning them over in her hands, she saw that she had in fact been given a 'Best of Dita Andreas Limited Edition Holiday Collection'. She blushed.

'Who sent me this?'

'I told you already. I have no idea. Who knows you're a Dita Andreas fan?'

No one. No one would have any reason to link me with Dita Andreas. Other than maybe my parents and a few old friends from Cambridge. But a friend wouldn't send me this. Besides, there's no postmark. It was hand delivered.

Oh shit. Her heart sank as the obvious truth dawned. Two minutes later she barged into Jackson's office, slamming the door shut behind her.

'Is this meant to be a joke?' She waved the DVDs in his face. 'Because it's not funny.'

Jackson leaned back in his chair, stretching his long legs out in front of him. 'I have no idea what you're talking about.'

'I'm talking about these.' She handed him the case. 'I know it was you who sent them.'

Jackson read the blurb on the back. *'Midnight's Children.* Now that was a good movie. One of her best. If you haven't seen Dita Andreas's shower scene with Leo DiCaprio, you haven't lived.'

'It won't work, you know,' said Sasha furiously, snatching back the case. 'These childish little mind games of yours. They won't get to me.'

Jackson laughed. 'Really? I'd say they already have. You know what your problem is, Sasha? You can give it, but you can't take it.'

'Excuse me?'

'It's fine for you to tell girls I'm seeing that I'm gay.' Sasha at least had the decency to blush. 'But when the joke's on *you, that's* childish. I must say, I couldn't believe it when I found out. After the way you've looked down at me from your moral high horse these past two years, like I'm the evil, selfish playboy and you're the perfect little saint. When the truth is you had an affair with a married man, then tried to claim his work as your own. I may be a playboy, Sasha. But I'm not a thief.'

'Neither am I!' Sasha was close to tears. When she moved to America five years ago, she'd tried hard to leave her past, or that chapter in it, behind. Until now, she'd succeeded. No one at Harvard Business School knew about the scandal that had ended her career as a physicist, and nor did anyone at Wrexall. In the States, the Cambridge court case was a footnote in Theo Dexter's history, nothing more. Or so Sasha had thought. 'Everything I accused Theo Dexter of was true. It *was* my theory. He's the thief, not me. He's made a fortune off an idea that doesn't belong to him.'

'Sasha, Sasha, Sasha.' Jackson shook his head, like a disappointed parent. 'You can't let it go, even now, can you? So sad. I guess it's true what they say. Hell hath no fury . . .'

Sasha stormed out, marching back down the corridor to her own office with Jackson's laughter echoing off the walls behind her. If there was one person in the entire universe she would have wanted *not* to know about her past with Theo Dexter, it was Jackson Dupree. She might as well take out a full-page ad in the *New York Times*.

This is going to be bad. Jackson's going to crucify me.

She wasn't wrong. Over the course of the next few months, the story of her scandalous past spread not just through Wrexall Dupree, but throughout the entire real estate industry. Jackson's taunting was relentless. Sasha would turn on her PC at work to find Theo Dexter's face loaded as her screensaver. Amazon delivered books to both her home and office: *How to Move On*, *The Married Man Addiction*, *Astrophysics for Beginners* and the newly published coffee table photo book by Mario Testino, *Dita Andreas: A Love Story*, in which Theo featured heavily looking brooding and intellectual – as intellectual as anyone *could* look with their top off and wearing only tight white boxer shorts that left little to the imagination. Most irritating of all, though, was Jackson's habit of humming the theme tune to *Dexter's Universe* under his breath every time he passed Sasha in the halls. It was *so* childish, Sasha knew she ought to have been able to laugh at it. But sometimes the urge to physically attack Jackson was so strong she had to lock herself in the ladies and deep breathe until she got it under control.

The office that had long been Sasha's sanctuary now became a torture chamber. As a result, she began doing more and more work from home, often poring over spreadsheets and making calls late into the night. With no time for dinner, still less wild nights of sex, her relationship with Grover Hammond soon fizzled.

The only chink of light in the gloom of Sasha's life that winter was the McKinley deal. Haverstock McKinley was the largest, most profitable construction firm in the United States. Jackson's father, Walker Dupree, had first flirted with McKinley over two decades ago, to try to develop a nation-wide chain of discount shopping malls. That deal had come to nothing, as had numerous other proposals for possible joint ventures since. But Sasha had come up with a new model, to build cheap, prefab strip malls on Indian reserva-tions. They would start in the desert states, Arizona, New Mexico, Utah, Nevada and eventually roll the programme out nationwide. If the deal came off – a big *if* – it would be the largest in Wrexall's history. With her new compensation deal (Sasha had taken a huge cut in base salary and fore-gone her bonus in exchange for a flat five per cent share in her revenues) it would also make Sasha personally an extremely wealthy woman.

Jackson knew about the McKinley negotiations, of course. Everybody did. Publicly, he shared the firm-wide excitement. But privately he was nervous about the degree of autonomy it gave Sasha's division.

'I know you think it's personal. But you're wrong,' Jackson told Lucius Monroe over a discreet lunch at the Harvard Club.

Lucius raised a wiry eyebrow. 'Am I?'

'Yes. I'm not going to deny the woman gets under my skin. But this goes way beyond our personal animosity. She's running that retail group like a private fiefdom.'

'A very successful fiefdom,' Lucius reminded him. 'One that we all profit from.'

'Yes. For now. But giving any one individual total control over a business area is dangerous. Our clients and our share-holders need to have faith in Wrexall Dupree. Not just Sasha Miller. She could leave us at any time, Lucius, and then where would that business be?'

Lucius Monroe sipped contemplatively at his martini. 'I take the point, Jackson. But these are good problems to have, don't you think? Employees who are *too* successful? Besides, Sasha's not going anywhere. Why would she? No other firm on the street would offer her what we do, a straight percentage cut. Sasha's very talented, but she has the Wrexall business card and the might of our balance sheet and reputation behind her. Without that, she'd be nothing.'

Jackson tried to feel reassured.

Lottie Grainger burst into the coffee shop, hopping from foot to foot with excitement.

'What's happened?' laughed Sasha. 'You look like you just won the lottery. Either that or there's a wasp up your shirt.'

The girls had agreed to meet at Bepe's, a hole-in-the-wall Italian espresso joint a block from the Wrexall building. At six o'clock on a Friday night the place was almost empty.

'Jackson just texted me. I'm going to Park City! He wants me to pack a bag and meet him at JFK in . . .' she looked at her watch, '. . . about three hours. Can you believe it?'

Sasha hesitated, not sure how to react. On the one hand it was obvious Lottie wanted her to share in her excitement. Jackson had a big series of meetings in Utah over the long weekend. Wrexall was involved in developing a new luxury ski resort to rival Deer Valley, and he was flying up to finalize the deal. On the other hand, Sasha knew better than anyone what a thumping great crush Lottie had on Jackson. She doubted very much it was the business opportunity that had put that shit-eating grin on her friend's face.

'That's great, Lots. Just be careful, OK?'

'Careful of what?' Lottie twirled around, a human spinning top of delight. Nothing would spoil her happiness today.

'Careful of looking so utterly ravishing at all times that he won't be able to help but fall madly in love with me? Or careful not to clinch the deal with my awesome marketing insight?'

Sasha laughed. It was impossible not to. Lottie's joy was infectious.

'Just be careful. And pack a lot of scarves. It's colder than a witch's tit up there.'

'And what will you be doing this weekend, my miserable, workaholic friend?' Lottie teased. 'I suppose it's too much to hope that you have anything actually *fun* planned?'

'That depends on what you mean by fun,' said Sasha. 'This McKinley thing could easily close on Monday. So yes, I will be working. As will you, remember? He asked you on a business trip, Lots, not a date.'

Lottie raised an eyebrow knowingly. 'We'll see. See if you can squeeze some hat shopping into your busy schedule. It's going to be a *very* formal wedding.'

Sasha watched her float out of Bepe's on a cloud, not sure why she felt so down. Was it because she was worried about Lottie, and the thought of Jackson breaking her heart? Or was it because her own life was so utterly devoid of passion and excitement? She downed another shot of espresso and pulled herself together. *Focus. Lottie's a grown-up. She can take care of herself.*

And you have work to do.

CHAPTER FOURTEEN

Jackson sat in the first-class lounge, watching Lottie helping herself to orange juice from the buffet counter. Her slim legs and high, tight bottom looked cuter than ever in the tight-fitting, forties-style Alexander McQueen skirt she was wearing, and when she turned around and caught his eye her smile lit up the entire room.

It's business, he told himself firmly. *She's here to sell these hotels to the city planning committee. Nothing more.* Still, he couldn't deny he was looking forward to the prospect of three days, and maybe longer, holed up in a hotel with the lovely Lottie Grainger. The recent tensions at work and with Sasha had been getting to him more than usual. Being around Lottie was like getting a massage for the spirit. *She's Valium and ecstasy rolled into one.*

'I got one for you too.' Lottie passed him a flute of orange juice and her fingers brushed the back of his hand. Jackson felt a jolt of desire shoot through him.

'Thanks.' *Get a grip. You'll only hurt her and you know it.* 'We should probably run over the figures again on the flight.'

'Right. Absolutely,' said Lottie, wishing that Jackson would run over *her* figure on the flight. 'We want to get it pitch perfect.'

You're perfect. Too perfect for me. That's the trouble.

They stayed at the Stein Eriksen Lodge, in the heart of the Deer Valley resort, a Nordic wood and glass structure with a three-storey atrium and spectacular mountain views. With its roaring fireplaces, intimate log-cabin bedrooms and the scent of pine and juniper infusing everything from the bed linen to the bath towels it was both luxurious and simple. Lottie thought it wildly romantic.

'It would be perfect for a honeymoon, wouldn't it?' She gazed up at Jackson dreamily at the check-in desk, but he was all business.

'If this deal comes off, it'll be one of our main competitors. That's why we're here. Hi, yes, we're checking in.' Jackson flashed a smile at the receptionist. 'The name's Dupree.'

The girl scrolled down on her computer.

'Here we are. Mr and Mrs Dupree.'

Lottie started to protest but the girl ignored her. 'We've held the Deluxe Mountain View Suite for the two of you for three nights.'

'You've made a mistake,' said Jackson tersely. 'We booked two rooms. We're not a couple; this is a business trip.'

'Oh.' The girl looked flustered. She clicked on her screen again. 'I'm sorry. I don't know how that happened, but I definitely only have you down for one deluxe suite.'

Jackson was starting to get angry. The last thing he wanted was for Lottie to think he'd tried to pull a fast one. Not that he was above such tactics – far from it – but he respected Lottie too much to try such a crass manoeuvre. Besides, he was going out for a late dinner tonight with an old friend from college, Piers Dellal. Piers had promised to bring some hot girls along ('Ski-bunnies, man, there's nothing like 'em. All that mountain air makes 'em hornier than bitches in heat.'). Somehow Jackson doubted that wholesome Lottie Grainger was into threesomes.

'Listen. I don't care what you have down. My office reserved two rooms. Two rooms is what we need. Close to the business centre if possible.'

The girl frowned. 'I am sorry, sir. But I'm afraid we're totally fully booked. The suite does have a foldout sofa bed in the living room if you need it. And the master bath is stunning. It's actually the nicest accommodation in the entire hotel,' she added helpfully.

'Which is what, code for the most expensive?' snapped Jackson. So much for his night of passion with one of Piers's hotties. He turned to Lottie. 'Sorry. Is that OK with you? I'll take the foldout, of course. The alternative is that I try to check in somewhere else, but at this time of night . . .' He looked at his watch.

'It's fine,' Lottie blurted. 'Really. It's totally fine.'

To Lottie's disappointment, and Jackson's relief, the suite was so huge that the makeshift bedrooms had an entire room between them, a sort of dressing-room-cum-study. 'This is great,' Jackson brightened, disappearing into the bath-room and emerging five minutes later with a towel wrapped around his waist. Lottie blushed to the roots of her chestnut hair, trying not to stare at his six-pack stomach, but Jackson seemed completely un-self-conscious, sauntering around the suite as if she weren't there.

I'm invisible to him, Lottie thought miserably. *Like his little sister or something.* She went into her own room and began to unpack. *I mustn't give up. This is my chance. If he doesn't see me as a sexual woman, it's up to me to change his mind.* Pulling out a pair of sexy, sheer La Perla panties with a matching lace push-up bra, Lottie slipped them on, admiring herself in the mirror. She'd been so excited when Jackson asked her on the trip earlier, she hadn't eaten all day so her stomach looked wonderfully flat. The clock by her bed said 9.45 p.m. Late enough to change into the new champagne silk robe that just brushed the tops of her thighs and lounge around in the sitting room 'working' before bed. Carefully tying the robe so that the lace from her bra peeked tantalizingly out at the top, Lottie tousled her cropped hair and spritzed herself with Gucci Envy, emerging into the sitting room just in time to hear the front door of the suite slam shut.

'Jackson?'

He was gone. A note on the coffee table said,

Dinner with friends. Don't wait up. See you at breakfast. 7.30 a.m., J.

After a fractured night, the first half of which was spent lying awake, listening for Jackson's return, and the second half tossing and turning with sexual frustration so bad she could have wept, Lottie came down to breakfast with huge dark shadows under her eyes.

'Are you OK?' Clean-shaven and rested, in a dark suit and tie, Jackson looked fabulous. 'You look awful. Like you caught the flu or something.'

'I didn't sleep well,' grumbled Lottie, pouring herself a strong black coffee.

'Really? I slept like a baby. The service here is shit, but I must say that sofa bed was damn comfortable. Now look, the planning meeting's been pushed back to ten a.m., so we've got an extra hour to polish our presentation.'

'I don't need it,' said Lottie. 'I've got it down.'

Jackson raised an eyebrow. 'Are you sure? I can run over things with you if you like, I have the time.'

'I'm sure.' If she couldn't seduce him sexually, she was damn well going to impress him professionally. The planning committee would be eating out of her hand.

'That was amazing!' Jackson hugged Lottie as they left the meeting. 'They loved you.'

Walking down Park Avenue towards the golf course, in downtown Park City, beneath a blazing bright winter sun, he felt elated. The deal would go through now, no question. Lottie had dazzled the committee with figures, and melted them with charm. Jack Brannigan, the chairman, a dour, fat, self-important little man, was notoriously difficult to please, but Lottie had joked and cajoled and – there was only one word for it – *flirted* with him until he rolled over like a puppy. It was a side to her Jackson had never really seen before. He'd always thought of her as so sweet, so pure. But she'd manipulated old man Brannigan like a pro.

'I'm serious, Lottie, you nailed it. I half expected Jack to propose marriage to you by the end of the meeting. He was drooling.'

Lottie blushed. 'He was *not*.'

'He was too. *Man*, I'm on a high! Of course, you realize this means we're going to have to extend our trip. Now we have verbal approval, I want to do as many on-site meetings as we can. Talk to all the bidders, the primary contractors, the subs. Can you stay?'

Lottie thought about her desk in New York and the mountain of work waiting for her. Then she thought about Jackson last night, and this morning, his utter sexual indifference. Did she really want to put herself through two, three, four more nights of mental and physical torture, lying awake, alone, while he ignored her?

'Of course I can stay,' she heard herself staying. 'No problem.'

'Great. We'll have dinner tonight and work out a schedule. In the meantime, I think we've both earned the afternoon off.'

Lottie beamed. 'Fantastic! Maybe we could go for a hike up in the pine forest? I've heard that the area right above our hotel has some stunning trails.'

'Sounds great,' said Jackson. 'You have fun. I'll see you at dinner. Eight o'clock, Mastro's.'

Before Lottie could say another word, he'd hailed a cab and disappeared.

Lottie tried to look on the bright side. *At least he wants to have dinner with me.* She looked at her watch. One o'clock. Seven hours in which to transform herself into a Jackson Dupree-worthy sex-siren. Last night had been a washout, but that was no reason to abandon hope. Tonight. Tonight was the night.

Mastro's was a bustling, modern steak and ribs joint attached to an achingly trendy bar. *The* place to see and be seen in the mountain resort, it was the sort of restaurant that Lottie Grainger usually avoided like the plague. Tonight, however, she felt confident and sexy and fierce. *I am one of the beautiful people. I belong here, just as much as the silicone-lipped twigs propping up the bar.*

In one afternoon, she had succeeded in effecting a very dramatic transformation. Marching into an expensive salon, she'd demanded the ultra-camp stylist cut her already short hair even shorter, into a spiky, boyish crop, then dye it from Lottie's natural chestnut to a shocking, peroxide-white blonde.

'Take a deep breath,' said the stylist, proudly handing Lottie a mirror. 'Ta da! What do you think?'

Lottie opened her eyes and burst into tears.

The poor stylist was horrified. 'Oh, no!' he wailed. 'Oh, please, don't cry, sweetheart. It's OK. We can soften the colour if it's too much for you. It's not a big deal, honestly.'

'It's OK,' laughed Lottie, wiping away the tears. 'It's a shock, that's all. I love it. I look . . . I look . . .'

'Fucking gorgeous?' the stylist preened. 'Yes you do, my angel. Yes you do.'

Next stop was the beauty salon, to get her nails painted the latest, hippest shade of gleaming, gothic black and to wax every hair on her body into oblivion. Finally, still smarting from the hot wax torture, Lottie bought a tight-fitting pair of black hipster jeans from Chloe Lane on Main Street, and a matching black mink cropped fur jacket from Alaska Furs that cost more than her last three months' salary, but that completed the glam-rock look perfectly. Dashing back to the hotel for make-up – smoky eyes were most definitely called for – and her highest pair of Louboutin spiky boots, Lottie finally arrived at Mastro's twenty minutes late with her adrenaline pumping.

'I'm here for dinner,' she announced to the hostess confidently. 'The table's booked under Dupree.'

'Oh yes, of course. Most of your party are already here, if you'd like to follow me.'

Most of my party? Lottie looked confused. Her bewilderment intensified as the hostess led her to a large, round table in the middle of the restaurant. A handsome man in a beanie hat was arguing loudly and pretentiously about art with two very young girls, both of whom looked like models and hung off his every word. Next to him, an older man in a crumpled suit looked up and smiled at Lottie. 'I'm Francis. I'm a friend of Jackson's. And you are?'

'Lottie. Lottie Grainger.' Lottie shook his hand and sat

down, biting her lip hard to stop herself from crying. How could she have misread the situation so badly? Jackson didn't want to take her out for a romantic dinner. He'd simply invited her along to join a group evening. *He probably felt sorry for me, stuck in the hotel on my own. He was being kind.* 'Jackson and I are . . .' What were they? '. . . colleagues.'

'Lucky Jackson.' Francis smiled wolfishly. 'And unlucky you. It's bad enough having to deal with his bullshit as a friend. If I worked with the arrogant son of a bitch, I'd shoot myself. What are you drinking?'

The table was already lavishly supplied with red and white wine, plus a jug of some sweet, fruity-looking cock-tail. Lottie was about to say, 'Nothing thanks, I'm fine,' but then suddenly changed her mind. *Fuck it. Why not?* Jackson might not want her, but she was looking drop dead gorgeous tonight, she'd just won Wrexall Dupree a vital piece of business, and someone else was paying. She deserved to celebrate.

'I'll take one of those.' She pointed to the red jug. 'A large one.'

Francis grinned. Pouring the drink he handed it to Lottie. 'That's the spirit. Thank God you've arrived. If I had to listen to this idiot spout one more line of crap about Kandinsky's genius, I swear to God I would have drunk the whole pitcher myself.' He looked at handsome beanie guy the same way he might look at a cockroach in his soup. 'They're all AA you know, this crowd, even the children. Nothing more boring than an ex-addict. I mean, really, who wears a fucking snowcap indoors?'

Lottie giggled. She enjoyed talking to Francis. It turned out he was an architect, rather a famous one, but he had no airs and graces. Tall and thin with an angular, intelligent face and eyes ringed with fans of laughter lines, he was neither handsome nor ugly, but he was so animated it was impossible not to look at him, and laugh with him. Francis met Jackson five years ago, when he designed a chain of boutique hotels for Wrexall Dupree in Polynesia, and he was in Park City for business, hoping to be brought on board as part of the design team for the new resort, if it ever got off the ground.

'Oh, it's off the ground,' said Lottie. 'It's flying.' She told him about her and Jackson's triumphant meeting with the planning committee today.

'You star! You actually got Jack Brannigan excited about something other than his own nose hairs?' Francis poured her another drink, her fourth at least. Lottie was vaguely aware of things around her starting to sway. How late was it? Maybe someone should order some food?

It was after midnight by the time Lottie staggered out of Mastro's on Francis's arm. Jackson had failed to show up at all, but after the first hour Lottie didn't even notice his absence. It was only when Francis had had to foot the entire table's bill that it occurred to Lottie to be angry at Jackson's rudeness.

'I don't care who he is, ish rude. Ish fuggin' disgraceful.'

'That's Jackson. I'm used to it,' laughed Francis. 'Besides, if I get a slice of this resort deal, it'll be well worth the cost of a few dinners.'

'Thash not the point,' slurred Lottie.

'It was worth it anyway. Meeting you. I had a great time.' He leaned in and kissed her. Lottie closed her eyes and sank into the sensation. It was rather wonderful, the combination of the chill night air and the warmth of Francis's body. He tasted of coffee and mints and smelled faintly of patchouli oil. Combined with her drunkenness the sensation was heady and delicious, as if all the pent-up tension of the last three days had been unlocked and was pouring out of her body into his arms.

'Lesh go to bed.'

Francis's kind, funny face lit up. 'Your place or mine?'

Five minutes later they were giggling and kissing their way through the lobby at the Stein Eriksen. Lottie was so drunk she kept bouncing off the walls. 'Ish these damn shoooooes!' she kept saying. In the end she sat down on the floor and had Francis pull them off, a process that produced even more fits of giggles.

'What the hell's going on?'

Jackson, who had just walked in with a used-looking blonde on his arm, marched over to Lottie and Francis.

'Oh, I remember you,' Francis teased him. 'Weren't you some asshole I agreed to have dinner with once?' Turning to the blonde he added, deadpan, 'Don't sleep with him, love. He's a martyr to his crabs, is our Jackson.'

Ignoring him, and the girl, Jackson grabbed Lottie by the arm and yanked her painfully to her feet. 'You're making a total spectacle of yourself. Look at you. How much have you had to drink? And what the fuck did you do to your hair?'

'I dyed it,' said Lottie. 'I wanted a change.'

'It looks like shit,' snapped Jackson.

'Hey.' Francis put his arm around Lottie and pulled her close. He was no longer smiling. 'Take it easy, Lord Capulet. For one thing, Lottie looks fantastic. And for another, what she does with her hair is none of your business.'

'Don't give me that protective crap,' snarled Jackson. 'You don't care about Lottie. You don't even know her.'

'As it happens, I've gotten to know her,' said Francis angrily. 'We had a long, *long* dinner at Mastro's, waiting for *you* to be bothered to show up. Where the fuck were you?'

'Something came up,' said Jackson dismissively. There wasn't a hint of apology in his voice. 'But it's nice to know I can trust my friends, Francis. You've clearly spent the entire evening getting Lottie drunk enough to agree to fuck you. Well, congratulations. It looks like you succeeded. She looks like a hooker, and now she's acting like . . .'

The punch was so quick and so forceful, Jackson had no time to react. Before he knew what was happening he was flying backwards across the lobby. Not knowing what else to do, the blonde gave a half-hearted scream, but her heart wasn't in it.

'Fuck you, Jackson.' Francis was shaking with rage. Lottie, who'd observed the whole scene with shocked dismay, felt herself sobering up fast. 'If anyone made a fool of themselves tonight, it was you.' Francis took Lottie's hand and led her towards the elevator. They'd only got a few paces when Jackson got to his feet, let out a roar of primitive rage and hurled himself at Francis from behind, bringing him to the floor in a flying rugby tackle, and knocking Lottie to one side. Seconds later the two men were writhing on the floor like wrestlers, throwing punches wildly.

'Stop it!' Lottie shouted. 'For heaven's sake. Can't anybody do something?' She looked around for any hotel staff. Finally, two barmen and the fat nightshift security guard at reception came over and broke up the fight. Lottie ran straight to Francis, who was bleeding profusely from what looked like a broken nose.

'We should get you to the Emergency Room.'

'I'll drive him,' said one of the barmen. 'You should go get some sleep, miss.'

Lottie protested, but Francis was insistent. 'It's OK. I'll call you in the morning.' Meanwhile Jackson's blonde was hovering around him like an ineffectual Florence Nightingale, murmuring 'poor baby' over and over and stroking his hair. Eventually Jackson turned on her. 'Look, Candice, I'm not in the mood, all right? Let's just call it a night.' Instantly the girl's face soured.

'Fine by me, dickhead. You probably *do* have crabs, anyway.' She turned on her heel and stormed out.

'Will you be OK, ma'am?' the security guard asked Lottie, eyeing Jackson warily. He knew that the two of them were in the Mountain View Suite, and was not at all sure of the wisdom of leaving them alone together there. 'If you like I'd be happy to accompany you back to your room. Just till things cool down.'

'I'm fine, thank you.' Lottie glared at Jackson. She wasn't about to give him the satisfaction of thinking she was afraid of him. 'I'll call if I need anything.'

Jackson and Lottie rode the elevator up to the fourth floor in total silence. The silence continued on the long walk down the corridor to their room, and was only broken once they got inside and Jackson unwisely asked Lottie if she would like to use the bathroom first.

'Don't speak to me! Don't even look at me! You are a total, *total* jerk.'

'Why? Because I told you the truth?' Jackson shot back. 'You were drunk and you were making an idiot of yourself. I know Francis O'Donnell a lot better than you do, and I'm telling you, he was trying to take advantage of you.'

'My God. Where do you get *off*?' Lottie didn't think she'd ever been so angry in her life. 'You of all people, judging someone else's sexual behaviour? Their morality? If it weren't so outrageous it'd be funny. No one was "taking advantage" of me. I was with Francis because I wanted to be. Because I was attracted to him.'

'I don't believe that,' said Jackson bluntly.

'Why? Because he isn't on the *New York Times*'s Hottest Bachelor List? Get over yourself, Jackson. The rest of us have.'

Stung, Jackson backed away. He knew he'd behaved like a moron this evening, insulting Lottie and getting on his high moral horse with Francis. But seeing Lottie like that, with her punk hair and sexy, tight black jeans, sprawled out on the floor . . . it had shaken him. Lottie was the good girl. Pure. Innocent. Some unnamed part of him needed her to stay that way. Certainly the thought of Francis O'Donnell's hands wandering over her naked body was more than Jackson's rational brain had been able to handle.

'I realize this may not compute for you, Jackson, but there are other qualities, apart from looks, that women can find attractive. Qualities that Francis has in spades, like decency and a sense of humour. Not to mention good manners. How dare you leave us all stranded at dinner like that? How dare you leave *me* stranded? Don't you care how rude you are?'

'OK, OK, give it a rest, would you?' he grumbled. 'You're starting to sound like Sasha.'

'Good,' said Lottie. 'You know, I've always defended you to Sasha. I've always said you weren't as black as she paints you. But I guess I was wrong.'

'Oh really? So you hate me now too, do you?' Instinctively, without thinking, Jackson grabbed Lottie and kissed her. It was so unexpected, her brain found it hard to make the switch from anger to pleasure. Certainly it was nothing like the kiss that she'd dreamed of every night for the last four years, since the day she started work at Wrexall. When he finally released her, Lottie burst into tears, overwhelmed with emotion.

'Oh, God, don't. Please don't cry,' said Jackson, hugging her. 'I'm an ass, I'm a giant ass. I was jealous and I . . . I didn't handle it very well.'

'Jealous?' Lottie dried her tears. 'I thought you weren't attracted to me.'

Jackson gave her a rueful smile. 'I'm a sighted, adult male, Lottie. In what possible alternate universe would I not be attracted to you?'

'Then why do you keep ignoring me?' sniffed Lottie. 'At work. Even here, this whole trip, you've looked right through me. I feel like a ghost around you.'

He kissed her again, more gently this time, his fingers lightly brushing the back of her neck as his lips pressed against hers. Suddenly Lottie wanted him more than ever. But then, just as suddenly, he stopped.

'You're not a ghost. I see you, Lottie. You don't need to do shit like *this*,' he touched her hair, 'to get my attention.' Lottie blushed but did not deny it. 'You have my attention. But you also have my respect. My friendship. I don't want to ruin that.'

'You wouldn't,' Lottie began, but Jackson cut her off.

'I would. You know, Sasha *is* right about me, on one level anyway. I'm not exactly the steady boyfriend type. I admire it in others, you know? My parents have been married forty years. But I think it's important to know your own limits. I'd make a lousy husband, Lottie. And with you, I wouldn't want to be anything less than perfect.'

Lottie stared at him, not sure whether to feel happy or sad. Jackson cared about her. Maybe even loved her. Move a few words around and that could have been a proposal. But they weren't going to be together. 'So what happens now?' she said glumly. 'I mean, what happens tomorrow? Do we just forget any of this ever happened?'

'Yes,' Jackson kissed her cheek. 'I think that's exactly what we do.'

'You'll have to apologize to Francis.'

That brought Jackson up short. 'Apologize? Uh uh, no way. I'm not apologizing. I never apologize.'

'Yes you are.' The shock of the last hour's events had sobered Lottie up completely. 'And you can prove you mean it by bringing him in to the new resort team.' Jackson opened his mouth to protest but Lottie stopped him. 'You owe me one, Jackson. In fact you owe me about twelve. If it weren't for me we'd still be stuck in never-ending planning and you know it. I want Francis on the team.' Her cute, pixie-like chin jutted forward defiantly as she drew herself up to her full five feet one inch. Jackson wondered how anyone ever refused her anything.

'Fine,' he said grumpily. 'You can have Francis stupid O'Donnell. But I want something in return.'

Lottie felt hope surge up within her. 'You do?' she trembled.

'Yes. I want you to keep Sasha Miller off my back and as far away from this project as humanly possible.'

Lottie flew back to New York the following evening. After everything that had happened, it felt too awkward to stay. Jackson stayed on in Utah for four more days. Officially he was tied up in a whirlwind of on-site meetings. Unofficially, he was taking his old friend Piers Dellal up on his ski-bunnies offer, ricocheting from party to party and bed to bed like a sex-crazed boomerang. By the time he'd worked off his sexual frustration over Lottie sufficiently to catch a plane home, it was Friday afternoon. He'd called a special meeting of the board, to discuss his triumphant new hotel deal, and stepped off the plane feeling more energized and alive than he had in months.

The feeling didn't last.

Jackson's first thought, on walking into Wrexall Dupree's offices, was that there must have been a fire. That or some sort of terror attack. On the street outside, crowds of people were milling around. On close inspection Jackson saw that well over half of them were press. When they saw *him*, they turned as one like a swarm of bees, jabbing microphones and cameras in his face and shouting questions that made no sense to him.

'What will the repercussions be for the new firm?'

'Will Wrexall do business with them?'

'Lucius Monroe this afternoon called the poaching of your clients "theft". Do you agree with that? Will you be making a statement?'

Pushing past the reporters into the lobby, Jackson ignored the receptionist's frantic arm waving, hopped into the nearest elevator and marched straight into his office.

'Would someone like to tell me what on earth is going on? It's pandemonium down there.'

Lise, his secretary, looked at her shoes. Even Bob Massey, not usually the shrinking-violet type, developed a sudden, burning interest in his cuticles. Standing next to Dan Peters, like Oliver Hardy to Peters' tall, lean Stan Laurel, Bob looked positively embarrassed.

Dan Peters was the first to speak. 'We've been trying to get hold of you. All day. Where were you?'

'What do you mean, where was I?' said Jackson, irritated. 'I was on a plane, as you well know.'

'We tried you first thing this morning, hours before your flight. And yesterday.'

'Jesus, Dan, what is this, the inquisition?' snapped Jackson, defensive because he knew he was in the wrong. 'I was in meetings half way up a fucking mountain, OK? No phone reception.' From the look on Peters' face, the lie sounded as unconvincing to him as at did to Jackson. Deciding that attack was probably the best form of defence, Jackson squared his shoulders belligerently. 'Now perhaps *you* wouldn't mind telling *me* what the hell's going on?'

At that moment an ashen-faced Lucius Monroe and most of the rest of the board filed in. Suddenly Jackson's palatial corner office was starting to feel like a sardine can.

'It's Sasha Miller,' said Lucius.

Jackson felt his heart tighten. 'Of course it is. Don't tell me. She's gone to one of our competitors and taken a bunch of the retail group with her? I hate to say "I told you so".' He looked at the shifty glances being exchanged between his fellow board members. 'What? It's worse than that? Don't tell me she's gotten McKinley to go with her?'

'No,' said Lucius cautiously. 'Wrexall retains eighty-five per cent ownership in the McKinley partnership. That was part of the deal.'

Jackson's eyes narrowed. 'What deal?'

'She left us with no choice,' said Bob Massey. 'It's an MBO.'

'A management buyout? Of what?'

'Of the entire retail division.'

Jackson laughed. 'Don't be ridiculous! That's the core of our business. It has been for almost a century.'

'They raised twenty per cent of the money themselves,' said Bob. 'McKinley fronted the rest. Evidently Sasha's become very tight with Joe Foman, their CEO. Very tight indeed.'

Jackson paused, trying to process this information. He knew Joe Foman socially, though not well. An aging roué, once extremely handsome but now a paunchy caricature of his young self, complete with slicked-back, receding hair and open-necked, wing-collar shirts, the idea of Joe Foman and Sasha being 'tight' made Jackson physically sick. Forcing it out of his mind, he turned back to business.

'It doesn't matter. So Sasha found the money and enough willing bodies to go with her. So what? She can't effect a buyout without unanimous board consent.' The shoe shuffling and awkward glances intensified.

'It's like Bob said,' muttered Lucius Monroe weakly. 'We had no choice. If we didn't agree to the deal, McKinley would have nixed the joint venture altogether. This way we get eighty-five per cent of the biggest transaction in our history. As opposed zero per cent of nothing.'

'And for what?' added Bob Massey. 'We'd still have lost the heart of our retail division. Sasha had a back-up offer from Jones Lang LaSalle and another from CB Richard Ellis Group, to take the team in whole or in part. They were out the door, Jackson.'

Jackson couldn't believe what he was hearing. 'So? So what if they were out the door? That's human capital. It's renewable! We could have rehired, we could have recruited. Instead you traded the living, beating heart of this company for a stake – a *stake* – in *one deal*! You must be out of your minds, all of you. Where's your backbone? Where are your fucking balls?' He waved an accusing arm around the room. 'Well, it's not going to happen. You know the statutes better than anyone.' He turned to look at Bob Massey, who blushed. 'I think you'll find they're very clear on this point. The board decision on any MBO must be unanimous and it *must* include the family vote. The family vote is me. And I vote no. Now where the hell is Lottie Grainger? I need to make a statement to those locusts outside, come to feast on Wrexall's remains.'

'It's too late for that, Jackson,' Dan Peters said stiffly. Dan had expected Jackson to take the news badly. They all had. But he for one was getting tired of being lectured by a long-haired upstart who couldn't keep it in his pants. If Jackson felt so damn strongly about the company's wellbeing, he shouldn't have spent the last three days screwing his way around a ski resort like a dog in heat. *'No phone reception'* *my ass.* Sasha Miller had put them in a unique position, both dangerous and potentially profitable. Yes, there were risks involved, on all sides. That was business. But the board had acted in Wrexall Dupree's best interests, and that was all there was to it.

'The deal was already signed, an hour ago. The board's decision *was* unanimous. And we *did* secure the family vote.'

'That's impossible!'

'Not at all. In the light of your absence and inability to be contacted, we put the vote to the next most senior family member with significant shareholdings, as we are legally entitled to do. Sasha Miller met with that senior family member this morning, explaining in full the relative advantages to Wrexall Dupree of this deal. After that meeting, he added his signature to our eleven. The deal is done. We believe it is a good deal. You may disagree, but the decision is nonetheless irrevocable.'

'Who added his signature?' Jackson's voice was barely a whisper. 'Who did Sasha go and visit, and bamboozle, and convince to sign in my name?'

With a small smile of satisfaction, Dan Peters said, 'It was Walker Dupree, Jackson. Your father.'

CHAPTER FIFTEEN

Sasha lay back on her bed, elated but exhausted. The last five days had been a whirlwind. She still had to pinch herself to make sure she wasn't dreaming. Have I really just bought out Wrexall's retail business? Am I really going to be running it as my own company?

She'd been fielding the same questions from the media all afternoon. Her phone hadn't stopped ringing: CNN, MSNBC's *Squawk Box*, *Forbes* magazine, the *Wall Street Journal*, and photographers were camped outside her luxurious Upper East Side apartment building. (She had finally allowed herself to move out of her pokey Brooklyn flat when Georgia, her old friend from St Michael's days, had flown out to stay and complained that the place was little better than a student squat.) The press all wanted to know just how such a young, not to mention female, Wrexall executive had managed to convince the board to sell out of one of their most profitable businesses. And of course, Sasha answered all their questions with the same, measured, poised responses: She hadn't 'outmanoeuvred' anyone. This was a great deal for Wrexall Dupree, as well as for McKinley and the new group, tentatively christened Ceres (after the small but fertile breakaway planet between Mars and Jupiter, a nod to Sasha's physics past). All sides felt that the time was ripe for a change, etc., etc.

In reality, Sasha had been overtaken by events almost as much as everybody else. Sure, she'd fantasized about one day running her own firm. But that was all it was, a fantasy. It was only as the McKinley deal drew to a close and Joe Foman, desperate to prolong his daily contact with Sasha, had started floating the idea of backing her, that she began to see the possibilities. Initially, Joe was suggesting that his private equity firm, Cosmos, fund a brand-new, start-up company with Sasha at the helm. As appealing as the idea was to Sasha's ego, it was far too high risk. Most start-ups sank without trace, however well managed they were; it was the law of the jungle. No, the ideal was a buyout, taking an established business with clients and a revenue stream and breaking it off from its parent. The problem was, of course, that parent companies tended not to want to let go of their most profitable divisions. They needed to be persuaded. And that's when the idea came to her: What if she were to link the entire $700 million McKinley deal with an MBO proposal?

Joe Foman loved the idea, and had no trouble selling it to the McKinley board. It was the Wrexall board that was always going to be tricky. Or so Sasha thought.

'How'd it go?' Joe Foman called her the second her meeting was over.

'Believe it or not, it went well,' laughed Sasha. 'I thought they'd throw me out of there on my arse, but by the time I finished the pitch they actually seemed kind of excited.'

'What did I tell you?' said Joe. 'Sure, they've got their pride. But eighty-five per cent of seven hundred million dollars buys you a lot of pride. So will they sign?'

Sasha sighed. 'No. We're short one vote. Jackson Dupree. He's out of town on business.'

'When's he back?'

'Tomorrow. But it doesn't matter. He'll never go for it.'

She'd hung up the phone from Joe Foman feeling deflated. She'd come so close, so close she could smell it. But of course *Jackson* would have to be the spanner in the works. It wasn't until much later that night, in bed, that it came to her. Using her security card to get back into her office, Sasha sat at her desk, poring over the company statutes into the small hours. At 6 a.m. she was on a plane to Martha's Vineyard.

The Duprees, Mitzi and Walker, had homes all around the United States, but they spent most of their time on their ten-acre compound on the vineyard. In the last five years, since Walker's health had declined, they had rarely left the island, preferring their own company and that of old friends to socializing in Manhattan or Palm Beach. Walker had a round-the-clock nursing staff living in at the house, a classic, white clapboard Cape home with dark green shutters, to-die-for ocean views and the most exquisite gardens Sasha had ever laid eyes on.

'It's so kind of you to come all this way to see us. You're a friend of Jackson's, you say?' Mitzi, an elegant woman in her early seventies with swept up grey hair and Katharine Hepburn cheekbones, poured Sasha a glass of hot home-made apple cider.

'Um, sort of, yes,' said Sasha guiltily. 'We work together.' She felt bad lying to this kind old woman. It didn't help that every inch of polished mahogany furniture seemed to be covered with silver-framed photographs of Jackson, reproaching her from all angles. There was Jackson as a baby, looking surprisingly fat in an old-fashioned, Oxford pram; Jackson, gap toothed and grinning on his first day at kindergarten; Jackson on horse-back, endlessly, holding polo sticks or trophies or both; Jackson graduating college, looking more like his dissolute, arrogant self with his long hair tied back in a ponytail and a taunting, *admit it, you want me* look in his dancing brown eyes.

'He's a good boy,' said Mitzi lovingly, noticing Sasha staring at the pictures. 'And so good at business, just like his father.'

Sasha glanced at Walker Dupree, the man who had once run Wrexall with an iron fist and whose name was still spoken of in the halls with a combination of reverence and fear. She knew of the rift that existed between father and son. Jackson never spoke of it, but it was common knowledge. Even so, disapproving of your child's lifestyle did not necessarily mean you stopped loving them. Sasha wondered what the old man's true feelings towards Jackson were. The mother clearly still doted on him. Sitting in an old-fashioned bath chair with a plaid blanket over his knees, Walker Dupree seemed barely aware she was there, gazing out of the window at the grey, misty ocean, pausing occasionally to smile at his wife.

'Walker and I are alone here most of the time now, but that suits us just fine,' said Mitzi, patting her husband's knee affectionately. 'Of course we'd like to see more of Jackson than we do. But he's so busy with work, it's not easy for him.'

Sasha thought of how easy it had been for her to hop on a plane from JFK this morning and wondered how such sweet, kind, *normal* people had produced such a selfish, egotistical son.

'But listen to me, prattling on like an old woman. You said you needed to talk to Walker about something?'

'Yes. It's nothing to worry about. We're trying to push through a deal, something that should make a lot of money for the company.'

215

'That sounds exciting, doesn't it, Walker?'

The old man's face remained impassive.

'It is exciting. But because of the size and nature of this deal, we need unanimous board approval, and the deadline is at one o'clock today. Unfortunately Jackson's away travelling and can't be reached.'

'Oh dear.' Mitzi wrung her hands. 'I do hope he's not pushing himself too hard.'

I expect he's been pushing himself very hard indeed, thought Sasha. *Right between some socialite's thighs.* Aloud, she said, 'We need another shareholding family member to vote in his place. I have all the paperwork with me, if you want to see it. But all we really need is Mr Dupree's signature, right here on the last page.'

Walker Dupree cleared his throat. Sasha jumped, as if a waxwork dummy had suddenly come to life. 'Mitzi, honey,' he said in his soft, gravelly voice, 'let me talk to the young lady alone, would you?'

Mitzi looked as surprised as Sasha. 'Sure. Of course, darling, if that's what you want. Would you like Mary Anna or one of the other nurses?'

'No, thank you. I'll be fine. We won't be long.'

Once Mitzi was gone and the living room door was closed, Walker Dupree looked Sasha in the eye for a long, long time. When eventually he spoke, he was not only lucid, but sharp as a tack and very, *very* mad.

'Now you listen to me. The next time you set foot in my house and try to get me, or any member of my family, to sign some bullshit piece of paper we haven't even read, I will set my dogs on you. Is that clear?'

Sasha blushed to the roots of her hair. 'Yes, sir. I'm sorry, Mr Dupree. I thought . . .'

'You thought I was mentally incapacitated. Yes, I know.

That's what makes it such a shitty thing to do. However, as you can see, I'm not.'

A frosty silence fell. Sasha didn't know whether to get up and leave, or apologize again. After what felt like years, but was probably less than a minute, Walker Dupree said, 'Show me the documents. All of them.'

Sasha did as she was asked. She sat and watched for twenty minutes as the old man read and reread the deal memo, his rheumy eyes scanning the figures and graphs, carefully extracting every ounce of meaning. At last he looked up.

'Explain to me in no more than three sentences why I should sign my name to this deal.'

Sasha took a deep breath. 'I can explain it to you in one sentence, Mr Dupree. Because it's the best deal you're going to get.'

For the first time since his wife had left them, Walker Dupree smiled.

'And if I don't sign?'

'Wrexall will lose the McKinley deal. And I'll leave the firm and take the retail group with me.'

'Take them where?'

'Jones Lang LaSalle, probably.'

'What makes you so sure they would go? Wrexall could counteroffer. Double their salaries if necessary. *We* could cut *you* out of the picture.'

Now it was Sasha's turn to smile. 'You could try, sir. But you won't succeed. You see, unlike every other business at Wrexall, we *are* a team and we watch each other's backs. It's not a concept your son believes in, but it's worked for me.'

Walker Dupree frowned and Sasha inwardly cursed her big mouth. *What did I have to go and bring up Jackson for? He's the man's son, for God's sake. Of course he's going to take his side over an outsider's, rift or no rift.* But Walker Dupree surprised her.

'You say you've been unable to reach Jackson. Where is he?'

'He's on business in Park City,' said Sasha, straight faced.

'You mean he's off somewhere partying his ass off?' Walker translated succinctly.

Sasha shrugged. 'Truthfully, sir, your guess is as good as mine.'

'I see,' said Walker. 'And you obviously believe my son would refuse to sign this deal if he *were* where he should be, at his desk? Otherwise you'd simply have moved the deadline and not bothered coming all this way to try and hoodwink me into doing it.'

Sasha was about to protest, but wisely thought better of it. 'I believe Jackson would refuse to sign anything that he felt *I* might profit from. However great a deal it might be for your company. Sir.'

'Ah.' Walker Dupree nodded in understanding. 'So it's personal.'

Sasha's heart sank. *That's it. I've blown it. He's not going to sign, not if it means backing me over his own heir.* At that moment Mitzi walked back in, carrying a tray of freshly baked cinnamon cookies. 'Anyone hungry? Business talk always makes Walker hungry.' She winked at Sasha. The smell of the biscuits took Sasha right back home to her parents' cottage in Frant. The combination of the nostalgia punch to the stomach and her disappointment about the deal was too much for her. To her great embarrassment, Sasha found her eyes welling up with tears.

'Oh, my dear, are you all right? Whatever is the matter?' said Mitzi.

'Nothing,' said Sasha unconvincingly. 'It's er, it's my

allergies. Thank you for the cookies, but I think we're done here.' She stood up to leave. As she headed for the door, Walker Dupree called after her.

'Haven't you forgotten something?'

He handed her the documents. There, on the last page, gleaming in fresh, bright blue ink, was his signature.

'I don't believe in letting personal feelings get in the way of business. And the best deal you're going to get is always the right deal.'

'Thank you . . .' stammered Sasha.

'If Jackson wanted to use his vote, he should have been at the end of his goddamned phone,' snapped Walker. 'Maybe this'll wake him up a bit. It'll certainly wake up those old fuddy-duddies at Wrexall. Companies need change, I've said it before and I'll say it again. It's what keeps 'em ahead of the game. Good luck with your new venture, miss.'

Lying on her bed now, it was hard to believe that that conversation had taken place this morning. The rest of the day had been one of the longest of Sasha's life, yet at the same time it had passed in a blur. As soon as the deal went through and was announced on Bloomberg, all hell broke loose in the markets, with both Wrexall and McKinley's shares fluctuating wildly before ending the day six and fourteen points up respectively. Sasha herself had been so overwhelmed with requests for interviews, she'd had to ask Joe Foman to loan her a full-time PR person to handle it all. It had been so crazy and so sudden, she hadn't even had time to call Lottie Grainger, the one person at Wrexall outside of her own group whom she was determined to poach over to Ceres. Reaching for her BlackBerry, ignoring the hundreds of unread messages and voicemails, she was about to call Lottie when she heard a loud banging at the door.

Instantly on her guard – no one should have been able to get up to her floor without security downstairs alerting her first – Sasha made sure the chain was on and the door double bolted before she looked through the spy hole.

It was Jackson.

'Open the door, Sasha. I know you're in there.'

Sasha left the chain on, unbolting the door and opening it about an inch so they could talk.

'How the hell did you get up here?'

'I took the fire stairs. Now are you going to let me in or what?' He looked tired and bedraggled, with deep purple shadows under his eyes and a sweat-stained shirt still crumpled from his flight. His face was flushed with anger and exertion. Sasha contemplated *not* letting him in. But she knew he was stubborn enough to hammer at her door all night, and besides, she would have to face him some time. She unhooked the chain and stood back as he stormed inside, pacing her tiny entryway like a caged tiger.

'You bitch,' he hissed at her. 'You set me up!'

'I did no such thing.' Sasha walked into the living room, keeping her cool. 'This was a good deal for all sides.'

'Don't give me that shit!' he roared. 'It was a good deal for *you*, at Wrexall's expense. My expense.'

'Don't take it so personally.' Sasha sat down on the couch. 'It was business.'

'It was blackmail! And don't tell me not to take it personally. You flew out to *my house* and turned my own parents against me. You call *me* unethical, but what the hell kind of a stunt is that?' He was still pacing, his arms flailing wildly, as if looking for a suitable object to punch. 'The old man only did it to hurt me. To try to claw back some of his power, his glory days.'

Sasha was shocked at the vitriol in Jackson's voice. 'That's

220

not true. Your father read the memo very carefully. He signed because he thought it was the best outcome for Wrexall Dupree, under the circumstances.'

'And what circumstances were those? The circumstance of you sticking a dirty great knife in all our backs? You disgust me. You're a total hypocrite.'

Stung, but not wanting to show him how hurt she was, Sasha lashed out.

'You know, your father *did* say that he hoped this might act as a wake-up call. That it might get you to start taking your role at Wrexall more seriously.'

'What do you mean by that? I take my role very seriously. Just because I play hard, doesn't mean I don't work hard.'

'You think your father doesn't know you were AWOL in some hooker's bed in Utah, enjoying yourself while Rome burned? You think the entire board doesn't know? I didn't "set you up", Jackson. You set yourself up. All you had to do was answer your phone and none of this would have happened.'

Furious, because he knew it was true – yes, Sasha had pulled a fast one, but he'd allowed it to happen, been the architect of his own undoing – Jackson instinctively drew back his fist. Sasha flinched, cowering against the wall. Jackson felt shame creep over his skin like hives. *What the hell is wrong with me? What, I'm going to hit a woman now?* Spinning around he slammed his fist repeatedly in the opposite wall until his knuckles bled.

'I think you should go.' Sasha's voice was firm but he could hear the tremble beneath. 'Please leave.'

'I gave you a job,' said Jackson. 'I brought you into this company. I *made* you, Sasha. And how do you repay me? You turn on me like a viper.'

'Bullshit! Yes, you gave me a job, and in return I made you a fortune. You're lazy and arrogant, Jackson. Loyalty is something you earn, you can't just demand it. My team is loyal to me because they see me work my arse off for them every single day. That's one of the most exciting things about Ceres. It's a real team effort.'

Jackson stepped closer to her, so close that Sasha could feel his warm breath on her collarbone. She was aware of her heart racing, a combination of physical fear – he still might try and hit her – and something else, something too disturbing for her to name. When he reached out and touched her hair, his strong hand gripping the back of her neck, she thought she might faint. He dropped his voice to a whisper.

'I'm going to crush you, Sasha. I'm going to blow Ceres out of the water. Obliterate it into so many pieces, it'll be like it never existed.'

His closeness, his physical presence, made it hard for Sasha to breathe. Tightening his grip on her neck, Jackson pulled her towards him and kissed her, once, on the mouth. Shocked, and horribly excited, Sasha squirmed away.

'Get out of my apartment.'

'Good luck,' said Jackson as he walked out of the door. 'You're going to need it.'

Out on the sidewalk, the cool night air brought Jackson to his senses, as if waking from a dream. He tried to process his feelings but it was impossible. *Did I really just kiss her?* Part of him hated Sasha, loathed her enough to want to hit her, to hurt her. Not just for today and what she'd done to him: landing a body blow to Wrexall and turning the board, and even his own father, against him on what ought to have been *his*, Jackson's, day of triumph. But for all the bickering

222

and sparring and fury of the last few years. Once upon a time she'd tried to destroy Theo Dexter's career and failed. Now, it appeared, it was Jackson's turn. What kind of a psycho was this woman?

But another part of him, a part he'd been denying since the day Sasha rejected him at Harvard all those years ago, another part wanted her so badly it made Jackson want to cry. *It's not love,* he told himself. *It's lust.* The competitor in him wanted to beat Sasha, wanted to win. He knew that the only way he would ever truly win was when he had her in his bed, naked and longing, begging him for more. Just picturing it now was giving him an incipient hard on that only added to his fury.

In his head, Sasha's voice taunted him:

You set yourself up.

You're lazy and arrogant.

You think the board doesn't know?

Too wound up to go home, he headed to the nearest bar.

Lottie sat at the kitchen table in her Brooklyn apartment, checking her messages on Facebook. 'Update your status!' the home page invited her. 'What are you doing right now?' After the words 'Charlotte Grainger is' Lottie typed '. . . wondering if it's ever going to end.'

It was Friday night, so officially her *week-us horribilis had* ended. But the aftershocks kept coming. Her kiss with Jackson – the kiss – had only been five days ago, but already it felt like a lifetime. Lottie hadn't seen him this afternoon since he got back. Understandably, he had bigger fish to fry. Such as trying to strangle Sasha with the nearest electric cord, presumably. Lottie was torn about the MBO and Ceres's violent birth. On the one hand she saw what a huge opportunity it was for Sasha. For some reason that Lottie had never understood, Sasha was obsessed with making money. Not just massive-salary-great-apartment-wardrobe-full-of-designer-clothes amounts of money. But serious, game-changing, corporation-controlling amounts of money. Enough money to wield 'real power', that was how Sasha described it. But power over what? Over whom? In any event, Ceres clearly represented a giant leap in the right direction, and to that extent Lottie was pleased for her friend.

On the other hand it meant that the two girls would no longer work together. And then of course there was Jackson. Lottie tried to believe that Sasha's coup had not been intended to wound Jackson personally. But given their history, she wasn't sure. What she *was* sure of was that the whole Ceres debacle had damaged Jackson's standing at Wrexall. Folk stories about exactly *where* Wrexall's not-so-golden boy had been while his former employee was busy taking apart his company had already begun doing the rounds on Wall Street. One of them involved a pair of Czech twins and a pet poodle. Another featured Senator Davis's soon-to-be-ex-wife Alana, a chalet hot tub and an overeager paparazzo. All of the stories left poor Lottie feeling as if she was undergoing open-heart surgery without anaesthetic.

Closing down Facebook, Lottie clicked onto Outlook and was astonished to see a new mail from Sasha flashing at the top of her inbox. Shouldn't she be on her way to a TV studio somewhere, or sipping champagne with that sleazeball Foman, toasting Ceres's future success?

In typical Sasha style, the email was two words long. It simply read, 'Join us?' A few moments later, a second message arrived, 'Name your price. S xoxo'.

Lottie flushed with pleasure, as if she'd just done something naughty but wonderful. Of course, she hadn't actually *done* anything. *I didn't say 'yes'. I just read it.* She was flattered to be asked, and tempted, not just by the idea of working for Sasha but by the 'name your price' part. That had an excellent ring to it! But of course it would mean leaving Wrexall, and the chance to work every day along-side Jackson as the new Park City ski resort took shape.

Shutting her computer, Lottie put her coat on. A walk would help to clear her head. Even in March, the greyest and drabbest of months, neither winter nor spring, Lottie adored her Brooklyn neighbourhood. Her apartment was the top two floors of a once grand old brownstone on a broad, leafy street that seemed light years away from the *Sturm und Drang* of Manhattan. She first moved across the bridge in her early twenties, when it was all she could afford. Now she easily earned enough to move to the West Village or some trendy loft in the meatpacking district, but you couldn't have paid Lottie to leave Brooklyn. As much as New York ever could be, it was home.

Turning the corner, she pulled up the hood of her jacket against the biting wind and trudged in the direction of the 7-Eleven, keeping her head down.

'Look where you going, would you?'

She'd collided with a drunk, heading down the hill towards the subway.

'Sorry,' she began. 'I didn't see you. I . . . Jackson? Is that you?'

'Lottie. Hello, Lottie!' Jackson grinned down at her like a simpleton. Dangerously underdressed for the weather in jeans and a crumpled Spurr shirt, he reeked of whisky, swaying from side to side like a seasick sailor. 'I was trying to find your street, butIgodabidlost,' he slurred. 'But you're here. Thass amazing! I must be getting warm, right?'

Not sure whether to feel excited (that he'd come to find her) or depressed (that he only ever seemed to come to find her when he was three sheets to the wind), Lottie wrapped a steadying arm around his waist and led him back to her place.

'It's not much,' she mumbled awkwardly, kicking a pile of mail off the floor in the entryway and moving a cold, half-drunk mug of this morning's coffee off the stairs before Jackson sent it flying. 'But at least we can warm you up. I'll make you some coffee.' She led a shivering Jackson into the kitchen and left him there while she disappeared to find a blanket. She returned to find him standing exactly where she'd left him, like a lost child at a railway station. 'Here.' She wrapped the blanket around his shoulders and pulled out a chair. 'Sit down. Tell me what happened.'

While Lottie brewed some fresh coffee, Jackson poured his heart out. About Sasha, and what a fool she'd made of him. About his father taking Sasha's side and going behind his back. Finally, he spoke about his own guilt, and fury at himself for not having been on the ball.

'I know I party too hard. I'm not stupid,' he said, chewing idly on a stick of stale French bread that Lottie had left lying around. 'I guess I just thought, after my big success in Park City, I could kick back a little, you know. Is that so terrible?'

'Hmmm,' said Lottie. *You mean* our *big success in Park City. I was the one who clinched us that deal. But you didn't see me 'kicking back'. It's back to work as normal for the rest of us lesser mortals.*

Reading her face, Jackson said, 'You think I'm arrogant, don't you?'

Lottie poured the milk. 'Well, I . . . maybe a little. Sometimes.'

'You think I'm arrogant and lazy and I don't care about my team.'

Lottie blushed. 'Sugar?'

'Oh God.' Jackson put his head in his hands. 'That's what hurts the most. Everything that bitch Sasha said to me is true. I set myself up. I did. I *let* this happen, and all for a few hours of lousy sex with a pair of . . .'

'OK, enough.' Lottie clamped both hands over her ears. 'I don't want to know.'

Jackson looked taken aback.

'I'll try to be your friend and to listen. I'll try to give you advice, if that's what you want, not that you ever listen to it, and I'll happily make you coffee and lend you my blanket, but I *will not* stand here in my own kitchen while you talk about your . . . your . . .' she struggled for the appropriate word, '. . . your *sexploits* with God knows who, twins or whatever ridiculous thing it was. I mean, really. *Really*. I don't want to know.'

She was so awkward and outraged and sweet, Jackson couldn't bear it. He moved towards her, an unmistakably predatory look in his eye. 'You're lovely.'

'No.' Lottie backed away. 'Stop it. You're drunk. This isn't fair.'

'I am drunk,' Jackson admitted. 'But I'm drunk for the last time. As of today, I'm gonna be a changed man. No more booze. No more partying. No more *sexploits*.' He was still moving closer. Lottie pressed her back against the kitchen counter.

'I'm happy to hear that, Jackson, I really am. But . . .'

He kissed her. 'I think we should be together.' Lottie started to protest but he stopped her. 'Please, hear me out. You're good for me. When I'm around you I feel calm. I feel content.'

And when I'm around you I feel like I'm about to burst into flames. Oh God, Jackson, I want you so much, can't you see it?

'I thought you said you'd make a lousy husband?' Lottie whispered. Jackson's body was pressed against hers now.

She could feel what little resolve she'd had crumbling like stale wedding cake.

'We'll work up to the husband part,' he grinned. 'One step at a time.' Slipping a hand under Lottie's sweater he reached for her bra strap, unclasping it with consummate ease. Lottie tried not to think about how many times he'd done that before and with how many women. There were a hundred and one reasons not to do this: Jackson was her boss, he was drunk, he was vulnerable, he was an inveterate womanizer who would sleep with her once, regret it and move on. Then his other hand slipped beneath her panties and none of the reasons meant anything.

'Jesus.' He looked up at her, startled. 'When did you get that done?'

Lottie blushed. She'd forgotten about the rather extreme Brazilian wax she'd had in Park City, the same day she dyed her hair. She'd been on such a high that day. But perhaps it *was* a bit slutty. 'Don't you like it?'

Jackson grinned. 'Are you kidding? I love it. It wasn't what I was expecting, that's all.'

Lottie closed her eyes and surrendered herself to the heavenly feelings washing over her. 'That makes two of us!' she gasped.

It was the last words either of them spoke that night.

Across town, Sasha lay in bed, staring up at the ceiling, whipsawed with frustration. It should have been one of the happiest nights of her life, the start of an exciting new chapter. But instead of focusing on her bright future, Sasha's head was full of images of two men.

Professor Theo Dexter: still happy, still rich and famous and successful, still living the dream that he stole from her.

And Jackson Amory Dupree, who'd kissed her, whose lips

she could still taste on her own, whose body heat still burned every inch of her skin. Jackson who had threatened to destroy her.

'I'm going to crush you. I'm go to blow Ceres out of the water.'

Sasha closed her eyes and said a silent prayer, the same prayer she'd said every night for the last ten years. *Help me, Lord. Help me to destroy Theo Dexter.* But this time she added a codicil. *And if it's not too much trouble Lord, help me forget about Jackson Dupree.*

PART THREE

CHAPTER SIXTEEN

Tokyo, five years later

Theo Dexter looked straight at camera, raising one eyebrow like Roger Moore's Bond and smouldering as only he knew how.

'*Driven,*' he whispered huskily, holding up a bottle of cheap-looking cologne. 'The smell of success.' He stood for five more seconds, his face frozen mid-smoulder, till the energetic Japanese director yelled, 'Cut!' Instantly Theo's features relaxed into their more familiar, petulant scowl.

'Very good, very good.' The director clapped his hands enthusiastically, and the Japanese crew did the same. 'All finish. Very good take, all finish.'

Thank Christ for that. Theo loathed Japan. A few years ago, Asia had excited him with its otherworldliness, its air of adventure. But by this point in his career, the novelty had well and truly worn off. If he closed his eyes and said the word Asia, four things sprang to mind. Humidity, cockroaches, stinking traffic and carbohydrates. (How the Japanese stayed so thin was a mystery to Theo. They seemed to eat rice or noodles with everything. He'd even come across a chicken noodle toothpaste, although that might have been intended as a joke item. You could never tell in Japan.) Despite staying at the uber-luxurious Park Hyatt, the hotel featured in the movie *Lost in Translation,* in a penthouse suite with spectacular views across the city all the way to Mount Fuji, he felt distinctly hard done by. Not least because Dita and the children were with him.

'Just think of the money,' Ed Gilliam told him cheerfully. Now in his late sixties and richer than ever thanks to his star client, Theo's agent still had the hunger for the next big deal. 'This commercial's earning you more than your entire last season's paycheck on *Dexter's Universe,* and three times what you made on *Space Suits.'*

Mentioning the name of Theo's last, ill-fated, straight-to-DVD feature film put him in an even worse mood. That was another thing he had to blame Dita for, pushing him into movies like some goddamn dancing monkey.

'I don't care. It's embarrassing. I feel like a used-car salesman.'

'Yes, well, get over it,' said Ed. 'All the big stars endorse over here. Clooney, Pitt, Cruise.'

'Maybe. But they don't have to live with Dita while they're doing it.'

After seven years with Dita, six of them married, the novelty of her celebrity had well and truly worn off. Not that Theo didn't still revel in the attention, the ubiquitous paparazzi who followed them everywhere, the throngs of screaming fans. But he resented the fact that his fame and Dita's had become so inextricably linked in the public imagination. Being one half of Hollywood's golden couple was wearing, particularly when the reality of Theo and Dita's domestic life was, at best, strained.

Sexually Dita could still do it for him. Unlike most exceptionally beautiful women, Dita was good in bed, a skilled and exciting lover. But although she remained a huge box office draw, physically she was past her prime. The tabloids and gossip magazines ruthlessly scrutinized her every, tiny flaw, photographing her at point-blank range and then printing the shots with red circles drawn around every incipient laughter line or prominent vein. Already deeply insecure, such criticism sent Dita into a frenzy of panicked exercising, Botox injecting and sarong buying. It also made her more than usually demanding of Theo's attention, a sure-fire way for her to lose it.

Theo couldn't remember exactly when he'd started cheating on Dita. Probably while she was pregnant with Milo, their eldest, now five. A sweet, sensitive but sickly child, Milo Dexter was allergic to everything and seemed mysteriously to have been born with the lung capacity of a gnat, necessitating frequent, stressful late-night trips to the Emergency Room, often followed by lengthy hospital stays. Dita doted on the boy, transferring all the attention she had previously lavished on Theo to their son. Of course, she still employed nannies, legions of them, which grew into full-scale battalions when their second child, Francesca, arrived two years later. It wasn't so much the *time* Dita spent with Milo, reasoned Theo. It was more the way she looked at him, the way they looked at each other, an exclusive little club of two from which he, Theo, would forever be excluded.

Francesca, known as Fran, was much more the sort of child that Theo could identify with. Confident, sensible and utterly self-reliant, she neither needed his love, nor asked for it, but rather accepted his affection as and when he chose to bestow it. If he'd known kids could turn out like this, he'd have adopted with Theresa years ago. Back then Theo would never have believed a three-year-old could be so politely distant, but that's how Fran was with Dita. Pleasant, unassuming, but fundamentally a little bored by her mother. It drove Dita crazy. 'Even my own daughter doesn't love me!' she would sob melodramatically to Theo, who was trying to download *Match of the Day* on his PC and wished to God Dita would find somebody else to emote to. Bringing the whole family to Tokyo had been Dita's idea, part of her drive to 'deepen my bond' with Fran.

'You can spend some time with Milo-pooks too. He's hardly seen you all year.'

'Come on, Deets. It's not my fault the boy's been in and out of hospital like an asthmatic boomerang. It's not me he wants when he's sick, it's you.' He didn't add, *and all the rest of the bloody time too,* but he felt like it. He knew it was ridiculous to be jealous of a five-year-old, but he couldn't help himself. 'Japan will be a nightmare. The jet lag, the paps, the kids going stir crazy in the hotel room. I'll be back in a few weeks.'

It was no good. Dita had insisted. Theo had had no choice but to call Cassie, his latest twenty-one-year-old bit on the side, and tell her their romantic trip was off. 'I'll make it up to you, angel, I promise. We'll sneak off to the Post Ranch as soon as I'm back.' Fuming, he'd climbed the stairs into the private jet with Dita and the kids feeling as if he was walking up to the guillotine. *This is going to be a nightmare.*

Then they got to Tokyo.

And it was much, much worse.

First, Milo picked up some bug on the plane and had to be rushed to the Hachioji children's hospital. Then Dita was photographed looking haggard and exhausted the day they discharged him, and the picture ran in *Star* magazine back in the States, alongside an airbrushed photo of Theo looking preposterously handsome, taken from his aftershave campaign. That evening Dita had screamed and screamed in their suite at the Hyatt until Theo had had to call a doctor to sedate her. She was so bad, the nannies had moved with the children to a different floor, as Milo particularly was getting very distressed. The next morning, Dita had refused to let Theo go to work until he'd made love to her, then afterwards sobbed in his arms for an hour. Despite his having come twice, Dita insisted he was 'faking it' and didn't really want her any more. It was mid afternoon before Theo got to the set. As ever, the Japanese crew were unwaveringly polite. But Ed Gilliam had ripped him a new arsehole.

'For fuck's sake, Theo! You're under contract. You can't just turn up when you feel like it. You realize there'll be a penalty, a big one. That fuck with Dita probably cost you two million dollars. I hope it was bloody worth it.'

'It wasn't,' said Theo grimly. On days like today, his mind sometimes wandered back to his first marriage. Theresa had been weak, and of course she did let herself go dreadfully towards the end. But she was also funny, and supportive, and never in the least part a drama queen. Even when the scandal with Sasha Miller had been all over the papers, when any rational wife would have had a good excuse to throw her toys out of the pram, Theresa had been so cool, calm and collected, it was almost regal.

Sasha Miller had been on Theo's mind too lately, for the first time in years. Bizarrely, his former student and paramour seemed to have reinvented herself as some sort of business mogul. Her property company, Ceres, had gone public a month ago, its shares floated at some astronomically inflated price, and suddenly Sasha's face was all over the business pages. Physically, she'd changed surprisingly little over the years. She still had that youthful, moonlight-white complexion, and of course those incredible pale green eyes that had once gazed into his with such trust and passion.

In her early thirties now, she wore her hair shorter than she had as a student, but it still gleamed the same lustrous tar black. Her body, if anything, looked better than it had back then, or at least more to Theo's taste, leaner, with less puppy fat. But if Sasha *looked* unchanged, appearances were obviously deceptive. You didn't get to that sort of position in business or in life without being a tough cookie. When Theo knew Sasha she'd been as soft and malleable as dough, but the intervening years must have baked her hard.

Theo's first reaction to Sasha's success was nervousness. The last thing he wanted was for some overenthusiastic journalist to start digging into Sasha's past and unearthing the stolen-theory scandal all over again. He raised his concerns with Ed Gilliam, but Ed was reassuringly sanguine.

'It's very unlikely. That was aeons ago. More importantly, it happened in England. Americans don't care about scandals in other countries.'

'Hmmm.' Theo wasn't convinced.

'Look, there's nothing you can do about it so you may as well stop worrying. What's the worst that can happen? Someone leaks the story, you and Sasha both make statements about bygones being bygones. If anyone's reputation's in danger here it's hers, not yours, right?'

'Right,' said Theo uneasily.

In the years since the scandal, *Dexter's Universe* and the theory that launched it had become so much a part of Theo's self-image, he'd almost forgotten its murky origins. Seeing Sasha Miller's face again stirred emotions buried deep in his subconscious – an uneasy concoction of guilt and fear that had begun to further sour Theo's mood. Combined with the increasing strain of dealing with Dita's meltdowns, and now this horrendous trip to Japan, he was feeling more restless and dissatisfied than he had in years. Ed Gilliam inadvertently made things worse by filling Theo in on the latest gossip amongst the Cambridge physics faculty. Apparently one of Theo's former students, Mike Green (now Emeritus Professor Michael Green) was sending shockwaves across the scientific world with his ground-breaking research into optical quantum computer chips.

'He's quite the new big thing,' Ed told Theo. 'I've got four publishers in a bidding war for his book. Of course Oxford, Harvard and MIT are all desperate to lure him.'

Theo consoled himself that Mike Green would never have a career like his. For one thing he was so shy he bordered on autistic, and for another he looked like a three-hundred-pound version of Daniel Radcliffe. No one wanted to switch on their television and be mumbled at by a morbidly obese nerd. Even so, Mike's success rankled. The public might never love him, but his fellow physicists clearly did. Much as he hated to admit it, there was a part of Theo Dexter that still craved approval from his peers. Grinning inanely at the camera today for three hours straight with a giant bottle of aftershave in his hands, Theo felt more nostalgic for Cambridge than he had in years.

One day I'll go back. I'll get back to my research, prove to all those envious bastards that I've still got what it takes. He turned on his phone. Six missed calls, all of them from Dita.

One day.

Horatio Hollander looked at himself in the bathroom mirror.

Not bad. Not George Clooney, perhaps. Not Theo Dexter, either. But not bad.

At twenty-two years of age, Horatio had finally (thank *God*) grown out of the acne that had plagued him as a teenager. Tall and skinny, with a shock of thick hair that had never been able to decide if it was red or blond, merry blue eyes and wide nose smattered with freckles, Horatio was generally referred to by girls as 'sweet'. In his first year at Cambridge, one of the prettier fresher girls had described him as looking a bit like a baby giraffe, and the phrase had stuck. A talented rower with a regular place in Jesus College's First Eight, Horatio's crewmates knew him only as 'Giraffe'. Horatio rolled his eyes, but secretly he rather liked the nickname. After six years of being called 'pizza face' and getting the shit kicked out of him at school (what sort of sadists named their son 'Horatio' then sent him to the toughest comprehensive in Leeds?), Giraffe was a refreshing change.

This morning, unusually for him, Horatio had made a titanic effort with his appearance. He wore his best tweed jacket, which only had a couple of tiny moth holes, a clean, ironed blue shirt and a pair of French Connection jeans that his friend Mary had assured him made his bum look great. 'More beefcake, less beanpole,' had been her exact words. *That's good enough for me.*

Of course the real question was whether they'd be good enough for Professor O'Connor. He'd waited long enough. It was time to screw his courage to the sticking place and ask her out before . . . before what? *What am I so scared of?*

Horatio had lost count of the nights he'd lain awake, his body racked with longing and his heart crippled with fear, imagining his Shakespeare tutor, Professor O'Connor – *Theresa* – locked in passionate embrace with another man. In his fevered imaginings, the other man always looked preternaturally handsome, and usually bore a strong resemblance to Professor O'Connor's ex-husband, the ghastly, white-toothed, perma-tanned Theo Dexter. Theresa had reverted to her maiden name after the divorce, largely to stop people making the connection between her and her world-famous ex. But of course, everyone at Cambridge knew.

This must be what Chris Martin felt, asking Gwyneth Paltrow out after she'd been engaged to Brad Pitt. But look at Chris, eh? He got the girl! Then again, he was a multi-millionaire rock star with legions of screaming fans. Whereas I'm a scruffy student from Leeds with an overdraft and holes in my jacket.

The thing was that Theresa had given him just enough hope – a smile here, a shy glance there – to make Horatio think that perhaps, just perhaps, by some miracle, his affections might be returned. Yes, she was his teacher. And yes, she was twenty years older than him – not to mention twenty times more beautiful and brilliant and funny and kind and . . .

'Get a move on, mate!' Jack, Horatio's roommate, was banging on the bathroom door. 'You can't polish a turd, you know. She'll either see past your ugly mug or she won't, so hurry the fuck up, would you? I need a slash.'

Jack was an engineer. Lovely bloke, but no soul whatso-ever.

Horatio opened the door. 'What do you think?'

'I think you've got no chance,' said Jack robustly. 'She's old enough to be your mother, she's sworn off men, which is probably code for she's a lesbo . . .'

'She is *not* a lesbo!' said Horatio crossly.

'*And*, she supervises you, which makes you even more off-limits.'

'Maybe that'll be part of my appeal?' Horatio smiled hope-fully. 'I'm a forbidden fruit.'

'You're a forbidden fruit-loop more like it,' said Jack. 'Nice jeans though. You don't look like as much of a scrawnster as you usually do.' And with that he shut the bathroom door, abandoning his friend to his fate.

Theresa unlocked the outer, heavy wooden door of her college rooms with the same, heavy, palm-sized metal key that its occupants had been using for over two centuries. The romantic in her loved the giant key. Like the rest of her rooms, the rest of Cambridge in fact, it felt magical, like something out of a fairy tale. The key to Rapunzel's tower perhaps, or to some lost city of gold. Once inside she turned on the lights and the fan heater. It was April, spring according to the newspapers, but Cambridge was still bitterly cold and the college authorities were notoriously parsimonious about luxuries such as central heating. Soon, however, the noisy little fan had expelled the chill sufficiently for Theresa to take off her duffel coat, turn on the kettle, and start leafing through her notes for this morning's session on *Macbeth*.

She had a one-on-one supervision this morning with her star pupil, Horatio Hollander, and she was looking forward to it immensely. Horatio's last essay, on Macbeth's classic 'Tomorrow' soliloquy, was so good it had moved her almost to tears. Then again, that wasn't hard. Yesterday evening she'd sobbed like a child watching Jenny's cat, a fat old tabby inappropriately named 'Ninja,' give birth to six healthy kittens.

'What'll you do with them?'

'Sell them, I suppose. Or more likely give them away. I doubt people pay for kittens any more. We might keep one, I suppose.'

'Oh, you can't do that!' protested Theresa. 'Look at them. They're a little team. They have to stay together.'

'I'm not housing seven cats, T,' said Jenny reasonably. 'JP would divorce me and I wouldn't blame him.'

'Well, at least take two,' pleaded Theresa, watching the blindly crawling fur balls through a haze of tears. 'They can be company for each other. I'll have the rest.'

Jenny laughed. 'All four of them? You're not serious?'

'Why not? I like cats. They're good company.'

'But you've already got Lysander. You'll be like the classic old cat lady, T! Blokes'll be too scared to come near you.'

'Perfect,' said Theresa, reaching down to stroke one of the fur balls. 'I don't want blokes coming near me. They can be pets, companions and bodyguards all in one.'

This summer it would be five years exactly since Theresa had last been on a date. Looking out over Cloister Court, with its medieval arches and cobbled paths worn smooth with age, the thought gave Theresa a warm glow of contentment. *I don't need a man. I don't even want a man, and that's the God's honest truth.* In the first couple of years after her divorce, she'd accepted occasional dinner dates, largely as a way to keep Jenny and Aisling and her other friends off her back. But as time went by and she settled once more into the rhythm of academic life, cocooned in beauty both at work and at home, Theresa began to take a stand.

'I'm not denying myself,' she would say, truthfully. 'I'm happy as I am.' Coming home to Willow Tree Cottage still made every night feel like Christmas Eve. After she had finally published her book on Shakespeare in Hollywood, the first really serious academic analysis of the modern media interpretations of the plays, to high critical acclaim. The book was never going to make her rich, but Theresa was inordinately proud of it. As a result, she'd been approached to edit and write an introduction to the new Cambridge University Press Shakespeare anthology, a huge honour and without doubt the crowning professional achievement of her life so far. *I have my work, my friends, Lysander, my perfect, chocolate-box home. What more could anyone ask for?*

If there were one thing she might have wished for, had someone presented her with a magic wand, it would probably have been a baby, although even that desire had softened over the years. It would not, under any circumstances, have been a boyfriend, still less a husband. Theresa had loved once, deeply, and she had lost. As far as she was concerned, that was that. Her feelings for Theo had also faded – when she saw his face on the television now it was like looking at a stranger – but the memory of the pain remained. Someone had once told her that that was the definition of a lunatic: someone who repeats the same mistakes over and over and over again. Well, Theresa O'Connor was not a lunatic. She was simply a single woman who *happened* to share her home with five cats.

A knock on the door disturbed her musings.

'Come in,' she trilled cheerfully. 'It's open.'

Horatio hovered in the doorway. Not for the first time, Theresa thought what a kind, intelligent face he had. *If I had a son*, she thought, *I'd like him to look like that.*

'Good morning, Mr Hollander. Can I offer you some tea?'

Horatio cleared his throat. 'Er, no. No thank you. I'm fine. Thanks.'

Theresa smiled. 'You look nervous. If it's about your essay I can assure you you have no reason to be. As usual you were insightful and to the point. I did want to debate a couple of your conclusions with you, however, especially your position in the final stanzas, where . . .'

'It's not about the essay.'

Pouring herself a cup of Earl Grey, Theresa noticed the boy's complexion had faded from its usual white to something closer to see-through. 'My goodness, Horatio. Are you all right?'

'Not really.' He walked over to where she was standing and gently took the mug of tea from her hands. Unfortunately his own hands were shaking so much, he instantly scalded himself, yelping with pain. Theresa shifted at once into motherly mode.

'Come on, come with me. I've some frozen peas in the

kitchenette, I think. I don't cook much in my rooms but I think they're still there. Stick it under the cold tap while I have a look.'

Horatio stood at the sink, oblivious to the burn on his hand, watching her. In a pair of slouchy jeans that looked in permanent danger of slipping off her slim hips, and a black polo neck sweater that accentuated her fragile arms, she looked (to Horatio's eyes) almost childlike. In the stressful wake of her divorce Theresa had shed all the weight she'd gained in America, and her students at Christ's had only ever known her as skinny. It was a joke amongst them that half Professor O'Connor's body weight had to be made up of hair, that trademark wild explosion of titian curls that today she wore piled up on top of her head in a messy bun.

'Here you go.' She pressed a packet of frozen peas onto his hand. It was an entirely maternal gesture, but Horatio seized the moment, and the physical contact, and clasped her hand in his.

'Have dinner with me,' he mumbled.

Theresa looked up at him, surprised, but said nothing. The tap was still running. Perhaps she hadn't heard him?

'I love you,' he said, more loudly, just as Theresa turned off the tap. The words boomed around the small room like a public announcement in a railway station waiting room. Blushing, Horatio continued. 'I'm in love with you, Profe . . . Theresa. I adore you. Have dinner with me.'

Now it was Theresa's turn to blush. It had not escaped her notice that Horatio Hollander was one of the more attractive of her students. Not handsome in any classical sense, but tall and kind and intelligent, the sort of man she might have gone for had he been twenty years older, and had she been in the market for a man, which, quite plainly, she wasn't.

'May I have my hand back, Horatio?' she said kindly.

Horatio thought about saying, 'Not till you give me an answer!' the way all the dominant, manly heroes did in romantic fiction novels. Mentally, he tried the words on for size, but from him they simply sounded ridiculous.

'Of course.' He released her hand. 'I meant what I said, though.'

'I can see that.' He looked so earnest, Theresa couldn't bear it. Part of her felt like kissing him right then and there, but it was a small part and she squashed it. 'You do realize how old I am?'

'I've no idea how old you are,' he lied. 'All I know is how beautiful you are.'

'I'm forty-three,' said Theresa. 'How old is your mother?'
Horatio hesitated. 'Older.'

'How much older?'

'Have dinner with me and I'll tell you.' He smiled, Theresa laughed, and mercifully the tension was broken. 'How can I persuade you? There must be something I can do.'

'There isn't,' she said, passing him back the peas and walking back to the sofa where she taught her supervisions. 'I'm your supervisor. I like you very much, Horatio. I mean that sincerely.' His face lit up. 'But you have to forget about this, or I won't be able to teach you any more.'

Morosely, he followed her into the sitting room and sank into his usual armchair. 'You think I'm an idiot for asking you.'

'Not at all,' said Theresa. 'I'm flattered. But you don't need an old woman like me, for heaven's sake. I'm sure you have a queue of drop-dead-gorgeous twenty-year-olds lined up outside your rooms as we speak.'

I wouldn't bet on it, thought Horatio.

'Now come on. *Macbeth*. Impress me!'

He watched her eyes light up, the way they always did when she spoke about Shakespeare, and felt himself fall a few feet deeper into the bottomless pit of unrequited love. *One day,* he vowed, *she'll look that way for me.*

There was a key to Theresa O'Connor's heart. There had to be.

All he had to do was find it.

At dinner that night with Jenny and JP, Theresa told them the whole story.

'I think it's adorable,' said Jenny, knocking back a second glass of Bordeaux. They were at Henri's, a new French bistro on Jesus Lane that JP had pronounced 'acceptable', his equivalent of at least two Michelin stars. '"From forth the fatal loins of these two foes, A pair of star-cross'd lovers!"'

'Don't be ridiculous,' said Theresa. 'Horatio Hollander and I are nothing like Romeo and Juliet. And please don't use the word "loins" when we're talking about my students. It's enough to put me off my foie gras.'

'Methinks thou art protesting too much,' teased Jenny. 'I'm sure you've mentioned this kid to me before. Admit it, you think he's cute.'

'He is cute. For a *kid*,' said Theresa. 'You aren't seriously suggesting I accept a dinner invitation from one of my students? My top student, as it happens.'

'But not your "on-top" student. Not yet, anyway.'

'*Jenny!*'

'Theresa's right,' said JP, scraping the last scraps of perfectly cooked entrecote onto his fork. 'This is a line it is best nevair to cross. Especially when one 'as *ambitions*.' He raised an eyebrow cryptically.

'Eh?' said Jenny

'What ambitions?' said Theresa. 'You make it sound like I'm running for office.'

Jean Paul reached into his inside jacket pocket and pulled

out a newspaper clipping from the latest *Varsity*. 'Per'aps you should be. Take a look at this.'

Theresa read the clipping. 'It's about St Michael's. Anthony Greville's finally stepping down as Master next year. I can't believe that old goat's still going. He was about a hundred years old back in Theo's day.'

'The college is inviting applications for the Mastership.'

'Yes, I know.'

'You should apply.'

Theresa laughed so hard she almost choked on her foie gras toast. 'Me?'

'Why not you?' asked Jenny.

'Why not me? Why not the dustman? Why not my mother? Why not Lysander, for God's sake! I'm far too junior. I don't have nearly enough experience.'

'Sure you do,' said JP. 'Graham North's put himself forward. He's in my department, engineering. I wouldn't hire Graham to unblock a drain, never mind run a college. The rest of the list are older but distinctly uninspiring: Andrew Gray. He's been at St Michael's so long they're about to name a library after him. Hugh Mullaney-Stoop from Robinson, which isn't even a real college.'

'Old Mulligatawny Soup's put his name in the hat, has he?' laughed Jenny. 'He's the dullest man in Cambridge. You'd be miles better than him, Theresa.'

Theresa laughed too. Some PA to the gods had obviously sent a celestial memo round that today was her day to be flattered. 'Thanks, guys. I appreciate the vote of confidence. But I am *much* too young, *much* too insignificant and, last but not least, much too female to stand a snowball's chance in hell of becoming Master of St Mike's. Now, who's for pudding? The hazelnut soufflé's supposed to be out of this world.'

* * *

Later that night, in bed in Willow Tree Cottage with the wind rattling the ancient leaded windows, Theresa lay under a mountain of blankets, thinking about the day. She'd managed to get through the rest of the supervision with Horatio Hollander, largely by avoiding eye contact as much as possible, but the poor boy's embarrassment was contagious. Afterwards she'd wondered guiltily if perhaps she'd somehow given him any encouragement – unconsciously, of course. The truth was she did enjoy his company. Theresa had come to look on her supervisions with Horatio as one of the highlights of her week, though in the past she'd always put that down to the thrill of working with an undergraduate capable of challenging her intellectually, of pushing the boundaries. Well, now the boundaries had been well and truly pushed. It was her job, her responsibility, to push them back. Even so, she couldn't help but take a tiny sliver of pleasure from the fact that this kind, brilliant, golden boy had fallen for *her* of all people. At her age, it was quite a compliment.

Then there was the day's other compliment, at the other end of the scale, Jean Paul's suggestion that she apply for the St Michael's Mastership. Theresa wasn't sure which fantasy was the more impossible to picture. Herself as Mrs Horatio Hollander, skipping down the aisle in a white dress, or herself taking the Master's seat at St Michael's high table. Both thoughts – the white dress and St Michael's – drew her mind back to Theo.

Theresa was no longer in love with him. Those days, mercifully, had passed. But occasionally, especially after a few glasses of Bordeaux, or when she saw pictures of his and Dita's adorable little children, fragile, blond Milo and the chubby-cheeked little girl, Francesca, she felt a sort of wistful nostalgia. *Those could have been my children,* she would think, before realizing that of course they couldn't, and that it was ridiculous and wrong to project her own frustrations or regrets onto two perfectly innocent little people whom she hadn't even met, and likely never would.

Tonight, as sleep crept over her, she wondered about Theo. Where he was right now, this moment, as she lay in bed in Grantchester. What he was thinking. She thought of how amazed he'd be if he were to read that she, Theresa O'Connor, had become Master of his old college.

As pipe dreams went, it was a good one.

CHAPTER SEVENTEEN

Jackson Dupree stood at the altar, staring down at his shoes on the polished parquet floor.

'You OK?' James Dermott, Jackson's second cousin and longest-standing childhood friend, nudged him in the ribs. 'Not thinking of doing a runner, are you?'

Jackson turned around. Behind him, over two hundred guests crammed into the pews of St Andrew's Episcopal Church, overdressed in garish hats and feathers and finery. More hovered at the back and in the side chapels, straining to catch a glimpse of the bride who had bagged herself the most eligible catch in Martha's Vineyard, and quite possibly the whole of America.

'I'd never make it out of here alive,' he joked. 'I'm trapped.'

Turning back to face the front, he started fiddling with his tie. The stiff collar of his formal shirt made him feel as if he was suffocating. At least, he chose to blame it on the collar.

'She'll be here in a minute,' said James. 'Do some deep breathing. Think of your happy place.'

My happy place, thought Jackson. *Isn't that supposed to be here? On my wedding day? The happiest day of my life?*

A collective gasp from the crowd indicated that the bride had arrived. Seconds later, the string quartet that Jackson's mother had hired from the Boston Philharmonic struck up the opening bars of the wedding march. *This is it.*

The last five years had been five of the most magical, and traumatic, of Jackson Dupree's gilded young life. When Sasha Miller spun off Wrexall Dupree's retail division to form Ceres, the company she walked out on was changed instantly and irrevocably. As Jackson predicted, the market soon forgot about the McKinley deal and the millions of dollars of revenue it had brought them. Instead investors and pundits alike watched with interest to see just *how* the new, slimmed-down Wrexall would compete; what their next move would be; and whether they would, as Jackson Dupree had famously and publicly threatened, 'go after' Ceres with all the fury of a lover scorned. Market-watchers hovered over Wrexall, not like an anxious parent concerned with its offspring's progress, but like a pack of vultures circling above their prey until they were quite sure it was dead.

In the first six months, the vultures almost got their way. While Ceres clocked up deal after deal, the seemingly unstoppable new kid on the block, Wrexall struggled to rebuild in retail real estate. First, their attempt to hire the CEO of Cityfleet.com, the online commercial real estate giant, backfired spectacularly and publicly when an overenthusiastic headhunter leaked information about his proposed multi-million-dollar compensation package to the press. Next they made the mistake of going head to head with Ceres over a transaction with Westfield, the Australian shopping mall giant, for a new mall outside Los Angeles.

'I don't understand,' Bob Massey complained to the head

of Westfield's West Coast operations when he called to tell him Wrexall's pitch had been unsuccessful. 'That was a strong pitch. You've been partners with us for over eight years, David.'

'Yeah. And everyone I dealt with at Wrexall for the last four of those years is now at Ceres. I'm sorry, Bob. It's nothing personal. But Sasha Miller really understands our goals.'

It was after Westfield fell through that the decline in Wrexall's stock price began in earnest. By that time they had belatedly rebuilt a retail division, hiring from all their key competitors (other than Ceres) and even bringing in fresh blood from other sectors, investment bankers and private equity guys. But it was too little, too late. If it hadn't been for Jackson's thriving hotels division and the gains they'd made in the residential sector, things might have got very bad indeed. As it was, they survived the year, bruised but still fighting and, at least in Jackson Dupree's case, determined to bring Ceres down.

'You know, they say the opposite of love isn't hate. It's indifference,' said Lottie over dinner with Jackson one evening. They'd been dating for a year by this point, and give or take a few slip-ups in the first few weeks, Jackson had been faithful, a personal best that those who knew him well viewed as little short of miraculous.

'You're maturing,' James Dermott told him.

'Bullshit. I've always been mature. I just never had a reason to stay faithful before. Now I do.'

This was partly true. Lottie had certainly played her cards well, firstly by refusing to move in with Jackson and secondly by quitting Wrexall Dupree and finding herself a new, highly paid job at a chic uptown art gallery. 'We can't sleep together and work together,' she told Jackson, presenting her resignation as a *fait accompli*.

'What do you mean? Of course we can. We've been doing it for six months, haven't we? It's been working out fine.'

'Not for me it hasn't,' said Lottie. 'You're my boyfriend, not my boss. *I'm* my boss.' Jackson pretended to be pissed off for a week, but Lottie completely ignored his cold shoulder so in the end he gave up. Besides, deep down he loved the fact that she was independent, that she challenged him. Deep down, he still occasionally worried that there was something missing between them. Sex was fine. It was regular and enjoyable, if a little on the straight side, at least in comparison to Jackson's prior tastes. But it lacked the spark, the passion, the addictive adrenaline rush he'd spent most of his adult life pursuing.

That's why this relationship is working, Jackson told himself firmly. *You like Lottie. You respect her. She's the best friend you always wanted, the sister you never had, the business partner you always needed . . . AND she's hot. Stop analyzing it to death and get on with it.*

Tonight, he'd taken Lottie out to Nobu in Tribeca to try to take his mind off of Ceres's latest triumph – their quarterly results, published today, had hugely outperformed even the most bullish analysts' estimates, and Sasha was once again riding high. As usual, Lottie did her best to calm him down.

'Have you ever thought the best revenge you could hope to have on Sasha would be to ignore her? Indifference, that's the key. Forget about Ceres. Focus on Wrexall, focus on your own business.'

Jackson speared a California roll morosely with his chopstick, wantonly destroying the sushi chef's work of art.

'The more energy you waste on hating Sasha . . .' Lottie continued

'I don't hate Sasha.'

Lottie raised an eyebrow, as if to say *not much.* 'Then why are you going after Raj Patel?'

Raj Patel, once Sasha's direct line manager at Wrexall, now worked for her as a key member of her senior management team at Ceres. Indian, Oxford educated, and devastatingly handsome in a softly spoken, intellectual Imran Khan sort of way, Raj had become almost as much the 'face' of Ceres as Sasha herself. The two of them were often photographed together, Sasha creamy skinned and seductive beneath her sleek black bob, and Raj dark and regal, his fine bone structure and strong aquiline nose belying his upper-class Indian heritage. If they ever got together sexually they'd make the world's most beautiful kids.

'That's business,' said Jackson. 'At Ceres, Raj will always play second fiddle to Sasha. Back with us he could run his own show.'

It sounded plausible. But Lottie didn't buy it. Out of loyalty to Jackson, she'd quietly dropped her own friendship with Sasha. There was no big bust up, no announcement. Both women understood implicitly that, after all that had happened, it was the way it had to be. Ironically, it was Jackson who kept Sasha's memory alive, to the point where Lottie sometimes felt, like Princess Diana, that there were three people in her relationship. Jackson hadn't seen Sasha in person for a year, but he carried her with him everywhere, lodged in his chest like a tumour. His attempts to poach back Raj Patel was just the latest in a long line of stunts aimed at hurting Sasha, humiliating her the way that she had humiliated him. Lottie prayed it wouldn't backfire as badly as all the others.

'About Raj,' said Jackson. 'I'm thinking of flying out to Barcelona next week.'

Lottie's eyes widened. 'You're not serious?' *Forbes* had

reported only last week that Ceres was holding its first global off site at the Hotel Majestic in Barcelona, Spain. Sasha Miller was to be the keynote speaker at a real estate conference that would be attended by the biggest names in the industry. 'You can't hijack Raj there, it's far too high profile. Remember what happened with Mr Cityfleet? If Raj doesn't come back to Wrexall, you'll end up with very public egg on your face. You're supposed to be being discreet.'

'I will be discreet,' said Jackson, knocking back the last of his sake and ordering another. 'I'll discreetly get him to sign his offer in Barcelona. Then I'll discreetly hold a press conference about it the morning of Sasha's speech and pull the rug out from under her Manolos.'

Lottie sighed. There was no reasoning with him in this mood: drunk and determined. She wished she could love away all the stress and anger Jackson seemed to carry around with him, like a backpack full of cement. Like him, in her darkest moments, she feared that there was something missing between them. There had to be, or he would have let go by now, given himself to her completely. But like him, Lottie put her fears aside. *I love him,* she thought. *He's already changed so much, come so far from the old playboy Jackson. This vendetta with Sasha is the last piece of the puzzle. He'll figure it out eventually, I just have to be patient.*

Sasha stepped out onto her balcony into the warm, Spanish night air and sighed a deep sigh of contentment. Barcelona had been one of her favourite cities since she came here as a teenager, on a school trip with St Agnes's. She remembered the wonder she'd felt back then, at the spectacular Gaudí architecture and the Plaça de Catalunya, not to mention the natural beauty of the ocean. There was a palpable sense of vibrancy in Barcelona, a feeling of life and youth and art that seemed to shimmer in the warm air along with the scent of jasmine and the mixed, mouthwatering smells of garlic and chorizo floating up from the tapas kitchens. As a school-girl, she and her friends from St Agnes's had stayed in a grotty little youth hostel, but Sasha had still adored the city. Now, returning not just as an adult but as a millionairess, a success beyond her or anyone's wildest dreams, she was staying in the most expensive suite at the Hotel Majestic, a neoclassical gem on Passeig de Gràcia that lit up at night like Harrods at Christmas time. Wealthy and famous visitors flocked to the Majestic to sample the Michelin-starred cuisine at the hotel's famed Drolma restaurant, widely considered one of the finest in Spain, and to enjoy its dated grandeur and old-world luxury. Sasha chose it because she remem-bered walking past it as a kid and wondering what the views must be like from the penthouse.

Now she knew. They were spectacular.

Tomorrow she had a full schedule of team-building events with her staff at Ceres. It was hard to believe that the company was only a year old. Already they had blazed a trail through the industry so bright that competitors twice their size and with ten times their experience had been left blinded on the sidelines, wondering what the hell just happened as Ceres won contract after contract, deal after deal. The media gave Sasha full credit for their successes, hailing her as America's new business genius, a female role model to rival Oprah or Martha Stewart. No one seemed to remember, or care, that she was, in fact, English. Not when she looked so ridiculously photogenic, standing arm in arm with her right-hand man, Raj Patel. A young woman and an Indian man; it was so politically correct, so perfect, it was as if Ceres had been dreamt up by someone at Central Casting. While the trade press salivated over Ceres's profits and Sasha's business acumen, the fashion magazines pored over her wardrobe choices, and the gossip rags speculated endlessly about her love life, or rather her mysterious lack thereof. A few months ago, someone had leaked the story of Sasha's scandalous past, and her connection to Theo Dexter, to one of the tabloids. Sasha suspected Jackson Dupree. True to his word, Jackson had pulled every stunt in the book to try to undermine her, personally and professionally, since she left Wrexall, but so far Sasha had managed to stay one step ahead. The stolen-theory story could have been a serious blow to her reputation and credibility. But with the help of a woman named Gemma Driscoll, a senior partner at the PR giant Fleishman-Hillard (and as far as Sasha was concerned, a genius) the mountain had morphed back into a molehill, '*Neutralized*,' as Gemma put it.

'The trick is never to try to cover up a story,' Gemma told Sasha. 'If a dog's got a juicy bone in its jaws and you start pulling, all he's going to do is clamp down harder.'

'So what do you do?'

Gemma smiled. 'Toss him a juicier bone.'

This she did by the simple but devastatingly effective means of falsely linking Sasha romantically with a string of eligible, newsworthy men. First there was the senator whose house Sasha went to once for dinner.

'I play tennis with his wife!' she insisted. 'He wasn't even home.'

'Ah, yes, but he might have been,' said Gemma.

Then there was the pop star, the Broadway producer, the Italian prince and the twenty-one-year-old heartthrob from NBC's new prime-time soap opera, *Brooklyn Heights*. Of course, there wasn't a thread of truth to any of the rumours. Sasha slept alone, with only her BlackBerry for company. But the stories served their purpose of distracting tabloid attention. Gemma finished the job with a series of 'teasers' about Sasha and Raj Patel, photo opportunities and interviews that suggested they might be a couple. *That* was the most ridiculous one of all. But as Gemma pointed out, 'The beauty of it is that it can run and run. You'll continue to be seen together. People will keep guessing. You're a public figure now, Sasha. You have to think of your life as a sort of reality show.'

'Reality?' Sasha laughed out loud. 'But everything you're doing is made up!'

'Exactly. Like I said. A reality show. I write the scripts.'

It was new world for Sasha, and one that, though she loathed to admit it, she found she rather enjoyed. She'd started Ceres for the same reason she joined Wrexall, the same reason she transferred to business school and moved to America: to become rich and powerful enough to destroy Theo Dexter. But as the years wore on, particularly with Ceres succeeding so spectacularly right out of the gate, she found the business becoming more and more of an end in itself.

Then, of course, there was Jackson. Every time Sasha got close to a deal, every time she made a hire or sniffed around some land, there he would be, bribing, badmouthing, conniving, doing everything he could do scupper her chances. Ceres was on a high right now, but Sasha had no illusions. At some point their new-kid-on-the-block sheen would wear off. Wrexall had multiples of their balance sheet. There would be instances, many instances, where Jackson would be able to outgun her. The fact that it hadn't happened yet only heightened the anxiety she felt daily, squatting in her chest like a loathsome toad, still and cold and heavy but always ready to pounce.

'Beautiful evening.'

Sasha spun around so fast she almost jumped out of her skin. There, standing on the adjacent balcony, looking lean and tanned in an immaculately cut Spurr suit and Harvard tie, stood Jackson Dupree. *It's like I jinxed myself. I thought about him and made him appear. Like summoning an evil genie.*

'It was,' she said coldly. 'What the hell are you doing here? Stalking me?'

'Hardly.' Jackson smiled. Suddenly Sasha felt like Little Red Riding Hood. *If he could he'd leap over here and eat me.* 'I have business here. A new hotel. Right opposite La Sagrada Família.'

'You'll never get permissions,' said Sasha. *He's cut his hair! I don't believe it. That's like Samson cutting his hair. Or Steven Tyler from Aerosmith.*

'Already got 'em.'

'Land'll be overpriced.' *It suits him though. I wonder if Lottie made him do it?*

'It's a luxury hotel.'

'Location's far too tacky for a high-end hotel. La Sagrada's the number-one attraction in the city. Fat kids in backpacks hanging around outside day and night, dropping chewing gum and crisp packets. It's like building a Ritz Carlton in Trafalgar Square.'

'Thanks for the advice,' said Jackson smoothly. 'It's been a while, Sasha.'

Sasha glared at him. 'Not long enough.'

'How are you?'

'I'm fine, thank you. I *was* fine. Goodnight, Jackson.' Turning on her heel, Sasha walked back into her suite, slamming the balcony doors behind her.

Arsehole. Luxury hotel, my arse. If he's here on Wrexall business, I'm Mahatma Gandhi. He's up to something.

She ordered room service and tried to settle down to the

mountainous pile of work she had to get through before tomorrow. But knowing Jackson was in the suite next door made it impossible to concentrate. *He looked so damn smug. What does he have to look smug about?* At one point she was sure she heard his shower turn on. As hard as she tried, it was impossible not to picture him naked, lathering shampoo onto his newly short, preppy haircut. He looked different to how she remembered him. The suit, the hair, the manner. *He's less of a boy and more of a man.* Sasha wondered whether that was Lottie's influence, and felt a pang of something painful. She hoped that it was her missing Lottie's friendship, but feared it might be something much more ugly: jealousy. Not that she was jealous of Lottie having Jackson. *I wouldn't want Jackson Dupree if he were the last man on the face of the earth. It can't be that. Maybe I'm jealous of other people having love in their life. Of other people being happy.*

On an impulse, she called Raj's room, but there was no answer. Disappointed, and irritated with herself, she put the work aside, popped a sleeping pill and defiantly turned out the lights. It was only 8.30 p.m., but she had a big day tomorrow. Barcelona was *her* city, this was *her* off site, *her* conference, *her* time to shine. Jackson could try his childish mind games until he was blue in the face. But he wouldn't ruin Barcelona for her. She wouldn't let him.

Raj Patel sat at an outdoor table at a quiet coffee shop on Barcelona beach, wondering if he needed to get his ears syringed.

'I'm sorry, Jackson. I think I must have misheard you. Did you just say fifteen million dollars? Fifteen as in one-five? Million as in *million*?' Raj's clipped British accent cut through the early-morning air like a scimitar.

Jackson sipped his espresso. 'It's a three-year package.'

'Guaranteed?'

'Of course. Guaranteed. Remember, you'd be running retail for us, lock stock and barrel. Given where we are today, and where I know we could be with you at the helm, I'd be disappointed if you didn't out earn those numbers.'

Fifteen million dollars. Fifteen million, guaranteed. I could fuck up as much as I like, make every wrong decision in the book, and I'd still get paid. Raj had always thought of himself as a risk taker. No, to hell with that, he *was* a risk taker. He'd taken a huge chance, tying his star to Sasha's and jumping to Ceres on nothing more than a wing and a prayer. That risk had paid off, in spades. Not only had it catapulted his career into the big leagues, but it had been a wild exhilarating ride, and Raj had loved every minute of it, the deals, the press attention, the camaraderie. Sasha Miller was a machine when it came to work – she never stopped – but somehow she still managed to make the atmosphere at Ceres fun. They were a young company, and a crazily young management team. No one missed the stuffiness at Wrexall, nor the bullying from the ageing, greedy board. Least of all Raj. There was more to life than money.

On the other hand . . .

'You're getting married, aren't you?' Jackson leaned back in his chair, stretching his long legs languidly like the king that he was.

'How'd you know that?'

'A little bird. How does your fiancée feel about all the brouhaha in the papers about you and Sasha?'

Raj stiffened. 'She couldn't care less. She knows it's all rubbish.'

'Really?' Jackson raised an eyebrow.

'Yes, really. We're colleagues, that's all.'

For some reason, Jackson felt relieved. *That'll make it easier to land Raj,* he told himself. *If they really were lovers, no amount of money would shift him.*

'Talk to your fiancée about the offer,' said Jackson. 'See what she thinks you should do.'

Raj laughed. 'Oh, I get it. "Honey, should I accept a cheque for fifteen million dollars no questions asked, or keep working on commission for a beautiful woman that half of America thinks I'm boning?" That's what you want me to ask her, right?'

Jackson laughed back. He genuinely liked Raj. Talking to him this morning, he realized how much he missed having him at Wrexall. With Sasha and Lottie both gone too, all the excitement had been sucked out of the place. 'Something like that,' he admitted. 'It's the truth isn't it? They tell me all the best marriages are based on trust.'

Raj's face fell. 'I'm tempted. Of course I am. But what about Sasha? She trusts me.'

Jackson put down his coffee and leaned across the table, like a chess grand master moving in for checkmate. 'Sasha is a businesswoman. At least, that's what she told *me* when she ripped the fucking guts out of my company, the company that gave her a start, the company that made her.' Raj was silent. Jackson had a right to be angry, but even so, seeing his rage in action was frightening. It was like a living thing, a being in its own right, hovering in the air between them like some malevolent moth. 'You're a young guy, Raj.'

'Young-ish. I'm thirty-three.'

'You're about to start a family and you have your own life to think about, your own career. Ceres has had an amazing start. You were a big part of that. But it will always be Sasha Miller's baby, and you know it. I'm offering you a chance to be master of your own destiny, at a firm with a century-old brand behind it. All the autonomy, all the financial upside and none of the risk. Sasha, of all people, understands what it is to be made an offer you can't refuse. This is it, my friend. This is it.'

He was right. Of course he was right. When Raj left Wrexall he was on nine hundred grand a year. That was less than fourteen months ago. He stared into the dregs of his coffee cup. 'I just don't know how I'm going to tell Sasha . . .'

'You aren't,' said Jackson firmly. 'I can have the contracts with you in an hour, but they're contingent on complete confidentiality. You say nothing. *I'll* handle Sasha.'

Back at the Majestic, Sasha was having a thoroughly enjoyable day with the Ceres staff, going over the past year's highlights and brainstorming their plans for the future. Raj had mysteriously disappeared, going for a run before breakfast and conspicuously failing to return. But Sasha was on too much of a high to care. Besides, Raj had earned the break. A large portion of her speech to the conference tomorrow would be dedicated to thanking him personally for his incredible contribution to Ceres's early success. Without Raj there she was free to ask the rest of the team for suggestions, little jokes and anecdotes that might help spice up her address. Though she wouldn't have admitted it publicly, Sasha had a fear of public speaking that bordered on the pathological. It was one of the reasons – one of the many – that she could have done without Jackson Dupree's presence. As if she weren't nervous enough already, without having to see his spiteful face in the crowd, willing her to trip up or say something foolish.

She'd half expected to see Jackson this morning at breakfast, and had made sure she looked immaculate just in case, washing and blow drying her hair and putting on her sexiest

Myla underwear, a feminine touch that always made her feel powerful and in control. *Nothing says world domination like a matching bra and knickers,* she thought to herself, laughing because of course it was ridiculous, but then wasn't everything about her life these days? When she walked into the breakfast buffet at eight thirty in a simple but sexy L'Wren Scott sheath dress, every male head turned to stare at her. But Jackson's wasn't one of them. After going to so much trouble, she felt oddly disappointed. Perhaps he really did have some hotel deal in the works, and had simply chosen to stay at the Majestic to irritate her? *Who cares what his motives are? Forget about him.*

She decided she would have dinner alone that night. Most of the Ceres crowd were heading into the old city for a night of drinking and dancing, but none of them had to give a speech tomorrow. Besides, Sasha had grown used to her own company over the years. She looked forward to eating alone, discovering new restaurants in exciting foreign cities, the way that other women might look forward to a romantic meal with a new boyfriend. Armed with a book or occasionally, as a guilty pleasure, a furtive copy of the *New Scientist* or *Physics Today,* she would settle down with a glass of Rioja and a plate of serrano ham and watch the world go by. Bliss.

After showering and changing into a simple, pretty floral sundress and sandals, she came down into the lobby, sticking her head round the door at the last minute on the off chance of catching the elusive Raj. Instead she saw Jackson, leaning against the bar in jeans and a faded grey t-shirt. He was saying goodbye to an older man, a Spaniard. Sasha was just about to creep away when Jackson glanced up and saw her.

'Sasha. Come on in. Can I offer you a drink?'

All this faux niceness was disarming. If she refused, she

would look churlish. If she accepted, he'd probably lace whatever she asked for with strychnine.

'This is Manuel Hormaeche. He's with Encerro, the company that sold us the land for that hotel I mentioned.'

So there is a hotel.

The Spaniard took Sasha's hand and kissed it. From an American or a Brit the gesture would have seemed forward, even creepy, but the Spanish seemed to do these things with such elegance. 'I look forward very much to your speech tomorrow, Miss Miller.' He pronounced it 'Mealer'. 'You 'ave done miraculous things with Ceres.'

'Thank you.' Sasha blushed. Jackson watched her as she chatted politely to Sr Hormaeche, exchanging business cards before the older man left. She looked different tonight. Perhaps it was the girlish dress? That and the lack of make-up, the flat shoes, the sweet, almost shy way she accepted the Spaniard's compliments. He had rarely seen this side to Sasha, the vulnerable, feminine side. It disturbed him.

'Two glasses of champagne please,' he heard himself saying. For some reason, he didn't want Sasha to leave.

'What are we celebrating?' Warily, she sat down beside him. 'Did you two finalize the deal?'

Jackson's stomach lurched. For one, mad moment he thought she was talking about Raj Patel. Then he realized she couldn't be. She must mean Hormaeche and the La Sagrada hotel. 'Not yet. But we will do.' The drinks arrived. He handed an ice-cold flute to Sasha. 'Manuel knows it's the best offer he'd going to get for that land. He's playing hard to get, but he'll give in eventually.'

Their eyes met. Sasha looked away first.

Since the night Sasha left Wrexall – the night Jackson had kissed her and she'd pulled away; the same night he'd got together with Lottie – Jackson had worked hard to stifle his desire for her. From that night onwards, he'd grown up. It was really very simple: Lottie was good for him; Sasha was bad. Lottie was loyal and supportive and loving; Sasha was a snake, a backstabber, a dangerous competitor who needed to be destroyed. Channelling all his sexual frustration into his efforts to undermine Ceres and rebuild Wrexall, he'd convinced himself that Sasha Miller no longer meant anything to him personally. But watching Hormaeche flirt with her before, he'd suddenly felt like a sixteen-year-old again. It was all he could do not to get up and punch the guy.

You need to beat her, that's all. Then she'll be out of your system.

Raj Patel's defection would devastate Sasha. Springing it on her here, tomorrow, in front of the entire industry, would ensure that the blow had maximum impact. It was the revenge Jackson had been waiting for, planning and fantasizing about for twelve long months. So why did he suddenly feel as if all the pleasure had been sucked out of it?

Sasha sipped at her champagne, cursing herself for feeling so awkward and praying that Jackson couldn't tell. Not knowing what else to say, she asked after Lottie.

'How is she? I hear she's running an art gallery now.'

Instantly Jackson's face clouded over. 'She's fine. She's well.'

'And the two of you?'

'We're good.'

Conversation closed.

For a full minute, neither of them said anything. At last Sasha drained her glass and got down from her bar stool. 'Thank you for the drink. Good luck with your deal.' She started to walk away.

Jackson called after her, 'Thanks. Good luck with your speech tomorrow, if I don't see you.'

Something about his tone of voice made Sasha uneasy. She looked at him, but his face was as blankly handsome as ever and gave nothing away. *You're imagining things,* she told herself. *He'll probably be gone by morning.*

Sasha woke at 3 a.m., 4 a.m. and 5 a.m., tormented by disturbing dreams in which she appeared on the podium naked, while Jackson Dupree pointed and laughed at her from the front row. At 5.15 a.m., unable to get back to sleep, she put on her running shoes and went out for a jog through Barcelona's deserted streets. The city looked totally different at this time, its cobbled alleys bathed in soft dawn light. The smells were different too, delicious aromas of baking bread and coffee combined with the rancid smell of fish from the restaurant rubbish bins, wheeled out for the early-morning garbage collectors. Sasha ran until her limbs ached and her mind was blank. Coming back into the hotel, she bumped into Raj Patel walking out.

'Hey, stranger,' she joked. 'What happened to you yesterday? I was starting to worry you'd been abducted by aliens.'

'Sorry,' Raj mumbled. 'I . . . something came up. Something personal. I got caught up.'

He looked away when he spoke to her, as if he were embarrassed, or even afraid. Sasha had never seen him look so awkward. 'Is everything OK?'

'Of course. Everything's fine. It's just . . . like I said, it's personal.'

'You'll be at the conference this afternoon, though, right?' asked Sasha. 'I could really use the support. You know public speaking scares the shit out of me.' During her sleepless night, she'd mentally rewritten the whole middle section of her speech into what she hoped would be a funny but inspiring little homily about teamwork. Half way through she was going to haul poor Raj up out of the audience like a magician's volunteer. Without him, the whole thing would fall flat.

'Sure,' said Raj. 'I'll be there.'

'Seriously,' Sasha smiled. 'I need you. Don't let me down.'

Raj walked away, wondering if it were too late to have Wrexall change the terms of his new contract to include a bonus of thirty pieces of silver.

The conference room at the Hotel Majestic was a grand former ballroom, high ceilinged and ornate with gilt inlaid panelling and a dais flanked by sumptuous, deep-red velvet curtains. By 2 p.m. the floor was packed with delegates, the most important seated at the front at round tables sponsored by their various companies, and the less well known fighting over the rows of plush cushioned chairs lining the middle and back of the room. Behind the dais, a large white screen had been erected to project a magnified image of each speaker's face to the more remote members of the audience.

Lunch had been served at 1 p.m., to the chagrin of the locals who viewed this as breakfast time, and a couple of dull speeches had been delivered while everybody ate paella and, in the case of the British and French delegates, got heavily stuck into the free-flowing Chablis. Waiting in the wings in a dark blue Balenciaga trouser suit, nervously scanning her speech cards for the hundredth time, Sasha could have murdered a stiff drink herself. It was only the thought of slurring her words in front of Jackson Dupree that made her hold back. *Afterwards,* she promised herself. *As soon as I step off that podium, I'll order a scotch.* Only a couple of minutes to go now.

Carlos Gallo, the dapper CEO of the Spanish real estate

giant Explorador and the master of ceremonies at today's event, tapped Sasha on the shoulder.

'Change of plan, *cariña*. We 'ave one other speaker now before you.'

Sasha felt sick. 'But I . . . I'm ready now. What other speaker? Can't they go later?'

'Unfortunately not. Mr Dupree 'as a plane to catch in a couple of hours. I know a lot of our attendees would want to hear Wrexall Dupree's take on the European market. Mr Dupree was kind enough to offer to say a few words and then introduce you.'

Peering through the throng of faces, Sasha saw Jackson a few rows back. He was chatting and laughing with a syco-phantic huddle of Eurotrash as if he hadn't a care in the world. Some sixth sense made him look up and catch her staring. He flashed her a maddening smile.

Before she had time to protest any further, Carlos Gallo was gone. She felt her sleeve being tugged. Someone was pulling her further back into the shadows, away from the stage. Turning around, she saw it was Raj.

'I don't believe it.' Sasha was shaking, close to tears. 'That bastard Jackson's asked to speak, *now*. He knows how hard I find this. He's done it deliberately! He's trying to throw me off.'

'I'm afraid it's worse than that,' said Raj grimly. 'Listen, Sash, there's something I've got to tell you . . .'

Two hours later and Jackson Dupree's roar could be heard through the floors of his eighth-floor suite, shaking light fixtures in the rooms below.

'You *fucker!*' he bellowed. 'You swore to me you wouldn't say anything! I hope you realize that your contract's now null and void? I'm not hiring you and I'm not paying you a damned penny. FUCK!' He banged his fist on the antique writing desk so hard it cracked like a stick of kindling. Raj, as ever, kept his cool. Jackson might want to throw his toys out of the cot because he'd failed to publicly derail Sasha, but Raj doubted the rest of the Wrexall board would back him.

'Don't be so childish, Jackson. You know I'm the best man for Wrexall. That's why you made me the offer in the first place. Clearly the board agrees or they'd never have signed off on the package.'

'I *trusted* you,' Jackson fumed. 'You warned her. You fucking warned her!'

'Yes, I warned her. She's my friend, and what you were trying to pull was just a shitty thing to do. You might not care whether the world thinks you're a card-carrying wanker, but *I* do. You were right, me leaving Ceres for Wrexall *was* a business decision. And I don't regret it. But throwing Sasha to the wolves like that? That's not business. That's spite. You know speaking in public terrifies her. It's that kind of shit that made us all leave Wrexall in the first place.'

'GET OUT!' Jackson yelled at him. 'Get the hell out of my sight!'

'Fine,' said Raj, unruffled. 'But you'd better get your shit together, Jackson. Or, money or no money, I *will* walk away. I *will* stay at Ceres – and don't kid yourself Sasha wouldn't have me back in a heartbeat – and I'll make sure the world, and the Wrexall board, knows why.'

He walked out, shutting the door behind him firmly but gently. In Jackson's current mood, even that felt like an affront. *Why can't he lose his cool like a normal fucking human being? Why can't he slam the door, or yell back. Why do I have to be the only jerk around here?* He kicked the leg of the desk he'd just broken and winced at the pain in his shin. He knew

Raj was right. He was being childish. And spiteful. And ridiculous. But he didn't care.

Jackson had taken the podium earlier full of confidence, praising Ceres for their innovative business philosophy while simultaneously undermining them brilliantly, constantly stressing their youth and inexperience versus Wrexall's maturity, longevity and rock-solid financial pedigree. Unlike Sasha, Jackson was an inspired speaker. Had he not gone into the family business he'd have made a terrific politician, masterfully shredding his opponents without landing any obvious or overt blows. In this case, however, after a carefully crafted speech that successfully belittled Sasha's achievements, he launched a full-frontal nuclear strike in the form of Raj Patel, whom he invited onstage, introducing him to a shocked audience and industry press as Wrexall's latest star hire.

Stepping down to gasps and thunderous applause, Jackson had taken his seat in the front row like a Roman emperor, waiting to watch Sasha being thrown to the lions. But instead of stammering confusion, he found himself watching a poised, thoughtful and above all gracious Sasha, deliver a speech that ultimately won her a six-minute standing ovation. Discarding everything she'd prepared, she spoke from the heart. About how much she owed Raj Patel, and how much she owed Wrexall Dupree. About how, as a young, experimental company, Ceres always pushed its people to accept new challenges, to move forward and be all that they could be. She joked about the tabloids painting her and Raj as a couple, pondering aloud whom she might be linked with next. 'I hear Rafael Nadal's single again,' she quipped, to ecstatic applause (the home-grown Spanish tennis champ had won the US Open two days before). 'Maybe I should stay in Spain for a while and work on my backhand?'

Seething with fury in the front row, the tennis analogy stuck in Jackson's throat. He'd just served Sasha what ought to have been a sure-fire ace. But here she was, lobbing it back to him with the effortless grace of a champion. So much for the element of surprise.

Up in his suite, the phone rang. Jackson answered with a snarl. 'Fuck off, I'm busy.'

'Aren't we all?' Lucius Monroe's reedy, elderly voice had lost none of its dry, sardonic humour. He didn't miss a beat. 'I was calling to congratulate you on landing Raj Patel. That's a great hire for us.'

'Thank you,' said Jackson grudgingly.

'You don't sound very happy about it, dear boy.'

'Sorry, Lucius. It's been a long day.'

'Well, go out and celebrate. Better yet, get Patel to pick up the tab. He can afford it on what we're about to pay him.'

Jackson hung up. Raj *was* a great hire. He knew he should be pleased, and focused on the bigger picture. But all he could think about was Sasha and the way this afternoon's conference crowd had lapped her up. Raj's defection should have been, at the very least, a PR nightmare for Ceres. But once again, Sasha had managed to turn things around.

The phone rang again. *If one more person calls to congratulate me, I'm pulling the cord out of the wall.* 'Yes?'

'You cunt.' Sasha's voice was quiet, but Jackson could feel the rage quivering in every breath. 'It wasn't enough for you to go after Raj. You had to try to humiliate me too, as publicly and painfully as possible. You knew how much I was dreading that speech!'

'Yes, well, thanks to Mr Patel's bleeding heart I never got the chance, did I? So I don't know what you're bitching about.'

'Don't know what I'm *bitching* about?' Sasha sounded as if she was about to erupt. 'Get over here.'

'Excuse me?'

'I said get over here! Walk next door to my room and tell me to my face that you don't know what I'm bitching about. You're a fucking coward, Jackson.' She hung up.

Six seconds later, Jackson was pounding at the door of her suite. *Coward, indeed. She thinks I'm afraid to face her? I'll face her. I'll tell her exactly what I think of her, right to her face.*

'I'm not here to apologize,' he announced defiantly. 'So if that's what you're hoping for you can kiss my ass.' Sasha had opened the door in a hotel bathrobe with a towel tied turban-style on top of her head. Clearly fresh out of the shower, she had no make-up on and looked more like an incensed fourteen-year-old who's just had her pocket money stopped than a beleaguered CEO. Jackson was just thinking how strangely sweet she looked when a sharp slap across the face sent him reeling. 'What the fuck?' He clasped his stinging cheek. 'You hit me!'

Sasha didn't answer, but let out a shriek that sounded like some sort of Maori war cry and flung herself at Jackson, punching, biting, kicking, flailing at him with her nails like a wildcat. 'You arsehole! You fucking arsehole!' It was so unexpected that at first Jackson barely reacted. In those few, precious moments of confusion, Sasha scratched at his face like a lunatic and landed one agonizing kick to his groin.

Jesus, he thought. *She's trying to kill me.*

By the time he regained strength and composure enough to overpower her, his face was covered in welts and the beginnings of a plum-coloured bruise was already forming on his forearm. Pinning her arms behind her back, he picked her up, legs still thrashing wildly, and put her on the bed face down, straddling her and holding her in place like a wrestler.

'Enough,' he panted. He released his grip a little and Sasha immediately spun around and bit him hard on the wrist. It was agony. 'Jesus!' Jackson screamed, restraining her again, harder this time with his knee in the small of her back. 'Stop it, Sasha. This is ridiculous. It's completely fucking ridiculous.' Beneath him he could feel her breathing slow and her muscles start to release. If he was exhausted, she must be about to pass out. Tentatively, he let go again and this time she made no attempt to relaunch the attack. Instead she turned and looked up at him, tears streaming down her face. Jackson was shocked. She'd never shown so much as one ounce of vulnerability in front of him before and now here she was *crying*. *Because of me?*

His voice softened. 'Hey, don't. Please. Look, I'm sorry, OK? Maybe I went too far.'

Sasha shook her head, too choked up to speak. Jackson didn't understand. How could he? What if losing Raj Patel was the turning point, the jinx, the beginning of the end for Ceres, or at least the end of their incredible beginning? For Jackson, business was a game. It was all about ego. Not for Sasha. All the adulation, the money, the fame, they meant nothing in themselves. They were a means to an end, an end that she already felt slipping from her grasp – getting her revenge on Theo Dexter. Somehow, in ways she couldn't explain, Jackson had come between her and Theo. Between her and her destiny, her purpose, her reason for existing. She wasn't crying about Raj Patel or even some stupid speech. She was crying because she didn't know who she was any more.

'I wanted to beat you.' Jackson's voice broke her train of thought. He sounded embarrassed. 'Just once. I wanted to beat you completely.'

'You did beat me,' muttered Sasha. 'You got Raj. Wasn't that enough?'

'No. It wasn't. I wanted to make you look a fool, the way you made me look a fool last year; in front of the entire industry. I wanted . . .' He looked her in the eye, and she knew he was telling her the truth. 'I wanted you to suffer because of *me*. The same way I suffer because of you.'

Sasha's tears stopped. She looked back at him. Still kneeling over her on the bed, she could feel the pressure of his legs against hers, his body warm from the exertion of fighting her off. Her eyes were drawn up, over his lean, suited torso to his face, the strong outline of his jaw jutting out like a ledge at the top of a cliff.

'I make you suffer?' she asked.

His hands stroked her tear-stained cheeks. 'Every day.'

Afterwards, both of them would try to remember how it had happened: who kissed who first? Did Sasha slip out of her robe or did Jackson undress her? But it was impossible to tell, like trying to untangle the roots of a single tree. All Sasha could remember was that, without time seeming to have passed at all, they were both naked.

Tentatively, she traced a finger down Jackson's bare back, wondering at the smooth tautness of his skin. He leaped at her touch as if he'd been scalded. Sasha drew back.

'Are you OK?'

Jackson nodded. 'I've waited a long time for this, that's all.'

Sasha laughed. *Not as long as me*, she thought, mentally trying to calculate exactly how many years it was since she had last had sex. Jackson probably logged his encounters by the week, if not the day.

As if reading her mind, Jackson said quietly, 'This is different.'

Gently, with a tenderness Sasha was surprised to find he was capable of, Jackson slipped a hand beneath the small of her back and pulled her down the bed until her hips were level with his own. She felt his erection nudging against her belly. All of a sudden, like being swept up in a storm utterly beyond her control, she found herself reaching for him, her legs opening wider, her hands grabbing his buttocks and pulling him greedily inside her. She'd expected Jackson's love-making to be polished and practised, an all-star performance from a seasoned lothario. Instead, he moved inside her with a wild need that she had not expected, grabbing at her hair, her back, her breasts. He fucked as if his life depended on it, like a thirst-crazed nomad stumbling upon an oasis. And Sasha responded in kind, wrapping her legs around him and arching her back with a hunger she could neither contain nor conceal.

'I love you,' Jackson moaned. He was on his back now, with Sasha above him, his hands on her hips as she rocked gently back and forth, utterly lost in her own pleasure.

I love you too, said Sasha. Except it didn't come out as words, but more of a sigh, a deep exhalation of all the frustration and longing and need she'd been carrying with her for years, since the day they met. Through the wall, she could hear a phone ringing from Jackson's room. 'Someone wants you,' she murmured.

Jackson thrust deeper inside her. 'I want *you*, Sasha. You're all I want.' He came then, his whole body shaking, as if in the throes of some delicious electric shock. Sasha bent low and kissed him lingeringly on the mouth. Neither of them wanted to move, both afraid to let the moment end, to break the spell. But a few seconds later, it was broken for them by Jackson's cellphone, trilling loudly and insistently from the pocket of his pants, now lying in a tangled heap on the floor. He reached down and picked it up.

'Hello?'

'Darling, it's me.'

Lottie's voice was like a glass of cold water in the face. Jackson pictured her at home in their apartment, loving him, trusting him, eager for him to come back to her. He winced. 'Hey. How are you? I was going to call . . .'

'Jackson, something's happened,' she interrupted him. For the first time he heard the trepidation in her voice. Some mad impulse made him wonder whether perhaps *she'd* been unfaithful? Then he wouldn't have to feel so bad. If she'd fallen for somebody else, someone decent and kind, someone infinitely better and more worthy of her than he was . . .

'It's your father.'

'My father?' Jackson frowned. 'What about him?' Ever since Walker Dupree had sided with Sasha and the Wrexall board over the Ceres deal, Jackson had barely spoken to the old man. Their relationship, strained at the best of times, had deteriorated to terse, business-related messages, usually delivered second hand via Jackson's mother, Mitzi.

On the other end of the line, Jackson heard Lottie's deep intake of breath. 'Jackson, honey, I'm so sorry. He died. About an hour ago. We've been trying to get through to you . . .'

Lottie was still talking but Jackson didn't hear her. He hung up and looked at Sasha. His face was blank, and when he spoke his voice was robotic and dull. 'My dad's dead. That was Lottie. I have to go home.'

Back in St Andrew's Episcopal Church, four years later, Jackson was dimly aware of his best man shaking him by the shoulder.

'Jackson. JACKSON! Are you with us, dude?'

'Hmmm?' Jackson opened his eyes. *Church. Martha's*

Vineyard. My wedding day. The Barcelona hotel room and Sasha's stricken face faded from mental view. That night had been the last time he'd seen her in person. *Four years ago! Why the hell am I thinking about that now?*

'Your mum got held up at the house.' James Dermott's voice sounded unreal. 'Something about flower arrangements. Lottie's car's gonna go round the block till she shows up. Ten more minutes, OK?'

'Ten minutes? Sure.'

It was after he flew back from Spain, after his father's funeral, that he'd proposed to Lottie. Ridden with guilt about sleeping with Sasha – not so much the act itself, though that was bad enough, but what it had meant to him, what he had felt – Jackson threw himself back into his relationship with Lottie with renewed determination. It was no longer a choice between two women. It was a choice between two versions of himself. There was the good Jackson, mature, responsible, kind, content, the Jackson that he was when he was around Lottie. And there was the bad Jackson, impetuous, restless, spiteful and passionate, the Jackson that Sasha Miller seemed to bring out merely by breathing. *It's not Sasha's fault. It's mine. We're bad for each other. Bad chemistry. Put us in a room together and we explode.*

Barcelona changed things. Jackson dropped his vendetta against Ceres. Raj Patel came back to Wrexall and had since done a stellar job, reinvigorating the business in ways that not even Jackson had imagined possible. When Jackson heard that Sasha had done a deal with Manuel Hormaeche behind his back (so much for La Sagrada being the wrong location!) he found himself chuckling at her chutzpah. A year earlier he'd probably have been hiring a hit man or boning up on the internet about how to firebomb Ceres's offices. And yet, on a personal level, both Sasha and Jackson behaved as if nothing had happened that day. Sasha sent flowers to Walker Dupree's funeral. Jackson thanked her. That was the last contact they'd had. Jackson didn't invite her to the wedding, and Sasha had not expected him to. Whatever had once been between them was in the past now, buried. Jackson felt relieved.

'Here she is.'

Jackson turned. His mother, Mitzi, took her seat, and as soon as she did so the entire congregation stood up. Lottie, smiling shyly like an angel on her father's arm, made her way up the aisle towards him. In a demure, handmade white lace gown with a full-length antique veil, she reminded Jackson of a nun taking orders: serene, certain, lovely. As usual she wore next to no make-up, and her jewellery, a simple Solange Azagury-Partridge cross set with a smattering of tiny emeralds, was as delicate and understated as only Lottie could be. As soon as he saw her, Jackson felt the tension ease, and the anxiety flood out of his body.

She's beautiful, he thought. *She's what I need.*

The wedding march was playing. His new life was about to begin.

CHAPTER EIGHTEEN

Sasha wandered around Terminal Three, aimlessly looking through the Duty Free shops. Her flight back to New York didn't leave for another two hours, and she was too antsy to read a newspaper.

Heathrow hadn't changed in the year since she'd last been here. Still overcrowded, with crazy queues for the lone Starbucks at all hours of the day. Still full of exhausted immigrant families asleep on the floors and benches, their thin brown arms draped protectively over suitcases held together with string, fighting for space with harassed business travellers looking bored or irritated as their eyes flickered between the flight information screens and their *FT*. Avoiding the Harrods outlet store, already crowded with a gaggle of giggling Japanese tourists, Sasha walked into a deserted Gucci. Picking out a deep purple handbag with an oversized silver clasp, she put it back when she saw the four-thousand-pound price tag. *Ridiculous.* She could afford it, of course, though she'd never been much of a consumer. Now that her life was consumed with deal making, analyzing the *value* of everything, it stuck in her craw more than ever to pay thousands of pounds for something that was probably made for forty. *Then again*, she thought morosely, *what am I saving my money for?* Today more than ever, Sasha was painfully aware that she had no children, no significant other, no one but herself to spoil. Once upon a time she'd believed that wealth would buy her power, the power to destroy Theo Dexter, the power to right the wrongs of the past, the power to seize her life back. Today it struck her with more force than ever. *This IS my life now. There's no going back.* For some reason, the thought was deeply depressing.

No doubt the fact that Jackson Dupree got married last weekend had had something to do with it. Sasha had come to England ostensibly to see her parents and to take a holiday, her first since founding Ceres five years ago. But she also wanted to be out of the States for Jackson and Lottie's big day, knowing what a huge deal would be made of it in the American press. In England, mercifully, nobody knew who Jackson was. He was like baseball or Thanksgiving, something that only Americans cared about.

Perhaps I'm becoming too American? Sasha thought idly. *I've gone native.* The past two weeks at home had left her feeling unsettled. As if she didn't really fit in anywhere, not in New York, not in England. Frant and her parents' cottage remained wonderfully unchanged, the sort of place where you could finish a mug of tea, put it down in a corner somewhere, then return a year later to find it exactly where you left it.

'Messy, you mean?' laughed Sue, when Sasha made this observation. 'A bloody pig sty? Well, you're not wrong, but *you* try keeping a house this small tidy when your father comes home every weekend with another sackload of old junk.'

'It's not *junk*,' said Don, a wounded expression on his face. 'Some of these artifacts are literally priceless. Look at this.' He thrust a mangled disc of dirty metal into Sasha's hands. 'That's pre-Roman, that is. Part of some sort of threshing device.'

Still a keen amateur astronomer, Don had recently added a new obsession to his repertoire: treasure hunting. Armed with a metal detector he'd bought at a boot sale in Tonbridge, he disappeared to the South Downs most weekends, returning with sacks full of what, to the naked eye, did indeed look like junk. A few days ago, Sasha had gone with him. She needed to get out of the cottage, and it was clear her dad wanted to 'talk'.

'So how are you, love? You happy?' Don asked, as his battered old Volvo spluttered through the Sussex country-side. Looking out of the passenger window at the green, wooded hills, peppered here and there with flint cottages or sturdy old Norman churches, Sasha felt as if her life in America was just a dream. Ceres, New York, Jackson Dupree . . . here, in her dad's car, they could all be figments of her imagination.

'I'm all right Dad.' She tried to sound cheerful. 'I'm a bit tired, I suppose. But the business is going well.'

'No offence, Sasha, but I don't give a monkey's nuts about the business,' said Don, keeping his eyes on the road.

'Thanks!'

'You know what I mean. I'm proud of you and all that, of course I am. But I'm your dad. I want you to be happy. A fat bank account never made anybody happy.'

Sasha wondered about the truth of this statement. It seemed to her that a fat bank account made plenty of people deliriously happy. But Don was right, it hadn't worked for her.

'How about your love life?'

'*Dad.*' She rolled her eyes.

'Still no one serious?'

Unbidden, and unwanted, an image of Jackson's face popped into Sasha's mind. 'No,' she said, irritated. 'I don't have time for all that, Dad. Building a business like Ceres is no joke. You're fighting to get to the top, day after day after day. Then when you get there, you think you can rest for a while, but of course you can't. Turn your back for a second and someone's stuck a knife into it. The retail real estate business is brutal. It's cut-throat and it's unrelenting.'

'It sounds horrible. You should jack it in.'

Sasha laughed.

'I'm serious,' said Don. 'You've made enough money, haven't you? Quit while you're ahead. Get a boyfriend, get married, have some kids. Have some *fun*. It's not too late to go back to science, you know.'

Yes it is, thought Sasha sadly. *It is too late. Life has moved on and there's nothing I can do to stop it.*

They'd arrived at Wilmington, a small hamlet famous for its Long Man, a giant human figure carved into the chalk hill like an oversized police drawing of a murder victim. No one knew for sure how old the Long Man was. Although it probably only dated from the sixteenth century, the area around it had been associated with religious rites and festivals since pagan times, and was a popular spot for local treasure hunters. Sasha used to come here as a kid to pick sloes, bitter, dark blue berries that Sue made into sweet sloe gin for Christmas. Stepping out into the cold, misty morning air, a wave of nostalgia hit Sasha like an oncoming truck. Out of nowhere, her eyes filled with tears.

'Are you crying?' Don's face clouded with concern.

'No! Why would I be crying?' said Sasha, forcing herself to snap out of it. It wasn't fair to worry her dad, especially as she didn't know herself what was wrong. 'The cold just made my eyes water, that's all. So come on then, where's this treasure? I was expecting Aladdin's cave of wonders, not some dreary old hills in the drizzle.'

The day passed pleasantly enough, with Don wisely dropping the serious father-daughter stuff and chatting away about local gossip. 'You remember Will Temple, that boy you were so mad about your last year at St Agnes's?'

It was a name she hadn't heard in a million years. Sasha blushed. 'Will! God, yes, of course I remember. Whatever happened to him?'

'He made a ton of money as a developer. Not in your league, I dare say, but he's a big cheese in this neck of the woods. Bought that lovely house in Tidehurst, the manor.' Sasha remembered it well, an idyllic Tudor pile with a maze and a walled rose garden. It was a wildly romantic house. The Will she remembered would not have appreciated it. 'Anyway,' Don went on, 'his wife left him a few months ago, ran off with a mate of his or some such.'

'How awful!' said Sasha sincerely. 'Poor Will.'

'Rattling round there alone he is now. Single dad. Very good looking still, according to your mother.'

It wasn't until this point that Sasha realized he was trying to set her and Will up. Reunite her with an old flame so she could move home to Sussex and live happily ever after. If only life were that simple. 'Oh Dad!' she grinned. 'You don't think . . .? Will Temple and I had nothing in common when we were kids! That's why we broke up. What on earth would we have to say to one another now?'

Don shrugged. 'You're both in the property business. You're both young and single and rich. And lonely.'

'I'm not lonely. I'm busy,' insisted Sasha.

'Anyway, I thought you broke up because of that wanker Dexter. Don't suppose you ever see him, do you?'

'No.'

Normally it amused Sasha the way that her parents seemed to think she might have 'bumped into' celebrities, simply because she lived in America and was now rich and well known herself. As if New York were like Frant, and she might pass the time of day with Tom Cruise or the President in the post office on a Tuesday morning. When it came to Theo Dexter, however, she couldn't see the funny side.

'Your mother and I saw him on some "Hollywood Special" the other night. I don't know what he's done to his face but he looks more and more like Joe 90 every time I see him, all waxy and frozen. No glasses though, obviously. Just those damn stupid teeth. You can see them from space, I bet, the colour they are. Looks like he's got a mouthful of burning magnesium. And his house was just ridiculous, all marble and gold, like a bloody brothel.'

'Hmmm.' Sasha did not want to talk about Theo Dexter. Not today, not ever. His continued existence, prosperity and apparent happiness all reminded her of her own abject failure.

'I wonder what his old muckers at Cambridge think of him now? Whether any of 'em have thought twice about what they did to you, taking his word over yours?'

'I doubt it,' said Sasha, unable to keep the bitterness out of her voice. 'He was part of their little boys' club. I wasn't. They were *real* scientists. I was just a kid.'

'Maybe, back then,' said Don. 'But no one thinks of Dexter as a real scientist now. He's more like an actor, isn't he? A *celebrity*.' Don's lip curled with distaste at the word. 'I'll bet they all hate him these days.'

It was an interesting thought, one that, oddly, had never occurred to Sasha. As she remembered, the Cambridge establishment was notoriously bitchy. Many of Theo's contemporaries had disliked him even before his big break, back when he was still a tutor at St Michael's, sleeping with all the prettiest students. She wondered if it ever bothered Theo, being cast out into the scientific wilderness, even if it was into the welcoming arms of Hollywood? Sasha herself had grieved intensely for physics and Cambridge and the life she'd left behind. At Harvard Business School she had recurring nightmares of the university court, her utter humiliation and devastation at being branded a liar, at seeing her work appropriated by someone else, someone she had loved. Back then she thought often of her fellow undergraduates, of Georgia and Josie and her St Michael's friends, but more often of her rivals in the physics faculty, guys like Owen McDermott from Caius or the fat, nerdy Hugo Cryer who spent his days locked in the particle physics labs at the Cavendish. What had happened to them? To their research? Had they gone on to make breakthroughs, to become professors, to make a difference in the physics world, the real world, the only world that mattered?

Over the years, Sasha had learned to stop tormenting herself with such thoughts. Her life had moved on, first to Wrexall, then Ceres, and soon there was no time to brood on what might have been, the doors left unopened. But it was curious to imagine Theo Dexter having the same thoughts. Most people, looking at his life, would have thought it laughable, the idea of a global TV star pining for academia. But Sasha knew better than anyone that wealth and fame weren't everything. Physics was Theo's first love, just as it was hers. You never got over your first love, not really.

'I read something the other day about St Michael's. What was his name, that old git who was Master there in your day?'

Sasha gritted her teeth. 'Anthony Greville.' The name would be engraved in her memory until the day she died. Greville had chaired the show trial that had ruled in Theo's favour, sealing her fate.

'Greville, that's it. Well he's finally retiring. They're holding elections for a new Master, next spring, I believe.'

'Oh,' said Sasha, not sure how she was supposed to react. It was getting dark. The mist sank lower over the rolling chalk hills, wrapping the landscape in a cold, wet blanket. Sasha shivered, thinking of her mother's homemade fruit cake and the crackling log fire that would be waiting for them back at the cottage. 'Come on, Dad. It's late. We should be getting back.'

They turned and walked back to the car, with Don still muttering, 'I'm serious about Will Temple, you know. You're a modern girl. Ask him out for dinner.'

'Virgin flight twenty-four to New York, boarding at gate twelve.'

The tannoy announcement brought Sasha back to her senses. Tired of window shopping she'd made her way up to the first-class lounge where she sat staring into space, an untouched plate of cheese and crackers in her lap. A number of her fellow passengers recognized her, but she'd grown adept at tuning out the nudges and whispers and disappearing into her own world.

Gathering up her hand-luggage bag, she made her way down to the plane where the upper-class passengers were boarding first. A kind-looking, slightly podgy stewardess showed her to her seat, her large bottom straining against the red fabric of her skirt as she bent down to offer Sasha various things she didn't want: a glass of champagne, warm cashew nuts, a hot towel. 'I'll just leave you these, and I'll get out of your way. They're all new,' she said cheerfully, dumping a stack of fashion and gossip magazines into Sasha's lap.

Sasha flipped through them idly. *Vogue's Ten Must-Have's for Winter!* Fashion had always bored her, and she found it bizarre the way that her own outfits were analyzed and commented on in the press. Most of the time her PA, Jeanne, shopped for her online. In winter Sasha wore whatever was nearest and warmest. Passing *Vogue* to her neighbour, she opened *People* magazine and immediately wished she hadn't.

'JACKSON DUPREE'S FAIRYTALE WEDDING TO LONG-TIME LOVE, CHARLOTTE GRAINGER!' There were six pages of it. *Six!* Despite herself, Sasha turned to them immediately, skimming through shot after shot of Lottie smiling beatifically. Jackson looked happy too, feeding her wedding cake, holding her close for the first dance as every socialite in New York looked enviously on. It did look like a fairytale. Just not hers.

'Excuse me.' Sasha stopped the stewardess. 'I don't need these.' She handed the magazines back to her. 'Do you happen to have today's *Wall Street Journal*?'

'Of course. I'll bring it right over.'

Work, that was what she needed. Tomorrow she'd be back in the office, back in the fray, with no more free time to think about things like Jackson and Lottie, or the St Michael's Mastership, or what Theo Dexter was or wasn't thinking.

Holidays were definitely over-rated.

'Come on, baby. Harder! Do it like you mean it.'

Even in bed she wants to direct, thought Theo with a sigh. Putting a hand over his wife's mouth – Dita wouldn't mind, she liked it when he was masterful – he continued fucking her. But his heart wasn't in it.

Yesterday he'd had a call from his accountant, Perry Margolis.

'I'm just going to give it to you straight, Theo. You're living beyond your means. Something's going to have to give, and fast. I'm not kidding.'

'But, Perry, how is that possible? My salary on *Universe* just went up. I've got the aftershave deal, Kenco coffee renewed. I know Sony haven't signed on the dotted line yet, but . . .'

'This is nothing to do with Sony. Your income's healthy, that's not the problem.'

Theo sighed deeply. 'I know.'

The problem was four letters long, and it was lying beneath him now, sucking the very life out of him like a fucking preying mantis. Dita's spending, always excessive, always impulsive, had recently become borderline pathological. It was as if there were a direct link between her self-esteem and the bills she ran up on her Amex card – one went down and the other went up. In the last six months, Dita had been passed over for two major movie roles, in both cases for younger actresses. The irony was that she still looked fantastic. But *keeping* her that way was like running a grand old stately home. It required an army of professionals, hairdressers, stylists, personal shoppers, make-up artists, trainers, facialists, yoga instructors and therapists just to get Dita out of bed in the mornings, and all of them were on full-time payroll. That was *before* you got to the nannies, tutors and tennis coaches for the children, the French ballet instructress for Fran, the twenty-four-hour on-call allergist for Milo.

'Your staff alone cost more than you're earning for the new season of *Dexter's Universe*,' said Perry. 'I've seen countries run more cheaply. You have to let at least a third of them go.'

Theo had broached the subject with Dita last night, and again this morning. 'No,' she said defiantly. 'I'm not going to live like a pauper because *you* can't manage our finances.'

Theo had lost his temper, pointing out that if it weren't for his earnings they would have lost the house years ago. Dita shot back that without her stardom, he would never have made those earnings; that all his endorsement deals, not to mention his film career, such as it was, were a direct result of his marriage to her; that he was little more than a gigolo – a gigolo who, quite frankly, had become lazy and boring and no longer excited her in bed. Theo raised a hand to slap her, Dita grabbed his arm, and before they knew it they were making love, clawing at one another like a pair of wild animals in heat.

The sex had been great until Dita started talking, goading and taunting Theo (she called it 'coaching') until he could happily have ripped her head off with his bare hands. Now it was all he could do to finish the job, forcing thoughts of bills and unpaid IRS demands out of his head and fantasizing about Lorna Fox, the teenage actress who had 'stolen' Dita's latest role, just to get himself to come.

Thankfully Dita came too, her nails digging painfully into Theo's buttocks as she moaned and gasped beneath him. 'Not bad,' she said, lighting a cigarette as he rolled off her. 'At least you're making an effort.'

Ignoring her, Theo walked into the bathroom. Pressing a button on the wall, a torrent of hot rain exploded out of the ceiling in the far corner of the room. The 'invisible shower' was another of Dita's extravagances, but in this case Theo wasn't complaining. The hot jets of water felt wonderful on his back, invigorating and relaxing at the same time.

His depressing conversation with Perry yesterday wasn't the only thing on his mind. Ed Gilliam had forwarded him an email, a news piece about his old Cambridge college, St Michael's. Apparently, old Tony Greville was retiring and elections were being held for a new Master. Ed had only sent it as a piece of idle gossip, something it might amuse Theo to know. But the news had opened up a floodgate of feelings in Theo that he'd barely had time to process.

He could picture St Michael's now, as if he'd never left. The ivy-clad, medieval courts, the formal gardens rolling down to the peaceful Cam, his rooms in First Court and all the exciting, intelligent, adoring young women he'd taken to bed there. He still had young lovers in LA of course, physically perfect specimens all. And Dita, to give her fair credit, was no slacker in either the looks or the lovemaking department. But it was a long time, a *long* time, since Theo had fucked a truly intelligent woman.

What would it be like to go back to Cambridge now? To return as the conquering hero? As a fantasy, it had a lot of appeal, though it was hard – impossible – to fit Dita and the children into that picture. Plus Perry had made it painfully clear that now would *not* be a good time for Theo to walk away from his lucrative endorsement deals, never mind jack in the TV show that had made him.

Drying and dressing in long shorts and a James Perse t-shirt, his LA uniform, Theo came down to breakfast in a thoughtful mood. Unusually, Dita was up already, wrapped in a silk robe and picking at a waffle with Milo on her lap when he came in.

'Hi, Dad,' Milo said shyly. It irritated Theo, the way the boy was always so nervous around him, clinging to Dita like Bambi to his mother, but he tried not to show it.

'Morning, Milo. How's that cough this morning?'

'Better,' he smiled wanly. 'I think I can go to school today. I feel fine.'

'That's great,' said Theo, but Dita shook her head.

'Not today, honey. Rosetta said he was wheezing a lot in the night,' she explained to Theo. 'I want Dr Gray to see him before we make any decisions.' She sprinkled powdered sugar into a square of waffle and fed it to her son, as if he were a helpless baby bird. Theo felt his anger building.

'He just said he feels fine.'

'Drop it, Theo, OK?' Dita snarled. 'You know nothing about how to care for Milo. You never have.'

Unwilling to be drawn into yet another fight in front of the kids, Theo changed the subject.

'I heard something interesting yesterday,' he said pouring himself a bowl of Kashi GoLean cereal and ruffling his daughter's hair. Throughout her parents' tense exchange, three-year-old Fran had continued happily stuffing her face with Cheerios, washed down with chocolate milk. 'St Michael's is looking for a new Master.'

Dita frowned. 'What is that, code? You wanna be a priest, now? Or a spy?'

Theo looked at her and thought, *You really are a deeply stupid person.*

'No,' he said patiently. 'St Michael's is a college at Cambridge university. My old college, as it happens. The Master is like the principal, the head of the college. It's a very prestigious post.'

Dita shrugged, bored. 'So?'

'I don't know.' Theo tried to keep his voice casual. 'I mean, it's kind of a crazy idea. But, you know, I could apply.'

'*You?*' Dita laughed insultingly. 'What the fuck do you know about running a school? You're a TV presenter.'

'Actually, I'm a physicist who happens to have a television career,' said Theo stiffly.

'Right. And I'm a NASA astronaut who happens to make movies,' taunted Dita.

'Is that so?' Theo shot back. 'When was your last movie role, darling? I forget. Perhaps it's time to give your old buddies at the Space Center a call.'

'Fuck you,' said Dita. Milo started wheezing.

'Don't shout,' he pleaded. 'I don't like shouting.'

'Sorry, my angel.' Dita smothered the boy in kisses, immediately switching into doting-mother mode. 'Daddy's being silly, that's all. Mommy's not really mad. Daddy was joking, weren't you, Daddy?'

Not trusting himself to say anything, Theo stalked out of the room, bumping into Rico, Dita's stylist, in the hallway. *It's like living in a fucking office,* he thought darkly. *I can't get to my own front door without tripping over the hangers-on.* 'Watch where you're going,' he barked.

Rico raised an overplucked eyebrow. 'Temper, temper. Looks like someone got out of her ladyship's bed on the wrong side this morning.' Rico, like the rest of Dita's entourage, who were all either female or gay, fancied Theo like mad. He couldn't understand how anyone could be dissatisfied with a husband as ruggedly handsome, rich and brilliant as Theo Dexter. As for that British accent, it was enough to give one a teeny orgasm on the spot.

'She's out of control,' said Theo, tearing at his hair like a man distracted. It was rare for him to confide in Dita's staff, especially the flamboyantly flaming Rico. But he needed to let off steam. 'The spending is beyond all reason. I'm not the Aga fucking Khan, and she's not the star she used to be. Someone needs to get that through her brainless, blonde skull before we're all living under a bridge.'

'So you'd rather I didn't give her these tickets for the preview of Marc Jacobs' Spring Collection, then? He's doing it in Rome this year. I thought we'd make a week of it, stay at the Hassler, you know, a spot of shopping on the Via Veneto.' He held up a pair of stiff, gold-embossed tickets wickedly.

Theo snatched them out of his hands and pocketed them. 'Not unless she's planning to swim there.'

Rico watched as he picked up his car keys from the hall table and swept angrily out of the house. He loved it when Theo got all macho. Dita must be out of her mind to push him the way that she did.

Outside, the blazing LA sunshine lifted Theo's spirits some-what, as it always did. It was impossible to pull out of the gates of his $15-million mansion in his new red Bugatti Veyron with the thick black centre stripe, and not to think of how far he'd come from his childhood in Crawley. Crawley where it always rained, and the height of anyone's ambi-tions was a souped-up Ford Escort and a paid-off mortgage.

Do I really want to go back to England? Leave all this behind?

He argued with himself all the way to his new offices on Canon Drive in downtown Beverly Hills. *It's not England. It's Cambridge. It's the Mastership.* Hollywood had plenty to offer, but that was something that couldn't be replicated. To be a living part of history, to perch triumphantly at the very top of academia's tallest tree. Best of all, it was a golden ticket back into the academic fold, the world that had turned its back on him, but it was a ticket that did *not* involve him having to go back to research or, heaven forbid, come up with a new idea. *I'm too old for that,* he told himself. *I've already earned my laurels. What I want now is to be able to rest on them.*

There were numerous hurdles, of course, and he ran through them mentally on the elevator ride to his twelfth-floor office.

The college might not want me. They might see me as too 'flash'.

I've got work commitments here and around the world I can't just walk away from.

Dita will divorce me. Although this morning that feels like more of a plus than a minus.

'Good morning, Mr Dexter.' The new receptionist, Candy or Kiki or some sort of stripper name, gazed at him adoringly. 'Your mail's on the desk. Can I get you anything this morning? Coffee? Bagel?' *Blow job?* her eyes added, brazenly.

'No, thanks.' He went into his office and shut the door. Turning on his computer, he clicked open his emails and scrolled down to find the one from Ed Gilliam, about St Michael's. *There must be a way. If I could fit the work around it somehow . . . shoot in the long summer vacation, come to some deal with the fellowship.*

He thought about Dita and their row this morning. The mockery in her voice. *'You?* What do you know about running a school?'

It was, Theo decided, high time he grew back a pair of balls.

Clicking on 'reply' he began to type.

CHAPTER NINETEEN

Theresa sipped her piping hot Starbucks cinnamon latte, warming her gloved fingers around the paper cup and humming joyously to herself as she crunched down Jesus Lane. 'Crunched' was the operative word. A thick blanket of snow had fallen overnight, carpeting Cambridge in white, like a Victorian Christmas card. Snow always made everything beautiful, but somehow it felt especially magical here. The ancient spires and steeples jutted up from the winter wonderland below into a piercing, bright blue sky. It was only a few days before Christmas, and all across the city bells were ringing, the same peals that had rung out in celebration for centuries. It was impossible not to feel happy, and excited, on a day like this, and Theresa O'Connor had no intention of trying.

Last week, she'd finally bitten the bullet and officially put her name forward for the Mastership of St Michael's. Braced for ridicule, she'd been astonished by how seriously the college seemed to take her candidacy, and by the overwhelming support she'd received from her students and colleagues in the English faculty. Horatio Hollander, who

Theresa knew for a fact hadn't two beans to rub together, bought her a beautiful dark green cashmere scarf as a congratulations present.

'Congratulations for what?' she laughed. 'I've only applied, Horatio. I'll not get the thing, you know. I haven't a snowball's chance in an oven.'

'We'll see,' he said loyally, refusing to take back the scarf and insisting she not only accept it but wear it. 'It's the perfect colour for you.'

Actually, it is the perfect colour for me, thought Theresa, pulling it up over her red curls to protect them from the newly falling flakes. She would miss Horatio over the Christmas break, she'd miss all her students in fact, although the five-week holiday did provide some much needed time to work on her own book (she'd started a new project on *Troilus and Cressida*) not to mention get going on the endless list of odd jobs that needed doing at Willow Tree Cottage. She'd turned the heating up full blast, and lit the wood-burning stove daily, but still barely a week passed when something didn't crack, buckle or fall to pieces with cold. Pipes, windows, floorboards; in a house this old nothing was safe. As soon as Theresa dealt with one problem, another seemed to spring up, and of course there was never enough time, or money, to deal with them.

Today, however, she'd determined to spend the whole day in college, catching up on paperwork and, hopefully, writing. With snow like this it was impossible not to be inspired, and if she stayed home she knew she'd end up curled up in front of the fire with a Jilly Cooper novel. Either that or on her hands and knees, defrosting some vital piece of plumbing with a kettle.

With the undergraduates all home for Christmas, and the thick snow like a layer of cladding on the ground, college was almost eerily silent. When one of Theresa's colleagues tapped her on the shoulder, she almost jumped out of her skin.

'Jesus, Harry, you frightened the life out of me. I never heard you coming.'

'I know. Brilliant, isn't it, the snow? Makes me want to skip about like a ten-year-old.' Harry Tremayne grinned. A sprightly sixty-year-old classics scholar, he was a throwback to another, gentler era, before graffiti and football hooliganism and internet porn, before ugly bendy buses belched their fumes onto King's Parade and undergraduates stripped topless every May Week and had their photographs published in *The Sun*. On a day like today, though, Harry's Cambridge felt within reach. Theresa could have hugged him. 'You look cheerful,' said Harry.

'I am.' Theresa glowed. 'I feel inspired. At least two thousand words today, I think.'

'Marvellous,' said Harry. 'I'm so pleased you aren't letting that vile ex-husband of yours dampen your spirits.' He started to walk away, but Theresa grabbed his arm.

'My ex-husband? You mean Theo Dexter?'

Harry looked puzzled. 'Do you have more than one?'

'No.' Theresa blushed. 'No. I just wondered what made you mention him, that's all. I mean, why would Theo be dampening my spirits? We haven't spoken in years.'

Harry's face fell. He looked like a little boy whose brand-new model aeroplane had just crash landed and was beyond repair. 'Oh dear. You haven't heard.'

'Apparently not.' Theresa felt her stomach lurch, like a plane suddenly losing altitude. She was both surprised, and irritated, that the mention of Theo's name could still do that to her. 'Come on, Harry, spit it out. It can't be *that* bad, surely?'

'Well, no. It's not. I mean it doesn't have to be,' Harry mumbled awkwardly. 'And, of course, I may be wrong. But I heard on the grapevine that Dexter's applied for the St Michael's job.'

Theresa laughed out loud. Well *that* was a relief! Clearly someone was playing a practical joke and dear old Harry Tremayne had fallen for it. 'Theo? Come back to Cambridge? Goodness me, Harry, I don't think so! I can hardly see Dita Andreas propping up the bar in the Senior Common Room at St Mike's, can you?'

'It is a rather incongruous picture, I'll admit,' said Harry. 'Oh well, I dare say I got the wrong end of the stick. Good luck with the inspiration!' He walked off smiling, treading carefully to avoid the slick patches of ice that lurked beneath the snowy paths. Theresa went up to her rooms. Switching on her computer, she settled down to work, but her encounter with Harry Tremayne kept bothering her. Of course he'd made a mistake. It was the only explanation. Cambridge was *her* world, not Theo's. Even when they were married, Theo used to go on and on about how happy he was to have 'escaped'. How much happier must he be now, ruling the roost in LA with his gorgeous film-star wife? No, Theo was already living his dream. What interest would he have in stealing hers?

Her phone was ringing. She *must* be distracted, normally she always turned it off when she was working. She was about to do so now when she saw it was Jenny Aubrieau. Thinking she could use hearing a sane, friendly voice, she picked up.

'Jen?'

'Oh, thank goodness you answered. I was worried about you. Are you OK?'

The hairs on Theresa's forearms stood on end, as if a ghost

had walked over her grave. 'Yeeeees,' she answered warily. 'Should I *not* be OK?'

'He's a real bloody bastard, isn't he? I mean he just won't go away,' Jenny ranted. 'He'll probably pull out at the last minute anyway. Some movie he has to shoot or some hapless third-world country he and Dipstick Andreas have to buy. Anyway, everyone at St Michael's hates him.'

Jenny's words faded. Everything inside Theresa's head was muffled, as if the snow were falling inside as well as out. *So it's true. Theo really has applied for the Mastership!* She could hardly have felt more heartbroken if someone had told her that Lysander had been squashed by a car. Except it wasn't her beloved cat who'd been squashed, it was her. Her life, her hopes, her peace of mind, snuffed out in an instant.

Theo had applied for the Mastership. The elections would be held in the spring, which meant he'd be here by then. *Theo* would be *here, IN CAMBRIDGE.* Even if, by some miracle, he didn't get the job at St Michael's, he would still be here, *living* here, with Dita and his children. *I'll have to leave. There's no other way around it. I'll have to leave Cambridge, sell Willow Tree Cottage . . .* her eyes clouded with tears. Dimly, she was aware of Jenny's voice, still talking to her.

'T? Are you all right, lovely? Do you want me to come over? I'd offer to pick you up but of course the car won't start. I could jump on a bus though?'

'No.' Theresa's voice was dull and flat. 'It's OK. I'm fine.'

'Well, will you at least come to ours for supper tonight?'

'Sure,' said Theresa, though she knew she wouldn't. 'I'll call you later.'

Horatio Hollander leaned morosely on the bar at the Mitre, staring into space.

'This is a pub, Horatio.' Jack, his friend and roommate,

had a job behind the bar. 'The general idea is that you come here to buy alcohol. Some people even come here to have fun.'

'I bought alcohol,' said Horatio. 'I bought this pint.'

'Yeah, back when dinosaurs roamed the earth,' said Jack, looking disdainfully at the dregs in his friend's glass. 'You've been standing there for over an hour. What do you want?'

'Fine,' grumbled Horatio, emptying both his pockets of change and dumping the contents noisily onto the polished wood of the bar. 'What'll that get me?'

'About half a pork scratching,' said Jack, scooping up the coins while the landlord glared at him, disapproving. 'For God's sake, I'll buy you a whisky myself but you have to promise to snap out of it. You're scaring away the paying punters.'

Jack was right. He was in a funk, and he did have to snap out of it. But it was easier said than done. It was all right for Jack. He had a girlfriend, Kate, who was mad about him. He also had rich parents who lived in Cambridge, which meant a warm, festive house to go back to every night, and a decent holiday job at the Mitre. Horatio, on the other hand, was living in an unspeakably dismal youth hostel until term started again, with no job, no money and, most depressingly of all, no girlfriend.

He *could* have had a girlfriend. Could have had any number of them, as Jack was fond of pointing out: Louise Halabi, Caitlin Grey, Jenna Arkell. All pretty, accomplished, fun-loving girls, all eager to show Horatio that there was life beyond the professor who barely registered his existence, still less his love. But to Horatio, that was like saying he *could* have gone home for Christmas. It implied he had control over his own actions. That he was the sort of person with willpower strong enough to tear himself away from the city where he knew Theresa would be; where he stood an off chance of bumping into her occasionally, or even arranging to meet over a mince pie on the pretence of developing his thesis.

It wasn't that he didn't hope his love for Theresa would lessen. Ever since she'd turned him down last spring, he'd been waiting for reality to sink in. He woke up every morning determined to get over her. But then he would catch sight of her again, papers fluttering out of her grip as she stumbled clumsily through college, like a beautiful mole unused to the sunlight, and it was all over. One taste of the sweet hopelessness, and he was lost, shipwrecked on a vast ocean with no land in sight.

'Get that down you.' Jack slid a single shot of whisky across the bar. Horatio sipped it cautiously. 'It's not poisoned.' Jack looked offended. 'You don't have to drink it like a girl.'

'I do if I'm going to stay here. I can't afford to order anything else.'

Jack's face suddenly darkened. 'Uh oh.'

Horatio looked up curiously. 'What?'

'If I tell you, you have to promise me you won't make a scene. I like working here.'

'I never make scenes. What?'

'Your Mrs Robinson has just walked in. Staggered in, actually. She looks three sheets to the wind.'

Horatio spun around so fast he slipped off his bar stool. There, indeed, was Theresa, standing by the door, swaying gently but rhythmically, like a sailboat in the breeze. Her divine mountain of red hair was wet and dark, stuck to her head with snow, and her long skirt and sheepskin boots were also soaked through to the point where they made a sloshing sound when she walked. Her pale cheeks were flushed, her eyes glassy. There was no question she was drunk. Horatio's eyes lit up with delight when he noticed she was wearing his scarf, but his happiness soon evaporated as Theresa staggered forward, falling into the arms of a surprised young couple enjoying their fish and chips by the fire.

'You'd better do something,' Jack whispered. 'The boss'll throw her out in a minute. He's clamping down on hurlers.'

The very idea that anyone might consider Theresa a 'hurler' filled Horatio with chagrin, but now was not the time to argue the point, especially as she looked as green as her scarf after her tumble and, if truth be told, distinctly nauseous.

'Let me help you.'

Theresa blinked groggily. 'Horay . . . Hooray . . . Horay-show? Whaddayou doing here? 'S Chrishmas.'

'I know. Here, take my arm.'

'Why? Where're we going? You shun't be here, you know. 'S Christmas. *'Tis* the season to be jolly, fa la la la *la!*' She dissolved into giggles. Jack shot Horatio a meaningful glance.

'I'm taking you home,' he said, ushering Theresa out into the freezing night air before she had a chance to resist. Outside the cold was sobering, but not sobering enough. At seven o'clock it had been pitch dark for hours. Street lamps flickered pale gold above the snowy cobbles. Somewhere in the distance, bells were still ringing. Theresa clutched Horatio like a drowning man reaching for driftwood.

'I'm drunk,' she murmured sleepily.

'I know.' Horatio felt the damp weight of her body pressed against his thick winter coat and felt weak with longing. All he wanted was to sweep Theresa up into his arms and kiss her, but of course he couldn't, not in this state.

''S'all Theo's fault, bloody bastard,' she mumbled into his lapel. 'Why can't he leave me alone? I mean, really, 'sthat too much to bl'dy ask?'

'Where do you live?' asked Horatio, who had no idea what she was talking about. 'It's too cold to talk out here and you're soaked to the bone. I could take you back to college?'

'No,' said Theresa firmly. She'd been drinking since noon, ricocheting from one pub to the next getting progressively more depressed at the thought of Theo's imminent arrival. Though extremely drunk now, she was not quite paralytic enough to think that staggering back to Christ's in this state, on the arm of one of her students, was a good idea. When she woke up tomorrow she would feel like death, but she'd rather feel like death in her own bed, with only her cats as witnesses. 'I'll go home. S'all right. I can get a cab.'

'Not in this state you can't, no one'll take you,' said Horatio matter-of-factly. 'I'll drive you. I'm parked round the corner and I've only had one beer all night.'

Too tired to argue, Theresa followed him. By day, Horatio's ancient Datsun looked like the death trap that it was. Right now, to Theresa's bleary eyes anyway, it looked like a welcoming oasis of warmth and safety. She climbed into the back seat, sprawled out across it and fell deeply asleep.

When she woke, she found herself on the couch in the living room at Willow Tree Cottage, wrapped in a blanket, a freshly laid fire crackling to life in front of her. Disorientated, she sat-up, and then immediately lay back down again, clutching her head and groaning.

'Here.' Horatio handed her some revolting-looking liquid, fizzy and amber-green. It reminded her of cat sick.

'No thanks.'

'Drink it. Trust me. I've made you Marmite toast for afterwards, to take the taste away.'

Like a child, Theresa drank. If possible, the liquid tasted

worse than it looked. She retched, but with an effort managed to keep it down.

'Good. Now try some toast. Small bites.'

The sour tang of the Marmite felt good, cutting through her nausea like a knife. 'Thanks,' she said weakly. She looked up at Horatio, who was smiling down at her, his kind eyes amused and compassionate at the same time. He was wearing a dark blue Guernsey jumper with holes in it and a tatty pair of grey corduroy trousers. Or was that three pairs of trousers? Her vision was still touch and go.

'What time is it?' she asked, closing her eyes and sinking back against the cushion that Horatio had arranged behind her head as a pillow. Before he could answer, another thought struck her. 'How did you know where I live? How did you get in?'

'It wasn't *that* much of a brain teaser,' he joked, sitting down on the other end of the couch, by her feet. 'After you passed out in the car I looked in your wallet. Your driving licence had the address on it.'

'Oh.' Theresa blushed. 'Of course.'

'I couldn't find a key in your pockets, thought I might have to jimmy open a window or something, but the place was unlocked. You should be more careful.'

His tone was admonishing, as if he were the teacher and she the pupil. It – all this, the knight-in-shining-armour routine – was a side to Horatio that Theresa had never seen before. As his three faces merged back into one, she watched him tuck the blanket around her feet and thought, *He's really very handsome.*

'You mentioned something outside the pub. About Theo.' The name seemed to stick in Horatio's throat. 'Is that why . . .?'

'I was drinking? Yes. Stupid, I know.' She ran a hand

through her drying curls. 'Getting hammered's not going to help anything. It's certainly not going to stop him coming back to Cambridge, if that's really what he wants. When Theo wants something he's like the Bad Rabbit. He doesn't say "please". He just takes it.'

Horatio missed the literary reference, but he got the gist of what she was saying. He looked almost as horrified by the prospect of Theo Dexter's return as Theresa had ten hours earlier. 'Dexter's coming here? *Moving* here? Why, for God's sake?'

Theresa told him the whole sorry story. By the time she'd finished she was fighting back tears again. Without thinking, Horatio leaned over and hugged her. Misinterpreting her distress, he said sadly, 'You still love him, don't you?'

'No!' Theresa pulled back, surprised by the vehemence of her own reaction. 'No, I don't still love him. Not in the least. In fact at this precise moment there's a possibility I might even hate him. And I make it a policy never to hate people.'

'A policy. I see. Like your "policy" not to date students, you mean?'

All of a sudden Theresa was aware of how close he was. She could see the stubble on his chin and jawline, smell the faint scent of aftershave on his skin. She looked up and his eyes were boring into her. This was *not* the Horatio Hollander she remembered. This version was a man, not a boy. And he was smouldering.

When she spoke, her voice cracked. 'Yes. Like that.'

'You have too many policies, Professor O'Connor.'

The kiss was so fast, and so bold, Theresa told herself she had no time to resist. The truth was, she didn't want to. It was so long since she'd been with a man, so long since she'd even thought of herself as a sexual being, she'd convinced herself that that part of her was dead. Apparently not.

Horatio's desire was intoxicating, far more of an aphrodisiac than the alcohol or the roaring fire or the romantic snowflakes still falling softly outside the window. He kissed her again, his hands caressing the back of her neck, then sliding down under her shirt, reaching for her breasts, stroking them briefly – too briefly – before he sat up.

'No!' *Was that my voice?* thought Theresa. 'Don't stop.'

Horatio grinned. 'I'm not stopping.'

Pulling his jumper off over his head along with his t-shirt and wriggling out of his jeans like an eager puppy, he was naked in seconds, revealing a body surprisingly strong and athletic. In the flickering firelight he looked like a marble sculpture, alabaster pale but exquisitely beautiful. It was a different body to Theo's. Taller. Leaner. *Younger.* Theresa tried not to look at his dick, but it was impossible, like walking round Trafalgar Square and ignoring Nelson's Column.

'Your turn.'

She started to unbutton her blouse, but Horatio was too quick for her, his fingers working expertly, opening the wet cloth to reveal an embarrassingly old grey bra.

'Sorry,' Theresa blushed.

'For what?' he asked incredulously. 'You are so fucking perfect I could cry.' And she knew in that moment that he meant it. That he wanted her, *really* wanted her, not as some passing student crush, but as a man, wanting a woman. She relaxed then, and he seemed to sense it, slowing down his movements, undressing her slowly, not tentatively, but with infinite care and wonder. Pulling away the pillow from beneath her head, he gently lifted her up and lay her naked on the floor. The worn Persian rug felt coarse against her back, but Theresa soon forgot any discomfort as Horatio stretched out above her, stroking the hair back from her forehead, and began kissing her cheeks, neck and breasts, working his way down slowly to her stomach. By the time she felt his warm breath between her legs, she was already squirming with excitement, longing for him to do what she knew *he* was longing to do.

'Please,' she murmured, 'now. Do it now.'

Horatio didn't need to be asked twice. Sliding back up so his face was over hers he slid inside her and began to rock gently back and forth. 'OK?' For the first time all night, he looked nervous.

'Perfect,' sighed Theresa. And it was. In that moment it was completely perfect. Perfect, and quick. Horatio had waited so long, and so hopelessly, it was all he could do not to jump for joy when he felt Theresa's breath quicken and her muscles tighten gloriously around him. He came the second she did, collapsing onto the floor next to her, afraid to open his eyes in case he discovered it was all a dream.

'Time for a policy review, don't you think?' he said playfully, once he'd got his breath back. But Theresa didn't answer.

She lay sprawled out beside him, soundly, drunkenly asleep.

'I'm not going.'

Dita Andreas was screaming. The veins on her forehead looked as if they were about to burst through the skin, and her usually flawless, porcelain complexion had turned an ugly shade of purplish red.

'I'm not going and nor are the children. I want a divorce!'

'You can have a divorce,' said Theo equably. They were sitting in a 'private' rooftop cabaña at the SLS hotel in Beverly Hills, although Dita's decibel level ensured that nothing about their conversation was private. 'Half of all my worldly goods – and debts. And good bloody luck to you.' Just to increase

Dita's fury, he lit a cigarette. 'As for the children, you can have Milo. But I'll fight you for Franny and don't think I won't.'

Dita gasped, genuinely shocked. 'That's a wicked thing to say.'

'Yeah, well, so's "I want a divorce". You're the would-be home-wrecker here, Dita, so quit trying to make me the bad guy. I made this move for all of us, not just me. You'll love Cambridge.'

'Oh no I won't. Because I'm *NOT GOING!*'

Theo sighed. This was getting them nowhere. 'Look. The actual election's not till April,' he said, trying to make his tone more conciliatory. 'It's not like we have to leave tomorrow. We have time to sort out schools, find a decent house, all of that business. It's not forever, sweetheart,' he added, bending to kiss Dita's flat stomach as she lay rigid on the sun lounger. That was a lie. If he got the Mastership – when he got it – it *would* be forever. But he would cross that bridge when he came to it. Moving his head lower, he started to peel down Dita's Missoni bikini bottoms and felt her writhe with anticipation, her thighs parting automatically. Oddly, the worse things got between them as a couple, the more thrilling the sex seemed to become. 'You can still fly back to LA regularly for work. We both can,' he purred, gently parting her newly Brazilianed labia and teasing her with butterfly kisses. Dita gasped.

'I hate you,' she whispered, her fingers massaging Theo's scalp and her back arching with pleasure.

Theo felt himself getting hard. 'I hate you too.'

Maybe, in Cambridge, away from all the Hollywood craziness, he'd finally be able to break away? If nothing else, he would get rid of Dita's entourage and decimate her spending. St Michael's had been surprisingly flexible about accommodating his filming schedule – 'Should you be elected, of course.' But both the college fellows and Theo knew that that was a foregone conclusion. Theo could open doors for St Michael's, in terms of funding and global PR, that no other candidate could possibly hope to match.

A uniformed waiter poked his head around the canvas walls of the cabaña just as Dita started to orgasm. Ever the exhibitionist, she turned and looked right at him, her pupils dilating wildly. He blushed scarlet.

'Oh my God! I . . . I'm so sorry, Ms Andreas.' He started backing out.

Theo looked up. 'Don't be sorry,' he said, deadpan. 'She loves it.'

Sasha heard the news that Theo Dexter had applied for the Mastership of St Michael's on Christmas Day.

Home alone in her Upper East Side apartment, more depressed than she cared to admit, she was sitting at her computer, gorging herself on Fortnum & Mason mince pies from the luxury hamper she'd had delivered to herself when her thoughts turned to England and home. Remembering the conversation she'd had with her dad a few months ago about St Michael's, she googled 'St Michael's Cambridge Master Election' and there it was.

'I don't believe it,' she said aloud. Her first reaction was horror. It was bad enough that Theo should still be alive, never mind richer and more famous and successful than ever. But that he should go back to Cambridge, and not just to Cambridge but to *St Michael's*? That he should be welcomed back into the academic and scientific fold? That was too much to bear. Sasha would have given away Ceres and every penny she'd earned to stop it from happening. But as ever, she was powerless.

Angry, frustrated and bitterly depressed, she pulled on her warmest Donna Karan cashmere coat and fur-lined boots and trudged out into the snow. *I'm like Mr Scrooge*, she thought, biting back her irritation as she watched smiling families building snowmen on the sidewalks, and tried not to glare openly at the elderly couple who wished her a Happy Christmas on their way home from church. *I have more money than I know what to do with, but I'm miserable as sin and all alone.*

Stalking past the cheery West Village store fronts with their bright holiday displays, Sasha tried not to think about Jackson and Lottie and how they were spending the day, but it was like trying to turn back the tide. She pictured them like Jim Carrey in the scene from *Dumb and Dumber*, in an idyllic log cabin somewhere, with Jackson in a snowflake sweater, gazing adoringly at Lottie as she sat by the fire looking wifely and blissful. She was probably pregnant already. Twins most likely, perfect, adorable little Jackson clones.

Turning the corner, she was mercifully distracted by the incongruous sight of a group of protesters. There were only ten or twelve of them, stomping their feet against the cold as they waved their homemade placards in the air, but their disgruntled faces cheered Sasha inordinately. *My people. The kind of people who bitch on Christmas Day.* She could have hugged them.

Crossing the street to get a better look, she saw that the placards read 'No Condos on Holy Ground!' and felt slightly less warmly disposed. God squadders had never been Sasha's cup of tea, and as a real estate developer she found it hard to muster enthusiasm for the no-building brigade either. But curiosity got the better of her.

'What's this about?' she asked one of the protesters, a pale, skinny girl with unfortunately prominent buckteeth.

'They want to build apartments on that lot over there, next to the church. The city's said they're gonna consent, because it's vacant land. But there are people buried there. It's consecrated!' She imbued the last word with as much outraged awe as her dental challenges would allow.

'Couldn't they move the bodies?' asked Sasha innocently. 'To some other consecrated ground?'

The girl looked as if she might burst into tears. 'How would you like it, if someone dug you up and dumped you someplace else, like some hunk of garbage? What if it was *your* mother down there?'

Thinking privately that, as she'd be dead, she'd probably be past caring, Sasha murmured something supportive and continued on her way. It was only after she'd gone another two blocks, and was thinking about heading home for a sixth mince pie and some Vicar of Dibley DVDs, that it suddenly hit her. An idea so radical, and yet so obvious, so *simple*! Running back to where the protesters were standing, she reached into her pocket and pulled out a wodge of twenty-dollar bills, thrusting them into the bucktoothed girl's bewildered hands.

'Thank you!' she beamed. 'Thank you, and good luck with your campaign! And Merry Christmas!' she added for good measure, skipping towards her apartment, her heart still racing.

'Er . . . you're welcome?' said the girl, watching the beautiful girl in the couture coat twirl her way down the street. She was sure she recognized her from somewhere.

Back in her apartment, Sasha kicked off her boots, dropped her coat on the floor and ran to her bedroom, bouncing up and down on the bed like a five-year-old, whooping and laughing until she was out of breath.

After all these years, just like that, she'd done it.

She'd figured out a way to get her revenge on Theo Dexter.

It wouldn't be easy, of course. Plenty of things could go wrong. But it was a chance, a plan, a window of opportunity she'd come to believe she would never be granted.

It was going to be a good Christmas after all.

PART FOUR

CHAPTER TWENTY

Theresa sat in the waiting room of the Bridge Street surgery, flicking through a three-year-old copy of *Country Life* and marvelling at how cheap the property prices were back then . . . back when they'd seemed astronomical. The property market had been on her mind lately, ever since an extremely polite American couple had knocked on the door of Willow Tree Cottage a few weeks ago and asked her at what price she would consider selling.

'It is just the most utterly charming house we've ever seen,' gushed the wife. 'We were planning to buy in the Cotswolds, you know, around Oxford?' She pronounced it 'Arksford'.

Theresa suppressed a smile. 'Yes, I know the area. It's lovely.'

'But then we came out here and Cambridge just blew us away, didn't it, Bill?'

'Blew us away,' the husband agreed. For a moment Theresa wondered whether he was being literal. She loved Cambridge as much as anyone had ever loved a city, but the February winds were brutally bitter. With its bare trees and grey, plaintive skies, and the last of the holiday snow turned to sludge in the streets, neither Cambridge nor Willow Tree Cottage looked at their best.

'You're very kind, but I'm afraid I couldn't consider selling,' Theresa explained, taking their telephone number and email address anyway because they were so insistent. Ironically, had the couple knocked on her door a few weeks earlier, she might well have entertained their offer. When she first heard that Theo had applied for the St Michael's Mastership, she'd jumped off the deep end, vowing to abandon her own bid for the job and leave the university altogether. As usual, it was Jenny Aubrieau who got her to see sense.

'Are you out of your mind? In fact, forget that, you can scratch the question mark. You *are* out of your mind.'

It was the morning after Theresa's passionate night with Horatio Hollander. Theresa had woken late, hideously hung over and in complete emotional turmoil. Thank God Horatio had left early. There was a note from him propped up against the butter dish on the kitchen table, but she didn't have the strength to read it yet. Last night had been amazing, incredible, a complete revelation and one of the most meaningful experiences of Theresa's life. But she already knew she mustn't repeat it. *What can I offer a boy his age? Once his infatuation wears off he'll want children and a normal family life. All the things I can't give him.* She pictured Horatio at forty, still handsome and youthful, pushing her around in a wheelchair. Admittedly, it was a bit of a stretch. When Horatio was forty, Theresa would only be sixty-one. But the basic truth remained: she was too old for him. He would grow to resent her, and rightly so. Downing two extra-strength Alka-Seltzer, she crawled back to bed but was woken by a phone call from Jenny, demanding to know where she'd been last night and insisting she come over for brunch.

'I really can't, Jen. I'm too ropey to drive.'

'Fine,' said Jenny. 'I'll come and get you. Throw on a sweater, I'll be there in five.' An hour later, fortified by a hefty slab of Jenny's homemade chocolate cake and numerous cups of hot, sweet tea, Theresa had confessed that she was thinking of leaving. 'I can't face bumping into him every day. Well, maybe I can, but I don't *want* to face it.'

'So you're just going to pull out of the Mastership? Roll over and let him win?'

'Come on, Jenny,' Theresa laughed joylessly. 'He's already won. You know how strapped for cash St Michael's is. Who are they going to want as Master, a penniless woman Shakespeare scholar no one's ever heard of, who's too inexperienced anyway, or a world-renowned superstar with a sex-symbol wife who can raise the six million they need to reroof the chapel just by fluttering his eyelashes? It's hopeless.'

'It's not,' said Jenny robustly. 'Not if you don't give up hope. Besides, isn't there a principle involved here?'

Theresa took another big bite of chocolate cake and tried not to think about principles.

'I mean, why should you give up everything you've worked for just because *he* has some passing whim about coming back to his roots? What sort of message does that send your students, especially the girls?'

'I've never set myself up as a role model,' mumbled Theresa guiltily, thinking about Horatio. What the hell was she playing at?

'Maybe not. But you've never been a coward, either, not while I've known you,' said Jenny. Theresa was shocked by the anger in her voice. 'You love your life here, you love your work, you love that house. Don't let him drive you out, T. Don't do it.'

And in the end, Theresa hadn't. She'd channelled her inner Blitz spirit and hunkered down at Willow Tree Cottage, working harder than ever on her book and her teaching, doing her best to impress the St Michael's fellowship with her quiet industry and determined professionalism. She'd also told a devastated Horatio Hollander that she couldn't go out with him. For a few weeks afterwards she would see him at supervisions, but it was torturous for both of them. Shocked by how much she thought about him, and horrified by the degree to which her ending their short-lived affair had affected him physically – hardly stocky to begin with, he'd become positively gaunt, his cheeks caving in like a prisoner of war – she was relieved when Horatio eventually requested a transfer to another professor.

'It's not personal,' he told her, sadly. 'Well, it *is* personal, but I'm not angry or anything. I just . . . can't.'

'I understand,' said Theresa. She felt as if she was going into a decline herself, although her version unfortunately involved eating rather than starving. While Horatio's ribs became more prominent daily, Theresa seemed to have developed a layer of blubber round the middle that no amount of brisk walks into college would shift. As the nights grew shorter and the weather progressed from chilly to cold to arctic, she would sit curled up by the fire at the cottage, eating Marks & Spencer's sticky toffee pudding and forcing herself not to think about either Horatio or Theo, whose arrival was now set for mid March, a mere three weeks before the actual elections. All the other candidates, including herself, had been diligently lobbying the college authorities for months, but not Theo. *Of course not. He'll just waltz in and steal it from under our noses, like the king that he is.*

'Ms O'Connor?'

The doctor's receptionist, a fat, surly jobsworth of a woman who revelled in the power she wielded over her tiny, linoleum-floored fiefdom, summoned Theresa imperiously to the desk.

'You didn't fill out your forms. I'm going to have to let this gentleman go in ahead of you. We'll try and squeeze you in before five, if you'd like to do these now and bring them back to me.'

'But my appointment was at three thirty!' said Theresa wearily. 'I've been waiting forty minutes already.' She wouldn't mind so much if she weren't so damn exhausted all the time.

The receptionist shrugged. 'We need the forms. It's part of our patients' charter.' She pointed to a laminated sheet on the wall.

Theresa returned to her seat and began ticking boxes murderously. *Patients' charter indeed. I'd like to show her my 'out of patience' bloody charter.* She'd been feeling low for weeks now, but had put off coming to see the doctor for fear he might advise rest (impossible with the election so close) or, even worse, a diet and exercise regime involving neither sticky toffee pudding nor sitting vegetable-like on the couch for three hours a night devouring old episodes of *Location Location Location*. By the time she'd finished the forms, provided a urine and blood sample, and exhausted the paltry supply of magazines – you know you're bored when you're reduced to skimming through a dog-eared copy of *Cambridgeshire Today* – the waiting room was all but empty when the doctor finally showed her into his office. A short, wisp of a man with the sort of pale, freckled complexion that looked even worse on men than it did on women, he nevertheless had a genial way about him, like a friendly leprechaun.

'Ah, Ms O'Connor. *Professor* O'Connor, isn't it?' He smiled disarmingly. Theresa nodded. 'Well, I must say, Professor, it is nice to end a long, dreary Wednesday on such a positive note.'

'Positive?' Theresa rubbed her eyes tiredly. 'I'm not with you. You mean you don't think there's anything wrong with me?'

'There isn't anything wrong with you.'

He was so definitive about it, Theresa found herself getting irritated.

'What you mean is, you don't *know* what's wrong with me. Because I can assure you, I'm not in here for the fun of it. I don't know what it is, if I'm anaemic or I've picked up some sort of virus. But my energy levels . . . *what*?'

He was laughing at her now, his pale blue eyes creased at the corners, chuckling quietly to himself. 'I'd stick to the literature if I were you, Professor. You make a lousy doctor.'

Too annoyed to think of a comeback, Theresa folded her arms sullenly.

'You're pregnant, my dear.'

Theresa went white. Without thinking, she grabbed the chair for support, sinking down slowly into it. It took a second or two to process what he'd just said. When eventually she spoke her voice sounded croaky and odd.

'That's not possible. I'm infertile. I tried for years . . . my ex . . . specialists.' Her powers of sentence construction seemed to have deserted her. 'There's no way. I'm forty-four.'

'Well, sorry,' the doctor shrugged. 'But you *are* pregnant. I can tell you that with one hundred per cent certainty. You'll need to have a scan but I would guess you're somewhere in the region of three months along. Does that ring any bells?'

Yes. Christmas bells. Horatio's loving, tortured face loomed into mental view. It was ridiculous, impossible. All those years of trying and hoping, of ovulation tests and IVF and sperm spinning and macrobiotic diets. And here she was, twelve years and one drunken one-night-stand later . . .

'You must have missed at least one period.'

'Probably,' Theresa mumbled. 'I'm so irregular anyway. I thought . . .' She laughed nervously. 'I thought it might be menopause.'

'Again, I'd stick to the poetry. So I take it the pregnancy is . . . unexpected?'

She nodded, stunned.

'But, you're planning to go through with it?'

She looked up as if she'd been stung. 'Go through with it? Yes. Of course.'

'Sorry,' said the doctor. 'We have to ask, NHS policy, I'm afraid. But I'm very pleased for you, really. Congratulations.'

Ten minutes later, armed with a stack of papers about nuchal scans at the Addenbrooke's Hospital maternity ward, Theresa walked down Bridge Street in a daze. Her heart was pounding so fast, she felt as if she'd just been chased by muggers. Adrenaline coursed through her veins until she wanted to laugh out loud, or shout, or run very fast up to a random stranger and hug them until she'd squeezed the breath out of their bodies.

Of course, this meant the end of the Mastership. She'd faced long enough odds as a woman in the first place, even before the whole drama with Theo. But a single mother in the Master's Lodge, pregnant by one of her students? Not even Jenny could tell her *that* wasn't hopeless.

Jen. I must call her! Jenny had been there all those years ago when Theresa had been trying so hard for a baby with Theo. Jenny had held her hand as her hopes soared and then dashed repeatedly, each failed implantation chipping away another tiny piece of her soul. After her divorce from Theo, Theresa had finally accepted defeat, grieving privately for the baby she had longed for but knew she would never have. It was hard at first, but over time the pain subsided. Eventually even the dreams stopped. Motherhood was not Theresa's destiny. Shakespeare was her destiny. Shakespeare, and cats, and sticky toffee pudding.

It was a strange feeling, to have the dream that you had buried and mourned handed back to you, alive and vibrant and suddenly miraculously real. The feeling was two parts ecstasy, one part terror. Theresa walked back to college in a dream, starting her car and almost killing two kitchen staff as she swerved wildly onto Jesus Lane. She had no recollection of the drive home, or of walking through her front door. All she knew was that she was suddenly there, in the living room, with Lysander and the other cats mewing for food like neglected children, curling themselves hopefully around her legs until she nearly lost her footing.

'Stop it! Go away, all of you!' she shouted, instinctively shielding her belly with her hands. Then she felt guilty and started pulling cans of Kitty Kat out of the larder, spooning them onto saucers. *It's not the cats' fault I'm up the duff. Maybe I should go and lie down?*

In the end, with an effort, she pulled herself together, lit a fire and did what every sensible Irishwoman does in such circumstances: put the kettle on. After two cups of PG Tips and half a packet of Hob Nobs, the fog in her brain at last began to clear.

I'm pregnant. I'm going to have a baby. Or am I? Suddenly she was gripped by panic. *I'm forty-four. What if there's something wrong with it?* She pictured herself at the nuchal scan, a nurse shaking her head as she ran the ultrasound machine over Theresa's jelly-slick belly, the doctor squeezing her hand.

'I'm so sorry, Professor O'Connor. I'm afraid there's no heart-beat.' It was ridiculous how much anguish she felt at the possibility of losing a baby that, until a few short hours ago, she hadn't the faintest idea existed. Then there were the practical things to be considered, a list that grew longer every time Theresa thought about it.

What about her job? How would a baby fit in to her clois-tered, academic life? Clearly the Mastership of St Michael's was now out of the question, but what about her fellow-ship, her teaching and writing commitments? Instinctively, she didn't want to tell anyone about the pregnancy until she knew the baby was healthy, except for Jenny, of course. But even that had its drawbacks. Naturally Jen would want to know who the father was. Which meant Theresa would have to confess about Horatio, and then what? Tell him, presumably, although just *how* she was going to do that she had no idea. It was all too much to take in.

Pushing aside the half-eaten packet of biscuits, she dialled Jenny's number and was half relieved when it went to answerphone. 'I've got some news,' she said cautiously. 'Call me back when you get this. Or better still, come over. I think I need some advice.'

Feeling relieved – Jenny was practical and organized, she would know what to do – Theresa slumped back against the cushions of her couch and promptly fell into a deep, exhausted sleep.

She woke to the sound of knocking on the front door. *Jenny*. 'Hold on!' Rubbing her eyes blearily, she looked at the clock on the mantelpiece. It was still only seven fifteen, so she couldn't have been asleep for long. Even so it was disconcerting, the way that tiredness seemed to overtake her these days. 'Just coming.'

The cats scuttled nervously out of her way as she heaved

herself off the sofa and out to the hallway, which made Theresa feel guilty again. *Must not become one of those horrid, cranky pregnant witches who snap at everyone. Must teach cats and offspring to get along by being an oasis of maternal calm at all times.*

Then she opened the door, and all pretence of maternal calm flew out of the window. 'Good God. What on earth are *you* doing here?'

CHAPTER TWENTY-ONE

Sasha took in the shocked, angry face glaring at her from the cottage doorway and thought, *I made a mistake. I should never have come.*

She'd been focused on this moment since she made the decision at Christmas. But there had been so much to *do* since then, finishing up her outstanding deals at Ceres, arranging for a three-month leave of absence without scaring her partners and investors (no mean feat when you can't tell anybody where you are going or why) that she realized now she'd forgotten about the biggest hurdle of all. What if Theresa Dexter didn't *want* her help? What if she refused to give her the time of day?

It hadn't been hard to find out where she lived. The porters at Jesus were more than happy to accommodate an 'old friend' and give out the Professor's address. 'It's not Dexter any more though, love. She goes by O'Connor these days. Must be a while since you've seen her.'

'It is,' said Sasha. *A lifetime ago.*

And yet now, shivering on the doorstep of Theresa's picture-perfect cottage in Grantchester, it was as if no time had passed, and the two women were facing each other once more across the Senate House, both of their futures in the balance.

'What do you want?' The anger in Theresa's voice was palpable. Sasha wondered what she'd been expecting. A warm welcome?

'I'd like to talk to you. It's about . . .' she was about to say 'Theo', then suddenly worried that it might sound over-familiar, '. . . about your ex-husband.'

Theresa felt her happiness bubble pop like a pricked balloon. Today of all days, Theo was the last person she wanted to talk about, and Sasha bloody Miller was the last person she wanted to talk about him with. Ever.

'No thanks.' She started to close the door.

'Please!' Sasha stuck out her arm, keeping the door open. It was an aggressive gesture, an intrusion. Theresa's eyes narrowed even farther. 'It'll only take a few minutes. I know you don't owe me anything but . . . I've come a long way,' she finished lamely.

Reluctantly, Theresa let her in. Angry as she was, she could hardly let the girl stay out there on the doorstep and catch hypothermia. Inside, in the light, the two women got a better look at one another. It had been a long time, more than a decade, since they'd seen each other last. On the surface, Theresa concluded with irritation, Sasha Miller had barely aged. She was thinner, and wore her dark hair in a shorter, more professional bob. Underdressed for the chilly night in an expensive-looking but thin black wool coat and suede pumps, her *style* was more urban and mature, but her alabaster skin remained resolutely line-less. And then of course there were the eyes, that wonderful, mesmerizing light green. Theresa had seen at the time why Theo had fallen for Sasha, and she could still see it now.

'Thank you,' said Sasha politely. She started to take off her coat, then hesitated again. 'May I?'

Theresa nodded. 'Sure. There's a chair over there with a bit less cat hair on it.'

Sasha laid her coat over the back of the chair. Beneath it she looked even thinner, too thin, in a pair of grey Gucci cigarette pants and a thin black polo neck sweater from Brora. Theresa felt like a whale swimming beside a baby eel. She wondered idly whether Sasha had been ill. Was that why she was here, to make amends because she had cancer or something awful? In Theresa's experience, only cancer or heartbreak could make a woman get that skinny.

'I'll get to the point,' said Sasha. 'I heard that Theo applied for the Mastership of St Michael's.'

'That's right,' said Theresa, warily.

'I also heard that you were in the running for the job.'

Theresa was about to say 'not any more' but thought better of it. She wasn't about to confide the most important news in her life to the girl who had been the beginning of the end of her marriage. Instead she folded her arms defensively and said, 'And?'

'And I would like to prevent Theo from getting the job. I would like to sabotage his chances. I would like to ruin him.'

Sasha said this last so matter-of-factly, it took a moment for Theresa to process her words. When she did, curiosity got the better of her hostility. 'Why?'

'Why?' Sasha looked genuinely surprised. 'Because he ruined my life, of course. An eye for an eye and all that.'

'Ruined . . . I don't understand. How did Theo ruin *your* life? You're the one who tried to steal *his* theory, remember?'

Sasha looked at her with incredulity. 'Do you still believe that? Honestly?'

Theresa looked perplexed. It was all so long ago. She hadn't thought about the case, or about the theory that launched Theo's career, for longer than she cared to remember. She'd believed Theo at the time. Then again, she'd believed Theo about a lot of things.

'I never took anything from Theo,' said Sasha, with unexpected vehemence. 'Never. He, on the other hand, took everything from me. My career, my future, my reputation. My heart, at the time,' she added bitterly. 'Look, if you don't want to get involved, I understand. I realize that you suffered too.'

'That's big of you!' Theresa spluttered. 'I was his *wife*.'

'I know,' said Sasha. 'And I'm sorry, I am. But I was eighteen. I was his student, I was just a kid.' Theresa thought about Horatio and blushed. 'I'd like to tell you the truth about what happened,' said Sasha. 'Of course it's up to you whether you believe me or not. Or whether you decide you want to help me, or you'd rather leave the past in the past. But I want you to know.'

Theresa hesitated. Leaving the past in the past sounded like a wonderful idea. Recently, however, her past seemed determined to hunt her down. She had a feeling if she turned Sasha Miller away tonight, she would only be delaying the inevitable. And despite herself, she *was* intrigued to hear the girl's side of the story. All these years later, how could it hurt?

'You'd better have a seat,' she said. 'I'll make us some tea.'

An hour later and Theresa was still sitting, spellbound, opposite Sasha as she finished her long, painful story. There were tears in her eyes by the end, as Sasha related what happened after the university court's decision – her struggle to get into another university, the hate mail she and her parents received from *Daily Mail* readers for years afterwards.

Until recently, when Jenny told her about him coming back to Cambridge, Theresa hadn't thought about Theo in years, and certainly not with any lingering feelings of pain or regret. Looking at Sasha Miller tonight, Theresa could see it had not been the same for her. Beneath her success, her beauty, her wealth, Sasha was still the same scarred, heart-broken nineteen-year-old from all those years ago. She had never got over him. It was tragic.

It was also quite clear to Theresa that Sasha was telling the truth. She hadn't seduced Theo. Of course she hadn't! It was entirely the other way around. Theo had lied to her and used her and strung her along, the same way he did with all his girls. But, of course, in Sasha's case, it was far worse than that. Theo had taken Sasha's research, her brilliance, and passed it off as his own. Everything he'd achieved since then, his fame, his wealth, his global stature as a genius to rival Hawking – it was nothing more than stolen goods. No wonder she hated him. That was a lot to let go.

'I'm sorry I was so stand-offish when I let you in,' said Theresa. 'I didn't know. Plus I'd already had a rather, um, surprising afternoon.'

'Please,' said Sasha. 'It's entirely my fault. I should have called.'

For a few moments silence fell, neither woman sure what was supposed to happen next. Finally, Sasha spoke. 'So what do you think? About the Mastership? Will you help me stop him?'

Theresa sighed deeply. 'I'm afraid that's a lost cause. Theo has money and a media profile, two things St Michael's need desperately. Short of a natural disaster, I don't see how anyone can stop him.'

'I am a natural disaster,' said Sasha. 'Think of me as Hurricane Miller.'

Theresa smiled. 'Even so.'

'I'm not expecting an answer now,' said Sasha, standing up to go. 'I've already taken up much too much of your evening. But if I *were* to come up with a way to stop him . . . *if* . . . would you help me?'

No. I can't get involved. I'm pregnant, for God's sake. I have enough on my plate.

'Yes,' Theresa heard herself saying. 'I would. If you can think of a way to get that bastard out of Cambridge and out of both our lives for good, I'll be right behind you.'

'No.' Jackson said the word with finality, leaning back in his chair and folding his arms to emphasize the point. 'We're not doing it.'

'Now, wait a minute, Jackson,' Bob Massey fumed. 'You can't just reject the proposal out of hand.'

'Yes I can. I'm chairman, I have a veto, I'm vetoing.'

'For God's sake!' Bob spluttered. The years had not been kind to Bob. Always short and with a tendency to run to fat, he was now properly obese. The fat hung off his jowls, giving him the look of an angry bulldog. An angry bulldog with mange, if the last remaining wisps of hair clinging forlornly to his bald head were anything to go by.

'Slow down, Bob.' Dan Peters, as usual, was the voice of reason. 'Jackson, can you tell us why you're so opposed?'

Ever since Lucius Monroe had dropped dead of a heart attack last year, and Jackson had assumed the chairmanship of Wrexall Dupree, the tension in the boardroom had risen exponentially. Jackson had never fully forgiven Bob Massey for trying to oust him years earlier. And Massey remained dismissive of Jackson's talents, and distrustful of his motives.

Today was a case in point. The entire board had voted in favour of launching a takeover bid for Ceres. Sasha Miller's inexplicable leave of absence had left the market jittery and the company vulnerable. There were sound business reasons for re-integrating what was still, at its heart, an ex-Wrexall group. By recombining the two companies, their position as market leader would be unassailable. Even Raj Patel was on board. It hadn't occurred to any of them that Jackson Dupree of all people might object. Jackson who had protested so much when they let the Ceres guys go in the first place.

'I think we'd all rest easier if we understood the basis for your objection,' Dan Peters said reasonably.

'It's not a good fit, that's all.' Jackson sounded defensive.

'Sure it is. Did you even look at the numbers?' snapped Bob.

'Numbers aren't everything. Those guys left us once, bleating on about our "hostile corporate culture" and what a nightmare we were to work for. We don't need that kind of attitude. Besides, Raj's division is doing great as it is.'

'They're number two in the sector,' said Dan Peters. 'Ceres is still number one. It's very unlikely we'll get an opportunity like this again, Jackson. With Sasha Miller gone they're uniquely vulnerable. In a few months she'll most likely be back, and then the window will have closed.'

'I'm not so sure about that.' Harvey Tyler, the newest and youngest board member, piped up from the back of the room. Harvey rarely contributed at meetings. He was more of the shy, cerebral, number-crunching type. Everyone turned to stare at him. 'The rumour on the street is that she's sick. It could be another Steve Jobs situation.'

Hearing him refer to the Apple founder's famously secretive battle with pancreatic cancer some years back made Jackson feel ill. *Who said Sasha had cancer? That was ridiculous. She'd taken a break for personal reasons and that was all there was to it.* He got to his feet. 'We are not going to launch a bid for Ceres. If you want a reason, Bob, try this: It's never the right time to buy the wrong company.' With this pronouncement he swept regally out of the room.

The board watched him go. A deep feeling of unease settled over the table. Inevitably, Bob Massey was the first to voice it.

'Am I the only person sick to my stomach right now? *Not a good fit!* It's the perfect fucking fit. What the hell is he playing at?'

'Maybe he knows something we don't,' said the head of compliance.

'Maybe he's just too fried to think about it,' suggested the CFO. 'My secretary heard from *his* secretary that his wife's pregnant. Apparently his stress levels are through the roof.'

'Yeah, well he can join the club,' said Bob Massey with feeling. 'We need to stand together on this. We should demand a clear, written analysis of his objections. Ceres is down, it's weak, it's on the goddamn floor. If we don't go in for the kill now, we will wind up regretting it for the next ten years.'

His colleagues nodded silently. They all agreed.

'You can go ahead and "demand" what you want,' said Dan Peters, gathering up his papers. He was as disappointed as any of them by Jackson's decision, but he was also a realist. 'The fact is, he has a veto and if he wants to use it, he will. Forget it, Bob. The deal is dead.'

Down the hall in his office, Jackson squeezed the executive stress ball Lottie had bought him until his fingers were numb. He knew that Bob Massey was right. They should go after Ceres. Sasha had founded the company by striking while *he* was absent without leave. What was stopping him doing the same to her, in the name of good business? Some misplaced idea about gentlemanly conduct? He didn't know himself, and that made him mad. *Why am I protecting her? If I can't stick the knife in, if I don't have the stomach for it, then I shouldn't be in the fight, still less commanding the troops.*

He thought about Lottie. When he left their apartment this morning she'd been on her knees, slumped over the toilet with morning sickness. But nothing could dim her happiness about the baby, her certainty that the little person growing inside her would bring the two of them closer together. Jackson tried to share her joy. He tried so hard, the effort of it made his limbs ache, almost as if he had flu.

I have to get a grip, he told himself. *It's my old fear of commitment, that's all, except this time it's fatherhood I'm running away from. I need to relax, go with the flow.* He was gripping the stress ball so tightly, it shot out of his hand and rolled across the floor. Wearily, Jackson walked over and picked it up. He knew he hadn't heard the last about a Ceres takeover. Bob Massey wasn't a man who gave up easily, especially when he was right. The longer Sasha stayed away, the harder it would be for him to defend his position.

Where the hell is she?

CHAPTER TWENTY-TWO

Theo sat by the fire in the grand drawing room of the St Michael's Master's Lodge, admiring the priceless artwork. There were two Constables on either side of the full-height sash window, and an enormous Turner hanging above the fireplace. *I could get used to this*, he thought, sipping his freshly filled glass of Château d'Yquem. *It already feels like home.*

Anthony Greville had thrown a small, welcome-back-to-Cambridge soirée in Theo's honour. Greville had made no secret of the fact that Dexter was his preferred successor as Master. He was supported in this by the bulk of the fellowship, who all wanted a share of the lucre they assumed a 'star' like Theo would bring to the college. But supporting Theo's candidacy, and stomaching him as a person, were two very different things. Jealousy and loathing hung in the air like thick cigar smoke.

'Didn't you bring your wife?' Thomas Dean, the Head of Engineering, was a new face since Theo's day. Thin to the point of emaciation, with ugly angular features and flaky skin, he reminded Theo of a statue he once saw at the Getty

Museum in LA, a male figure made out of wire coat hangers. 'She's the big draw, you know. It's Dita we all want to see, not your ugly mug!'

It was delivered as a joke, but the hostility beneath Tom Dean's yellow smile was transparent.

'She'll be joining me in a few weeks,' said Theo smoothly, 'once the children start spring break. We don't want to unsettle them more than we have to. Not until we're sure we're moving here permanently.'

'Nonsense.' Anthony Greville tottered over. *Christ, he looks old*, thought Theo, *like he might drop dead any minute*. 'Of course you're moving here permanently. The whole college supports you, isn't that right, Johnny?'

Another frail elderly man had joined the group by the fire. It took Theo a moment to recognize him as Jonathan Cavendish, Head of History and one of his *bêtes noires* from the old days.

'Hmm?' Johnny tapped his hearing aid. 'Oh, yes, yes, jolly good.'

The Johnny Cavendish Theo remembered was a booming, Friar Tuck of a man, hugely fat, drinking and smoking himself to an early grave. Or so Theo had thought. *How on earth did he make old bones?*

'Not the *whole* college, Anthony. You really must try not to be so sweeping.'

Theo looked up. Now *that* was more like it. A very attractive blonde woman in her early thirties was helping herself to a canapé from the tray next to him. She wore a subtly clinging grey jersey dress with black tights and boots, and she positively radiated disapproval.

'I don't believe we've met.' Theo stood up and offered her his hand. 'Theo Dexter.'

'Georgia Frobisher,' said the blonde, shaking hands stiffly.

'And we have met, as it happens. Many years ago. I was an undergraduate here when you were teaching.'

'I don't think so.' Theo looked at her meaningfully, giving her the benefit of his practised Hollywood smoulder. 'I wouldn't have forgotten a face like yours.'

The blonde's look of disapproval intensified. 'You didn't teach *me*. You taught a friend of mine. Sasha Miller.'

The smile melted on Theo's face. 'Oh.'

'Professor Frobisher is our Director of Studies for Architecture,' said Anthony Greville, without enthusiasm. 'Our resident feminist, aren't you, Georgia?'

'Fuck off, Master,' said Georgia robustly, helping herself to two more smoked salmon blinis before walking away.

Theo raised an eyebrow. You wouldn't have got away with insubordination like that in his day. *When I'm Master, she'll be the first to go.*

The elections were in three weeks' time. Three weeks in which Theo intended to make the most of Dita's absence and enjoy all that Cambridge had to offer. She'd agreed to make at least one trip over, to help him campaign, but it shouldn't be for more than a few days. He wondered how hard it would be to seduce the prickly Professor Frobisher before then. Fucking her *and* firing her would be double the thrill. But perhaps he should make life easy on himself and stick with pretty undergraduates instead? That was like shooting fish in a barrel – all the satisfaction, but none of the challenge.

He was thinking wistfully about a redhead he'd seen walking across Second Court only this morning when he realized he was being spoken to.

'. . . reach our fundraising targets. I'd like to carve out some time with you if I may. There are a number of urgent projects we need to prioritize . . .'

Dominic Lawless, the college bursar, was as dull an accountant as one could ever hope to meet. Theo struggled to focus on his monosyllabic drone as he wittered on about interest rates and alumni donors.

'Of course, Dom. That's a priority for me, too.'

Theo was well aware that his support base for the Mastership was founded on a belief that he was wildly wealthy, with access to mythical, limitless amounts of cash, cash that he would be happy to channel into St Michael's College coffers. Had any of the fellows seen Dita's latest, livid-red credit card statement, not to mention the lawsuits pending against Theo's production company for a web of unpaid loans, their enthusiasm for his candidacy might well evaporate.

For the next month Theo would have to walk a tightrope, hinting at money and connections while keeping his specific promises vague. Then, after he was Master, he would gently lower expectations. After all, it wasn't as if he were broke or anything, and he *could* raise St Michael's profile, something that the other candidates, including poor old Theresa, had no hope of doing. Hugh Mullaney-Stoop from Robinson was greyer than a misty morning in Scotland, the sort of man who faded into a crowd even when there was no one else in the room. Graham North was an engineer, which everyone knew was code for 'autistic social inadequate'. He could barely make eye contact, never mind raise money. Andrew Gray, the other St Michael's fellow who'd been in the running, had pulled his name out once he heard Theo had applied for the job. It was fair to say they weren't exactly awash with options. Theo had come back to Cambridge to save money, not spend it. Poor Dom was in for a shock.

'This week I'm completely snowed, as you can imagine,' he said soothingly. 'But maybe we can sit down next week. Get a handle on the big picture?'

'Sure, sure, absolutely.' Dom nodded like a dashboard dog.

Theo was used to obsequiousness. The world of television was full of yes-men. But it wasn't the same as being kow-towed to by one's intellectual equals. He had missed Cambridge more than he realized. It was good to be back.

Theresa pushed her trolley down the frozen-food aisle at Waitrose, trying to think of anything she was allowed to eat that didn't make her feel nauseous. It wasn't easy, partly because her obstetrician had given her a printout as long as her arm about avoiding mercury, vitamin A, uncooked this and overcooked that, and partly because most days even the thought of food made her sick as a dog. All the advice on pregnancy seemed contradictory. Keep active but don't over exercise. Eat fish, but avoid mercury. Eggs are good, but easy on the cholesterol. *It's a wonder anyone ever had a healthy baby, with this minefield to navigate. Never mind actually held down a job.*

Listlessly picking up a four-cheese pizza, trying to remember which cheese she was allowed and which, according to the scaremongering leaflets at the doctor's surgery, was the equivalent of feeding the baby arsenic, she became aware of a group of undergraduates staring at her. Inevitably, the battle between Theo Dexter and his ex-wife for the Mastership of St Michael's had become *the* hot topic in *Varsity*, the student newspaper. Theresa was aware she was the underdog. If she were honest, she knew she had already lost. But Sasha Miller's arrival in Cambridge in particular had strengthened her resolve not to give up without a fight. Since their first, bizarre meeting, when Sasha had shown up on the doorstep at Willow Tree Cottage, the two women had formed an unlikely but blossoming friendship. Sasha was staying at the University Arms hotel, and seemed to spend most of her days holed up in mysterious meetings with developers, city councillors, and a slew of local politicians. Quite how this was supposed to help get Theo out of Cambridge, Theresa had no idea, but Sasha's quiet confidence was contagious.

Of course, Sasha didn't know about the baby. Apart from Theresa's doctors, the only soul on earth she had told was Jenny Aubrieau, and even Jenny had had to swear that she would keep it from JP. 'I haven't told the father yet,' Theresa blushed. She was sure Jenny must know that Horatio was the dad, but she didn't want to confirm it, not until he knew himself. 'And he should really be the first to know.'

'So tell him.'

'I can't.'

'Why not?'

Theresa had used the Mastership race as her excuse. She wanted to keep the pregnancy a secret until elections were over. While this was true, it conveniently saved her from having to admit the *real* reason for keeping quiet. Once Horatio knew, he would want to be involved. Not just want. He would insist. He would want them to be together, and Theresa knew she couldn't do that, she couldn't give him what he wanted. Just thinking about it made her heart ache and her hormone-overloaded body push her to tears.

Wantonly throwing the pizza into her trolley without resolving the cheese issue – every trip to Waitrose felt like Russian Roulette! – she pushed round the corner away from the gawking students. Pulling her baggy sweater down over her swollen middle, she realized that pretty soon her secret would be out of the bag whether she liked it or not. It was astonishing how quickly she was gaining weight, particularly since she felt as if she threw up a good half of what she ate every day. At not yet four months gone, her bottom already looked like a giant, cling-film-stuffed bag of porridge. As for her breasts, she'd seen smaller mounds on an Ordnance Survey map. *Was that what those kids were staring at? Can they tell?*

She was so busy thinking about her whale-like frame, that at first she didn't hear him.

'Theresa!' The voice was louder this time, almost a shout. 'It *is* you! My goodness, how are you? Long time no see.'

Standing at the checkout with a packet of Jaffa Cakes in one hand and a pizza in the other, Theresa froze. There, like a vision from another planet, was Theo. In a dark suit with a bright blue shirt and St Michael's College tie, he looked tanned and relaxed and at least ten years younger than she remembered him. When he smiled, she noticed that his teeth were even whiter than they used to be. He smelled of Gucci aftershave, confidence and money and in his single shopping bag was a six-pack of protein shakes and some smoked salmon.

'I knew we'd run into one another eventually, but I didn't think it would be here.'

'No.' His friendliness was so disarming, Theresa found herself tongue-tied.

'You look, er . . . well.' His eyes swept over her figure. In a threadbare, man's sweater, long tweed skirt with a comfy elasticated waist, and the sort of scuffed lace-ups that Theo used to refer to as 'lesbian shoes', Theresa knew she looked a wreck. To add insult to injury, her pregnancy hormones had given her spots. Not expecting to run into anyone remotely interesting at the supermarket, she'd come out without make-up and with her hair scraped up in a messy bun, so that every last zit was on display.

'I've been busy,' she mumbled.

'The election. Of course.'

'On top of my regular workload. Those Shakespeare papers don't mark themselves you know,' said Theresa, instantly regretting sounding so defensive. *What do I care if he thinks I look awful? Or that I'm some downtrodden, haggard old spinster who can't cope?* she told herself. *His opinion means nothing to me.* But the pity in his eyes still irked her. Why did he have to show up here, of all places, and looking so unreasonably handsome?

'I know what you mean. I'm on my way to London actually. Got an interview at Television Centre in two hours,' said Theo cheerfully. 'It never stops, does it? Anyway, good to see you.' Before Theresa could move he was kissing her on both cheeks, as if they were old friends. 'Take care, T, and best of luck . . . you know. May the best man win and all that. Bye-eee.'

She watched him go, still rooted to the floor, like a frightened cow watching something spectacular and unexpected, like a passing cyclone.

'D'you wan' any cashback?'

'Hmmm?' said Theresa vaguely.

'Cashback. You wan' any?' the surly girl at the checkout repeated herself.

'Oh. No. Thank you. I'm fine.' Grabbing her shopping bags she practically ran outside. The streets were thronged with lunchtime shoppers. Theo, thankfully, was long gone. Their encounter had been surreal. Not upsetting exactly, but jarring and, for some reason Theresa couldn't put her finger on, depressing. *Once upon a time we were everything to each other.* Ridiculously, she found herself thinking about Horatio, wishing he were here to hold her and hug her and tell her she was beautiful, even when she looked like an acne-prone shot-putter. Just then her phone rang. Already annoyed that she wished it were him, her heart sank still further when she saw 'Sasha mobile' flash across the screen. Sasha had been lovely these last few weeks, a human injection of energy and confidence and sisterly spirit. But Theresa couldn't face a rousing pep talk just now. All she wanted was to crawl under a duvet and eat Jaffa cakes.

Guiltily pressing 'ignore' she switched her phone off. She realized that the dampening of her spirits was nothing more than a dose of cold reality, delivered face to face when she'd least been expecting it.

Theo was here.

He was going to win the election and become Master of St Michael's.

Theresa was either going to have to come to terms with that – with running into him in the supermarket, at university functions, on the street – or she and her baby were going to have to move somewhere and start afresh.

Sasha kept telling her she could do it, she could stay and beat Theo and become Mistress herself. Theresa wanted to believe it. But who were they kidding? Just looking at Theo today brought it home to her. She didn't stand a chance. Besides, Sasha had her own agenda. *She's here because of Theo, not me. She wants to hold on to the past, and I want to escape it.*

In a week, the whole Mastership debacle would be over. But Theresa would still have some tough decisions ahead.

Anthony Greville shouted into the phone, 'That's not possible, do you hear me? Not possible!'

On the other end of the line, a patient female voice assured him that not only was it possible, but it was an indisputable fact. 'Check it out for yourself, Master, but my source is one hundred per cent accurate.' The girl was a journalist, from the local city newspaper. She seemed not in the least bit bothered that she had ruined Anthony Greville's day. In fact, she seemed to take great pleasure in the conversation, pushing him for a juicy quote to top off her scoop. 'The land has been sold to a private buyer, and preliminary permissions have already been granted. They'll be the first new luxury apartments to be built in the old town since the St Frideswide's Church conversion in the eighties. But these are new build. "A sympathetic addition" the planning committee called them.'

'A sympathetic . . . *what*?' the St Michael's Master spluttered. 'That land has been green space for seven hundred years! This is outrageous.'

'The college will be appealing then? You'll protest the development?'

'Most certainly we'll protest it. More than that, madam, we will prevent it,' Greville seethed. 'Who is this private buyer?'

For the first time, a note of disappointment crept into the girl's voice. 'I've no idea, Master. I was hoping you might be able to shed some light.'

Anthony Greville hung up. He was about to reach for the phone again and dial the head of the Cambridge City Planning Committee, when a small voice in his head made him hesitate. It was he, Anthony Greville, who had sold the two-acre plot of St Michael's land back to the city in the early eighties. Back then the college had been in deep financial trouble. Even so, he'd been roundly opposed at the time by many of the fellows, who saw the sell off as the 'thin end of the wedge'. The controversy over the sale had died down years ago. The city had preserved the open space, and life continued much as it had before, except with the college a much-needed four million pounds richer. These days Anthony Greville's Mastership was widely viewed as having been a prosperous, stable period for St Michael's. But if this deal went through – if a block of modern apartments were really to be built *overlooking* the college's ancient, tranquil courts! – his reputation would be left in tatters.

He might have sounded off to the young journalist, but the truth was he had no specific right of appeal. He'd sold the land to the city free and clear. Their undertaking to leave it green had never been anything more than a gentlemen's agreement, one that, in this latest financial crisis, *they* could no longer afford to honour. As tempting as it was to vent his spleen to the planning committee, Anthony Greville knew better than anyone that he would need a better plan than that. He needed a knight in shining armour, and quickly. The council was unlikely to be out-argued. Their 'private buyer' could, however, be out-bid.

He called for his secretary. 'Yasmin,' he said imperiously. 'Get me Theo Dexter. Try all his numbers. Go to his home if you have to. Tell him I need to see him urgently at the Master's Lodge.'

'Yes, sir. Should I say what this is concerning?'

Anthony Greville thought about it. 'Tell him it concerns his future and the future of the college. Tell him if he wants my job, he's going to have to earn it, and he's going to have to start now. Oh, and Yasmin?'

'Master?'

'Tell him to bring his cheque book.'

CHAPTER TWENTY-THREE

Theo Dexter walked out of Television Centre onto the South Bank with the sort of spring in his step he hadn't felt in years. London looked beautiful in the late-afternoon sunlight. Below him, barges slowly chugged along the silver Thames. Above him, a surprisingly blue sky shimmered over modernist glass towers and grand Victorian mansion blocks, that mish-mash of eras and architectural styles that made the city so vibrant and unique.

Theo's interview with Connor Greaves, ITV's new 'face' of late-night talk, had gone remarkably well. So well, he could almost have done it live, although as usual Ed Gilliam had insisted on the slot being pre-recorded, 'Just in case. You never know when someone's going to try to stitch you up.' In fact, Greaves's questions had been softer than a gay man's dick on his wedding night: How did it feel to be back home after such a long sojourn in Hollywood? What did Dita think about living back in Blighty? Would Theo be making a return to British screens any time soon, or would his academic ambitions preclude that?

Theo could hear his own voice now, soothing and

mellow. *You know, Connor, I think Cambridge is moving with the times along with the rest of the world. I've always seen myself as a scientist, first and foremost. But if I have an opportunity to share that passion, that vocation, with ordinary people? That's something that I think the university and St Michael's College would both be excited by.* He pronounced it 'exci*did*', the faintest twang of an American accent creeping into his voice. In the US he worked hard to sound as clipped and British as possible, but here a little hint of Hollywood went a long way. In fact the interview had gone *so* well, he'd gone further than he intended, referring repeatedly to the Mastership as if he'd already been appointed. He'd been careful not to stray into arrogance though, talking pointedly about his desire to 'give back'. *I've been very blessed, Connor. I've reached a point in my life where I can afford to think of others. I see myself as very service-oriented. It's all about service, you know? To your country, to science, to the next generation.* The housewives would love it. So, hopefully, would the St Michael's fellows. With any luck this was just a taste of the great PR he could get for them once they appointed him Master.

It had been surreal, running into Theresa earlier. By God she'd looked a fright! She must have gained a stone at least since he'd last seen her, and aged too, with those deep, dark circles under her eyes, not to mention the old-lady clothes she was wearing. Any lingering doubts he'd had about her prospects of beating him to the job had been well and truly dispelled. She might have Georgia Frobisher and the rest of the politically correct feminist brigade on her side, but she couldn't seriously hope to be appointed Master looking as if she'd just broken out of the local lunatic asylum. *Thank God I got rid of her when I did,* he shuddered, imagining for a second how different his life and career might look today had Theresa, not Dita, spent the last decade on his arm. Of course, Dita bored him now too. It was time for a new chapter. But as a strategic alliance, that marriage had certainly served its purpose.

Walking over Waterloo Bridge, Theo's thoughts turned to this evening. He was meeting some friends, including Ed Gilliam, for dinner at the Chelsea Arts Club. Helena, a stunning undergraduate he'd met at the university library last weekend, was catching the train up to town to join him. After making his friends suitably jealous, he would take her on to Annabel's afterwards, then hopefully back to his serviced apartment in Mayfair to continue the night's entertainment. It was a long time since Theo had looked forward to an evening more. His excitement was heightened by the knowledge that this would be his last night of fun for a while. Dita arrived in Cambridge tomorrow morning, just in time for the college's official launch of the Mastership election, a grand lunch party-cum-press junket in the grounds. Dita had made it plain that she was coming on sufferance.

'You know I hate to leave Milo,' she'd whined on the phone last week.

'So bring him. It's only for a few days and they'll be moving here soon enough anyway. Bring them both.'

'*Bring* him? To that wet, damp, toxic climate? Do you *know* how bad his asthma is right now, Theo? Do you care?'

Theo was tempted to hit back that as the boy was being raised in one of the smoggiest, most polluted cities on earth, he was hardly surprised, but he restrained himself. Soon, if things went according to plan, he would be free of Dita's tantrums forever. Just a few more weeks of making nice . . .

Turning his mobile phone back on, he saw he had a string of messages. Two from Ed, asking how it had gone with Connor Greaves. Theo texted back 'Stellar'. One gloriously X-rated message from Helena – perhaps he'd nix Annabel's and take her straight home after dinner? – and a fourth, terse voicemail from Tony Greville's office at St Michael's.

'This is Yasmin Jones. Please call the Master as soon as you receive this message.'

Irritated, Theo switched the phone back off. *Fuck you, Greville. I'm not at your beck and call.* If it were that urgent, the old lech could pick up the phone himself.

It was starting to rain. Theo felt the first heavy, ponderous drips on the lapel of his cashmere coat and stuck his hand out. 'Taxi!' A black cab appeared immediately, its orange 'For hire' light glowing in welcome. Theo hopped inside.

'Mayfair, please,' he said brightly. This really was turning out to be an excellent day.

Three hours later, having showered and changed into jeans and a grey Armani Exchange polo neck sweater that the salesman had told him made the blue of his eyes pop, Theo swaggered into the Chelsea Arts Club with Helena on his arm. Ed Gilliam was already at the table, with a group of hangers-on.

'My, my,' leered Ed, drooling unashamedly at Helena's legs in the ultra-short yellow sixties mini-dress she was wearing. 'Does Dita know?'

'Helena's a friend of mine,' said Theo smugly. 'We met at the library in Cambridge last week.'

'Helping her with her GCSEs, were you?' Ed lowered his voice. 'Or was it her eleven plus?'

Theo couldn't resist a grin. 'Now, now. Jealousy'll get you

nowhere. She's a second-year undergraduate. King's, I believe. As it happens we have a lot in common.'

'Like what?' Ed guffawed. 'Genitals?'

Dinner went swimmingly. The men around the table made no effort to hide their desire for Helena, nor their envy that Theo was quite clearly bedding her. Everyone asked about his interview, due to be aired tomorrow night, and what it felt like to become Master of a Cambridge college after so many years in the spotlight.

'It's humbling,' said Theo, looking about as humble as a pig in shit, and plainly delighted by the attention. The only irritating thing was his telephone, which buzzed ceaselessly in his pocket throughout dinner. He'd agreed to keep it on in case there was a problem with Dita's flight, but every single call had come from St Michael's. In the end he gave in, stomping outside onto Old Church Street and grudgingly returning Anthony Greville's calls.

'For fuck's sake, Tony, I'm having dinner. What's so bloody urgent? I'll be back in Cambridge tomorrow, can't it wait until then?'

'If it could wait, do you think I would have wasted my evening calling you? How dare you screen my calls!' The Master's voice quivered with rage. Theo quickly backtracked.

'I wasn't screening. I'm in a club, there's lousy reception here. What's up?'

'What's *up*? I'll tell you what's up, Theo. Either you wire Dom Lawless eight million pounds first thing tomorrow morning, or you can forget about taking my place next year. And that's a promise.'

He filled Theo in on the sale of the land adjoining the college, and the council's outrageous plans to build apartments there. 'They've got some mystery foreign buyer, Arab or Russian I assume, and they're rushing this thing through. The local press have already got wind of it. Our only hope is to outbid this person and buy the land back ourselves.'

'I see.' Theo paused. He could hear the anxiety in Greville's voice and he understood it. The old man's entire legacy as Master was at stake. But the plain truth was Theo didn't have eight million pounds. Even if he had, he wasn't about to hand it over to St Michael's. Nor did he appreciate being threatened. 'Let's not do anything rash, Tony. The council may yet be open to persuasion. I have influence in media circles. We can make this look very bad for them, defacing the university's heritage and all that jazz.'

'Don't try to fob me off, Dexter!' the Master wheezed furiously. 'Either you come up with that money or there is no "we". I will personally see to it that the college transfers its allegiance to another candidate.'

'Bullshit,' said Theo firmly. 'Like who? Theresa? That geek from Robinson? You think *they're* going to pull you out of this hole? It's your balls on the line here, Tony, not mine. So if you want my help, I suggest you play nice.'

There was a sharp intake of breath on the other end of the line. Theo could hear the old man's mind whirring as he weighed up his options. Finally, very quietly, he said, 'Be in my office, nine a.m. tomorrow. We'll talk.'

Walking back into the club, Theo felt an initial glow of satisfaction. He had called Greville's bluff. Taking the wind out of the old bastard's sails had felt good. But it only took a few moments for doubts to start creeping in. What if Greville *did* turn on him, out of pure spite? Theo knew there was no love for him at St Michael's. That the fellows only supported him because they believed he would bring money to the college. If the ship were going down, perhaps they would prefer it to go down with one of their own at the helm? A nice, committed academic? Like Theresa . . .

Suddenly he wished he had not waxed quite so lyrical about his future at Cambridge on Connor Greaves's couch. If the interview aired and Anthony Greville turned on him, he'd become a laughing stock, not just at Cambridge but all over England. He'd have to return to LA and Dita with his tail between his legs.

'Are you OK?' Helena met him at the door, snaking a proprietorial arm around his waist.

'Not really,' snapped Theo, removing her hand and handing her a twenty-pound note. 'Here. Get yourself a cab back to Liverpool Street.'

'But . . . but . . . what about our night together? I thought . . .'

'Sorry, sweetheart. I'm not in the mood.'

Grabbing his coat from the cloakroom, Theo stormed off into the night.

Ed Gilliam could see to the bill.

The next morning dawned misty and grey in Cambridge. People loved to moan about the weather, but Theresa adored these sorts of days. The way the fog hung low over the river gave everything a mystic, ethereal look. Plus the drizzle gave one a cast-iron excuse to sit inside wrapped in blankets, eating biscuits and reading, surely one of life's greatest pleasures?

Today, however, she felt less joyful than usual. Bumping into Theo yesterday had put a dampener on her spirits that no amount of stiff talking-tos had been able to shift. On top of that she'd slept badly, and woken at five gripped by the sort of nausea normally associated with violent sea crossings or Indian stomach flu. Pulling on a dressing gown weakly, she'd finally managed to stagger downstairs at seven and make herself a cup of black tea and a piece of dry toast. But by the time the post arrived at eight, she still felt distinctly sub par. She had a million things to do today, including an antenatal appointment at Addenbrooke's this morning, and of course this blasted lunch at St Michael's for the official launch of the election. In an ideal world she should wash her hair and dig out her barely used make-up bag. As it was, she barely had the strength to switch on GMTV, never mind shuffle over to the front door and sort through her post. How she was going to grin and bear it for the press at St Michael's she had no idea.

Chucking a pile of bills onto the hall table, she returned to the couch with the new copy of *Varsity*. It was a student paper really, with little in it written directly for the faculty, but Theresa had always enjoyed the gossip and enthusiasm that crammed its pages. Flipping through a piece on *Footlights'* latest production, she turned to page three and froze.

'Oh my God,' she said aloud. 'Oh my God, no!'

Sasha was still in the shower when she heard the phone ringing. Running across her hotel room carpet, naked and dripping, she hunted for it under the mound of papers on her desk.

'Hello?'

'Sasha, it's me.' Theresa was hyperventilating so hard, it took Sasha a moment to recognize her voice. 'Listen, I . . . I have to pull out of the race.'

'No!' It was almost a shout. 'Why? You can't. I have news for you, really great news. I was trying to reach you yesterday, didn't you get my messages?'

'Sorry,' Theresa said guiltily. 'Yesterday was kind of a bad day. But it doesn't matter anyway.'

'It does matter! You don't understand.'

'No, Sasha. *You* don't understand. I'm pregnant.'

Sasha was silent for a moment. Then she said, 'That's great, isn't it? Congratulations.'

Theresa gave a short, cynical laugh. 'Thanks, but I'm not sure the St Michael's fellows are going to be congratulating me. Not when they read the piece in this morning's *Varsity*.'

She began to read. When she'd finished, Sasha sank down slowly on the bed.

'Yikes.'

'Yeah. Yikes. There's no way I can go to the lunch today. Not now.'

A small, insistent beeping interrupted their conversation. 'Theresa, I have my office on the other line,' said Sasha. 'Just don't do anything rash, OK? Let's talk again before the lunch. I still think you should go.' Theresa started to protest, but Sasha cut her off, pushing her wet hair out of her eyes as she switched calls. 'Hello?'

'Sasha. Thank God.'

It was Doug Carrabino, her CFO and one of her top right-hand men at Ceres.

'I take it you heard the news?'

'What news?' Sasha picked up a towel from the floor and wrapped it around her shivering body. 'I just woke up. Hold on, isn't it the middle of the night where you are?'

'Yeah, it is, but none of us are getting much sleep. Wrexall is launching a bid for us.'

Sasha's heart skipped a beat. Was he kidding?

'We won't get the official numbers until markets open tomorrow, but word is they're pulling out all the stops.'

'Jackson,' Sasha muttered. *I don't believe it. I thought all that was behind us. I thought we'd buried the hatchet.*

'Actually, I understand that Jackson Dupree fought his

own board on this,' said Doug. 'That's the rumour, anyway, that he doesn't want us back, after all the bad blood.'

'Of course he wants us!' Sasha snapped. 'We're the best.'

'Maybe. But we're vulnerable, and they know it.' Doug countered. 'Look, I don't know what you're doing over there, Sasha – nor does the market, that's the problem. But if you want us to have a fighting chance of beating Wrexall off, you need to come back to New York. Right now.'

He was right, of course. Sasha had left herself wide open, and Jackson had taken a shot. Why wouldn't he? It was business, after all. Hadn't that always been her mantra?

'I'll be there as soon as I can,' she said guardedly.

'As soon as you can? What does that mean?'. Doug Carrabino was incredulous. 'Call a taxi and get to the nearest airport, for God's sake. We'll have to give a statement by the end of the day tomorrow . . . I mean today. We need you, Sasha.'

'I know,' said Sasha. *But I need to do this. I've waited my whole adult life to get my revenge on that bastard. I can't stop now.* 'Whatever their offer is, we rebuff it. I'll draft you a statement right now. I'll be there soon, Doug, OK? I promise.'

She hung up.

Yesterday, everything had been falling into place. Today, all her carefully laid plans were crumbling into dust. Ceres was under attack. Theresa was pulling out of the Mastership race. Theo was going to get what he wanted after all. And Jackson . . . no, she mustn't think about Jackson.

Marching to the wardrobe, Sasha pulled out her smartest cream wool Dior business suit and the killer Jonathan Kelsey heels that made her feel like Alexis Colby on a mission.

She was on her way to St Michael's. It was time to close the deal.

Back at Willow Tree Cottage, Theresa had put the phone down feeling more confused than ever. Sasha still wanted her to go to the lunch at St Michael's, but how could she? Everyone would be staring at her, judging her. She'd be a laughing stock.

She picked up the *Varsity* piece and read it again. The headline alone was enough to bring on her nausea: 'ST MIKE'S HOPEFUL PREGNANT AFTER AFFAIR WITH STUDENT'.

Theresa O'Connor, a respected university Shakespeare professor and contender for the Mastership of St Michael's – in competition with her famous ex-husband, Dr Theo Dexter – is reportedly four months pregnant, after an affair with one of her students. While Varsity *has learned the name of the student, we understand from our sources that the young man himself may not be aware of Professor O'Connor's condition, and for this reason we have declined to identify him. We can reveal, however, that he was directly supervised by Professor O'Connor, and that he is more than twenty years the professor's junior.*

Who? How? Jenny would never have said anything, that much she was sure of. Walking upstairs in a dream, she pulled on a t-shirt and sweater, both of them inside out, and a pair of corduroy gardening trousers. She tried to clean her teeth, but gagged when she realized she'd squeezed moisturizer on the toothbrush. The moment she finished spitting it out, the doorbell rang.

'Go away!' Theresa wailed, putting her hands over her ears. 'Whoever you are I don't want to talk to you.'

'Too bad,' a voice shouted back at her. 'I want to talk to you.'

Horatio! Oh Christ. He sounded angry. Of course he was angry! He must be bloody furious, poor boy. She'd deliberately deceived him. But she'd done it for his own good, for both their goods . . .

'Open the door, Theresa.'

She ran downstairs and opened the door. Horatio was still in his pyjamas, with a pair of wellington boots, a sweater and a raincoat pulled on over the top. On anyone else, it would have looked ridiculous. But on him it looked . . . perfect. Normal. Theresa longed to throw herself into his arms. Instead she said meekly, 'You'd better come in.'

'Is it true?' He stood in the hallway dripping, a small puddle forming on the flagstones at his feet.

Theresa nodded miserably.

'Were you ever going to tell me?'

'Yes. No. I suppose so. I don't know.' She sat down on the wooden chair in the hallway, then she remembered it was covered with post and stood up again, wringing her hands awkwardly. 'I hadn't thought it through that far. It was a shock.'

'A disappointment.' The bitterness in his voice was heartbreaking. 'The end of your Mastership hopes! Is that why you kept it secret?'

'I couldn't care less about the stupid Mastership!' Theresa's eyes welled up with tears. She could take censure from anyone but Horatio. For him to think that she was disappointed by the baby, that she didn't want it . . . it was unbearable.

'You couldn't care less about me either, could you? What was I, just some sad sperm donor? Go for someone young and healthy with a decent IQ, never mind about *his* life, *his* feelings . . .'

'I did mind about your feelings! Very much. I'm over the moon about the baby, but what right did I have to saddle you with a child and a family, at your age? And with *me*, twenty years your senior as whoever wrote that article so graciously pointed out! It was a mistake, Horatio. *My* mistake.'

'*Our* mistake actually.' Standing in the hallway, shaking with emotion like a tall, wet tree, he suddenly looked a lot older than twenty-three. 'You're keeping it?'

Theresa nodded. 'Yes. Definitely.'

'Then I want to be involved.'

'All right.' There didn't seem much else to say. He hadn't said 'I love you' or 'Let's get married' or any of the things she'd feared. But now that he was actually here, in her house, *not* saying those things, she realized with horror that she wanted him to say them. She had no right to the fairytale, to steal his youth just for her own happiness. But in that instant, Theresa knew that she wanted it. She wanted *him*. But it was too late.

'Will you still stand as Master?'

She shook her head. Horatio nodded, absorbing the information.

'Will you stay in Cambridge?'

'No. Probably not.' As she said the words, Theresa realized that they were true. She had no idea where she would go. But she couldn't stay here. Not now. 'We can talk, later,' she said. 'But I have to go. I . . . I've got a doctor's appointment.'

'Fine.' He couldn't even bring himself to look at her, he just turned and opened the door. *He hates me*, thought Theresa. *I've ruined his life.*

'I'm sorry,' she sobbed as he marched off down the path.

Horatio turned. Theresa couldn't tell if he was crying or if it was rain pouring down his face. 'Me too.'

* * *

Dita Andreas admired her reflection in the full-length antique mirror. In a vintage Dior suit, navy blue with red piping, red leather gloves and a smart navy blue pill box hat, she looked understated but sexy. 'How do I look?'

'Very Carla Bruni.' Theo kissed her approvingly. 'You look perfect, actually.'

He'd been so wound up after his dinner last night, and his tense conversation with Anthony Greville, that he'd driven himself straight back to Cambridge and spent the night in his rented townhouse on Portugal Place. He'd been woken at 7 a.m. by Dita's arrival, confidently expecting her string of complaints to begin the moment she dragged her six Louis Vuitton suitcases through the door. Instead she'd climbed quietly into bed beside him, having evidently already showered and beautified herself in the first-class lounge at Heathrow, and proceeded to give him one of the best blow jobs he'd had in years. As if that weren't miraculous enough, she then got up, went downstairs, opened the fridge with her own, perfectly manicured hands and cooked him a full English breakfast, bringing it back up to the bedroom on a tray.

'What happened?' said Theo, eyeing his plate of bacon and eggs appreciatively. 'I thought you were furious with me for dragging you here.'

'I was,' Dita shrugged. 'But I got over it. I'm tired of being a bitch. For the moment. And I realized I've missed having sex with you. It has been a few weeks you know.'

'I know,' said Theo, noticing the fact that she'd said she'd missed having sex *with him*, and wondering who else she'd been warming their marital bed with while he was away. He was surprised to find that the thought of Dita with another man made him simultaneously jealous and horny. That was the amazing thing about Dita. Every time you thought you were finally over her, she would turn around and surprise you. It was disconcerting, but, this morning anyway, rather delightful.

'So what time's this lunch?' Dita asked, applying a slick of bright red movie-star lipstick to her bee-stung pout. 'And is your dreary ex-wife going to be there?'

'One o'clock, and yes, probably.' Theo straightened his tie. 'Do *not* make a scene.'

'A scene? *Me*?' Dita fluttered her false eyelashes innocently. 'How is dear old Theresa these days?'

'Fat,' said Theo. 'Fat, old and dishevelled the last time I saw her. It's really a shame. She was a terrific-looking girl in her day.'

'I suppose it's all relative,' sniffed Dita.

'Something else you should know. The current Master, Anthony Greville, has got himself into some hot water about a piece of land he sold years ago. To cut a long story short, he's trying to sting me for the money to buy it back. Last night he threatened to withdraw his support for me if I didn't write him a cheque on the spot.'

Dita's face lit up. 'How Machiavellian! What did you do?'

'I told him to stick it, obviously. But things might be a little tense today. I need you to charm them all, darling. Will you do that? For me?' Theo walked over and pulled her violently towards him. Yanking up her skirt, he slipped a hand inside her panties and began to stroke her possessively. Dita's eyes glazed over with lust, her pupils dilating wildly. Thank God she'd left the children behind! They needed this.

'Of course, Theo,' she murmured. 'Charm's my middle name.'

When St Michael's College pulled out all the stops for a special event, there was nowhere more beautiful in

England. Owing to the misty weather and intermittent rain, today's lunch had been moved indoors, to Formal Hall. The long oak refectory tables had been polished until they gleamed like newly opened conkers, and set with a dazzling array of the college's finest silverware. Glass vases of white roses overflowed onto the three-hundred-year-old Flemish lace tablecloths. The air was filled with riches and history along with the mouthwatering scents of côte de boeuf and fresh white truffles, imported from Italy especially for the occasion. After lunch, the fellows, guests and invited members of the media would wander out into the flower-filled courts, where tented canopies had been erected to help shield them from the elements. Champagne would be served and entertainment provided by some of St Michael's many world-class musicians, actors and dancers. There would be punting on the river, and traditional games for the children present, including a coconut shy and pin the tail on the donkey.

Today was not a day for speeches, but for celebration, the imminent dawning of a new era. It was also a final chance for the candidates to canvas votes and try to win support amongst the college council. The actual election was to be held on Wednesday, four days from now, at a formal general meeting of the college authorities. Students could attend, but not vote. For the election of the Master, all fellows, no matter how junior, had a vote and all were expected to attend. The candidates themselves would not be present and would be informed of the college's decision at 6 p.m. that same day.

By noon, most of the fellows and all of the press had arrived, drawn by the prospect of free booze, the intoxicating smell of white truffles, and the chance to ogle Dita Andreas in the flesh. Thanks to the latest *Varsity*, today's

362

event had been livened up still further by the delicious prospect of a bona fide Cambridge scandal. No institution on earth thrived on gossip more than an Oxbridge college. St Michael's enjoyed a juicy story more than most. It gave them a chance to sharpen their *schadenfreude*, and to use words like 'sexploits' in ordinary conversation.

'Has anybody seen her yet?' A junior philosophy fellow asked his friend, knocking back a third free glass of vintage Chablis.

'Who? Dita Andreas or Theresa O'Connor?'

'Theresa, of course! Everyone knows Dexter's got the job in the bag, which means we'll be seeing Dita Andreas every day next year. It's Mrs Robinson I'm interested in. Do you think she'll bottle it?'

'I dunno. I would. Who's the daddy?'

'No idea. There's only twelve English postgrads at Jesus though, so shouldn't be too hard to find out. Poor kid.'

'Poor kid my arse. *I'd* shag Theresa O'Connor given half a chance. Her tits are sensational, and redheads are always amazing in bed.'

Anthony Greville mingled amongst the throng with his wife, Brenda, a fixed smile glued to his face. This morning's sensational news about Professor O'Connor had given him some breathing space regarding this blasted development. But this being Cambridge, the news was sure to leak out sooner rather than later. He'd called the chairman of the city council, demanding a private meeting, and one had been scheduled for Monday, two days before the election. But Anthony Greville already knew that nothing would come of it. The sale to the private buyer had already gone through, on the basis of planning approval being granted. Unless the college bought the land back, those flats would be built.

Across the court he saw Theo Dexter arriving, hand in hand with his slutty actress wife. The pair of them stopped and preened like peacocks in a mating dance, while photographers clicked and whirred away. This is what the college had to look forward to if Dexter became Master. Paparazzi everywhere, swarming the courts like locusts. *If* he became Master . . .

Watching Theo smile for the cameras, Anthony Greville felt a pang of something close to loathing. *I made you. If it weren't for me, you'd never have been appointed a fellow here in the first place, never mind be standing for Mastership! It was me who ruled in your favour all those years ago, when that girl accused you of ripping off her thesis. Me who gave you a career. And now you think you can turn your back on me? Put your hands in your pockets, when you know we* need *that cash, and move into the Master's Lodge anyway? Pride comes before a fall, Theo.*

'You must be Tony.'

The Master turned. The slutty actress wife had somehow materialized at his elbow.

'Dita Andreas. I've heard *so* much about you.'

Close up, even Anthony had to admit that she was an attractive woman. There was something of the fifties sex-siren about her, almost a Monroe quality. His own wife, Brenda, had a number of fine attributes, but it would be fair to say that she had probably never been compared to Marilyn Monroe.

'Would you mind awfully if I stuck with you for a while? Theo's off doing his thing,' she nodded towards the press pack who were still surrounding Theo like a shoal of piranhas, 'and I'm terrified his ex-wife is going to march up to me and start hitting me over the head with her purse or something.'

'I highly doubt that,' said Anthony, deciding that there

was no point in being standoffish towards Dita. A beautiful woman was a beautiful woman, after all. It wasn't her fault that her husband was a backstabbing bastard. Theo would get his comeuppance soon enough. 'I'm afraid it looks likely that Professor O'Connor – Theresa – will withdraw her candidacy. I'm certainly not expecting her to make an appearance today.'

'Oh?' Dita arched a perfectly plucked eyebrow. 'Why's that? Not on my account I hope.'

'Oh no,' Anthony assured her, filling her in on a précis of the scandal. 'This is all hot off the press this morning, so as you can imagine it's caused quite a stir. Theo doesn't know then?'

'Not yet. I suppose . . . I know it's awful to say this, but does this strengthen his chances?'

Unless he prises open that Fort Knox of a wallet of his, he has no chances to strengthen. And he'd better be damn quick about it.

'That's a matter for the General Meeting of the college, my dear,' said Anthony smoothly. 'Have you met my wife?'

Lunch was a drunken, gossip-fuelled affair. Theresa's chair, predictably, remained empty. The other three candidates, Theo, Graham North and Hugh Mullaney-Stoop, were all able to relax and enjoy themselves, Theo because he knew he'd won, and Graham and Hugh because they knew they'd lost. After pudding and port, Anthony Greville made a short, boring speech. On his way out of Hall, swaying slightly and visibly the worse for wear, he grabbed Theo by the arm.

'I'd like a word.'

'Certainly.' Theo pushed back his chair, stretching out his long, lean legs but pointedly not getting up. 'What's on your mind, Master?'

'You know very well what's on my mind,' Greville hissed.

'I have a meeting with the council on Monday. I need you to be there.'

'I'm afraid I'm tied up on Monday.' Theo smiled arrogantly. 'Dita wants to do some sightseeing. I promised to take her to King's Chapel.'

'Don't push me, Dexter. I can still pull the rug out from under you, you know. You are not the only contender.'

Theo swivelled in his chair to look across at his rivals. Hugh Mullaney-Stoop was asleep in his chair, head thrown back, triple chins quivering gently with each drunken snore. Graham North was staring at the wall, quietly picking his nose.

'I think we both know that's not true, Tony,' said Theo smugly. 'At a pinch you might have persuaded the college to go for Theresa. But as she'll be elbow deep in dirty nappies by autumn . . .' He left the sentence hanging, rudely turning around to join Dita's conversation and leaving Anthony Greville standing there, his anger burning his cheeks a deep red.

'Master?' Yasmin, Greville's secretary, tapped him on the shoulder. 'There's someone to see you in your office. She says it's urgent.'

Glad of a chance to escape, the Master followed her out of Hall and back to the Lodge. 'Who is it?' he asked as they walked, imagining Theo Dexter's head impaled on the spiked railings that lined the riverbank. He hoped it wasn't that reporter again, digging around the development story. Then another thought occurred to him. 'It's not Professor O'Connor, is it?' He didn't think he could face an emotional, pregnant woman today. Not after three glasses of port, washed down with a bitter dose of humiliation from Theo Dexter.

'No, Master. The lady didn't give her name. She said she was an old friend, and you would want to see her. That was all.'

They walked into the Lodge. She was waiting in the hallway, outside his office, her face turned away from him. As Anthony Greville approached, she suddenly looked up. *Good God,* he thought. *After all these years.*

'Hello, Master.' Sasha Miller smiled sweetly. 'It's been a long time.'

'I'm afraid it's out of the question.'

The Master sat behind his grand oak desk, running a gnarled hand over its beautiful inlaid panels. He would miss this desk, this room. He would miss everything about St Michael's.

'I will happily withdraw my support from Theo Dexter. That's not a problem. And I'm confident I can get a majority of the college council to do the same. Dexter is not well liked here. But it will be a cold day in hell before I'll see an unmarried mother in the Master's Lodge. The woman had an affair with one of her students, for God's sake!' He curled his upper lip in distaste.

'So did Professor Dexter, many years ago,' Sasha reminded him. 'It didn't seem to bother you unduly back then. As I recall, the entire college rallied around him.'

'Yes, well,' Anthony Greville mumbled gruffly. 'That was different.'

Sasha stood up. 'Thank you for your time, Master. I'll see myself out.'

'What? No, no, wait. Sit down, Miss Miller. I'm sure we can come to some . . . accommodation.'

Sasha stopped but did not sit. It was enjoyable to see the panic written across the old man's features. The last time she'd seen him, it had been her life, her reputation that hung in the balance. Now the tables were turned.

'I'm not here to negotiate,' she said brusquely. 'I've made

you an offer. I will gift that land back to the college if, and only if, Theresa O'Connor is appointed Mistress. Make that happen and you're off the hook. Fail to make it happen, and I can offer you first refusal on a lovely two-bedroom penthouse apartment with *spectacular* college views.'

'It's not that simple,' the old man spluttered. 'The university will have a say in this. There may be a disciplinary hearing. Professor O'Connor could be barred from teaching undergraduates altogether.'

'So?' Sasha shrugged. 'I shouldn't think she'll have much time for teaching anyway, will she? What with the administrative pressures of running the college. Oh, and taking care of the baby.'

'The college will never stand for it!'

'According to the 1923 Universities of Oxford and Cambridge Act, as long as she holds a Cambridge degree, she is eligible for the Mastership. And according to *this*,' she pulled out a sheaf of papers and dropped them casually on the desk, 'I am the legal owner of that land, with a legal right to develop it.'

Anthony Greville looked at the papers. 'This is straightforward blackmail.'

'Yes.' Sasha smiled sweetly. 'I like to keep things straightforward when I'm doing business. I've made a lot of money that way. I'll leave those with you.' She turned to go. 'I'm taking the originals back with me to the States.'

'You're leaving?'

'Yes. I have an evening flight to New York tonight. Urgent business. But I'll be watching the election results with interest. By Thursday morning, life might look very different for all of us. Goodbye, Master.'

Anthony Greville watched her go.

A disgraced, single mother as Mistress of St Michael's.

Even if he did as Sasha asked, could he get the rest of the fellowship on board?

Yasmin knocked on the office door. 'The Dexters are leaving, Master. Theo wants you to pose for pictures with him at the front gate. A sort of informal handover shot. It's for tomorrow's *Sunday Times*.'

'Certainly.' He got to his feet. After the day he'd had, he deserved *some* pleasure. If Theo Dexter wanted to hang himself, Anthony Greville would gladly hand him the rope. 'Tell him I'll be right out.'

CHAPTER TWENTY-FOUR

Theresa walked down the Fulham Road, idly looking in the windows of some of the more froufrou baby shops. Were there really people prepared to pay a hundred and twenty pounds for a pair of cashmere booties? She supposed there must be.

She'd come to London to get away. There was no way she could stay in Cambridge after the *Varsity* story broke. After Horatio left Willow Tree Cottage, Theresa drove straight to her antenatal appointment and promptly burst into tears all over her obstetrician.

'Professor O'Connor,' the doctor told her sternly, when Theresa finished explaining what had happened, 'you must rest. Your blood pressure is elevated. Clearly you are in great emotional distress. Is there somewhere you can go, for a few days at least? Somewhere quiet?'

Willow Tree Cottage was quiet, but it wouldn't be for long. By this evening she would have become a local celebrity of the worst possible sort and the phone and doorbell would not stop ringing. She could go to Jenny and JP's, but the Aubrieau household, though welcoming, could hardly be described as 'quiet', still less restful.

'Ideally, you should get out of Cambridge.'

Theresa's thoughts immediately turned to Aisling. Her old friend's house in Parsons Green had been a sanctuary once before when her life was falling apart. *Not that my life is falling apart,* she told herself firmly. *I'm having a baby and I refuse to be unhappy about it.* But still, things were undoubtedly complicated. Sasha Miller called as Theresa was leaving Addenbrooke's, begging her not to withdraw her name from the St Michael's Mastership ballot.

'If I don't withdraw voluntarily they'll kick me off,' said Theresa. 'I'm not sure how much humiliation I can take in one week.'

'They won't kick you off. I promise you that.'

'But how *can* you promise me? There are rules, Sasha . . .'

'Which you haven't broken,' Sasha interrupted.

'. . . and traditions, which I certainly *have* broken. Truthfully, I don't even know if I want this any more. Perhaps Theo *is* more suited to the job than I am.'

In the end, Sasha had been so insistent, so vociferous, that Theresa hadn't the energy to fight about it. Sasha had problems of her own to deal with, some work crisis or other, but she'd made Theresa promise not to withdraw before she left. That afternoon Theresa caught the train to King's Cross, confidently expecting her phone to ring at any moment and Anthony Greville to start delivering the inevitable blow: 'Under the circumstances . . . college's reputation . . .' but miraculously the call never came, not that day, nor the next. It occurred to Theresa that perhaps St Michael's Master couldn't get through, what with all the other calls she'd been getting, from the English faculty, the university authorities, the Jesus College Council, not to mention friends, family and, of course, the press. The only person who hadn't called was Horatio. Horatio, and Anthony Greville.

This morning was election day. After Theresa's phone rang three times during breakfast, Aisling leaned across the table and swiped it. Switching it off, she slipped it into her jacket pocket.

'That's it. I'm confiscating this bloody thing.'

'You can't confiscate my phone, Aisling!' Theresa laughed. 'I need it.'

'Bollocks. You need to rest. That's what you're here for. Besides, I just did confiscate it. Go and have a facial or something. Go shopping. Go do whatever it is you do to relax.'

Unable to think of anything except curling up in Horatio Hollander's arms by the fire at Willow Tree Cottage, Theresa turned on the television. She was immediately punished by seeing Theo's face twinkling back at her. The morning shows were running highlights from his interview with Connor Greaves, which had drawn huge ratings last weekend. Listening to him witter on about 'coming full circle' and his 'need to give back', Theresa wondered how she had ever been in love with him. Everything about him, from the words coming out of his mouth, to his Hollywood-white smile, and perfectly youthful blond mop of hair, was fake. She touched her belly lovingly and switched him off.

'Come on, baby. Let's go for a walk.'

Strolling past Bambino, possibly West London's most overpriced baby shop, she stopped at a second-hand book store and picked up a couple of dog-eared Dr Seuss books – whatever kind of sprog she produced, she could not imagine it turning its nose up at *Green Eggs and Ham* – and then ducked into a Starbucks for some tea and cake. She thought idly about Sasha and her work crisis. It was strange how, for all her money and success, Sasha hadn't been able to let Theo go. *She cares more about the Mastership of St Michael's than I do*, thought Theresa, picturing Sasha at a desk in some palatial, glass-walled corner office, waiting anxiously for tonight's results. She hoped she wasn't going to be too disappointed.

Sasha *was* sitting in a palatial, glass-walled corner office. And she was disappointed. But it had nothing to do with Theo Dexter.

Last night, Ceres's senior staff had voted overwhelmingly to accept Wrexall's offer. After Doug Carrabino's call, Sasha had rushed home to fight off a hostile takeover bid, only to discover that her colleagues seemed to view it as a love-marriage. Sasha felt like a jilted wife, watching her husband run off into the sunset with his mistress.

'You still have a controlling share of the company,' Doug reminded her. 'You can veto.'

'And what, watch all my people start hating me? Sit here while they leave, one by one? I'd rather be shot in the heart than slowly bleed to death.'

'Don't you think you're looking at this a little bleakly?' said Doug. 'Wrexall Dupree made us a great offer. You're going to make a ton of money, have a seat on the board of the biggest real estate giant in the world. The synergies are incredible . . .'

'Please.' Sasha held up a hand and fixed him with a gimlet eye. 'Do *not* say "synergies". You sound like a business school handbook.'

'I know you've had your issues with the culture there. But we can change them.'

Sasha laughed. 'Sure, Doug.' How many dynamic boutique companies had sold out to leviathans like Wrexall, doped up on promises that they could preserve their culture, their uniqueness, their entrepreneurial spirit? *Give it a year and*

Ceres'll be completely subsumed. Two years and no one will even remember the name. We didn't get married. We got eaten.

But no one else saw it that way. The markets roared their approval of the 'merger'. Sasha's phone had been ringing off the hook all day with excited *Wall Street Journal* reporters wanting a punchy, upbeat quote from the woman who was about to become one of the wealthiest on Wall Street. But both Sasha Miller and Wrexall's Chairman, Jackson Dupree, had remained bizarrely silent, letting their henchmen give the statements and do the cartwheels for them.

At 6 p.m., Sasha left the office, still looking like a woman in mourning. It was election day at St Michael's today, but there would be no result for hours. Since she got back to New York, Sasha had been plunged so deeply into crisis management, she hadn't had a second to think about what was happening in Cambridge, still less to chase Anthony Greville. Would he be able to bring his colleagues round and get them to vote for Theresa? Sasha figured his chances at 50/50. Of course, if he didn't, and if Theo Dexter was appointed Master, she still had no intention of building those apartments. She didn't need the money, that was for sure. Even if she had, she wouldn't have wanted to be the woman who defaced the most beautiful town in England. But Greville didn't know that. He would try his best. The only question was whether his best would be good enough.

Outside on Wall Street, the warm, late-spring evening seemed to have brought the usually weary commuters to life. Some were heading home after a long day at their computer screens. Others were on the way to the bar, secretaries in laughing, sisterly groups, traders sparring with each other as they walked, still pumped full of testosterone and unexpended energy from the high-stakes tension of the day. Too depressed to go straight home, but too morose for company, Sasha decided to do something she never did. Go shopping.

'Bergdorf Goodman, please,' she told the cab driver, jumping into the first car in the long, yellow line outside her office. Everyone kept telling her how rich she was about to become. It was time for a little retail therapy.

All the way to Fifth Avenue, Sasha tried to think about clothes, things that she wanted. Half of America seemed to view her as some sort of fashion role model, but the truth was she'd never been very interested in the things other women were interested in. Shoes, handbags, Chloé cocktail dresses and Balmain smoking jackets, it was all just so much *stuff*. Still, she had nothing else to do. And perhaps if she looked good, she might start feeling good? She had yet to officially decline Wrexall's offer of a seat on the board. Until the deal went through it would be foolish to rock the boat. But she knew that there was about as much chance of her working with Jackson Dupree every day as of America winning the World Cup. No, the merger would be the end of an era for Sasha. She must find something else to do, something else to live for. She realized with a sinking heart that she had no idea what that something might be.

They'd arrived. Pulling herself together, Sasha handed the driver a twenty and stepped outside. Just as she did so she was almost knocked flying by the woman taking her cab. 'Hey! Watch where you're going,' she said indignantly. The woman was more shopping bag than person. Every time she turned she was in danger of knocking another hapless pedestrian off their feet.

'Sorry,' yelped a voice from beneath the pile of bags. It had been years, but it was a voice Sasha knew instantly.

'Lottie?'

'Sasha?'

The cab driver was getting impatient. 'Hey. Lady. D'you want a ride or not?'

'Not,' said Lottie, absentmindedly. Dropping her purchases with a clatter she stared at Sasha as if she'd just seen a ghost. Sasha stared back. On Lottie's tiny frame the bump was unmistakable. Either she'd just shoplifted a basketball, or she was pregnant. *A baby. Jackson's baby.* Just at that moment, like a walk-on cameo in some terrible, predictable horror movie, Jackson himself emerged from the store.

'Hey, Lottie, did we forget the . . .' The words died on his lips. Unlike the two women, however, he managed to recover himself sufficiently to speak. 'Sasha. How are you? I've been meaning to call you directly. I should have, I know, but this deal's had me swamped and I . . .'

'I know. It's OK. I understand,' said Sasha. She couldn't bring herself to look at him. Lottie's swollen belly had a lock on her eyes like some kind of torturous magnet. She felt like Luke Skywalker being sucked in towards the death star.

'Congratulations on the merger.' Lottie finally found her voice. 'Everyone seems pleased.'

'Thanks,' said Sasha. There wasn't much else to say. Jackson was staring at her so forcefully she had no choice but to look up. When she did she saw an expression in his eyes that she couldn't read. It was part anguish, part anger, as if he were making an important point but she'd failed to understand him.

'I didn't vote for it, you know. The merger. It was Bob Massey's baby.'

Sasha's eyes narrowed. *Unbelievable! He wants to wriggle off the hook.* 'You're the chairman. You could have vetoed.'

'So could you,' said Jackson.

Sasha opened her mouth to say something, then closed it again. Partly because he was, of course, right. And partly because she realized that she didn't care any more. Merger or no merger, Lottie was still standing there, still pregnant, still about to get into a car with Jackson and drive away, forever. It took every ounce of Sasha's strength to look Lottie in the eye, smile, and say what she should have said the moment she saw her.

'Congratulations on the baby. When are you due?'

'August.' Lottie's eyes lit up. She wasn't gloating, she wasn't capable of it. She just radiated happiness. *That pregnant glow.*

'We should be going.' Jackson stepped forward, relieving Lottie of her shopping bags and helping her into a cab. He was frowning again, angry, though at what Sasha had no idea. Surely if anyone had a right to be upset it was her? 'Nice to see you, Sasha. Take care.' And with a slam of the car door, they were gone.

Sasha stood on the sidewalk for a long time, unsure what to do. She could hardly go in and buy dresses. But where else should she go? The urge to burst into tears was getting stronger and must, she realized, be resisted at all costs. People were already looking at her oddly as they walked past. Many of them, she knew, must recognize her. *I have to get out of here.* Finally she jumped in a cab and went home. Once safely inside the cocoon of her apartment, she kicked off her shoes, walked into the kitchen and unearthed a year-old bottle of scotch. Pouring it into a mug as if it were tea, she sank down at the table and took a long, deep slug. It burned, but it was good, warming, comforting. She drank again, and again, and with each swallow the image of Jackson's face faded. When the mug was finished she poured herself another. Soon Jackson Dupree, along with everything else, was gone.

* * *

The noise was getting louder. Buzzing like a fly. No, a wasp. It was getting closer, so close she could feel the vibrations of its wings. *Oh My God it's in my ear! It's in my fucking ear!*

Leaping to her feet, kicking over the kitchen chair, Sasha ran around the room, heart and head pounding, shaking her head like a dog that'd just been swimming. It took a long time – ten full seconds – for her to realize that there was no wasp in her ear. That the buzzing was coming from her cellphone, which had spilled out of her purse onto the table. She grabbed it, jabbing buttons frantically, anything to make the noise stop.

'Hello?'

On the other end of the line, a woman was screaming. Not shouting, or whooping or laughing. Screaming, as if someone were slicing a razor blade into her eyeballs. Sasha felt the first stirrings of panic. She also felt unbearably nauseous. She didn't dare look at the whisky bottle to see how much she'd drunk, but as she had clearly passed out cold at the table it must have been a lot.

'Who is this?'

More screaming, then silence.

'If this is some sort of crank call, you have lousy timing,' said Sasha crossly, trying to make herself less afraid. At last the screaming stop, or rather it morphed into a more familiar sound – laughter.

'I'm sorry. It's only me.'

Relief flooded Sasha's body. 'Theresa?'

Theresa was laughing so hard on the other end of the line, she could hardly croak out a 'yes'.

'Are you drunk?'

'Of course not,' she giggled. 'I'm pregnant. What sort of an irresponsible mother do you think I am? Besides, that's hardly an appropriate question to ask the Mistress of your former college.'

'You got it?!' For the first time in three days, Sasha smiled.

'I got it. Thanks, I can only assume, to you, although God only knows how you did it. Tony Greville sounded like he was choking on a wasp when he told me!'

Wasp . . . Sasha clutched her head again, then her stomach.

'That's brilliant news, Theresa. I'm thrilled for you, really. But I'm afraid I *am* drunk. I have to go and throw up now.' She dropped the phone and ran, only just making it to the bathroom in time.

Ten minutes later, weak and exhausted, she crawled back into her bedroom. Pulling the covers up over her head, as she had done when she was a child, she curled up into a ball and prayed for sleep. It was late, past midnight, and she was shattered, but her mind would not switch off. Through a woozy, whisky haze, she pictured Theresa celebrating and Theo Dexter, somewhere in Cambridge presumably, reeling from the shock. Would Anthony Greville tell him what had happened? Would he let Theo know that it was Sasha who had destroyed his chances, Sasha who had robbed him of his life's ambition and made him look a prize fool into the bargain? *Of course he will, the vindictive old bastard. He won't be able to help himself.* For a brief flicker of a second, the thought made her smile. But then the image of Theo's furious face receded, replaced by Jackson Dupree's scowl as he helped his wife into the cab this evening.

His wife. His pregnant wife.

Sasha fell into a fitful, broken sleep.

CHAPTER TWENTY-FIVE

'Can I get you anything, sir? A glass of champagne perhaps? Or anything else?'

The BA stewardess was sexy in a used, slutty, over-made-up sort of way. Normally Theo would have taken her up on the 'anything else' and slipped back to the galley for a quick blow job. Today, however, Gisele Bündchen could have dropped to her knees naked right in front of him and it wouldn't have lifted his foul mood.

'No, thank you. I'm fine.'

Theo was not fine. He was furious. He'd been humiliated, publicly and deeply embarrassingly. He'd been made to look a fool among his peers, and to the British public at large. Even Dita, who this time last week had been so eager to please him and make amends, now seemed to look at him in a different light: the grim pallor of failure. It was not a look that suited him. Nor was it one that Theo intended to wear for long.

He was on his way to New York to have things out with Sasha Miller.

'I don't know what you expect to happen,' Ed Gilliam had

warned him, advising strongly against the trip. 'The college has made its decision. The most you can expect from the woman is an apology, and given your history together I'd say you were spectacularly unlikely to get even that. Forget it, Theo. Go home. Rebuild. No one outside of England has even heard of St Michael's College. It's all a storm in a teacup.'

But Theo couldn't forget it. When Ed said, 'Go home', he meant Los Angeles. But despite having lived there for half his adult life, LA would never be Theo's home. He knew that now better than ever. Of course Dita was in seventh heaven, the children too. She'd got what she wanted without even having to try. But for Theo, losing the Mastership, to *Theresa* of all people, was a bitter blow. He didn't realize quite how keenly he'd wanted it until it was gone. When that shit Tony Greville had told him it was Sasha who had bought up the adjoining land, Sasha who had held a gun to his head and effectively foisted Theresa on the college council, it was as if someone had poured sulphuric acid into an open wound. By some sick twist of fate, Theresa and Sasha had apparently become unlikely BFFs, united in a desire to bring him down. Livid with rage, Theo stormed out of the Master's Lodge and immediately placed a call to Ceres, only to be told that Sasha was on indefinite leave while some bloody merger was being finalized.

'Listen, you cretin, I don't give a fuck about your merger,' Theo roared at the Ceres receptionist. 'This is Theo Dexter calling. *Theo Dexter.* Do you know who I am?'

'Yes, sir,' came the weary reply. 'You're the TV space guy.'

That was like a slap in the face. Theo visualized the words on his gravestone.

'I demand to speak to Ms Miller, immediately.'

'I'm sorry, sir. As I've explained, that's not possible. If you'd like to leave a message . . .'

Theo left a message. It was not a message to be repeated in mixed company, nor was it a message to which he had expected a reply. But to his surprise, not two hours later, Sasha returned his call.

'I'd be delighted to talk to you about Theresa's success, or anything else you'd like to talk about. Unfortunately I'm rather tied up in New York at the moment.'

Her sang-froid had momentarily thrown him off guard. Theo knew about her achievements in the business world, of course. But in his mind, he still pictured her as the naïve teenager he'd charmed into bed all those years ago.

'Fine,' he heard himself saying. 'I'll come to New York. I'd rather do this face to face anyway.'

'Perfect. I'll expect you next week. We can have dinner at my apartment. Avoid the press.'

Theo stared out of the grimy plastic porthole window at the anonymous cloudscape below. In five hours, he'd be in New York. In eight, he'd be sitting across the table from Sasha Miller. Ed Gilliam's words came back to him. 'I don't know what you expect to happen . . .'

Theo didn't know either. But if Sasha Miller, if *anyone*, thought that they could screw over Theo Dexter and walk away Scot free, they had another think coming.

Sasha woke up that morning with a renewed sense of purpose.

He's coming. Not just to my city. To my apartment. He's coming here to see me, to talk face to face. It was a meeting that she had fantasized about for so long that now that it was actually about to happen it felt completely unreal. While she was in Cambridge she'd prepared herself mentally for the possibility of bumping into Theo, not sure whether she hoped for such an encounter or dreaded it. But never, in her wildest imaginings, had she envisioned this scenario: that *he* would come looking for *her*. That he would come when he was defeated, angry, volatile, when he believed he had nothing to lose. But, of course, he still had everything to lose. This was Sasha's chance, perhaps her only chance, to make sure that he did. The tension was overwhelming.

The first thing she did was go back to Bergdorf's, pushing all thoughts of Jackson and Lottie from her mind, and head straight for the lingerie department.

'I want something sexy, but understated. Nothing red, nothing crotchless, no tassles. I'm thinking silk, lace, tiny.'

The gay salesman's eyes lit up. 'Honey, you are *soooo* in the right place.'

After that it was downstairs to ready-to-wear. Sasha opted for a subtly clinging grey jersey dress from Donna Karan, the fastest way to look a million bucks without looking as if you tried. The next stop was Dean & DeLuca for something simple and delicious – asparagus and mint salad, poached salmon and a wicked-looking tiramisu – then on to Morrell's wine store for two bottles of vintage white burgundy, Puligny-Montrachet. Theo had always been a crashing wine snob, and would insist on white with the fish. Tonight, Theo Dexter would get everything he wanted. But he would get it at a price.

By the time seven o'clock rolled around, Sasha felt oddly calm. All the nervous energy she'd been running on since breakfast seemed to have magically evaporated. Both the underwear and the dress felt incredible next to her newly showered, moisturized skin. After trying on six different pairs of shoes, she decided to go barefoot. It wouldn't do for him to think she'd gone to too much effort, and it made her feel sexier anyway. She'd just had time to pull out a couple of salad plates and check that the wine was properly chilled when, right on cue, the doorbell rang.

'You made it.'

'Of course.'

He was wearing dark jeans with a Brooks Brothers shirt and Hermès tie, like an investment banker on casual Friday, and he was scowling. Sasha studied his face. There were more lines, of course. The frown didn't help. But, as with most men, maturity seemed to have improved Theo's looks. Sasha had seen his face on the screen countless times over the years, but she was unprepared by how attractive he still was in the flesh. A little bland, perhaps, a little plastic. He had none of Jackson's animal magnetism. And yet she remembered, instantly and quite clearly, why it was she'd fallen in love with him.

Theo looked at Sasha, too, his seasoned eyes evaluating her figure the same way a farmer might evaluate a cow. *Her tits are still good. Flat stomach. You can tell she hasn't had kids.* But it was her face that really surprised him. Used to Dita, and all the legions of bleached-blond LA girls who started Botox at twenty-one, it was a long time since he'd seen such a naturally beautiful woman. Sasha's skin positively glowed, as pale and creamy and smooth as it had been when she was nineteen. Her hair was the same gleaming black, and her eyes were still the two deep-set emeralds he remembered.

But he wasn't about to let a pretty face distract him from his anger.

'I want to know what the hell you think you were playing at.'

Sasha smiled, gesturing towards the couch. 'Come in. May I offer you a drink?'

'You blackmailed Anthony Greville! You forced him to back my ex-wife over me!'

'I did, yes,' said Sasha sweetly. Her demeanour was

designed to irritate Theo and it was working. She was acting as if they were discussing the weather.

'What the hell business was it of yours?' he snarled. 'And since when were you and Theresa so tight?'

'Since we realized we had a lot in common,' said Sasha, handing him a chilled glass of white. Theo took the wine and sat down. He knew he had to rein in his temper, especially if he were going to persuade Sasha to admit what she'd done. He'd convinced himself that if it became public knowledge that the Mastership vote was effectively rigged, Theresa's appointment might be declared void.

He looked around the apartment. It spoke eloquently of the life of its owner. Everything in it was expensive, from the imported antique lighting to the hand-sewn velvet curtains. The couch he was sitting on was B&B Italia, a model Theo had considered buying himself. But at the same time the room was stark, barren, empty. *She's lonely*, he thought. Sasha sat down next to him and instinctively he put a hand on her leg. Close up her body really was quite extraordinary, and gift wrapped to perfection in that tight grey dress she was wearing.

'To the casual observer, I'd say you and Theresa had nothing in common.' His voice was deep and gravelly. The desire was unmistakable. 'You look terrific.'

'Thank you.'

Sasha felt her heart pounding. They hadn't even had dinner yet! She'd hoped Theo would make a pass at her at some point in the evening, that she'd be able to play him, win him round – that was part of the plan – but not even she had expected a move in the first five minutes. She wasn't ready.

'Will you excuse me just a moment? I need to see to something in the kitchen.'

Theo waited while she clattered around behind him in the open-plan room. He took a sip of wine and began, slowly, to relax. This evening was going to go better than he'd expected. Not only had Sasha chosen a damn good burgundy – another surprise – but she was clearly still attracted to him. That much was evident from her flustered response on the couch just now, the way she'd let his hand stay on her leg but then got nervous and made an excuse to get up. Perhaps this whole business with the Mastership had just been an elaborate attempt to get his attention? If so, it had succeeded admirably. He would make love to her first, taking his time, savouring every inch of that incredible body. Then, once he'd shown her what she'd been missing, he would figure out exactly *how* he would get her to help him unravel this mess back in Cambridge.

'There we are. Done.' She was back on the couch, flushed (*blushing?*) and wearing freshly applied make-up. He was almost disappointed it was going to be this easy. *Like taking candy from a baby.*

'You know, I was so angry when I came here,' he whispered, taking her hand, 'I'd almost forgotten how fucking sexy you are.'

Sasha looked down at her lap. She was trembling. 'It's been a long time, Theo.'

Gently, he reached under her chin and lifted her face to his. Then he kissed her, a long, slow, teasing kiss. She kissed him back, passionately at first, her hands stroking his face, exploring, rediscovering. But then, just as suddenly, she pulled away.

'What's the matter?' He snaked a hand around her waist, edging slowly upwards towards her breasts. *I wonder if they'll be as good once I get her bra off?* 'Are you nervous? Come on, Sasha. You know you want it as much as I do.'

His hand was on her shoulder now, peeling down the top of her dress. *Jesus,* thought Sasha helplessly, *I do want it!* She hated him, loathed him as she had never loathed another human being. But at the same time the power rush it gave her, knowing she was turning him on, knowing how desperately he wanted to fuck her in that moment, was almost stronger than the hate. It was a physical force, like an orgasm but better. It took all Sasha's willpower to focus on what she needed to do.

Straddling him, she leaned forward and whispered in his ear. 'I don't trust you.'

Theo kissed her neck. He could feel himself getting hard. His appetite for conversation was dwindling by the second.

'Why not?'

'Why not?' Reaching down, Sasha stroked the outline of his rock-solid erection through his jeans. Theo groaned. 'You know why not, Professor Dexter.'

'Stop talking.' He flipped her over, pushing her down onto the couch. 'I want you now.'

'No.'

The violence of her voice surprised him. He stopped, pushing himself up on his forearms, looking at her with a combination of curiosity and intense frustration.

'Not until you apologize.'

He laughed. '*Me* apologize? For what? You're the one that screwed me out of the Mastership just so you could get me back into your life. Into your bed.'

His arrogance was so breathtaking, Sasha stifled a gasp. She mustn't break the spell now, she mustn't ruin the moment. 'You stole my theory. I want you to admit it. I want you to admit you took the credit for my idea, and that you set me up.' She wriggled out from under him until she was sitting on the floor. Theo, still on the couch, sat up and ran his hands through his hair. *Fucking little prick-tease.*

'Sasha. Are we really going to go over all this again? Look at where you are in life, sweetheart. Look at what you've achieved. Surely, whatever happened back then worked out for the best, for both of us?'

Sasha said nothing. Instead, very, very slowly, she began to peel off her dress, Limb by limb her lithe, silken body emerged from its grey cocoon. Theo stared, mesmerized as she stripped down to her underwear: a minuscule bra in the softest, grey-pink lace with matching panties, which showed the faintest shadow of neatly trimmed pubic hair beneath the silk. She eased one bra strap down over her shoulder, then the other. Theo could hardly breathe. Reaching back to undo the clasp, she stopped, looking him right in the eye.

'I want to hear you say it,' she whispered. 'The truth.'

'Fine.' His mouth was so dry he could hardly get the words out. 'I lied. I lied to you, I lied to everybody, OK? I stole your theory and I claimed it for my own. And you know what, Sasha? I'd do it again. I'd do it again in a fucking heartbeat. How's that for an apology?' Leaping off the couch like a cheetah, he pounced on top of her, tearing off her clothes and his own, deranged with excitement and his eagerness to get inside her.

Sasha was excited too. She wanted this as much as he did. In fact, she wanted it more. Closing her eyes, she screamed with pleasure as he pushed himself into her body, fucking her with the passion that only hatred could inspire. Theo hated her, and Sasha hated Theo. *Hated* him! But it was the best, most animal sex of her life. Better even than it had been with Jackson. When she came, she sobbed, her climax seeming to go on forever.

I've got you, you bastard. She hugged him tightly, biting down hard on his shoulder. *I've got you.*

Behind her, on the kitchen counter, a Dictaphone silently turned, hidden behind the food they'd never had time to eat.

It had recorded every word.

CHAPTER TWENTY-SIX

Three weeks later, Los Angeles

Dita Andreas was having an awesome day. She woke up late to blazing sunshine pouring through the bedroom window (nothing unusual there) and a note from Theo on the pillow: 'Taken Milo to softball. Back around 2.' (Very unusual).

The fact that Milo was well enough to make softball practice was miracle enough in itself. But for his dad to take him, willingly and without being asked? That was unheard of. Theo had certainly been in a strangely good mood since he got back from his New York business trip. Before New York, Dita had wondered if he would ever get over this whole debacle with the Cambridge job. There had always been a direct link, like an invisible fishing line, between Theo's confidence and her attraction to him. After the old fogeys at St Michael's College turned on him, Theo's temper had soared but his confidence had plummeted to new lows, and looked set to take their marriage with it. He and Dita barely spoke on the plane home to LA. But then he'd dashed off to New York to meet some production company or other, and returned two days later energized and positive, his libido raging. Life with Theo had always been a rollercoaster, but that was what kept it interesting.

Rolling out of bed and into the shower, Dita dressed and came downstairs to find a note from the nanny. She and Fran had left hours ago for the playground. Dita had the day to herself. Feeling like a teenager again, she grabbed the keys to her white Porsche Boxster and headed for Beverly Hills. A stack of gossip magazines, a pedicure on Rodeo, a hot stone massage at the Peninsula and a spot of light shopping at Barney's on Wilshire. What could be more perfect?

There was a newsstand just outside Bristol Farms supermarket. Slipping on her largest, starriest shades and a headscarf, Dita pulled up and began scooping up all the week's new editions: *US Weekly*, *People*, *Star*, *OK*, *Life & Style*. It wasn't until she got to the cash desk that she noticed the picture of Theo.

'You wouldn't believe it, would you?' said the cheerful young Mexican man on the till. 'Married to Dita Andreas and he's *still* playing away.'

Dita felt her heart tighten. Theo's affairs were no surprise to her. All men were the same in that regard. But she did expect him to be discreet, as she was.

'And that's not the worst of it. Have you listened to the tapes?'

Dita pulled her headscarf lower over her face. 'What tapes?'

'There's a telephone number in there,' said the man helpfully. 'You can call in and listen. Apparently Dexter stole the theory that made him famous from *this* woman.' He pointed to a picture of Sasha Miller, looking business like and serious in a black Armani Privé suit. 'He admits it all on tape. *Dexter's Universe*, the whole thing – it was someone else's idea! Can you believe that?'

Somehow Dita made it to the car. Shaking, she turned to page six of the magazine and dialled the three-dollar-per-minute number they had so thoughtfully provided.

Two minutes later, she called Theo.

'Hi, honey. Milo's doing great. You should see him out here on the . . .'

'You idiot.'

'What?' Theo sounded annoyed. 'What's the problem? I thought you'd be pleased I took him to practice.'

'She taped you, you moron! Your new girlfriend. The tabloids are charging a fortune for people to call a hotline and hear you admit you stole her theory. You're a fraud, Theo! You're a fucking fraud!'

The line went dead. In Brentwood Park, Theo Dexter watched a softball soar high into the blue sky and then tumble inevitably to the ground. It was his life, flashing before his eyes.

'Get in here, honey! You should see this.'

Two days later, Lottie Dupree was watching TV in her apartment, calling to Jackson in his study. 'Sasha's wiping the floor with this guy.'

'I'll be there in a minute.'

Jackson had tried to avoid the coverage of the Sasha Miller–Theo Dexter scandal but it was impossible. Not since Tiger Woods was caught with his pants down had the nation been so gripped by a story. Even Jackson had to admit it did have all the elements of a good soap opera: a glamorous heroine, a charming but dastardly villain, a lie perpetrated for decades and finally avenged thanks to an illicit sexual affair, a betrayed movie-star wife. The irony was that Jackson had known about Sasha's history with Dexter forever, since the earliest days of their rivalry at Wrexall. He'd chosen not to believe her when she protested her innocence – yet another of his poor choices where Sasha Miller was concerned – but it turned out she'd been telling the truth all along.

In the last forty-eight hours, Theo Dexter had seen his wife leave him, he'd been fired by two major television networks, and dropped by all but one of his commercial sponsors. He'd been roundly condemned by the scientific community, and lampooned by every late-night talk-show host in the country. While his embattled lawyer gave statement after statement, protesting his client's innocence, Sasha had been on every televised couch from *The View* to *Ellen*, telling her side of the story. Right now she was on *Oprah*. Lottie was glued.

'Jackson, come *on*. She's talking about their affair now. The first one. This is killer stuff.'

Jackson stood stiffly beside the couch, listening to Sasha talk about how Dexter had seduced her as a teenager, and admitting that they had slept together again the night she taped his confession.

'I'm sure it's hard for people to understand how that happened. It's hard for *me* to understand. This was the man who destroyed my life, after all. But maybe it's *because* of that. There's always been a connection between us.'

'Do you regret it?' Oprah asked. Lottie held her breath.

'I do,' Sasha said sombrely. 'I regret that part of it. He was married, after all. It was wrong, but it happened. It will certainly *never* happen again!'

The audience laughed. So did Lottie. Jackson felt his jaw tighten like a vice.

'But you know, maybe without that he would never have opened up the way that he did? I needed to hear him admit that he'd lied. I needed the world to know that I *hadn't* lied. And Dita Andreas has called me since, offering her support.'

Jackson picked up the remote and switched the TV off.

'Hey!' Lottie protested. 'What are you doing?'

'Let's go out,' he said briskly. 'I need some fresh air.'

'After the interview,' said Lottie, turning the TV back on. 'You know, I hate it when you do that.'

'Do what?'

'Make decisions for both of us like that. I was watching. I'm interested.'

'Fine,' said Jackson petulantly. 'Suit yourself.'

A few seconds later Lottie heard the front door slam. She tried to refocus on *Oprah* but it was impossible. Once again, Jackson had spoiled the moment.

In the kitchen of the Master's Lodge at St Michael's, Theresa was watching the recording of the same *Oprah* interview with Sasha, curled up in an armchair by the Aga with four cats asleep at her feet. It was so gripping, she kept forgetting to chew her Monster Munch crisps so they fizzed and melted in her mouth and lost all their crunch.

Lysander, the oldest and fattest of her feline family, hopped up onto her lap and Theresa stroked him mindlessly. She was happy for Sasha. There was no doubt who was the victor in this explosive media war. But the vilification of Theo had become so intense, she was reaching the point where she almost felt sorry for him. All those years ago he'd seduced Sasha and tricked her out of her life's work. This time, it was Sasha who had seduced him, falsely won his trust, and destroyed *his* life's work. There was certainly a satisfying symmetry to it all. Some might call it justice. But all the betrayal and seduction left a bitter taste in Theresa's mouth that no amount of Monster Munch could fully eradicate.

Suddenly Lysander leaped to his feet with a screech and jumped to the floor. Theresa put a hand on her belly and laughed out loud. Either she had some extremely serious digestive problems, or the baby had just kicked for the first time. She turned off the television and sat very still, willing him – for some reason she had come to think of the baby as a 'him' – to do it again. Sure enough, about a minute later, her stomach jumped visibly. This was not the 'fluttering sensation' she'd read about in baby books. This was a very firm, apparently deliberate punch. A 'hello, I'm here' punch, not painful, but decidedly *solid*.

Theresa felt a wave of happiness rise up within her. Then, looking round the kitchen still piled high with unpacked boxes, she realized with a pang that she had no one to share it with. Her girlfriends were all AWOL. Jenny was out of town at a conference. Aisling, who'd phoned a lot since Theresa was appointed Mistress of St Michael's, was on a romantic break in Tahiti with her husband. And Sasha, who Theresa did now count as a real friend, was doubtless in another TV studio somewhere in America, throwing another live grenade into the shattered remains of Theo's career.

But it wasn't her girlfriends that Theresa wanted.

Horatio had officially dropped out of college the day after Theresa moved in to the Lodge. He'd written her a sweet letter, enclosing a cheque for two hundred pounds that she knew he couldn't afford, and promising to be back in touch before the birth. 'I need some time to get my head together. And get a job,' he wrote. 'Many congratulations on your job, by the way. You deserve it.' But that was it. Since the letter she'd heard nothing, and had no idea how to get in touch with him should she need to. They still hadn't spoken about anything practical, such as when he was going to see the baby, or whether he would want to be at the birth.

You did the right thing, Theresa told herself firmly. *You had to let him go.*

She hoped that some day soon, she would start to believe it.

'So are we done with the interviews? You want me to tell Conan O'Brien no?'

Sasha's newly appointed, temporary media agent, a pushy, powerhouse of a woman named Sarah Rosen, failed to keep the disappointment out of her voice. She wished all her clients were like Sasha Miller. The woman just had to sit down on camera and people fell in love with her.

Sasha was in bed in her apartment, with the phone in one hand and a tub of Cool Whip in the other. She had realized about an hour ago that, unless you counted coffee, she hadn't eaten in almost two days and was suddenly feeling ravenous.

'Yeah, tell him no. We did what we set out to do.'

'OK.' Sarah Rosen hadn't known her client long, but she was a seasoned enough agent to appreciate when no meant no. 'And what about the business shows? The Ceres sale went through today. MSNBC *Squawk Box* has been calling me. You wanna do that?'

'No.' This time she was even more categoric. 'I gave a statement. I'm cashed out of the business. I'm officially retired.'

'Lucky you,' said Sarah, though she knew in her heart that retirement was just another word for death. When the time came, someone would have to prise Sarah Rosen's Rolodex and BlackBerry out of her cold, dead hands. But maybe retirement would suit Sasha Miller? She was still a young woman. She could do what she wanted, travel, adventure, get married, enjoy her life. 'Good luck, Sasha. You know where I am if you need me.'

Sasha threw the phone onto the pillow beside her and ate another spoonful of Cool Whip. It was done. Over.

Theo Dexter was discredited. More than that. He was ruined.

Sasha's reputation, as a scientist and as a person, was fully restored.

Theresa O'Connor, the other woman Theo had betrayed, had been given her happy ending.

And at the close of markets today, on paper anyway, Sasha was worth over two hundred million dollars.

If ever there were a time to feel truly, deeply happy, surely this was it?

That's the trouble with closure, thought Sasha. *It means something's finished. It's accomplished. It's done.*

So what happens now?

She'd already decided she would go back to science. Astronomy was her first love, and it called to her now more loudly and plaintively than ever. She would probably also go back to England. There was nothing here for her now. *I'll look for a research post somewhere – they won't have to worry about funding me! I'll spend the rest of my life devoted to something important, something more meaningful than numbers on a balance sheet.*

It was the life she'd always dreamed of. But something was missing.

Something will always be missing.

CHAPTER TWENTY-SEVEN

Three months later . . .

'Keep pushing, Theresa! Keep pushing! You're almost there.'

It was the 'almost' that really rankled. That and the implied suggestion that she could do anything other than keep pushing. It felt as if someone had inserted a melon in her cervix, for Christ's sake. What was she going to do, suck it back up?

'Hold my hand. Squeeze it.' Jenny Aubrieau tried to distract her from the midwife's irritating coaching.

'It hurts,' Theresa groaned weakly.

'I know it does, darling. Next baby, go for the epidural.'

Next baby?! Despite the agony, Theresa laughed, immediately triggering another contraction. Seconds later she felt a slithering sensation between her legs and a cessation of pain so blissful it made her want to cry.

'Oh, T, it's a boy!' gasped Jenny.

The midwife stepped in and did her thing, patting the baby's back, expertly checking his reflexes.

'A boy? Is he all right?' Theresa sounded panicked. 'Why isn't he crying?'

'He's fine,' said the midwife, scooping the baby up and

laying him on Theresa's chest. 'Breathing beautifully. Not all newborns cry, you know. Looks like he's happy to be here, aren't you, chicken?'

Theresa gazed down at the scrunched, bloody face of her son. She couldn't speak. She couldn't even cry. No reaction, no gesture could come close to conveying what she felt in that moment.

'I'll leave you alone for a few minutes,' whispered Jenny, backing quietly out of the door. Theresa didn't even notice her go. Nor did she notice it five minutes later when the door opened and a man walked in. *Blasted doctors. Why can't they leave us alone?*

'I missed it. I don't believe it. How could I have missed it?'

Horatio looked terrible. His hair, never neat at the best of times, was too long and sticking out at more than usually gravity-defying angles. He was wearing a pair of dirty wellington boots, two pairs of tracksuit bottoms pulled on one over the other, an inside-out sweater and a parka coat of some indeterminate colour best described as sludge.

Theresa's eyes lit up. Too happy to be cautious with her emotions, she couldn't hide anything today.

'It doesn't matter,' she beamed. 'You're here now. Come and meet him.'

Horatio walked over to the bed. His son was basically a white, blanketed cocoon with a small circle of mottle-skinned face poking out at the top. His eyes were tightly closed, and his miniature, rosebud lips twitched in his sleep, presumably sucking on an imaginary nipple. 'He looks a bit like a glow worm.'

Theresa gasped. 'He does not look anything like a glow worm! He looks lovely.'

'You look lovely,' said Horatio. He kissed her on the lips,

gently at first, then passionately, holding her face in his hands. Theresa didn't stop him. 'I love you,' he said, as he pulled away.

'Horatio …'

'No, stop it. I've had enough. If you really don't love me, you need to tell me now, to my face.' He looked at her defiantly. To his dismay, she burst suddenly and violently into tears.

'I can't tell you that,' she sobbed. 'I *do* love you. But it would never work.'

'Oh *bollocks*,' said Horatio, kissing her again. 'It would work. It *will* work. You, me and William. It'll be perfect.'

'William?'

'William.'

Theresa looked down at the baby's face. It *was* rather William-ish. Just then a midwife bustled in, followed by the obstetrician and rather sheepish-looking Jenny.

'I'm not interrupting anything vital, am I?' she asked, beaming at Horatio. 'It's just JP called a minute ago, he was trying to heat up some mince pies in the gas oven and somehow managed to cause a fire. Half the kitchen's burnt to a crisp apparently, they had the fire brigade out and everything.'

'Go,' said Theresa. 'We're fine.'

'Actually, we're better than fine,' grinned Horatio. 'We're getting married. First church we can find after Christmas. Aren't we?'

He turned to Theresa.

And in that moment she knew.

'Yes,' she laughed. 'We are. We absolutely, definitely are.'

CHAPTER TWENTY-EIGHT

It was a beautiful Christmas morning in Sussex. Snow had fallen two days before Christmas Eve, blanketing the wooded countryside in a magical frosting that had melted even the most cynical of hearts. New York Christmases were magical in a different way, but for Sasha there was nothing to beat the smell of wood smoke wafting over the village green and the festive sound of the church bells pealing their traditional yuletide song.

The autumn had passed slowly for Sasha. She'd had plenty to keep her busy: moving out of her apartment in New York, shipping a decade's worth of stuff back to England, visiting Theresa and Horatio and her adorable new Godson, William. At three months the baby already looked hilariously like his father, right down to the shock of strawberry blond hair and the freckles. Sasha had never seen quite such a happy family and her heart thrilled for Theresa. But her own capacity for joy seemed to have shriveled away to nothing.

Concerned for their daughter, Sue and Don Miller had gone all out to make this a traditional family Christmas par excellence. Knowing that Sasha was depressed, they'd insisted that she come home for the holiday, and from the minute she walked through the door of the tiny cluttered cottage she'd been roped in to tree decorating and mince-pie making, dragged out to sing carols at the village school and generally plunged into Sussexy, home festivities whether she liked it or not. Sasha appreciated the effort. She had more money than she could ever want, let alone need, but it couldn't buy her this: the love and care of a family. Unfortunately, though, she wasn't a child any more. Grateful as she was, it wasn't her parents' love that she needed.

In the kitchen, Sue Miller was checking her turkey. Closing the oven door – it still needed a few minutes – she turned around and screamed. A strange, long-haired man was standing in her kitchen.

'Get out!' she yelled, grabbing the heavy frying pan she'd used for this morning's bacon. 'My husband's upstairs, you know. Get out of my house this minute!'

'Please!' The man ducked from the frying pan. 'The door was open. I only …'

Just then Sasha came flying into the kitchen. 'Mum? What's wrong? Are you hurt? Did you burn yourself?' Then she saw the man. 'Good God. What are you doing here?'

The two of them stared at one another. Slowly, Sue Miller lowered the frying pan. 'You know him?' she asked Sasha.

Sasha nodded, too dumbstruck to say anything.

'How do you do, Mrs Miller.' Jackson stuck out his hand. 'Jackson Dupree. I wondered if Sasha and I might have a word in private.'

'Oh … yes … of course.' Flustered, Sue started taking off her apron.

'Don't worry, Mum,' said Sasha. 'You stay here. Jackson and I will go for a walk.'

* * *

Outside, the village green was quiet. A few children were chucking snowballs at each other in the lane, but other than that the village was indoors, huddled round fires drinking, cooking, unwrapping presents and watching *Vicar of Dibley* reruns, the closest most of them would get to a religious experience this Christmas. Sasha crunched over the snow in silence waiting for Jackson to speak. When, after five minutes, he still hadn't said anything she decided to break the ice.

'I hope you didn't mind coming out. There's no such thing as a private conversation in that house.'

'I can see that,' he nodded. 'It is kind of small.'

'I offered to buy them somewhere bigger,' said Sasha quickly. 'Mum would have liked to, I think, but Dad wouldn't hear of it. I was relieved in a way.'

'Really?'

'Yeah. You know, it's home.'

They walked on. With nowhere particular to go, they headed for the churchyard. After yet more silence, Sasha blurted, 'I applied to Oxford for a research fellowship. I start in January.'

'Oh.'

Jackson stopped walking. Standing in the snow with his hands in his pockets, Sasha looked at him properly for the first time. He was wearing a long, dark coat and a thick grey scarf, but even under the layers she could see he'd lost weight. His cheeks looked hollow and sunken. If he'd slept in the last week, it didn't show. He certainly hadn't shaved.

'How are you? How are things at Wrexall?' she asked, randomly, wondering if he could hear the desperation in her voice. She knew she should ask how Lottie was, and the baby. She knew they'd had a little girl, Serena. But she couldn't bring herself to do it. 'How's business?'

'Business is fine. Wrexall's fine.'

It was no good. She couldn't take it any longer.

'For God's sake, Jackson, put me out of my misery! What are you *doing* here? It's Christmas Day! Has something happened? Do you want to buy me out of my stock, or ...' She stopped. His face had crumpled. Whatever it was, it clearly had nothing to do with stock.

'I'm in love with you.'

He said it so quietly, Sasha wasn't sure if she'd misheard him.

'I'm sorry ... what did you say?'

Jackson ran a hand through his hair. 'I should never have married Lottie. It was a mistake. She's an amazing, wonderful, incredible girl and she deserves someone who loves her. It just isn't me.'

The surge of happiness flooding through Sasha was so violent she almost lost her footing. She knew it was wrong, to delight in the end of someone else's marriage. Especially someone as good and kind and decent as Lottie. But she couldn't help it. The missing jigsaw piece to her happiness had just fallen out of the sky and landed in her lap. With an effort she managed to control herself. She mustn't jump to conclusions.

'Have you told her how you feel?'

Jackson nodded grimly. 'She was very good about it. We agreed to spend Christmas apart. She's with her family. And Serena, of course. We'll work out the details when I'm back in New York.'

'You must miss her. The baby, I mean.'

'I do,' he said with feeling. 'She's the light of my life, that girl. Well.' He looked at Sasha. 'One of the lights.'

They moved towards each other, like two figures in a dream. Jackson pulled her close and hugged her as if she were a life raft. Sasha could feel how frail he was. As if reading her mind, he said 'I haven't been eating much. I couldn't. Not till I knew what you were going to say.'

'What I was going to say?' repeated Sasha. 'Say to what?'

'Say to this.' He sank down on one knee, making a deep hole in the snow. Behind him the church steeple Sasha had known since childhood stood proud and strong. To Sasha it looked benevolent, a smiling God looking down on them. 'I've loved you since the day I met you, Sasha. Will you marry me?'

She paused, smiling, not wanting this moment to end. Mistaking her silence for hesitation, Jackson started panicking.

'Please, Sasha. I know I can be a pain in the ass at times. But, you know, so can you.'

Her eyes widened. 'Is this still part of the proposal?'

'You're ambitious, you're stubborn. You slept with Theo Dexter!' he blurted, to his own horror as much as Sasha's. The stress of proposing seemed to have given him some sort of emotional Tourette's.

'Well, *you* slept with every woman you ever met!' she shot back. 'Talk about pot calling the kettle!'

'Aw, shit. It wasn't supposed to come out like this.' He grabbed her hand. 'Look, you can still take the job in Oxford. I'll move. I'll quit Wrexall. I'll do anything, Sasha, please. Just tell me you love me. Tell me you love me, and you'll marry me and you'll stay with me forever. Ideally before my balls drop off with cold.'

It wasn't the most romantic proposal in the world. But it would do. Kneeling down in the snow beside him, she threw her arms around his neck.

'Do you promise never to mention Theo Dexter's name again?'

'Promise. Cross my heart and hope to die.'

'And will you definitely try to work on some better romantic lines before the honeymoon?'

'Definitely. I will. I promise.'

'And do you …?'

'Sasha?' He looked at her pleadingly. 'I wasn't kidding about my balls.'

'Merry Christmas, Jackson.'

She kissed him, and he kissed her back, and suddenly the cold didn't matter any more.

It was going to be a very merry Christmas indeed.

Tilly Bagshawe
exclusively answers our
SCANDALOUS
questions...

When did you first know you wanted to be a writer?

For me, it happened rather late...and gradually. I had given up a very high-powered, high stress job in the city and was taking a career break. I have always enjoyed writing (I did English at university) so I thought I would try to write a few feature articles and see if I could sell them. I was extremely lucky in that I was able to sell my first published piece to the Sunday Times Style Magazine, and after that began writing semi regularly for them. I was a full time journalist for about a year before my sister Louise suggested I should try and write a novel. So, like many things in my life, the writing sort of evolved out of a combination of circumstance, accident and good luck.

Do you think it's important to have a regular writing routine?

Every writer is different, but it is vitally important to me. I am a very routine sort of a person, and very disciplined about my writing. I write Monday to Friday, rain or shine, and I have a set word count per day which I make sure I finish.

Are any of Sasha's experiences at Cambridge University based on your own memories of studying there?

Well, none of my tutors ever came on to me, if that's what you mean! But yes, generally speaking, I based a lot of the

Cambridge scenes on my own experiences there, which were magical. I will never forget the feeling of arriving at Cambridge for the first time, the wonder and awe of it all. I was seventeen and pregnant when I applied to St John's College. Without their support, both financial and emotional, my life and my daughter's life would no doubt have turned out very differently. I think people generally have a lot of misconceptions about Cambridge, that it is snobby and elitist and unfriendly. That was certainly not my experience.

You always write about such fabulously glamorous worlds. How much of it is based on your own life?

Sadly not much! I am lucky though, in that I live in two exciting and glamorous cities, London and LA, both of which provide perfect fodder for my books and characters. For me, fiction is about fantasy. I want my stories to be larger than life, not just a reflection of reality.

You've lived in both America and the UK. How are they different and where do you call home?

They are SO different, it's hard to know where to begin. LA is all about the 'lifestyle', the sunshine, the beach, surfing, skiing etc... I feel healthy and productive when I'm out there, and there is a lot of creative energy and positivity in the city. But England is home, without question. I am probably the most quintessentially English person I know, and I miss it dreadfully when I am away. I actually do cry with happiness every time I land at rainy Heathrow, which is a little sad.

Do you find it easy to come up with new ideas, and where does your inspiration come from?

I wouldn't say I find it easy, exactly, but I do think that coming up with new stories, and starting a new book, is the most exciting and fun part of my job. For me, inspiration almost always comes from the characters first, and the plot usually grows from there. So, I picture a new heroine, or hero, and then sort of see where they take me. Inspiration is all around, you just have to look up.

Can you give us any hints about your next book?

Hmmm. How much should I give away? It's very Hollywood. Lots of suspense, drama and (of course) sex. It's actually a story idea that I've been wanting to write for a few years, but I only worked out the missing pieces to it while I was writing *Scandalous*. There are movie stars, orphans, aristocrats and some seriously evil villains. And that's as much as I'm going to tell you!